PRAISE FOR

CW01391530

"There's no better escape th[...] seductive thrillers. She'll hook you with an intriguing mystery, but she'll keep you up with her fabulous characters, with all of their weaknesses, spite and charisma."

Abigail Dean, bestselling author of Girl A

"A cultish, moreish page-turner. Lizzy's very engaging writing style combined with the sinister plot is the perfect combination."

Emma Curtis, bestselling author of The Commuter

"Lizzy Barber's novels are so well written, gripping and emotionally intuitive, I read each one in awe and then eagerly await the next. *Be Mine* is a tense, richly textured and unsettling novel that will linger in my mind for a long time. Appointment reading for fans of complex characters and compelling human dramas."

*B.P. Walter, Sunday Times bestselling
author of* The Dinners Guest

"Lizzy Barber returns with a thriller that's as chilling as it is addictive. Set against the stylish backdrop of San Francisco, this novel hooks you from the start, pulling you deeper with every twist and turn. The last quarter will have you gripping your seat as secrets unravel at breakneck speed. Prepare for an expertly crafted mystery that's as sophisticated as it is suspenseful – a treat you won't be able to put down."

Emily Freud, author of Her Last Summer

"A brilliant and elegant read – what happens when wellness

steps over into something sinister. Atmospheric and gripping, *Be Mine* is perfect for 2025 summer reading!"

L.V. Matthews, author of The Twins

"Topical, intriguing and highly original, Barber's signature classy writing elevates this dark story of manipulation and secrets above the crowd of thrillers in this space. I was transported to San Francisco and fell deep into the world of Elixir. This is a must for those looking for a compelling summer read!"

Charlotte Duckworth, USA Today best-selling author of The Perfect Father

Lizzy Barber

BE MINE

DATURA

DATURA BOOKS
An imprint of Watkins Media Ltd

Unit 11, Shepperton House
89-93 Shepperton Road
London N1 3DF
UK

daturabooks.com
It Works.

A Datura Books paperback original, 2025

Edited by Gemma Creffield and Alan Heal
Cover by Mark Swan
Set in Meridien

ISBN 978 1 91552 351 8
Ebook ISBN 978 1 91552 352 5

Printed and bound in the United Kingdom by CPI Group (UK) Ltd, Croydon CR0 4YY

The manufacturer's authorised representative in the EU for product safety is eucomply OÜ – Pärnu mnt 139b-14, 11317 Tallinn, Estonia, hello@eucompliancepartner.com; www.eucompliancepartner.com

9 8 7 6 5 4 3 2 1

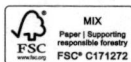

For Juniper

2014
Marin County, San Francisco

The sound of the party pulsates throughout the mansion. Literally. When she puts a hand to the room's thin walls, she can feel them vibrating. A low-level quiver, one that beats in time to the whomp of music blaring through the Sonos speaker system: Kanye West, Grimes, Frank Ocean – California-cool tracks ripped from a Pitchfork-approved hit list, a posturing of taste rather than the actual demonstration of it.

When she dares to peek outside the window, she can see that they are already gathering. A sea of figures: men and women, young and beautiful, fit to within an inch of their lives. Holding ice-cold vodka shots – their signature – the muscles of their upper arms taut, skin dewy and noticeably sun-kissed against the white cotton fabric they are all, unanimously sporting.

No sign of the sacrifices they have made to be there. The cruelties they have endured. And inflicted.

They stand around the perimeter of the vast rectangular pool that was such a constant of her time there, and as she watches their figures flicker in the water's reflection, memories seep into her: the lazy afternoons drifting into its cool centre, the mornings wrenched from her bed, dragged unwilling into its depths.

The water is still now, though, almost peaceful. It bounces the light from the hurricane lamps that surround the pool, casting a shimmer across the wide flagstone terrace and a warm glow across the faces of the guests. Below the terrace, tiki torches line the path to the beach, where the ice-blue waters of the Pacific are rendered dark and menacing by the night sky, the susurrant waves becoming a warning hiss.

She allows the soft burble of her former friends to find her ears. Almost, almost, has the urge to join them. Stares down at the dress she is clutching in her right hand – white, cotton, sheer. Imagines how easy it would be to slip it on, take her position among them.

They are happy, she knows. Excited. It's a celebration. And they all love a celebration.

Stop. Come on. Get a grip.

She doesn't have long. There is only a small window of time. A precise and distinct moment between their puffed-up distraction and the realisation that she is missing. If she loses the opportunity now, it may be gone for good.

She sees movement, the synchronised shift of their bodies as they turn towards the sliding French doors, their floor-to-ceiling glass offering uninterrupted ocean views.

He's arrived.

She watches him moving through the crowd. And she feels it: the hard stone of hate that has formed gently but stubbornly in her pit. It makes her dizzy, lightheaded, as though she's stayed under the ocean too long.

But it also gives her the final push she needs to act.

She lets the curtain fall, slipping her jumper over her arms and pulling the hood tightly over her hair, picturing him snaking his way through his adoring fans, greeting each one by name. Because he knows each one by name. He knows them all, intimately.

She steels herself. Moves towards the bedroom door and, with a final motion, flings the white cotton dress onto the bed, where it falls to petulant rest.

She takes hold of her small backpack, the one that contains only the most essential items, the ones she hopes will save her. Feels the weight of it. The clunk of the heavy metal object at the bottom. The one she has no idea in hell how to use, and may have only one chance to.

But it's not enough just to leave.

She needs to make him pay.

She pictures it now, so palpably she can almost taste it. The warm sea breeze, blowing with it the smell of iodine, mingling with the clary sage and eucalyptus that seem to emanate from their pores now. The murmuration of the crowd, parting as one.

Tate will turn, lynx-like as always. The sheen of his blond hair will catch the light, the glow of his California tan and millionaire arrogance reflected back at her.

"Well, there you are," he'll say in his perfect accentless English, lip curling with typical insouciant satisfaction. "We've been waiting for you."

"Goodbye," she will say, heart pounding, hand reaching, fingers crimping around the handle of the gun. "And go fuck yourself."

1
Muswell Hill, London
July 2023

∞

A shriek rips through the blackness.

I struggle to process it in the muddy depths of sleep. A fire alarm, maybe, or a car backfiring? It is familiarly unfamiliar, a continuous rasping cry, insisting itself on me even as I beg it to retreat.

But then my brain starts to clear and I recognise it: the rawness of my own voice, echoing back at me in the disorienting dark.

"Where is she? Where is she?"

The sound is coming from me.

I rake through the bed sheets, animalistic. *"I fell asleep. I must have fallen asleep."* The pads of my hands pressing into the softness around me, searching the emptiness, finding... nothing. *"She was here, right here, in my arms! Did I roll over? Did I... Oh, God, did I–"*

"Beth? Beth! *Elizabeth!*"

At the sound of the name in full, I freeze, a Pavlovian reaction that makes my skin itch. Twists of bed linen are still squeezed beneath my fingers.

A shadowy figure looms over the side of the bed.

Another sound joins my own: a low, insistent wail.

The figure turns. Bends. Reaches.

"She's *in the cot*." The speech is urgent, hissed. "She was *asleep...*" The implication is unspoken: *until now.*

"She's... here?" My words are thick, caked in sleep.

"Yes. See?"

I unspool myself from the tangle of sheets. Rouse fully upright as the mass is handed to me. Feel the weight of it, heavy and fragile all at once. A wriggling, furious thing. A creature that smells of lavender fabric softener, the sickly curdle of milk and, uncannily, of me.

"It must have been a dream." The voice soothes, gentler now, more forgiving.

And somehow it is the smell that crystallises me fully, that makes my body respond, my mind unfurl.

She's here. Etta's here. She was in her cot. Safe. As always.

Etta cries, louder now. And with more action than thought, I pull at my top and curl her into my chest, feel the tension in the black room dissipate as the baby quiets, sucks.

The figure stands beside us for moment, watching – and then yawns, retreats. "Will you two be all right now, darling? You know I'd help, but I have that meeting first thing. Besides, you know it's you she really wants..." Adam, my partner. His words already sleep-slurred. I feel the depression of the bed as he returns to his side, rolls back into the night.

And so I remain, cradling my daughter in the darkness until she is content. Slip Etta softly into her crib and shush away the grunts of protest.

But when I can finally reclaim the night as my own, I can't sleep. Adrenaline quivers through me, won't let my mind rest. It unearths the miasma of past fears that cling to me, tells me that I'm not safe. That none of us are safe.

That maybe I'll never feel safe.

When I finally wake for good, daylight spills across the room, seeping under the too-thin blinds. The room is airless, muggy. The heat always swells in our small attic bedroom, like a bottle with a cork in it, and I can already feel the dull ache of dehydration throbbing at my temples as I blink my eyes open.

Adam stands at the door, holding a mug of tea. Places it on my bedside table. "I thought you'd like a lie-in," he says with a verbal eyebrow raise, "seeing as this one's obliged."

He's already wearing his suit, a tie loose around his neck, but his hair is still damp from the shower, spraying droplets of cool water over me as he bends down to kiss my forehead. He smells of the mint shower gel he likes, fresh and clean, making me even more aware of my morning breath, my creased T-shirt, maternity bra half-unclipped beneath it.

I look to my left, where Etta snoozes peacefully in her crib, as though her antics in the night were all imagined. There had been more wakings, innumerous, all blurring into the endless stop-start of what nighttime has now become, although the last one, at five am, has at least afforded me a window long enough to reclaim sort of rest. My eyes are still desert-dry, the bitter taste of bad sleep lingering in the back of my mouth, but I feel at least as though I can paper over the cracks of the day until the whole thing begins again, on repeat.

But I shouldn't – can't – complain. The me of a year ago, exhausted from blood tests and pessaries, pills and patches and injections, would have resented a woman like the one I am now, for having anything negative to say, for having the gall to look at the privilege of motherhood in the face. To not cherish every single moment.

I love Etta, with every ounce of my being. But it is *so hard*.

I reach for the mug of tea. My hand shakes slightly as my fingers grasp the handle and I hope Adam doesn't see.

Is it me? I often wonder in snatched moments of quiet. *Am I uniquely unable to cope?* The sheer magnitude of responsibility for preserving another human being. The constant anxiety over whether I am doing the right thing. The nagging fear that I have no right to do this, that I can't do this. How the hell did I think I could do this? If only I had someone I could talk to. Not Adam – I can't burden him more than I already have. Someone who understands. A place where I can truly be myself.

I take a sip of tea.

Don't mind that it scalds my lips.

Welcome the way it stuns me into wakefulness.

I watch Adam from the bed as he opens the wardrobe, adjusts his tie in front of the mirrored inner door. His movements are unthinking, the muscle memory of the action well honed, and as I drink I can't suppress the jealousy that pools acidly in the corner of my mouth, envy of the world he is about to walk into so effortlessly. Coffee cups and laptops, meetings and lunch breaks: his days have sharp edges, clearly defined. Mine are marshmallow: nappies and milk and laundry, each hour blurring softly into the next.

In another life, it could have been me. Before. I'm no stranger to hard grind. Even in my most recent job – admin for a small travel agency in West Hampstead – the work had been uniform and unhurried, just busy enough that my mind didn't wander. And the move to flexible working had been ideal, affording me a borderline anonymity that I had worn like a comfort blanket. Sidebar sniggers during boring Zoom calls with the boss – a consequence-free way of attempting a social life.

Now that has been stripped away, my even newer identity – Beth the mother – feels more formless than ever.

"I've got back-to-back meetings today." Adam's groan breaks my thoughts in two. "What have you got planned?"

"Oh…" I flail, weighing up the blank canvas of the day. "The usual. Maybe we'll go to Alexandra Park if it stays nice."

"Again?" His face wrinkles, and my stomach fillips. When I say nothing, he fiddles with the tie, looping his index finger into the knot and pulling. It's a tell of his when he's annoyed. I wonder if he's aware he's doing it. "We should have done that antenatal course like I suggested."

I put my mug to my lips. Look down in surprise, finding it empty. I didn't realise I'd finished it.

"You know I didn't want to." I begin my well-worn argument slowly, putting the mug aside. "I didn't want to sit through ten hours of different birthing methods, listening to other mothers scaremongering. I didn't want anyone to change my mind. Natural birth – that's what I wanted."

I hold his gaze.

No hospitals. No doctors. The added benefit of not needing to make myself more visible than was one hundred per cent necessary.

A risky choice that came back to bite me.

Surprisingly, our fertility doctor, Dr Stone, had agreed. He'd even found me a doula well-versed in home births, although I'd quickly skirted his suggestion of hypnobirthing, the mention of "affirmations" making my palms sweat.

Adam nods silently.

The memory of the ambulance careening in the race to the hospital sits in the empty space between us. The blaring hospital lights, my eventual emergency C-section. I will never get his look of terror out of my mind. Or my own secret fear, hounding me until we were finally discharged, that this would be the moment I would finally be tripped up.

"Okay, so maybe not for the advice," he says eventually. "But don't you think it would have been nice to have a change of scene? Hang out somewhere new?"

And now it is my turn to sigh.

Me and Adam. The social butterfly and the wallflower. He'd said that was what had attracted him to me when we'd first met, a chance encounter in the pub, work drinks for both of us – my leaving do, in fact, having found myself getting a little too cosy in a job. He'd tripped over my feet carrying a bucket of beers to his table. Somewhere between the ice being cleaned and my tights drying, he'd asked me out.

I like that he is uncomplicated. That he doesn't speak in riddles or aphorisms. He says he likes my reserve. That I don't say things unless I mean them. That I don't nag when he wants to go out with his mates – that, in fact, I'm delighted.

He thinks he's brought me out of my shell, and I let him.

Because he doesn't know that the shell I wear is forged in iron. That it protects me from far more than simple social interactions.

I watch him shut the wardrobe door and step over to the crib, a hand agitating the dove-grey fabric, causing it to sway on its rocker. I instantly feel bad for making him stressed before a big meeting.

"I promise you, we're doing just fine," I insist. "And we *will* get out. Just let me do it in my own time. For now, this is the only little stranger I need to get to know."

For a moment we are both silent, looking over at the sleeping creature who has knitted us into a family. Her lips are slightly parted, emitting a light snore, arms above her head, fists curled. We share a smile of adoration. However different our personalities are, Etta makes us whole.

"She's your spit, isn't she?" Adam moons, stroking her cheek softly.

"She'd better be," I snort lightly, "after all the effort."

Adam sits on the edge of the bed, nudging himself in beside the crib. "It'll get easier," he says gently. "Nobody says the first few months are fun. But the important thing is, we have her." He takes my hand. Squeezes it.

"I know." I squeeze back. "You shouldn't worry so much about us. I promise, we're doing okay. Good, even. You never know who Etta might get talking to at the park," I wink, deflecting. "You should go. I'll see you tonight." Adding, as if to prove that I am worth keeping around: "I'll go to the shops. Make something nice for dinner. Thai green curry – your favourite."

"Sounds great." He raises himself up, kissing me on the cheek. "All right, I believe you. No more about NCT classes. Just… message me if you need me, won't you? I'm never too busy to hear from my girls."

I nod. "We'll be fine. *Go*. You're going to be late."

I watch him retreat. Reach for my mug, blinking as the touch of cool ceramic reminds me that it's empty.

I relax into my pillow, sinking into the silence of the room, ear instantly tuned to Etta's snuffles, the hum of cars from the street below.

It is good, this life we have created. Simple. Quiet. The only demons here are in my mind.

My eyelids feel heavy, and I am wondering if perhaps I can chance a nap when I hear the beat of footsteps on the stairs once more, see Adam's face appear in the door frame.

"Sorry." He fiddles with something in his inner jacket pocket, slightly out of breath. "I almost forgot to give this to you. It was in the post this morning." He walks over to the bed, proffering a thick white envelope. "Looks fancy." He hands it over with a rough glance at it. "Okay, now I really am going to be late. See you later."

He's out of the door quickly enough that he doesn't see the expression on my face as I take the envelope between my fingertips. Doesn't hear the beat of my heart quicken.

Or the breath that punches out of me as I turn the card over.

Because the front of the envelope isn't so remarkable: textured ivory card, name and address calligraphed in black.

But the back… It is the back that makes my head spin, my eyes blur, so that I have to grip the edge of the mattress.

I hold it closer. Hoping I might have got it wrong. Misseen.

But it is undeniable.

There it is.

That symbol.

The endless double loop, embossed in gold, stamped onto the envelope's closure. As indelible there as it is in my memory.

ELIXIR.

2
San Francisco Bay Area
May 2013

∞

It started with coffee.

Along with every other twenty-something Bay Area dweller, Beth was standing in the snaking line at Blue Bottle, at 8:30 a.m. on a Tuesday morning, debating whether to give up.

She bent down to retie the lace on her trainers, glancing first at her watch and then the length of the line. Tried to calculate whether she'd have time to shower before work or whether she'd have to remain in the funk of post-run sweat until noon.

She stood, shivered involuntarily as the open air of the Ferry Building wicked the sweat from her bare arms. Cursed herself for not having brought a jumper.

"California!" they'd said, and "Sunshine!" she had presumed, not knowing that San Francisco was renowned for almost year-round fog which settled over the city throughout the day like a loosely blown tablecloth. Persistent cool breezes raked in from the Pacific and competed with the bright sunlight, resulting in an almost constant Goldilocks-esque swing between being too hot and too cold. "Wear layers!" would have been a far more practical exclamation.

The person behind Beth gave her a nudge and she shifted to look at him, removing the earphones that were still blasting a heavily curated "2012 Running Playlist."

"Sorry?"

"The line," he inferred. A brief nod before looking back down at his iPhone.

She turned to see the single space that had opened up in front of her. Shuffled forwards a step.

The mission for a third-wave hipster coffee took no prisoners.

She had been in San Francisco for three weeks.

Three weeks.

Which meant it had been three months since she had found out: Matt and Kate, her boyfriend and her best friend – the oldest of cliches.

Three months since her world had imploded.

Which meant it had been two months and twenty-eight days since she'd packed the last of Matt's things off to his new life while trying to make sense of the fragments of her own.

Two months and twenty-six days since she'd opened her eyes in the hospital, body numb, thoughts jangling, her mother's broken expression staring down at her. Her words, carried on an exhale, "Beth, what on earth have you done?"

Two months and twenty-two days since she'd been discharged.

Two months and fourteen since she'd finally escaped her mother's home for her own.

And approximately one month, thirteen days and nine hours since she'd taken a seat in the HR office of her former

London consulting firm, high on grief and no sleep, and watched her line manager and HR representative press their fingertips together, heave concern onto their faces as they leaned forward; offered – as the official line dictated they must – "What can we do to help?" And she had replied, with surprising alacrity: "Send me somewhere. Anywhere that isn't here."

San Francisco was, for want of a better phrase, a mindfuck. Unlike London, prone to tradition and stagnation, here optimism crackled in the air like electricity. In her first few days in the city, she'd seen a woman walking a micropig and a man riding a skateboard completely naked except for a strip of tinfoil wrapped around his private parts. The cars of a new taxi company all sported giant furry pink moustaches to court attention, and everyone seemed to know someone who worked for Google. Former abandoned buildings had been taken over by soft-serve ice cream vendors. Street food trucks peddled every conceivable foodie fantasy: tacos, dumplings, crème brûlée. The Tenderloin – arguably the Bay Area's sketchiest neighbourhood – now housed an award-winning speakeasy. Here, it felt like everything that could be, had been disrupted.

And if anyone was in need of disruption, it was Beth.

But so far none of it was working.

True, she liked the promise of sea salt that was carried in the air. The monolithic presence of Golden Gate Bridge, reproduced ad nauseam on postcards and T-shirts and chocolate bars. She liked her one-bedroom apartment on North Beach, which bore no trace of her old life – even though the rent was half her salary, especially now she wasn't splitting in two. She liked the anonymous bed, which wasn't tainted with her discovery of a bracelet, the

"K" pendant that may as well have been a scarlet letter. She couldn't help but like the overwhelming possibility of the Trader Joe's supermarket, with its entire aisle dedicated to nut butters and ten different kinds of hummus. And she liked her daily run out to Chrissy Field, back along the Embarcadero to the Ferry Building, where she was standing now, grabbing something known as a cold-brew coffee before the ten-minute walk to work.

But she couldn't help thinking that she was missing something. Some vital thought or feeling that would catch hold of her. Grab her by the shoulders and say, "You're going to be okay."

"Excuse me?"

She felt the tap on her shoulder again. "I'm fucking moving, all right?" Took an exaggerated step forwards – the Brit in her not quite erased – and connected, hard, with the foot of the woman in front of her.

"God, I'm so sorry," she blabbered as she rebounded. "Are you okay?"

To her credit, the woman barely flinched. Pretzeled herself in two to rub the top of the offended area, where Beth had left a dirty trail on the bare skin of her tanned, flipflopped foot. "No harm, no foul," she shrugged Beth off cheerily, running a hand through abundantly long hair, which had a glossy sheen Beth had never managed to attain and smelt strongly of something medicinally minty. Just before she turned back around, the woman cocked her head to one side, surveying Beth. "Hey, cute workout pants."

"Oh, thank you." She glanced down at her new running tights – an expensive gift to herself on her first, disoriented walk around the city – and in the same second took in the form-fitting pastel blue leggings that showed off the other woman's neatly muscled legs, the matching crop top that betrayed more than a peek of tanned abs.

"So, you like working out?" the stranger asked as the line inched forward, and Beth began to smell the bitter tang of coffee for the first time.

"Running, mostly. I love it." She always had. She liked the singularity of it, the focus. The seamlessness of how, if you planned it right, it became exercise and transport in one. Matt had not liked running. More specifically, he did not like *Beth* running – how she would favour it over an extra half hour with him in bed or refuse to stay out drinking when she had miles to conquer the next day.

But there was no Matt now. No one to annoy. Or, indeed, to care.

"I so admire that," the woman gave Beth a soft smile. "I personally find it so boring."

Beth held up her phone. She'd removed the headphones, looping them around her neck. "I like zoning out. A good playlist is all I need."

"Wait, is that a British accent?"

Beth nodded. "England, born and bred."

"That's cool." The woman nodded back appreciatively. "Very cool. I've never even left the state."

As the line juddered forward, they fell into a rhythm of conversation. Beth learnt the woman was Marissa and that she was from Palo Alto but had been in the Bay Area a year. She didn't ask Marissa's age but pitched her a couple of years older than herself, in her late twenties.

"I came to San Francisco for a fresh start. I needed a bit of luck, and it turned out luck found me." Marissa raked a hand through her hair, flashing an enigmatic smile. As she brought her arm down to her waist, Beth clocked the various pieces of intricate, expensive-looking gold jewellery that jangled on her wrist. She didn't say it, but Beth got the distinct impression that she either came from or had made decent money.

However, it wasn't what Marissa looked like that drew Beth to her – though the woman did possess a natural, wholesome beauty, all strong cheekbones, wide clear eyes and dewy skin, like a better version of what Beth could look like if she tried – but rather the aura Marissa gave off. Beth could tell almost instantly that she was an easy conversationalist, good at deploying information about herself without seeming egocentric, at asking questions without it being an interrogation. She had an innate warmth that made Beth open up to her, and although she couldn't bring herself to tell Marissa quite everything about her recent past, she found herself speaking about Matt and Kate and her subsequent Stateside move, her father's death, her mother's hasty remarriage and the "late lamb" second child, so that she almost didn't realize they'd reached the front of the line until the barista interrupted them, asking once, then twice, "What can I get you?"

Beth blushed, paused mid-flow. Found the boldness to turn to Marissa, ask, "What would you like?" Pressed, when her companion demurred, "Come on, it's the least I can do. I stamped on your foot and told you my life story. I should be paying you for a therapy session. Coffee's a lot cheaper."

"Oh, go on, then," Marissa laughed, a toss of her head sending blonde highlights cascading over her shoulders. "If you insist."

"I'll have the New Orleans Cold Brew," Beth instructed the barista clearly, aching to impress. She had cribbed on Eater.com and knew it was a specialty. "And a...?"

"Oh, hey, Enrique." Marissa fluttered her fingers in familiarity. "Have you got any of the Embu Gikirima beans left in stock?"

"Oh, hey, Marissa. How's it going? Let me check for you." He smiled warmly at her, turned to call back to one of the guys behind him. "Guys, any of the Kenyan roast left?"

"Creo que sí!" a voice called back.

Enrique gave her a thumbs-up.

"Great." Marissa reached into her tote bag, handed over a glass mug with a pink rubber lid. "Here's my KeepCup."

Game, set, match.

"So, what are you doing now?" she asked after Beth paid and they were walking through the Ferry Building, past the dollhouse-perfect cakes at Miette Bakery, the stacked displays of artisan cheeses at Cowgirl Creamery.

"Work," Beth screwed up her nose. Marissa was the closest approximation to a friend she'd had in three weeks, and the thought of the conversation ending brought a stale taste to her mouth.

"Oh, silly me, I didn't ask: what do you do?"

"I'm in consulting. JE&G?" Beth checked the time on her phone, noting as she did Marissa's impressed nod. They were a top-tier firm, making waves in San Francisco tech. "And, shit, I'm going to be late."

She'd lost track of time, and her ten-minute walk was looking more like a five-minute sprint.

"Shame," Marissa sighed, with what sounded like genuine disappointment. "I was gonna say, if you like working out, I teach this class over in SoMa – I was just on my way over there. I wanted to ask you to come check it out."

"Oh," Beth stuttered, torn. "I'd love to, but…"

Marissa held her hands up in submission. "Totally, I get it. Work."

They both fell silent.

Beth reluctantly opened her mouth to say goodbye, but as she did Marissa cut in. "Only, I think you'd be super into it. It's more than just a workout. It's mind, body, soul – the whole package. I only started classes last year, but it changed my life. That's why I began teaching. It's the whole reason I decided to stay in San Fran."

"Wow." Beth widened her eyes, remembering her mum's old Jane Fonda videotapes, wondering how an exercise class could have such power. She offered, graciously, "It sounds cool." To be fair, Marissa did seem to have herself together.

"Super-cool," Marissa nodded. Paused, holding up a finger as though she'd just remembered something, before her hand delved into her bag and re-emerged with a clean, white business card between her fingertips. "Look, I don't give these out to just anyone, but something tells me you just have the right kind of energy to really benefit from the class, so you take this." She proffered the card. "I teach another one at eight tonight. That one's actually a Beginner Plus." She winked. "But something tells me you're going to be a natural. Tell them at reception Marissa sent you. Show them the card and the first class is free. All the info's on here."

"Oh, great. Thanks." Beth reached out, fingers touching the cool, cream card. "What did you say it was called?"

"Here." Marissa turned the card over, pointed a French-manicured nail to the word written below an embossed gold symbol. "It's called Elixir."

3
Muswell Hill, London
July 2023

∞

The unopened envelope burns a hole in my pocket until I manage to get Etta down for her morning nap.

I have resisted leaving the house as long as possible. Procrastinating. Changing Etta. Dressing her. Playing with her. Changing her again. But then 10 a.m. rolls around and my resistance wanes: my stubborn child will only nap on the move. Staving off the thoughts that have rattled around my mind all morning has been exhausting. At least nap time will be a change of scene.

Besides, now there is no longer any guarantee that we are safer at home than out in the world.

Trying not to linger outside our building for too long, I take a firm grip of the pram and loop us onto the northern strip of the Parkland Walk, heading for Alexandra Park.

It is the stretch I have loved since the moment I laid eyes on it: emerging from Highgate Woods and up onto an abandoned viaduct, so that you're looking down on crowded rooftops, before climbing higher, ducking under an old railway arch and then finally being spat out into the shadow of Alexandra Palace. A secret trail that puts you both in the heart of the city and above it, the natural and the urban world enmeshed.

Hiding in plain sight.

When we'd first talked about moving in together, I quietly suggested to Adam that we moved to the countryside, somewhere quaint-sounding with *shire* in the name. I had visions of taking long country walks with a pram, not another soul in sight.

Adam had laughed bemusedly at me. Asked how he was supposed to take over his firm – a small local accountancy dealing mainly in tax returns – from a barn. Teased me over my pronunciation of *Gloucestershire*.

So, for now, the Parkland Walk has to do.

Once upon a time, city life had energised me. I had sunk my fingers deep into it. Gripped hold of the fog and the noise and the people and breathed in all their glorious, anonymous cacophony.

Now, the buzz is deafening.

It is July, warm in that muggy-London-pollution kind of way, making your skin clammy, the kicked-up dirt sticking to it. The sunlight has baked the wet earth and fecund plant life so that the smell of mud and abandoned dog poo lingers in the air. I wrinkle my nose against it as we emerge up out of the woods. Promptly walk into a cloud of midges; stop and spit, flailing my arms about my face so that Etta pauses her grizzling long enough to gaze at me in confusion.

"It's okay. Mummy's okay. Shh, shh, shh," I chant at her, wiping a dead midge from inside my bottom lip as I jiggle the pram and watch her calm, smile.

"Excuse me, is this yours?" a woman with a baby tucked in a sling calls out to me a few feet from the exit. I flinch involuntarily but look up to see she's holding a muslin that must have fallen out from under the pram.

"Ah, yes." I take it from her. She lingers for what feels like a second longer than necessary, fingers still grasping the muslin, and I don't like it. I snatch it from her and stuff it under the pram.

"You're welcome," she tuts into the breeze as I hunch over the pram in the direction of the park, realising, too late, that a 'thank you' was all she was after.

By the time we're in the shade of Alexandra Palace, Etta's lids are heavy, and by the time we've dipped down into the open parkland, I am confident that she is deeply enough asleep that I can stop walking, breathe, take stock.

I park us in the shade of an oak tree, the green leaves paintbox-perfect; sink to the grass and remove the envelope from a pocket in the hood of the pram, turn it over and allow my fingers to loop over the gold infinity symbol on the back. I curl my arm to see the skin on the inside of my wrist, where a one-inch patch of flesh has been etched in the same design; the memories crash into me – good, bad: that was the bittersweetness of it. For a while, I was convinced it was the answer to everything, that I had been incandescently happy.

Could Adam have seen the envelope? Made the connection to the tattoo I've always explained away as a sign of a misspent youth?

Surely not. To the untrained eye, it's just an eight on its side, a standard infinity symbol. It could represent anything – a clothing brand, a bathroom company, a myriad of other savvy marketing firms trying to trick homeowners into thinking they've received something special.

But I know it's not any of those. I know it's not an eight, or just an infinity symbol.

But my past catching up with me. As I always knew it would. A sign of everything I've tried to forget.

I feel my pulse quicken as I lace my fingers under the envelope's closure, steeling myself. The flap grazes the tip of my finger pad and I suck air, watching a seam of blood form. I curse, wipe the blood on the grass and look back to the envelope. Opening it will be like unleashing a Pandora's box, but I have to see what's inside.

And so, grounding myself with all my internal strength, I find the lip once more. Pull.

Inside, a plain white card. Plain black font. No embellishment or aggrandisements apart from that looping infinity symbol emblazoned in gold, burning itself into my retinas.

∞

SAVE THE DATE
10th Annual Founder's Day Celebration
29th July 2023

I drop the card. Fling it away from me as though the words themselves have the power to leap from the page; ensnare me.

Every hope. Every foolish notion that I've got it wrong, that I've misunderstood, is thrown back in my face.

The sheer *arrogance* of it! The lack of details – no name, no location, no contact information – almost makes me laugh.

It's really true. He knows where I am.

Perhaps he always has.

Nine years. For nine years I have been so careful. Lived my life on the fringes whenever I could. London: too busy, too anonymous to be singled out. Too many people preoccupied with their own lives to be concerned about me. Changing jobs whenever anyone got too close. An obscure email address. No social media accounts. And I had told no one about that time – especially not Adam. Where would I have even begun?

But I knew I had never gone far enough. I have always known, deep in my core, that he could find me. He wasn't stupid. Certainly didn't lack resource. I'd just convinced myself he didn't want to.

The words on the card taunt me. The Founder's Day Celebration? Why would he invite me to that? Why now?

I look up at Etta's sleeping form and my stomach knots.

A runner skims past and I instinctively grasp for the base of the pram, but the woman doesn't even glance at us, fists balled, face set with determination. I look down at the maternity leggings I haven't quite got out of the habit of wearing, swallowing down a pang of envy at her freedom, her drive. I can still remember that feeling: the surge of adrenaline, the whir of blood in my ears. But it is abstract, the coil of a person buried somewhere in the softness of my postpartum body; buried, in fact, under so many other layers of me – the person I am now, the one I became, because of them.

She heads down the hill and I let out a heavy sigh into the muggy air.

Beside me, Etta lets out a whimper signalling she's on the verge of waking up. Has it been an hour already? I can't help the frustrated tears that sting my eyes. I haven't even had time to think. She begins to fuss, her little legs flailing against the cellular blanket prison I've tucked around her. I know I should get up, reassure her before she begins to cry, properly, becomes impossible to settle, but I can't help resisting, eking out the final moments of uninterrupted thought. I'm suddenly battered by a surge of tiredness, the fluid inside my brain sloshing around like I'm on a ship.

"Sleep when the baby sleeps," they say. Maybe I should have stayed home and napped, too? Maybe if I put her down for naps in the cot she'd sleep longer? Maybe I should look into co-sleeping; give us all a better night's sleep? Or baby-wearing? Or a night nanny? Or...

Etta mewls.

I think of Adam's argument this morning. I should get out more, find friends with children Etta's age. Someone who could reassure me my frustrations are entirely normal. That was the beauty of Elixir, wasn't it? That shared experience, the feeling of belonging.

The groupspeak that obscured the truth.

Just like that, I've convinced myself I'm better off alone.

The mewls turn to wails. I try jiggling the base of the pram, hoping it'll buy me five minutes. It works sometimes. Doesn't it? But now the noise agitates something hardwired inside me: anger and fear intermixed, making me want to both panic and protect. I curve into a ball, hands pressed against my temples, Etta's cries underscored by my own relentless tune: I can't think; I think; I'm so tired; I'm just so fucking *tired*.

"Excuse me?"

A voice pulls me out of myself. I unfurl. It's the jogger, her cheeks red, strands of hair plastered to her forehead. "I was just wondering if you happened to see an AirPod lying around? It's fallen out and I've been searching for it but I just... Oh gosh, I'm sorry, are you all right?" The woman bends towards me before I can hide the card, or the fact that I'm crying, but instead her head turns from me to the pram, face creasing into reassurance. "It's so hard, isn't it, the first few months? I remember it so well. It feels like it's going to go on forever, but I promise you it gets better. Mine are both in school now, and look at me – free!" She waves her hands in the air.

Free. The word makes my throat constrict harder.

"Thank you," I manage. My voice clings to a web of saliva in the back of my throat, comes out hoarse. "I'm sure you're right." I make a show of casting my eyes around, hoping to dispatch her. "I'm sorry, I haven't seen your AirPod."

"Never mind, I'm sure it's here somewhere." The jogger puts her hands on her hips, showcasing her matching running clothes – mottled teal-and-maroon leggings, a tightly fitted running top. I search the outfit for an Elixir insignia, shoulders loosening when I spy the reassurance of a white Nike tick. "And don't worry about the party," she continues. "I'm sure you won't miss out."

I feel my body tense. "Sorry… what?"

"That invitation. It looks like a special occasion." She nods at the card, resting on the grass by my right ankle. "I know it can feel like you're missing out on the whole world right now, but if you're important enough, I'm sure your friends won't let you go."

Before I can reply, she swoops down, plucks something from near the path. I resist the urge to flinch. "Oh look, there it is – thanks!" She holds the AirPod aloft.

"No problem," I bleat, her previous statement still hanging in the air.

"Well, best crack on." The woman takes off before I can reply, her figure blurring into the green of the parkland as Etta's cries crescendo and she manages to kick the blanket to the floor in fury.

It was just an innocuous comment, wasn't it?

The park suddenly feels overwhelmingly large, the wide expanse of oaks and redwoods casting black shadows onto the cool grass.

Anyone could be there. Hiding. Waiting.

An involuntary shiver runs down my spine, but I force myself to shake it off.

It's just an invitation. Marketing bumf. It means nothing. Doesn't it?

Unconvinced, I rise, go to Etta. Clench the pram's handlebars as I steady myself.

"Hello, sweetheart. It's okay." Force lightness into my trembling voice, steering the pram towards home. "Mummy's here."

4
San Francisco Bay Area
May 2013

∞

The card sat in the groove of her keyboard, nestled below the Escape button and number strip. Threatening to tip when she pressed the keys too enthusiastically.

She had nearly forgotten it. In her race to shower in the office's slick basement gym before the clock hit nine, she had been hastily shoving her running top into her backpack when the edge of card had peeked out of the pocket. It nicked the skin between her thumb and forefinger, making its presence known like the scratch of an attention-seeking kitten.

Now it caught the light from the artificial spots overhead, the looping gold figure of eight making her eyes blur when she stared at it too hard, zoning out of Excel spreadsheets and PowerPoint presentations. Her job was monotonously familiar no matter what city she was sat in.

She'd never intended to be a consultant. She wasn't sure anyone had. It was one of those jobs where you seem to go to sleep one day, wake up the next to find it's been five years. She was always smart and driven – good grades, good degree, a typical Type A. But when university graduation was approaching and she began to feel a blind panic about what her next step would be, she applied for all the graduate schemes she could think of and landed at JE&G.

But the job did have a certain synergy with her personality. Matt had called her a "joiner." She was totally uncreative but was energised by hard work. She got a sense of fulfilment from completing a project and having another on the horizon. And she liked the measurable goals, the process of annual reviews and peer-group assessments that told her how she was doing. She would be lying if she said she didn't like the money.

But even out there, in the tech gold rush of San Fran, where she was working on biotech and helping a partner pitch his former Stanford colleague's venture-capital business rather than the dental-chain downsizings or rail-load modelling she was doing in London, she had to admit that the day-to-day work was leaving her cold. In fact, since leaving Matt, she'd found it hard to summon the enthusiasm for anything much. It was as though all her senses had been dulled, like there was a smudge on the camera screen of her life that she couldn't wipe off. However dazzling San Francisco was, it was as though she was observing it from a distance, going through the motions in the hope that something would penetrate.

She blinked, realising she'd been staring at the same page of a PowerPoint presentation for forty-five minutes without making a single change. Her eyes felt sucked dry; she scrunched them, trying to blink them back to life.

Around her, her colleagues sat hunched over their desks, echoing her posture. They were largely North American with a smattering from India and the UAE, plus a seven-foot-tall Swede called Karl – all, without exception, Ivy League or the equivalent. San Francisco was an attractive place to work; the only reason she happened to be able to transfer was because they'd recently doubled in size to meet the demand from tech companies springing up in Silicon Valley. That, and the period of personal leave she'd taken, the recent swelling of graduate burnout cases in the sector making her new employers think they should watch their step.

They were all friendly enough. She'd join them occasionally to grab lunch; was even invited to a rooftop barbecue the previous weekend, where she'd played beer pong and politely declined the advances of a Canadian called Chad. But something was holding her back, and, looking at them all now, she was hit with a sense of ennui. The names and faces may have been different, but they were really all just variations of her life in London. She had come to San Francisco seeking change, but nothing felt much different.

She plucked the card from the keyboard, ran her finger over the embossing. What was it about Marissa that had been so attractive? Yes, she was friendly – in the manner Beth had come to expect as second nature from Americans, rather than the cynical strangers of her homeland. But there was something else about her – something vital that Beth wished she could emulate. A calm confidence that had energised her, made her want what Marissa had. If that class was what did it, hell, she wanted to drink the Kool-Aid.

Mind, body, soul – the whole package.

The English woman in her wanted to balk at it. Californian mumbo-jumbo. A green juice served with a side of Taylor Swift lyrics. But then she thought of Marissa glowing with energy. The doldrums of her own current existence.

What if a bit of Californian pep was exactly what she needed?

Somehow, five o'clock arrived: the afternoon slump when Beth and her colleagues tended to either drown themselves in caffeine or sneak into one of the bathroom stalls for a nap. Her legs felt heavy, and she had that familiar pinch between her shoulder blades from sitting at a desk all day. She would be there for another five hours at least, even if four of those were spent scrolling the internet as she waited for a partner to come back with comments on the pack or tell her she could finally leave.

Forget it, she told herself, removing the card and placing it out of sight in her desk drawer. She wouldn't make it there for eight, and besides, she had no idea what the class even entailed. What if she was terrible at it and everyone laughed at her?

She stood up, stretched. Anika, on the desk opposite, caught her eye and took out an earphone. "Coffee?"

Beth nodded.

When they came back, she noticed she'd left her desk drawer slightly ajar and couldn't resist the urge to open it fully, retrieving the card.

"It changed my life," Marissa had said. What if it had the power to change hers?

At 6:15 p.m., she craned her head to look across the room where her case manager, David, sat in the corner of the open-plan office. He was still going through the pack, which meant it hadn't even reached the partner yet. She had some calls she could make, but no one would be answering now.

At 7 p.m., David had finished the pack, but the partner was on a conference call with the New York office and Beth was at inbox zero.

At 7:30 p.m., she rose, determined to ask him if she could

step out… and then promptly talked herself down, fetched a glass of water instead.

At 7:40 p.m., she'd played three rounds of Solitaire on her computer and couldn't take it anymore. She pocketed the card and walked over to his desk.

"Um, David?" She cleared her throat.

"Elizabeth." As he looked up, she noted his tone was pleasant, which meant she couldn't have done too bad a job. "How can I help?"

"It's just Beth," she reminded him gently, noticing there was still a feather of spinach in his teeth from the half-eaten salad bowl that had sat on his desk since lunch. She liked David, a Korean American who kept a photograph of his wife and two young sons on his desk, which she hoped meant he hadn't yet cheated on her. He was a decent manager, but he was part of that old-school generation who thought of the weekend as taking time off and nicknames as a suggested serve.

"Is it okay if I pop out for a bit?" she asked. "I've been really struggling with missing home recently, and I was hoping to catch my mum on her lunch break. Since my dad died, she's all I have." She let her eyes rest on the family photograph for effect. David blinked at her, and she could see him internally processing her request. She didn't know exactly how much he knew about her, but he tended to regard Beth with a sort of anticipatory panic. Perhaps it was unfair of her to play the mental-health card when JE&G had been so good to her, but it was the only ace she had. "I'll stay late to finish any edits needed before tomorrow."

"Um." He itched his cheek – Beth heard the rough scritch-scratching of nail on his five o'clock shadow. Looked across to the partner's office, where the echo of the conference call was still reverberating through the closed door. "Yes. Yes, that's fine. Just... make sure you complete the pack. The client is quite difficult about timing."

"Yes, of course. Thank you!" She suppressed her excitement, subdued her expression. "I'll be back before you know I've gone."

At seven minutes to eight, she was standing outside Elixir.

5

Muswell Hill, London
5th July 2023

∞

I distract myself by cleaning the flat. Vacuuming. Wiping down surfaces. Fluffing sofa cushions. Deep cleaning the hob. Removing the entire contents of the fridge and spraying it down before carefully replacing each object in precise, linear fashion. Most of it is entirely unnecessary; I'd done the same thing yesterday.

It's an old habit, and one I probably shouldn't do quite so obsessively – my hands are permanently dry and cracked, despite the organic cleaning products I switched to when I was pregnant. But the flat – a second- and third-floor maisonette in an otherwise unremarkable converted terrace – is like my own personal panic room. Keeping it neat is my way of being in control.

I feed Etta, imagining, as I am always compelled to, my mother's voice in her ear: *"Why don't you give her a bottle? I don't see what the big deal is. You were bottle fed and you're fine."*

My mother would never commit herself to any act she couldn't delegate.

"And she certainly wouldn't care about all the benefits,"

I stare down defensively at Etta's wisp-covered head. "All the things it protects her from."

"You can't protect her from everything," comes my mother's imagined response.

When it is time for Etta's lunchtime nap, I realise I've forgotten my promise to Adam to cook something nice for dinner. I glance out the window into murky afternoon light, not wanting to leave the sanctity of the flat. We could order in, but Adam could never conscience the expense midweek, and how would I justify it? His basket-case of a partner can't even manage to cook a meal?

Etta grizzles, making her opinion known.

"I know, I know." My voice sounds oddly flat in the empty living room. I finish the sentence silently: *We can't stay inside forever.*

I stand, decisive, before I can regret it. Grab a tote bag hanging from a cupboard door and pull Etta into my arms.

I'm catastrophising, surely. There is no one "out to get me." My life is not a movie. If anything, they're just toying with me, sending an idle threat. And wouldn't it be just their style not to waste their precious time by following through. They know the real me, maybe better than anyone; know well enough that just the simple reminder of their existence would be all it would take to plant a bomb under my fragile existence.

I don't entirely believe it, but what other choice do I have?

I pull my jacket tighter as I steer the pram towards the high street; walk briskly, my gaze fixed on Etta, as we make our way to the shops.

When we return, unharmed, an hour and a half later, I heave a loud sigh as I drop the heavy shopping bags at my feet; lay Etta down on her stomach on the play mat in instigation of the much hated "tummy time." She starts crying instantly, rubbing her cheek against the mat's fuzzy surface. She only slept for forty minutes; it should have been an hour and a half at least. Now she'll be out of sorts all afternoon. My temples throb in anticipation.

"There, there, there," I cluck, willing myself to move through the noise. We have been to the shops and back and nothing has happened. I want to live in this small victory whilst I can. "It's not so bad."

When the bags are empty, I scan the surfaces, seeing what else I can rectify. I pick up a plate with a banana skin, realise that's all I've eaten today. Search myself numbly for hunger cues, dulled from the years I've spent training myself to ignore them.

Sighing, I take the plate to the counter and pluck an avocado from the fruit bowl, slicing it in half and scooping out the creamy flesh, not wanting to think about how many grams of fat it contains, how many calories, how once upon a time every ounce of it would have been weighed, measured, recorded.

I brush the waste into the clutch of my hand and move to the bin, depressing the pedal. Am about to throw the lot inside when I stop. Stare.

Inside, a flyer: a glossy A5.

I let the rubbish go – the avocado pit landing with a heavy *thunk*. Remove the flyer, wiping the slick of avocado and banana on my hands down the side of my leggings.

TINY SPARKS, sunshine-yellow letters advertise. *Mummy and me playgroup to light up your little sunbeam*. There is a photograph of a group of women sitting cross-legged in a circle. Each of them holds a beaming baby in their lap, their hands poised in mid-clap. They all look so relaxed, so happy.

I know the place: it's a church hall just up the hill.

Funny, I didn't remember seeing the flyer before. Adam must have put it there. Guilt nibbles at my sides. It probably came with the post, and he was going to suggest it. That was probably why he brought up the NCT classes. And then I'd been so adamantly opposed he'd chucked it in the bin without even mentioning it.

Etta lets out a squeal. She has rolled onto her side, can't right herself.

I hurry to rescue her, but once she's sorted, my fingers curl tighter around the paper, the sunshine-yellow blaring. Because hadn't I changed the bin that morning, *after* Adam had left for work?

I reach for a memory, but it's fuzzy, indistinct – the days are all so similar that what I've done when is impossible to pinpoint. *Think, think.*

And I am sure I can see it now – walking down the stairs, the cut of the plastic straps against my left palm as I'd balanced Etta on my right shoulder, worried the weight of it might make us fall. But it was today, surely, *before* I'd opened the envelope – I'd marked it when we'd gone to the shops, how much easier the journey was without the added weight of the bag.

So I *had* changed the bins.

Which means Adam couldn't have put it in there.

And I am almost certain I haven't seen the flyer until now.

The pappy smell of avocado and banana lingers on me as I stalk to the sink, scrubbing at my hands, the stain on my leggings. Wipe soapy water across my lips to rid myself of the nausea that threatens.

It wasn't Adam who put the flyer there.

And it wasn't me.

...was someone else inside the flat?

6
San Francisco Bay Area
May 2013

∞

SoMa – the more glamorous contraction for "South of Market" – was a former manufacturing district to the north of the city. It seemed an odd place to have a fitness studio, but as Beth threaded her way past the towering, mirror-glass office blocks, blue chip logos suspended over the entrances – Black Rock, PWC – she wondered if perhaps the choice was deliberate.

The address on Marissa's card didn't take her to a tower block, though. Instead, she arrived at a squat warehouse building clad in an ugly off-white, housing a paper supplies store on the ground floor. She couldn't help feeling disappointed. But as soon as she'd walked up the echoing concrete corridor to the second floor, heaved opened the wide sliding door with the looping symbol painted in gold, she understood that Elixir would all at once exceed and confound her expectations. Because what greeted her behind those doors was energy – pure, effervescent energy, grabbing her by all the senses and propelling her inside.

In this era of industrial chic, the Elixir studio was the pinnacle of cool. The vast warehouse space had been left almost entirely unadulterated, the exposed brickwork painted with upbeat aspirational sayings: *It's not how you start, it's how you finish. Respire, Aspire. You got it, dude.* The wryness of the last, a catchphrase from the San Franciscan sitcom *Full House*, made her smile. So they had a sense of humour. Light flooded through the double-height windows, bouncing off the orb-like lights which hung between the pipework running the length of the ceiling.

As she stepped fully inside, she was hit with a whack of the same minty, herbal smell she had noticed on Marissa, looked up to see great bunches of eucalyptus hanging from the rafters. House music thumped through the speakers at a volume just loud enough that she felt it in her chest; a rhythmic RPM which seemed to charge the people who gathered in the space, threading across the concrete floor or settling onto pastel coloured lounge furniture as though they were all part of some low-effort flash mob.

She took them in – their easy manner, their bright eyes – and realised there was something ineffably similar about them. Whether they were tall, short, man, woman, black, white or anywhere in between, they had something in common. What united them, she realised – and them with Marissa – was that they all seemed to have that *glow*.

And then she saw Marissa herself, standing behind a white Formica reception desk in the far corner of the room. She must have felt Beth's eyes on her – or, rather, gawping at her – because she placed a hand over whatever paperwork she was looking at and raised her head to meet Beth's gaze.

"Beth, you came."

The statement was simple, confident. As though she'd never had any doubt. But as Beth crossed the distance and let Marissa wrap her thin arms around her shoulders, she noticed the tightness with which Marissa held her, the distinct pleasure – erring on relief – with which she whispered, "Thank you."

And if Beth wondered, at the time, what it was that made Marissa so grateful, she soon forgot it, caught up as she was in the flurry of movement that followed. A form to sign – the usual stuff: name, email, emergency contact. A health waiver which may have bordered on too much if it hadn't been California, where no-win-no-fee lawyers grew on trees with the oranges. A tour of the space – a juice bar peddling five dollar ginger shots, co-working desks lined with the latest MacBooks, their owners hunched down, barely visible. A changing room so discreetly tucked away she wouldn't have known where it was if Marissa hadn't pointed it out, stocked with Elixir products.

When she emerged, clad in new butter-soft activewear purchased hastily from the onsite shop (Marissa's smile had tightened when she'd pulled out her sweaty running gear, "Oh Beth, you can't wear *those!*"), she took her place in line as Marissa directed, rolling nervously on the balls of her feet. As she did, she noticed a small commotion at the far end of the studio, a confluence of people that seemed to come together and then almost as seamlessly ripple apart as a body strode through them. A man – tall, lean, with a pair of Aviators pushed back over his neatly combed hair and, curiously, bare feet – made his way purposely towards the exit, eyes fixed straight ahead, as though he didn't see the heads that turned towards him, the stammer of voices that called out to him.

The effect was unanimous. All around her, people seemed to adjust their posture, raising themselves straighter, inspecting their clothes as though looking for any sign of imperfection. On their lips, a word, whispered in reverence: *Tate, Tate, Tate.*

"Who is it?" Beth asked sotto voce, leaning towards Marissa, quivering at the front of the line.

But Marissa didn't answer. Her gaze was locked on him. Eyes burning a hole into the back of his head until he'd vanished out of view.

"Okay, come on you guys," she snapped the moment the doors shut behind him, evidently disappointed, but then quickly heaved a smile on her face. "Sore tomorrow, or sorry today: which is it gonna be?"

The aroma of eucalyptus was even stronger in the studio, almost stinging Beth's eyes as she watched Marissa take position on the small white podium mounted on the front of the room, adjusting the ear mic that circled her right lobe. She looked across at Beth and another ten almost identically clad classmates as she pressed her palms together in prayer.

There was no sound. No music. The only thing Beth heard as she saw Marissa close her eyes, urging the class to follow suit, was Marissa's long, slow inhalation and eleven other sets of lungs doing the same.

"Welcome, friends, old and new," she began, and Beth felt Marissa's eyes resting on her; involuntarily raised herself a little straighter, glowing under her gaze. Marissa's voice had taken on a resonant tone that struck Beth's ear differently to her previous preppy chatter, and she found herself soothed by it, tuning in to the aura of calm in the space. "Whatever resistance you have brought with you today, I ask you to leave it outside this door. Here, we say: give in. Give in to yourself. Because Elixir has the power to change. But the change begins with you."

I needed this. The thought whispered through Beth, raising the fine hairs on the nape of her neck. She had sought change – leaving Matt, leaving London – but it hadn't been enough. Her mind and body were a mess of unanswered questions about herself. Perhaps Elixir could be the answer.

Slowly, slowly, she found herself nodding.

Marissa cocked her head. Held out her palms to the spellbound room.

"Okay," she breathed. "Let's begin."

Elixir Manifesto
by Tate Larsen

#ItWorks

I see you.

The same sad you, staring back in the mirror each morning as you say to your reflection, "I guess I'll just give up."

I see the failed diets. The gym memberships that have drained your wallet. The dates that haven't worked out. Promotions you've been passed over for.

But what if I told you that you don't have to give up?

That I have the answer?

And the answer is Elixir.

But what is "Elixir?"

Elixir is transformative. It is healing. Life-giving.

It is ancient. A 13th century medieval Latin alchemical substance thought to be able to change base metals into gold. Later, it referred to a substance thought to be able to prolong life indefinitely.

A cure-all. The ultimate remedy.

Elixir is perfection.

And I know what you're thinking: "Perfection? Surely that's unattainable. How can I possibly achieve that?"

To which I reply: Why should you accept anything less?

Too many people allow the convenience of modern life to make them lazy, to lull them into a meaningless existence – a life of monotony, every day the same.

We are fatted with the spoils of technology. Food orders on speed dial. Twenty-four-hour streaming. Transportation available at the click of a button.

Our brains and our bodies are rotting. And we allow them to.

But if we want to transform ourselves, we have to *do* something about it.

We have to act.

And here you are, acting. So, congratulations. Just by reading this, you have made the first step.

Now, are you ready for what comes next?

Because I'm telling you, it won't be easy. The path to perfection is *Hard. Work.* It takes grit. It takes determination. It takes mental fortitude. It means rising to challenges you don't think you can endure, and believing there is light at the end of the tunnel even when all around you seems to be darkness.

If you come on this journey, you won't just be succeeding in Elixir. You will be succeeding in *LIFE*. Elixir can give you more knowledge, better health, a better body, deeper friendships, clearer skin, a total understanding of yourself and your relationships, more confidence, complete control over yourself and your choices.

Elixir will make you your best self.

But only if you're willing to commit.

Does that sound like too much effort? Then go. Give over to your weakness. Sink back into the abyss that is mediocrity.

BUT. If you are willing to make these sacrifices, you have the Elixir guarantee: #ItWorks.

The journey up any mountain begins with a single step.

At the summit is perfection.

Are you ready to climb?

7

Muswell Hill, London
5ᵗʰ July 2023

∞

By the time Adam comes home, I've searched the flat from top to bottom, seeking out some hint, some small sign of disarray, to suggest an external presence. But there's no trace of disturbance. I'm meticulous enough to know when something is out of place. There is no one here now, but I can't quite let go of the sensation of intrusion, that something isn't quite right.

Instead, I distract myself, folding myself into the familiar routine of making dinner. Nearly ten years on and I still can't eat meat, which I've told Adam is for ethical reasons. He's lactose intolerant, so the veggie curry is a clear winner.

Maybe I really had put the flyer in the bin, I muse as I chop an aubergine and rinse a pack of baby corn; feel the heat rise in the room as I sizzle onions in a pan, add coconut milk, stir. Lord knows it's difficult enough to keep my memories straight when I'm sleep deprived and all the days look roughly the same. As if to prove it, I reach for the wooden spoon I thought I'd left on the counter, find it in the sink instead.

Adam bustles through the door, eager to see us as always,

and rushes over to Etta, fingers poised to tickle, eliciting such shrieks of delight from her that my whole body radiates warmth.

"Dinner smells good," he comes up behind me and kisses me on the cheek, smelling of the outside – of the Tube in the heat and Pret sandwiches masked with chewing gum. "Why don't you go have a bath? I'll bring her up to you in twenty minutes or so and she can have a rinse with you?"

And I am so grateful to him that I go without protest, desperate to wash away the grime of the day, the smell of fear that has sweated through me.

By the time he brings Etta to me, I am feeling... well, if not fully restored, then some approximation of *better*. As I cradle Etta's warm body against me in the steamy air, I feel the tension I'd been holding release. The skin-to-skin contact makes my body hum, a reminder of how far I have come. I have made it, no matter how circuitous the route has been.

And somehow, Etta goes down obligingly in the bedroom upstairs with little fuss, so we have the peace of dinner to ourselves. Adam even sets the table. And I light candles, smiling shyly at him over their yellow glow as I take a sip of the alcohol-free wine he's poured for me, so used to it now I can barely remember what the real stuff tastes like. I know they say it's okay to have the occasional glass or two while breastfeeding, but it's not worth it – not worth anything happening to Etta after wishing for her so hard.

Adam holds up his own glass and we clink. It feels like an age since we've had time like this, just the two of us.

"You seem... I don't know, different?" he observes, taking a bite of aubergine and chasing it with a swig of wine. "More relaxed?"

I find it ironic that today, of all days, this is how I seem to him. Wonder if there's something transcendent about having prepared so long for the worst only for the worst to actually happen.

"It's really nice, watching you with Etta," I offer. "It makes me happy, seeing you together."

"A proper family," he agrees, reaching his hand across the table to take mine. "Like we've always wanted."

Adam isn't close to his family. An older sister lives in Scotland – I've spoken to her a couple of times, stilted Christmas Day chats over Zoom – but he barely speaks to his parents. "No great reason," he always shrugs when I push. "They felt they did their part by raising me. Once I turned eighteen, I was on my own. Any success I have is down to me."

I think it made my trouble getting pregnant even more upsetting for him: all he wanted was to create a family of his own. Familial disappointment is one of the things we have in common.

"I think I'm going to go to that baby group after all," I squeeze his hand, wanting to give this to him.

In the mellow evening light, it seems ludicrous to think that someone had, what, broken into the flat without leaving any trace? Put a flyer in the bin because they were so desperate for me to get some mum friends? Ridiculous. I must have mixed up the days and taken the rubbish out on a different day. And the more I think about it, the more I wonder if Adam is right, that I'm driving myself crazy spending day after day alone with Etta. Perhaps this class is what I need to stop myself from tipping over the edge.

Adam focuses his attention on scooping up a spoonful of rice. "What baby group?"

"The one you found in the post this morning." Noting his

coyness, I walk over to the fridge, where I'd stuck up the flyer. "Little Sparks. Here."

I sit down again, reach for my fork, only to find I've put it on the wrong side of my plate. I shake off the strangeness of it, pricking a piece of corn hard as Adam turns over the flyer in his hand.

He frowns. Sets the flyer aside. "Hmm. No, I don't remember seeing that." He spoons more rice into his bowl, chews a mouthful nonchalantly. "I don't think there was any junk mail this morning."

I set the fork down. It clinks on the side of the bowl. "It was in the bin," I persevere. "I saw it when I was cleaning up. I know you probably thought it was a non-starter, but I think it's a good idea. It would be good." I look at the monitor next to my plate. Etta is sound. "For both of us."

Adam reaches for the knot of his tie. Tugs. "No, there definitely wasn't any junk mail this morning. It was just some bills and that envelope for you. What was that, by the way? It looked important."

"No, I definitely found it in the bin." The need to be right insists itself on me. "I know I didn't put it there, so it must have been you. You were distracted this morning. The meeting. You must have forgotten. Look." I thrust it at him.

"Darling, I see it." Adam holds up his palms and shrugs. "I said I didn't put there. Maybe you chucked it in there and don't remember? You know lack of sleep literally damages your brain cells? And you've been so exhausted…"

His calm reassurance somehow makes me more stressed. I had settled on a theory, and now it has been debunked. I feel disoriented, as though my sense of reality is slipping away from me.

"I said wasn't me." But even as I say it, I'm second-guessing myself. I retrace my morning movements. At some point, I'd made a cup of peppermint tea before we left for the park… or maybe it was after we'd got back? I'd eaten the banana. That must have been after the park and before going to the shops, because the dishwasher was on when I got back, and the peel had been there for a while. I remember the limp warmth of it in my hand…

Oh, God! How is it I can remember that so clearly and not this? I try again to summon an image of the flyer there this morning, or what else I had thrown away, try to elicit the feel of the paper in my hand or the sound of the bin lid opening. Perhaps I can? Perhaps Adam's right?

"Beth… do we need to talk about this?"

I see the concern on Adam's face and feel my own grow hot. "No. Let's just drop it, okay?"

"It's just… I'm getting a little concerned about you," he says gently. "It's only a flyer. It couldn't have… flown there?"

I force a laugh, too late; the joke lands flat. The spice paste is suddenly overwhelmingly pungent, the coconut milk sitting heavily on my stomach. I push my bowl away.

Adam swallows. "Seriously, Beth, there must be a simple explanation. Do you think maybe you got in one of your tizzies about tidying up and scooped it up without realising it? It could have been stuck to something else. You know you're such a clean freak–"

"I'm not a freak, Adam." I don't know why I say it so vehemently. I don't know, truly, why that particular comment irks me so much.

"Hey, whoa." He holds his hands up in submission. "I'm sorry. I shouldn't have said that, Beth. Of course you're not a freak." He lets out an awkward laugh, trying to defuse the situation. But then he casts his eyes down, toying at the grains of rice on his plate with the tines of his fork. I scratch at the dry skin on my left hand, leaving a graze of white. "I *am* worried about you, though. It's been a lot, all of this. And you've been acting more and more… I don't know, paranoid, lately. I wonder… Maybe we should think about getting you some help again–"

"No!" I choke. I feel as though a lead weight is pressing onto my chest, crushing the air out of my lungs. I had tried it once, when we were struggling to conceive. A nice woman in a nice office near Harley Street who specialised in fertility counselling. I told myself it was nothing like Elixir, nothing like an Extraction session, but the moment I'd felt the soft depression of the couch against my thighs, I felt my throat tightening. I'd stuttered an excuse and bolted, gulping the polluted London air as gratefully as though I was on a Swiss mountain top.

"Okay, okay," Adam holds his hands up again. "Can we just roll back here a second and breathe?" He waves his arms across the table, signalling a clean slate. "Please, let's go back to how it was when we sat down. It's been so nice."

I sigh. Press the heel of my hand to the corner of my eyes, stemming the fragile tears that have sprung. Adam is right. It had all been so nice, and now I was spoiling it for nothing. Why does it matter which of us put the flyer there? Maybe I'm just looking for an excuse not to go to the class.

I take his apology, move the conversation on.

We have sex that night. Quietly, in the dark. It feels wrong, doing it with Etta asleep beside us, but she doesn't stir. And Adam is keen, and I am eager to make up for earlier.

I still feel uncomfortable, revealing my new body to him.

The flesh that was once taut and lean – at my lowest point, too much so – now soft and yielding. The elongated half-moon scar on my lower abdomen marking Etta's entrance into the world is bumpy and sensitive, only just beginning to fade from an angry red to a softer pink, a whisper of the brown linea negra still visible on my stomach. But he doesn't say anything. He never has. He reaches for my hand, pulling me close to him before stopping to look at the looping black mark on the inside of my wrist, running the pad of his thumb over it, making me flinch. Is this when he'll notice, make the connection to the envelope? But he moves his hand up, circling around my waist, pulling me close.

"Teenage kicks, huh?" he murmurs into my neck, recalling the fumbled lie I'd once told him about a drunken night's visit to a tattoo parlour. "Glad it wasn't that bloke's initials."

My insides squirm. A violent ex-boyfriend. That was what I'd told him, explaining away at least some of my strangeness. How right and wrong that was.

"You know you're the only bloke for me." I manoeuvre myself on top of him, obscuring the thing from view.

"I'm sorry for pushing you," he says after, as I rest my head on his chest. "About getting to know other mums. If you don't want to go to that class, it's fine. I understand."

I feel the weight of it – the pressure and the guilt – squeezing my chest. Because he can never understand, not fully. I wish so hard that I could show him the person I once was, that he could have met me nine years ago. Before. Before that person was taken from me.

I press my cheek into his chest, feeling the reassuring thud of his heart. *Adam is here, Adam is real, and he deserves better. I need to start living for him and Etta rather than in my past. After all, I made it here, didn't I? Still standing.*

"No, no," I charge my voice with conviction. "I want to go. It's lonely, being here all day on my own. And Etta's getting older – it's time she learns how to socialise or she'll end up a recluse like her mother. *Joking*," I add, before he can protest.

"Okay." He swallows, thinks. "Well, if you're sure?"

I nod into his chest before I can change my mind.

"That's great then, Beth. I just want you to be happy."

I stretch to wrap my arms around him, pull his lips to mine. "I am," I insist, glad he can't read my expression in the dark.

We lie like that, his left arm curled around my back, my head tucked into the crook of his shoulder, listening to his breathing deepen and slow. When he commences a thin, whistling snore, I know he is asleep.

I should be too. I should take the opportunity before Etta wakes again. But I can't.

I look across at Etta. We've begun "dream feeding" her – instigating a late-night feed while she's barely awake, in the hope that we'll claim at least the first few hours of sleep for ourselves. The clock on my phone says it's not yet midnight, so I should be safe for a snatch of time at least.

I swing my feet over to the carpeted floor and move to the door, listening for the creak of floorboards as I adjust my weight.

Adam snorts but doesn't stir.

I pad downstairs to the living room, put the front door on the latch and creep down the communal stairs in my bare feet, listening out for the sound of our neighbours, Ingrid and Hardeep, in the ground-floor flat. There's no light under their door, but I can hear the muffled sounds of the

TV, like someone speaking underwater, and slow my steps, not wanting to disturb them, or them me.

I didn't bring a light – my phone is charging on the bedside table – but I find my way to the pram easily, reaching under the base for the sharp corners of the card. My fingers go rigid when they touch nothing but air.

"What?" I whisper into the silence, bending to feel with both hands, squinting into the darkness in the hope I'll catch a glimpse of whiteness. There's nothing. "No… I put it there. I *definitely* put it there."

My breathing shallows as I search the pram, reaching around the corners of the bassinet. I think of the jogger from before. Could she have taken it? Replay the scene again, picturing the woman leaving, myself packing up to go, putting the card underneath only after she was gone. Could it have fallen out? Maybe. Could Ingrid have taken it? Could Adam?

No. Why would Ingrid be messing around with the pram? And Adam had asked about the envelope himself that evening; he would have brought it up, surely, if he'd seen it.

I grasp the bonnet of the pram, prepared to yank it down. As I do, I feel something stiff in the hood pocket. Find the zip, fingers clumsy with adrenaline, yank it open and reach inside.

The invitation is there. The top of the envelope is folded over it, exactly as I'd left it. *Where* I must have left it.

But the relief I expect to wash over me doesn't come. It's like the flyer all over again. I'm so sure I put it under the pram, but obviously I didn't because here it is.

"This confirms it," I mutter to myself, recalling the argument with Adam earlier. "I am losing my mind."

Is it *really* just that?

"Paranoid," Adam had called me, stumbling into a deeper insight than he realised.

It is true that I'm exhausted. That even before the invitation arrived, I had been struggling to keep myself together. Having Etta has ripped open the seam I carefully threaded around my fabricated life. What if I can never sew it back?

No. For the first time today, there is something else bubbling inside me aside from fear. *I won't let them do this to me, let* him *do this to me – make me paranoid, make me question what's real and what isn't. Take what I know is right and twist it. Not again.*

I shut the front door, secure all the locks. In the safety of the flat, I walk over to the kitchen and turn a knob on the cooker, listening for the click and hiss as the gas connects, ignites.

I won't let him win.

I will go to that class. I will make friends. I will forget all about this petty attempt to get my attention and live the life that I have salvaged.

I hold the paper over the hob, watching the flame take hold, burn.

See the infinity symbol catch the light of the flame.

Wink.

EXTRACT

Glowess.com
June 3rd, 2012

MORE THAN SKIN DEEP

Tate Larsen is shaping up San Francisco and beyond, teaching those in search of the body beautiful that perfection lies in more than a sixpack. Glowess.com editor-in-chief Rachel Cho sits down with the fitness and wellness entrepreneur and founder of Elixir to find out what gives him that glow.

The first thing I notice about Tate Larsen is that he isn't wearing any shoes. The second thing I notice is that he doesn't take no for an answer.

"Come on!" he chuckles. His voice is melodious, his English accent so perfectly neutral it can't be native. "You have to at least try it. It's everyone's favourite."

Larsen is standing in the entrance of the Elixir HQ, a three-thousand-square-foot loft space in the Bay Area's SoMa, and the "it" in question is a so-called "green juice," confected at Elixir's onsite juice bar. The ingredients are apple, pineapple, ginger, kale, and celery.

Only... I hate celery.

"Go on; you might surprise yourself." A smile carves across his clean-shaven face a little devilish, and I find myself magnetised to take the cup.

Cautiously, I sip.

And... he's right. The drink is delicious. Fresh and zingy, the fruits and ginger masking the offending vegetable. As I take another sip, I see Larsen nod approvingly, a tease sparkling in his Pacific-blue eyes.

"See? I told you. Sometimes you need to overcome the unpleasant parts to get to the good stuff."

It's a philosophy Larsen has taken to heart in the foundation of Elixir, a combination fitness studio and wellness centre designed to address both the inner and outer self for the ultimate "whole package."

"Too many gym programmes focus only on losing weight or building muscle," Larsen, who is Harvard educated and made his first million at twenty-three with his marketing company, Thirsk, says. "And too many wellness programs concentrate on mental agility, or nice scents, without addressing physical grit and strength. I wanted to create a system that harnessed the two."

The comment about scents is a wry one. The loft space smells intoxicating: fresh eucalyptus hangs from the rafters while Elixir's new line of organic and ethically sourced bath and body products has its own fan base.

But Larsen knows his audience. The recent tech gold rush has brought a new breed of cool to the Bay Area, affluent and dedicated, with a discerning palate and money to burn. Cutting their teeth on a diet of Apple products and private members' clubs, they want to set the trends, not follow them. Throw in a raft of celebrities and socialites looking for the Next Big Thing, and it's easy to see the magic that underpins Elixir.

And it's working. Membership is up 30% this year, with studios planned in major cities across America. Although, with some course fees starting in the triple figures and a pair of signature Elixir leggings setting you back $75, you may not be giving up your Gold's Gym membership just yet.

But Larsen is the first to admit the programme isn't for everybody.

"Hard work is the foundation of what we do. It requires sacrifice. Commitment. Is it tough, changing your entire mindset? Challenging yourself to your very core to become the best you that you can be? Yes. Does it work? Also yes."

The calm determination in his steely blue gaze makes me believe him.

"You finished your juice." He nods, reaching to take the empty cup.

I look down. Only an inch of green froth remains. "Oh… Yeah."

Larsen grins, warmth spreading across his impeccably smooth skin. "So maybe I'm right and you like celery now after all?"

"Maybe you're right," I agree, seeing first hand his powers of persuasion in action.

He winks, enigmatic as ever. "Perhaps you'd like to sign up to one of our courses…"

Article continues on page 17.

8

San Francisco Bay Area
May 2013

∞

When Beth left the class, she was dripping with sweat. Endorphins crackled through her, giving her a crazy high. But it was more than that. More than the aftereffects of the physical exercise – a curious blend of blood-pumping cardio and Pilates-like strength training she had tried her best to keep on top of, each exercise paced to a small sand hourglass placed in front of each of them at the start of the class – it was the things that Marissa had said as she took them through the class. The way she had made them search inside themselves to find beauty in their ability and strength in their pain.

She was exhausted. But for the first time since leaving London, she felt alive.

She made the journey in reverse. Showered, lathering herself in Elixir's own-brand willow bark and chamomile organic body wash. Dressed and stepped back into the evening half-light, into a world that now felt too real, dirty and polluted, the fog infused with the scent of rubbish bags, of cigarette smoke and leftover Chinese-takeout cartons. Part of her wanted to turn right around and go back.

But then she was back at her desk at JE&G. A pack was

waiting for her, a Post-It note from David scrawled on the top: "Needed by tomorrow 7am." His seat, empty. And she slipped, automatically, back into the motions. Finished the edits. Shut down her laptop. Transported herself home, where she fell into a thick, dreamless sleep.

The next day, she did it all again: harder, faster, pulled along by the treadmill of life. So that, by the end of the week, Elixir had slipped so far away from her that it seemed a sort of fever dream. A quirky, one-off experience that perhaps she would one day slip into an anecdote about "funny things that happened to me that time I lived in San Francisco."

She missed it, though.

A dull ache. A craving, for an ineffable something she wouldn't or couldn't get back.

Marissa's card had been lost, swept into a wastepaper bin somewhere in the debris of life, but the glow of the gold symbol still lingered in the periphery of her mind, like she'd stared at the sun too long, spots forming in her vision.

But then, the following Monday morning, after a weekend of interacting with no one outside of cashiers and shop assistants, she powered up her emails and there was Marissa's name lingering in her inbox like a nonchalant fingertip wave. And she felt it: a stirring inside her, a quiver of excitement that something in her numbing routine was about to change.

"Dear Beth Myers," the email began, her full name inserted crudely, after too big a gap, suggesting automated coding. As she scrolled through the rest of the neatly formatted and heavily branded page, she realised she had been added to a marketing newsletter. "Congratulations on beginning your Elixir journey. You totally smashed it! Book your Beginner Class Package now for just $99.99 a month and you'll receive 10% off all Elixir-branded products. Just use my exclusive booking link, Marissa999, to receive this offer." It was signed "Marissa, your Elixir rep." Underneath Marissa's name, a hyperlinked box urged her to BOOK NOW.

She clicked off the email. Stared blankly at her inbox.

It had just been a marketing ploy. Marissa didn't want to be friends. And on reflection, had she really even *liked* the class, or had she just been caught up in the moment? All that empowerment stuff – wasn't it a bit… silly? Where had her British cynicism gone?

No. She didn't have the time or inclination to start spending a hundred dollars a month on a gym membership she probably wouldn't even use and would waste time and energy trying to extricate herself from.

She moved her cursor to the box beside the email, quickly clicked Delete.

She was about to get up. Had her fingers wrapped around her glass of water, ready to refill it from the tank in the corner, when her inbox blinked, refreshed. Marissa's name appeared again. The subject line read, "Hey!!"

Hey hey Beth! It began. And it was her – really her, not some CRM system; Beth could hear the California drawl in her ear. *How are you? Hope you don't mind me emailing you. We're not really supposed to use client emails personally because of data protection, but I just had such a great time meeting you last week and I was sad not to see you again in another class. I miss you! What's up? Didn't you enjoy it?! I'd love for you to give it another try. I didn't even get a chance to tell you about the one-on-one sessions we do when you start Beginners Plus – they're the real deal. They're called "Extraction" sessions, and they're a bit like therapy – only better. I could take you through one, and we could hang out maybe, after? It would be a shame to let those leggings go to waste…*

Despite herself, Beth felt the blood whooshing in her ears. She glanced around the greyness of the office floor, at her co-workers performing the same dull tasks they'd been at all morning: reviewing their packs, mining survey results, cold calls. In contrast, Elixir's vivid branding and jazzy wording seemed like the moment in *The Wizard of Oz* when the film switched from black and white to Technicolor.

Marissa said she missed her. She wanted to "hang out." They'd had a connection; Beth had felt it.

She found herself navigating to the Trash, retrieving the original email.

$99.99 a month really wasn't that much. She was sure membership to Equinox or one of the other fancy gyms was at least double that. Plus, there was a ten per cent discount. And it wasn't "just a gym class." It was so much more.

Before she could change her mind, she found the link in the newsletter. Clicked.

And then she returned to Marissa's email and hit reply, fingers dancing over the keyboard as she tapped out an overenthusiastic response.

She was in.

EXTRACT

Elixir Manifesto
by Tate Larsen

"Extractions"

You know what is the easiest thing to change about yourself?

Your body.

Your self – your physical self – is merely a lump of clay. With the right diet, the right exercise, anyone (yes, anyone) can mould their outer form. Any excuse is just laziness in disguise, a justification for giving up.

So, this is why we begin with the body. It's an easy first step to fulfilling your true potential, to making a small but visible change.

But changing the body alone is not enough.

You can alter your physical self to become an athlete, a model or a body builder, but if you don't change your mind, you will only find yourself falling back into old ways, repeating the patterns of failure you've performed so many times before.

Which is why, once we address the changes with your physical self, we go deeper. Unlocking the underlying weaknesses that are holding you back, the negative energies that are preventing you from achieving greatness.

We call these sessions Extractions.

Once you graduate to Beginner Plus, we will assign you a personal coach to tackle the issues that are holding you back in one-on-one sessions that are handily included in your membership package.

Together, you will work through those unhealthy thoughts, those past experiences that go all the way back to your childhood; a miasma that clings to you, preventing you from achieving all you can.

Think of Marilyn Monroe, James Dean, Amy Winehouse – countless other beautiful celebrities whose lives were cut short, their ultimate success mired by the trappings of their inner self. If you don't clear the fog, those negative thoughts will drag you down, no matter how great you look on the outside.

This is the aim of our Extraction sessions: to remove that negativity and help you move on.

Elixir is not a religion. It is a belief structure firmly grounded in corporeal reality, in the here and now. But by working together to get your body and mind in full working order, we can create in you something far richer and purer that that outdated concept known as the soul.

Mind + body = Elixir.

That is your *true* self.

That magic. That spark.

It's nothing fantastical.

It's you.

9
Muswell Hill, London
6th July 2023

∞

The church is on the corner of Muswell Hill roundabout. I walk past it three times before going inside.

They've always freaked me out, churches. The buildings usually austere relics from the past, filled with rituals and routines I have played no part in. We weren't a religious family, growing up. I guess I would vaguely consider myself Christian, although the closest my mother got to a house of worship was a regular appointment at the nail salon. I have no idea what faith, if any, my father ascribed to. Adam had proposed, when I was pregnant with Etta, but although I hadn't exactly said no, I somehow couldn't bring myself to commit, to hitch him with such finality to all that I am.

And so it is with this sense of trepidation that I traverse around the church's Gothic façade, search the cool, echoing hall for the Little Sparks playgroup. I must look lost, because a woman with a kind expression and a blue rinse asks if I need help. She directs me around the corner to a modern extension where there are, reassuringly, no crucifixes or organs in sight.

The building smells of school: industrial cleaning supplies and whiteboard pens. The walls of the reception area even look like school, lined with leaflet-plastered corkboards touting the local community's wares: conversation classes and computer repairs, ballet lessons and carpet cleaners – life's full spectrum. The distant sound of babies chattering confirms that I'm in the right place.

I look down at Etta, chewing on edge of the new pram toy now clipped to the hood. Swallow down the urge to turn us both around and run. But she's been difficult all morning, fussy and discontented – teething or a regression, although really, it could be anything – and now that the idea of other parents has entered my head, I crave the reassurance from something, someone, external to myself.

I suppose I have always needed other people's approval.

It has been a week since the card arrived, and radio silence from Elixir. Long enough that the hard edges of that initial threat have been softened in the silence that followed. Not so long that the threat has disappeared entirely. But I am sick of hiding. If he wants something from me, he can damn well say it to my face.

As I push the glass doors open fully, the sound intensifies. About eight or nine other mothers sit in a wide circle, babies in various "stages of man" around them – cradled in arms, sitting, attempting to crawl.

I put the changing bag on one of the plastic chairs surrounding the perimeter, fussing with the contents. Stalling. But as I divest us of our debris and hoist Etta into my arms, I see her eyes widen, her little head wobble round to see what's going on, and know I can't deny her the involvement. Realise with a pang of guilt that this is the first time Etta has been outside the pram anywhere that isn't the park or the flat. She is so clearly her father's sociable child. Keeping her from this has been entirely selfish.

"Welcome." A woman – presumably the teacher, her hands resting possessively over a wicker basket stuffed with plastic instruments – gives me a warm smile. "I'm Sally. Is this your first time?"

"Yes."

The circle of mummies twist in their places, observing me, judging me, asking themselves if I fit in. I feel my face grow hot, something about the whole process tugging at me uncomfortably.

"Can I take your name please, love? Mark you off?"

"Sure – it's Beth."

Sally scrolls through a list on her phone. "Elizabeth Harris?"

Another woman in the circle holds up her hand. "No, that's me."

"Yes, sorry." Sally returns to her phone. "I've marked you off already. Beth... Myers?"

Slowly, I nod. As I do, I notice another woman turn to look at me. A little girl with a shock of white-blonde hair is sprawled across her lap.

"Great." Sally distractedly taps at her phone before setting it aside. "Grab a space on the floor and we'll begin in two minutes."

Somehow the circle shuffles apart, and I find myself sitting beside the woman with the blonde daughter.

"You said your name was Beth Myers?" she asks, and my skin bristles.

"Yes," I say slowly. I snatch a glance around the circle, expecting them all to pounce, the bear trap to be exposed, but they're all preoccupied with their babies.

"Sorry." The other woman waves her hand in the air. "I knew someone with the same name. Beth Myers." She chews her mouth around the words. "Not you, obviously. A long time ago. It just spooked me, hearing it here."

"Right. Sure." I give her a wary smile as I cross my legs on the ground, holding Etta tighter in my lap.

But as soon as the class begins, something strange happens, and I feel myself loosening. The persistent knot that lives between my shoulder blades eases. As we clap hands and wave our arms in the air, sing nursery rhymes in silly, overzealous voices, I forget all about the card. About him. I forget about myself. I have fun.

And then I realise what it is that makes me feel this way: Etta. Propped up between my knees, waving a maraca frantically in her fist, Etta is, quite simply, having the time of her life. She beams at her surroundings, lets out little squawk-like giggles, twists her head to look at me as if to say, "Look, Mummy, look! Can you believe what's happening?"

And I feel it fully: that outpouring of love so deep it is as though my heart might break, it clenches so tightly. The one that is so hard to feel in the thick of it all, knee deep in dirty nappies and so sleep deprived my brain aches in my skull. The one that tells me I would do anything for this child. Die for her. To keep her happy and safe.

Etta, my darling, I think, waving a hand across the wispy baby hair at her temples, *I wanted to protect you, but in doing so I've deprived you of the world.*

When the class finishes, it's like lights turning on at the end of a school disco. I return to myself, blinking, reluctant.

The circle breaks. Mothers scoop up babies, depositing them in slings or prams. The musical instruments are returned to the wicker basket, and soon the room is righted to its original anonymity.

I find myself drawn into idle chatter – poo-namis and preschool places, the best zip-up sleepsuits, weaning. Feel something I had almost forgotten existed: a sense of belonging.

I linger. Despite myself, despite all my misgivings, now that I've made it there, I don't want to go.

And then Etta cries.

"Hey, what's the matter?" I coo tentatively, embarrassed. Convinced that Etta is the only baby making noise, that I am the only parent who doesn't have their shit together. But the cooing only makes Etta's protests louder, my mollifications more frantic as I move us over to our things and, with increasing desperation, check her nappy, offer her a feed, bounce her in my arms with the signature "shush shush shush" that has become almost second nature. I have half our belongings in my arms, awkwardly trying to keep hold of them and Etta, and feel my jumper slipping from my grasp.

"Are you all right?"

I turn. It's the woman who made space for us at the start of class. Her own baby is resting placidly on a blanket by her feet.

I notice the dummy in her mouth. I had told Adam, "Strictly no dummies;" they mess with their teeth, cause nipple confusion. Now I look at the pastel-pink contentment longingly.

"Do you need help? I can hold her if you like, while you get sorted?"

The woman holds her arms out and I hesitate, look her over with uncertainty. But then the jumper falls. And I feel my phone go with it.

I give her a shy smile. "Actually, if you don't mind…"

Before I can change my mind, she takes Etta and places her gently onto her shoulder, turning so that she's facing the mirrors that line the back of the studio.

"Hey!" the woman calls, her voice mellow and sweet. "Hey, who's that?"

I hold my breath. Observe Etta's reflection in anticipation, and then in amazement, watching it turn from pinched and pissed off to intrigued, stretching out a balled hand to touch the glass, squealing with confused pleasure when her mirror image does the same.

I pull on my jumper, cram everything else under the pram as quickly as I can and proffer my arms to have Etta returned to me.

"There, isn't that better?" the woman sing-songs.

"You're a genius," I stammer, poised for Etta to erupt again, delighted when she remains calm.

"It's nothing." The woman gives a casual shrug, picks up her own child. "The crying doesn't get to your core the same way when they're not your own. I think it's a primal thing."

I watch her, too nervous to go anywhere in a hurry in case I unsettle Etta again. The mother is young, I notice, and lithe, her body betraying none of the lumps and bumps of childbirth that mine can't seem to smooth out. I wonder if that's what gives her this confidence. I see it in the way she holds herself, the deftness with which she manoeuvres her baby into one of those soft cotton slings that have always got me hot and bothered, how dexterously she folds a muslin square into one of the pockets of her changing bag where I would have just stuffed it in a wad. I feel all at once frumpy and useless and a mess when the woman turns to me, cocks her head.

"What are you doing now? Fancy getting a coffee?"

"Oh." My heart gives an involuntary jitter. "Well, nothing, I guess."

"Great! Have you been to that fancy new soft-play café that just opened around the corner?"

I shake my head.

"Oh, my goodness, you'll love it. It's amazing. I go at least four times a week."

The jitter becomes a jig. This was a mistake. What does she want? "Actually, y-you know, I should probably... but..." The woman's smile falters, and I feel my cheeks pinken. I give myself a mental shake. I'm being ridiculous. It's just coffee. "Yes. That sounds nice."

"Okay, great." She hoists the bag over her shoulder. "This is Astrid, by the way," she says with a smile. "And I'm Mia."

"This is Etta." I make her hand wave in the other child's direction. "And I'm Beth."

The woman gives me a strange look.

"You said that already, remember? Beth Myers." Her expression freezes for a fraction too long. Adds softly, "Like my friend."

Transcript
Audio Recording

Elizabeth Myers, April 2012

[Footsteps. The sound of chairs being scraped back. A cough]

Marissa Reid: So! Welcome. How are you feeling today?

Elizabeth Myers: Um, yeah. I'm feeling... good? [laughter] Sorry. I don't know why I'm laughing. I just... I'm a bit nervous, I guess. I... [exhales] Yeah, I...

Marissa Reid: That's okay. Relax. It's totally normal, just... [blows air] shake it off. [sound of jewellery clinking, hands shaking] Yeah, just like that. That's great. There's nothing to be scared of. This is a safe space. This is about you.

Elizabeth Myers: I know, I know. [swallows] Sorry. I'm ready. Let's start.

MR: Great! You're doing great. So, just for the purposes of this recording, we start each session by confirming your name, age, and the date.

EM: Okay.

MR: [laughs] So... can you do that?

EM: Oh. [laughs] Yes, sure, sorry. I didn't know if...

[pauses] So. Yeah, I'm Beth Myers. I'm twenty-six years old and it's… the thirtieth of April.

MR: So, April thirtieth.

EM: Yes, that's right. April thirtieth. God, I sound so English when I say it like that. Sorry, can I just ask, why do we record these?

MR: [sighs] Don't stress about them. It's part of the process. By recording the sessions, we're effectively exorcising your negative thoughts. The separation gives you physical distance from them, so that if we need to revisit unpleasant memories, you won't have to deal with them with the same level of trauma as if you were physically retelling them. It makes total sense, doesn't it?

EM: Yes. Sorry. And the tapes are kept…

MR: They're kept on file, totally safe, under lock and key. Nobody has access to them except you and me. Oh, and Tate, of course.

EM: Tate listens to this?

MR: Of course. How else can he provide help? He guides us all with best practice to help you move forward. Is that going to be an issue?

EM: No. No, of course not. I didn't realise, that's all. Just… wanted clarity.

MR: Totally. I'm an open book. [a pause. Clears throat] So, anyway, Tate says that the purpose of these sessions is to try and help you work through the past traumas that have been holding you back. It's about apportioning as much value to your inner self as your physical self. He says that so many people only focus on their shell, their outer body, but our past experiences, our negative beliefs about ourselves, these can all hold us back just as much as our outward perception of our self. A negative self-image can literally, physically weigh us down. It prevents us from moving forward and ultimately restricts us from having success. So, in these sessions he wants us to work on removing or extracting those adverse thoughts, preventing those dissenting voices so that you can heal yourself from the inside out. You see?

EM: Yes. Yes, absolutely.

MR: Great! So, let's begin…

10
San Francisco Bay Area
June 2013

∞

Beth didn't know when exactly the scales tipped.

When exactly did she move from attending weekly to almost daily classes? The fifth class? The fifteenth? How long was it before the direct debit doubled and she saw her bank balance depleted by more each month, as prominent a drain as her rent and utilities? How many washes before those leggings – the ones Marissa had persuaded her to buy – became worn through, replaced by five, ten more pairs? Before Elixir turned from *lifestyle* to *life*? All she knew was that, at the beginning at least, Elixir answered a call she was aware she was making but didn't quite know how to articulate.

And it worked.

With a regular evening class harder to commit to, she began a new regime: setting her alarm for 5 a.m. to jet over to the SoMa warehouse, hauling her sleep-fogged body through the first class of the day, before arriving at her desk ready to greet a day of client meetings and Excel spreadsheets. Then hurrying to the studio once more to fit in whatever evening sessions she could before collapsing, exhausted, into bed, ready to wake up the next day and do it all again.

The one-on-one Extraction sessions with Marissa helped. Together, crammed into a small office at the back of the studio amid lever-arch files of marketing materials and cascading monstera plants, they would talk. About her past, her present, what she wanted for her future.

At first, she was resistant, her natural hard edge wanting to put up a barrier to anything that smacked too much of therapy. But the sessions were rooted in the practical: helping her address her work-life balance, suggestions of Elixir-based coping methods and prioritising strategies developed by Tate's years of experience in high-level corporate firms. They helped. They worked. Even if she wasn't quite ready to divulge the whole truth about what had led her to San Francisco, what had driven her so far over the edge of her old life that she was compelled to start anew.

But Marissa was so easy to talk to, so candid. She told Beth about her own upbringing, her wealthy-but-absent divorced parents, who found it easier to send a car on her birthday than a card. The time she drank champagne before grade school one morning because the tap was broken and that was all there was in the fridge. About when she was left alone in their Palo Alto mansion for an entire weekend, each parent thinking the other had her, too selfish or too lazy to check.

"By the time I was an adult, I thought I was the only person I could rely on. I had money, yes, but no direction. My relationships always ended. My friendships seemed so superficial. I couldn't hold down a job. I had no motivation. I was totally lost." She picked at the corner of a nail, and Beth saw in Marissa the shade of the little girl she had once been – adrift, alone. And then she shook it off and was her strong, confident self once more. "Elixir found me."

She couldn't believe how much of Marissa's feelings mirrored her own: treading water, buying time rather than truly living life. And then she looked at who Marissa was now. Could it really be that easy? Was Elixir the answer?

She might not have been able talk about London yet, but hearing about Marissa's childhood prompted Beth to unpick her own, telescoping back to the day of her father's death, a week shy of her tenth birthday.

"I'd had a ballet exam – which I bombed, by the way. My mum didn't even wait until we got home." Beth toyed with the black Elixir hourglass in her hands. She'd been required to buy one when she'd signed up for membership ("A tennis player wouldn't expect to play without a racket!") and it had become a talisman to her now, even when not in class, its soft curves a comfort. "She told me in the car. I could still smell the rosin on my ballet slippers. She'd told me to stuff my feet into my outdoor shoes before we left the studio, slippers and all. She was so impatient with me, when I tripped at the door on the way out. I never took a class again."

"I'm so sorry." Marissa wrapped her soft hand around Beth's own. "The way our parents handle such important moments like this is vital. When they screw up so badly – pardon my language – it affects our behaviour in the long term. She really messed up."

In a later session, playing the recording back to her, Marissa explained how the collision of the two major and minor events gave Beth the unquenchable fear of failure. She made her see how her mother's hasty remarriage, followed so soon after by the birth of her half-sister, planted a notion that would flourish into a deep-rooted sense that she would never be good enough.

"You need to own it, Beth," Marissa urged as Beth found herself unexpectedly crying, the half-moons of her nails digging into her palms as she gripped the hourglass. "Listen to yourself. Learn from it."

"I know it seems ridiculous, but I always felt like if I'd just tried harder," her voice, tinny through the cassette player, echoed back at her. "If I'd paid more attention in class, or done more practice…"

"It wouldn't have stopped him dying, Beth. But that feeling of perseverance, of overcoming failure? Grasp hold of it. Use it to make you stronger. You owe it to yourself."

Her head pounded from the thick air in the room, from the confrontation of it all. But once the session was over, she felt lighter.

"That's Extraction," Marissa promised, looping an arm around her. "We draw out all those toxic elements and heal you from the inside out. It's exhausting." She nodded sagely. "But it works."

And then she progressed, moving to the Intermediate class – smaller and more intimate, with classmates whom she began to address by first name, and then by nickname: "Jojo," "Benjy," "Red." The classes became more frequent, and mostly at night, so she started sneaking out of work – in the dinnertime lull when no one would be any the wiser – before racing back to JE&G to complete whatever was required. Afterwards, she would rejoin Marissa and the others, often heading back to someone's apartment, where they would talk and drink until the pale orange sunlight began to bleed through the fog.

The faces changed. Some she'd see only once. Others

moved on after a while, because, as Marissa phrased it, "they couldn't hack it." But the ones who stayed were her people, sharing her drive, her energy, her zeal. Through them, she began to fall in love with San Francisco, to relish her good fortune to have found herself in this city at the forefront of the innovation.

She switched her drink order, mimicking Marissa's: "I'll have a neat vodka, please. On the rocks. A tonne of ice." In a week, her skin looked clearer, the banishing of craft beers also eliminating the toxic sugar and yeast that came with them.

On the advice of the Intermediate-class joining literature, she went vegan. Why would she pollute her body with animal fat? Her body was a temple. Animal fat causes high cholesterol, heart disease, and numerous other harmful chronic illnesses and inflammation. And she didn't need to eat so much, either; that whole two-thousand-calories-a-day thing was a myth. She needed to question what was really underpinning her desire to fuel herself – was it hunger or something deeper? She became adept at halving her meals, setting her knife and fork down precisely in the centre, to avoid eating the rest.

And it was good.

She laughed.

She hadn't laughed since London. Since before.

Everyone told Beth how great she was doing. Marissa said proudly that she was the quickest person to move through the course levels since she herself had joined, and Beth felt proud too.

She was sleeping better, even though she was sleeping less, and she was looking better. Her face lost the last of its pallid, puffy greyness. She'd shed half a stone without stopping to think. She was even working harder and faster at JE&G. Even David noticed, slipping into the seat next to her at a client meeting and noting, "San Francisco seems to be suiting you."

Sometimes, but not often, she would catch glimpses of Tate. His presence blessed the whole studio, and she would know, even without looking, when he was there – voices would become hushed, bodies straining for a glimpse. The lucky chosen few allowed to speak to him hurried their tread to keep up with his purposeful glide.

"I'd love to meet Tate sometime," she'd said foolishly before a session, hinting at an introduction.

Marissa had placed a hand over hers – gently, as though indulging a child. "You will. When the time is right."

"When will the time be right?" she'd pushed.

But Marissa had just smiled a prosaic smile. Turned towards the tape recorder, finger poised over the record button. "Have faith."

Meanwhile, Beth was bathed in Elixir (literally – she used their signature bath and body wash at least twice a day), and she was loving it. All that time she had spent in San Francisco before felt like she had been suspended in jelly, unable to free herself from the numbness of it all. Now she was achieving things, going out, meeting like-minded people. And she was so good at it! Beth could see the way Marissa looked at her from the front of the class with a sort of maternal pride when she gritted her teeth to hold a pose or complete a drill, even when sweat ran into her eyes and she thought her legs might buckle.

"You're amazing!" Marissa would cheerlead, a warm palm on the small of her back. "A complete natural. I'll be out of a job if you keep this up." And she felt herself grow three feet taller in the warmth of Marissa's praise.

She even influenced her first customer. A girl she'd accidentally walked into when leaving class one Saturday, still dressed in her Elixir workout clothes.

"Can I ask where your pants are from?" the girl twirled a tight curl of hair around her index finger, looking pointedly at the aqua-blue Lycra that encircled Beth's newly toned thighs.

"Oh." Beth blinked at her. She'd been lost in her own world, trying to work out how to get out of a client dinner that night in the Mission – a cool startup disrupting the DJ space, so David wanted some of their "sparkier" (i.e. younger) consultants present – in order to go to a concert with Marissa and others from class. "Thank you. They're Elixir." When the girl stared at her blankly, Beth cocked her hip, placed a hand on her waist, feeling the hardness of bone and taut muscle. She sometimes couldn't believe Elixir wasn't a global phenomenon. "The exercise class?"

The girl shrugged.

"Just up the road?"

Nothing.

"Well, I swear by it." She tossed her head. "It changed my life."

And Beth felt the girl taking her in. The look of awe, a touch of envy. And she felt a trill of excitement in her chest.

"Here." She reached into her bag, pulled out a pen and an old receipt with a blank reverse side. "I don't have any cards, but I'll write down the address. Mention my name – Beth – and ask for Marissa. I'm sure she'll look after you."

A few days later, when she went into the studio, she saw Marissa behind the desk, her finger curling in a wordless beckoning.

"What?" Beth asked. The blood rushed to her ears.

Marissa reached behind the desk, pulled out a slip of paper and inched across the desk to Beth with the tip of her middle finger. The receipt.

They locked eyes, and Marissa's lips quirked into a smile.

"I think it's time you met Tate."

11
Muswell Hill, London
6th July 2023

∞

By the time we reach the café, Etta is asleep, exhausted from the morning's social whirl. Part of me is running through the list of all the things I could be doing with the time – cleaning the flat, worrying about that goddamn card still, weighing up the arguments for whether I really am going mad – but I push the thoughts down in favour of a far greater win: the chance to have a conversation with a grown-up, a real actual grown-up, in the middle of the day.

I hadn't realised how much I missed it.

A bell jingles overhead as we step through the café's entrance, and I see instantly why Mia was so enthusiastic about it.

The front operates like a normal coffee shop, but at the far end is an area demarcated by a low wooden fence, beyond which sits a vast area floored with artificial grass and decked out like a faux garden, with a mural of trees painted on a hazy blue wall, a wooden house-shaped play structure and ball-pit "pond" complete with plastic ducks, all decorated in pleasing shades of Scandi neutral. Babies lie on their backs among a selection of wooden toys or toddle over to the plastic-free sensory boards mounted to the walls. Mothers in various states of exhaustion stack pastel-coloured blocks on the peripheries, drinking coffee like it's ambrosia.

Mia jerks her head towards a couple of toadstool-shaped chairs. "Why don't you grab us some seats? Coffee? I'm buying."

I hesitate, mentally calculating the caffeine in the cup of tea I've already drunk that morning, how many more I'll need to get through the afternoon slump. "I shouldn't really." I look down at my chest. "I'm breast feeding."

"Oh." Mia gives a shrug of her shoulders. "I never fancied the idea of it."

In the face of her insouciance, I feel obsessive. I am struck with the sudden, desperate urge for her to like me. Which I'm sure she won't if she knows the true level of my mania.

She looks at me expectantly, waiting – I realise a beat too late – for me to give her an order.

"I'm sure one more coffee won't hurt." I shrug, trying to replicate her casualness. "A flat white, please." Add, before I can truly give over, "Single shot."

I wheel Etta over in the pram and park it next to the fence. Glance warily at the other mothers before taking a seat and making a pretence of looking at my phone. My rational mind knows there won't be harm in taking a one-off extra shot of coffee, but I can't help myself. It's not just the worry that it will be harmful to Etta. The daily caffeine count has dusted off my un-exorcised mania for control. That time in my life when I could reel off the nutritional value of everything – fifty-two calories in an apple, seventy-five in a slice of brown bread, a hundred and ninety (gasp!) in tablespoon of peanut butter – as easily as the four times table.

"Your accent. Are you American?" Mia returns with the coffees.

I feel myself turning inwards. Every time I think I've erased every trace, that I've shaken off that time, something pulls me back, trips me up. "I spent some time in the States." I shrug. Hesitate, then explain carefully, "The accent grows on you like mould."

I like that expression. It's one Adam used when we were first dating and sharing our history, or as much as I dared to reveal. "Gosh, that accent must have grown on you like mould."

"Oh, that's cool! Whereabouts?"

I stare intently at the cup in my hands. The skin around my cuticles is ragged, turning white. I should use some of Etta's E45 cream.

"California." It's always easier to stick to fact. In case I'm caught out later.

"Wow. I've only been there once. San Francisco."

My fingers grip tighter around the cup. I bring it to my lips. Wet them. Buying time. "Oh. Yes. I know it."

"Didn't like it much."

In my periphery, I see Mia screw up her nose. "No." I take a careful sip. Swallow. "Neither did I."

Coincidence, I tell myself. Millions of people have been there.

"Astrid's beautiful," I say, fumbling to move the conversation on. I nod at Mia's daughter, sat in a sponge floor seat, fisting a rusk into her gummy mouth. "Does she look like her dad?" I ask it tentatively, realising Mia will know what I'm implying: that the two look nothing alike.

"Right?" Mia runs fingers through the sleek brown hair that is the antithesis of Astrid's candyfloss curls. "I must have a Viking relative hiding in the family tree. If she hadn't physically come out of me, I would be quite suspicious." She laughs and I join in eagerly.

"How was all of that?" I wave a hand in the air in an attempt to approximate the conversation I imagine normal mothers must have. "The birth, et cetera?"

"Oh, it was fine." Mia takes a sip of her coffee, allowing the foam to rest on her top lip for a moment before licking it off. "Nothing compared to what some people go through. A home birth. Eighteen-hour labour. Small tear but it healed quite quickly."

I'm flooded with visceral memories of my own labour. The merciless heat of it. Fingernails clutching into Adam's upper arm as the doula announced the ambulance was arriving, and my own voice, distant, desperate, "Please don't let her die."

Mia sneezes, bringing me back to the room. "After having got over the shock of actually being pregnant, anything else was going to be a breeze."

"Shock?" I try to read something beneath the shadow that crosses Mia's expression. She has a pleasant face, I notice, long and narrow with delicate features, her eyes slightly too wide, giving her a doll-like sweetness. There is something familiar about her. It caught me when I first saw her, and I'd spun frantically through my memories, feeling relief when I couldn't place her. But I now put it down to her resembling an actress whose name my frazzled mind can't place – the one who was in the period drama we'd watched last Christmas Day.

Whatever thought washes over Mia's face now causes those wide-set eyes to knit together, her neatly plucked eyebrows to furrow. As quickly as it settles, her face brightens. "Maybe shock's the wrong word. I just hadn't really decided whether I wanted to have kids. At least not yet – I thought I'd be at least thirty. My boyfriend's really busy with work. He travels a lot, and…" There it is again, that look. But before I can gauge its meaning, it's gone. "Well, he didn't know where my head was at. But turns out we get on just fine, don't we, Asty?" She bends to plant kiss on the baby's plump cheek. "I think it must always come as a bit of a surprise, though, finding out, right? The moment when you look down at that stick and realise your whole life is about to change?"

I think of the number of tests I took when we were trying. How hard I had willed each one to change my life for good. How, until Etta came along, I had just about convinced myself that being childless was my fate, that it was what I deserved.

"I never did a proper pregnancy test, actually. Well, not with Etta." I take a sip of my flat white, trying to inject my voice with some of Mia's nonchalance, but despite its liquidity, the coffee manages to get stuck in my throat and the words come out choked. "We did IVF, so I officially found out about Etta through a blood test – a beta test, it's called. I took them after, though. I kept taking them." I blush, confessional. "I had to keep making sure."

I think of the HCG tests that I'd caved in and bought during the two-week wait. Squinting at the white strips each day, trying to work out if I could see a faint line, if it was getting darker or if it was my eyes playing tricks. And then the bloods, three in total, holding my breath each time Dr Stone called, praying my numbers had doubled. It took months before I finally, safely, felt pregnant.

"Oh, my goodness, I'm so sorry." I see the change in

Mia's expression, the awkward down-casting of her eyes I recognize from acquaintances who had enquired similarly, unwitting colleagues who seemed to ask repeatedly, "So, are babies on the cards or…?"

"It's fine," I breeze over it, fix a smile on my face. "We're here now, aren't we?"

There didn't seem to be a reason for why I couldn't get pregnant. We'd done the requisite trying for two years, twenty-four months of tracking my cycle, peeing on ovulation sticks and googling *fertility-boosting supplements*. There was the obligatory sex, which seemed like silly fun at first, then "as good an excuse as any," then soon turned into work. I'd had some tests. There was a concern about the thickness of my uterus lining – a worry about something called a "trilaminar pattern," which rang alarm bells, at least for me. Questions were asked about my past history – any operations, past procedures that might have caused trauma or scarring – that I had answered in the appointments Adam had missed. But nothing conclusive.

It was nothing compared to what some women went through. And I know I should consider myself lucky never to have suffered the miscarriages that seem almost frighteningly commonplace among my generation – or perhaps we just feel freer to talk about them. But as each unsuccessful month turned into the next, it became increasingly easy to turn inwards, to find myself, and my past, at fault.

It was Adam who wanted to go private rather than continue with the NHS. He'd read about wait times stretching into years, particularly with the backlog from Covid. He had friends who'd gone through all we had plus another twelve cycles of artificial insemination before being finally granted IVF. As I ebbed first closer and then past thirty-five – the age of the fabled "geriatric pregnancy" – and with my mental state growing increasingly bleak, he hadn't wanted to waste any more time. I think he'd been a little insulted when I'd quietly questioned if the problem might be him.

"He even found the doctor, when I couldn't face thinking about it all," I tell Mia, treading lightly over the memories, not wanting to be dragged back to the place I'd been in then. "Made the appointment before I even had a chance to think about it. And Dr Stone was fantastic: did all sorts of tests, figured out there had been something wrong with my oestrogen levels, and then it worked first time round."

"I'm really sorry you went through that." Mia gives me a kind smile. "But your partner sounds great – so supportive. You're lucky to have him."

I think I catch something in the corner of Mia's eye, a glint of something undefined that I hope isn't pity. But then Astrid throws the half-chewed rusk across the floor, and when Mia rises from retrieving it, the glint has gone.

We finish our drinks slowly. Etta wakes up cheerful, mesmerized by the people, the noise, gold pendant lights that dangle overhead. For the first time in a week, I forget to look over my shoulder.

We try to move off the topic of babies, both of us seemingly eager to prove that we're more than just the sum of our maternal parts, then laugh good-naturedly as we inevitably find ourselves circling back.

Mia is so easy to talk to. Despite her comparatively young age – twenty-seven, nearly the same age I was when… – she seems so relaxed about being a parent, so comfortable in her own skin. I allow myself half a fantasy that, by virtue of merely being in her presence, Mia's good nature and ease will rub off on me.

We exchange numbers. Make promises about future coffees, play dates. A trip to the Barbican Squish Space, which Mia assures me rhapsodically is "magical."

When we stand up to leave, I feel as though I've emerged from a long sleep, rested and restored. No; as though some long-forgotten part of me has resurfaced and clicked into being, the part of me that always relished connection.

I leave Mia outside the café, glued to her phone. Probably on Instagram. I bet she's an influencer; that must be how she knows all these places to go. She was snapping away at Astrid inside; I'd had to plead her to keep us out of it. "Paedophiles," I'd said, with a manic cackle I hoped would cover up my real distress.

I'm halfway home when I realise I've left my cardigan on the back of the chair at the café. I check my watch. I could go back another day, but Etta shouldn't need a feed for another half an hour or so, so I turn reluctantly around.

I'm just round the corner when I spot the pastel pink of Mia's cable-knit jumper. She's still there, standing outside the café, her back pressed against the glass. I raise my arm to wave, hoping to catch her eye, when I notice there is a man standing with her. I Grind to a halt when I see he has the sleeve of Mia's left arm clutched in his fist. His face is too close to hers. Instantly I veer from wanting Mia's attention to avoiding it, stepping behind a shop A-board to mask myself from view.

The man is tall and dark, his hair falling in tight curls. It must be Mia's boyfriend. I think about the look on her face when she mentioned him and hesitate, not wanting to pry but compelled to watch, scanning their lips but unable to catch fully what they're saying. It's obvious the man is angry, though, or at the very least annoyed, removing his hand from her long enough to shake his finger into her face. She resists, weakly, worrying her head at him, turning her cheek to the side as he grips the point of her jaw between his thumb and forefinger, jerks her face back towards him. When she tries to loosen herself from him, he grips hold of her shoulder and pulls her towards him with such force that she stumbles off her axis, instinctively cradling Astrid's head, burrowed in the sling. I have to look away. If this is Mia's partner, no wonder she was undecided about having children with him.

When she looks back, Mia is righting herself. She looks into his eyes. And then lowers her head, nods.

He says something. I squint to make it out.

"I won't," I thinks she replies. "I promise I won't."

A moment later, he turns and walks away.

A moment later, Mia follows.

VitalWoman
Empowering Health and Wellness for Her

Quickfire Qs with Ruby Rae

VW *gets the skinny on what gives California's queen of pop folk her spark.*

What beauty product do you never leave the house without?
I don't wear much makeup unless I'm on stage – I take good care of my skin and like to keep things au naturel, but I love my Nars Afterglow lip balm in Turbo for a pop of colour.

What's your drink of choice?
I'm not a big drinker – clean body, clean mind – so I like to keep it as pure as possible with an ice-cold vodka on the rocks. I get the day going with green juice: apple, pineapple, ginger, kale and celery. I hated kale when I first started having it, but now I love it!

And your guilty-pleasure snack?
I recently decided to go vegan and thought it would be really hard, but I've been so surprised. I love Naturale's quinoa chips and PlantPower's almond-milk dark chocolate bites,

but honestly, I've found all the plant-based food I've been eating so filling and nutritious, I barely think about snacks!

How do you relax?
I don't have much time to relax at the moment, as I'm in the studio working on my new album and about to go on tour, so for me the biggest luxury is a long soak in the tub. Actually, what I'm loving right now is Elixir's new Almond & Oat Indulgence bath crystals – in fact, I love the Almond & Oat line so much it's going to be the official scent of the tour!

Okay, so it sounds like you may not be able to pack it in, but how do you work out?
Well, I believe you can always find the time to work out if you truly want to make it work, which is a guiding principle I've learned since taking classes at Elixir. Their 30-Minute Fast & Furious lunchtime workouts are easy to fit into even the most packed of schedules, and I love them so much I'm even offering *VitalWoman* readers an exclusive offer: book a class at any Elixir studio before the end of the month and use code RubyRaeLovesVital for 10% off. I promise you, it works!

So, we take it you're a fan of Elixir! Do we dare ask what your go-to active wear is?
Ha-ha, you got me! It's got to be the Elixir Original Active range. It's made of 100% LightesseTM fabric and, I swear to you, it feels so good it's like being naked. I've bought up one set in every colour to take on tour. Not only are they perfect for working out, but they're so soft and buttery they're ideal for downtime too. They sell out quickly, though, so you've been warned!

Thank you for making time in your busy schedule for VitalWoman, *Ruby Rae – it sounds like you have a jam-packed schedule and are totally loving life! And we know our readers will love your exclusive offer!* 😊

12

San Francisco Bay Area
July 2013

∞

The longer Beth went to Elixir, the more Tate Larsen became a mythical creature in her mind. A physical sighting was as awe-inspiring as witnessing the moon landing first hand, but even when he wasn't there, his presence was all around – his signature printed on every Elixir beauty product, his genius attributed to the aphorisms used in class, his name spoken with reverence by those on the higher levels. The Juice Bar even had a green juice named after him: the Tate. It was, unsurprisingly, their best seller.

But when Marissa talked about him, it wasn't in this ethereal way. To her, his greatness was grounded in fact. He was highly intelligent, with an MBBS from Cambridge and an MBA from Harvard, along with several other qualifications Beth couldn't begin to wrap her head around. He was altruistic, having put his former nanny's daughter through college. He spoke seven languages!

"He's lived all over the world!" Marissa enthused while sitting cross-legged on the floor of her apartment after a late-night studio session. It was always Marissa's apartment they went to, never Beth's. She said Beth's

North Beach studio depressed her. That she could smell the fried onions from the Italian restaurant across the street and she was sure someone had taken a piss in the stairwell. That it felt cluttered (this she said apologetically; she was a self-confessed clean freak). Marissa's two-bed was on the top floor of a pastel-blue-fronted Queen Anne in Cow Hollow, with a view of the bay from the master bedroom. "His parents are Scandinavian diplomats, but he came here for college and stayed to start his own business. He made his first million when he was twenty-three. Twenty-three! Just wait till you see The Jungle. It'll blow your mind."

The Jungle, as it was affectionately termed by those in the know, was Tate's coastal mansion, which he generously threw open the doors to for the annual Founder's Day celebration. And it was there, Marissa promised, that Beth would finally be able to meet the myth-made-flesh.

The trip would necessitate a three-day weekend, which was a stretch given that JE&G employees had only ten days of annual leave, which were regarded more as a privilege than a right. Plus, a ticket for the party – deemed by Marissa to be "like the best festival you've ever been to in your life!" – cost half a month's salary. She would have to dip in to her savings to cover it, but, as Marissa put it, "Can you really put a price on your well-being?"

She thought about how happy she'd been since joining Elixir.

Transferred the deposit without a second thought.

They left at 8 a.m. on Friday morning, just minutes after sunrise. Marissa picked her up, giggling when Beth spotted her in the driver's seat of an open-top red Mustang, the paintwork gleaming in the early morning sun.

"This is yours?" Beth asked, slinging her bag onto the back seat.

"Mm-hmm," Marissa tongued the lid of her KeepCup before replacing it in its designated holder.

Beth had asked her once how much she earned from her Elixir salary. It still wasn't clear if her apparent wealth came from that or family money. Marissa had told her that "wealth is in the eye of the beholder," but that she'd give it all up for true body and mind fulfilment, and Beth had mentally scolded herself for acting so mercenary. Now, her friend pulled her sunglasses down from the top of her head, the interlocking gold Chanel CCs catching the light, and revved the engine. "Come on, let's roll."

The day was fresh but still bright for July in San Francisco, the sky softening into the colour of stonewashed jeans. And as they wended around Russian Hill and past the quiet fishing boats in the marina, Beth tipped her face back, allowing the pale early-morning light to kiss her cheeks. She hadn't set foot outside the Bay Area since arriving in California, and now, as they approached the orange behemoth of the Golden Gate Bridge, Beth twisted to watch the city, a cramp of skyscrapers, disappear behind them. She felt something lift within her, the final tightness in her chest releasing.

The day before, in their last Extraction session before the trip, Marissa had finally asked her.

"Beth, why did you really come to San Francisco?"

Beth had sat there, listening to the whir of the cassette tape recording her every move. "I told you, a job opened up."

"That was it? You decided to uproot your whole life and move across the Atlantic for a job?"

She looked down at the hourglass in her hands. Noticed a piece of dry skin around her thumbnail and began to pick. "Matt and I had broken up." Marissa knew the bare bones about her ex-boyfriend's betrayal. "The timing was right, and–"

"You're withholding, Beth." Marissa took the hourglass from her, tipped it over and placed it on the countertop beside them. "Can't you feel the tension in your shoulders? Don't you feel it crippling you, making you weak?"

Beth watched the crystals of sand converging at the neck of the glass, rushing into the base.

"Let it out, Beth. Let it go. You can't go into this weekend carrying secrets like this. You need to have a clear mind if you want to truly heal. *It works*, remember?" Marissa nodded sagely. "Come on. Before the timer runs out."

"It works," Beth echoed, anticipation tangling around her, making her palms sweat. "Okay," She swallowed. "You remember what I told you about Matt and Kate?" Marissa had leaned closer, and Beth realised her voice had quietened to a whisper, the memories a vice grip around her throat. "It wasn't just the breakup. He didn't just sleep around. I... I took a bunch of pills." Tears stung the corners of her eyes. "I don't even know why I did it. It was about a week after we broke up. Matt was coming round to drop off some stuff of mine that had got mixed up. I was waiting for him and then he called saying he'd got caught up, that he'd be late, and I *heard* her in the background and just felt so forgotten, so... discarded. And it *hurt*. And I wanted him to hurt, too." She sniffed. Hard. "Anyway, when I woke up, I was in the hospital. I found out afterwards that it was him who found me. But he hadn't even bothered to stick around. My mum was there, though. And…" She tried to find the words, but she couldn't. Her eyes followed the rush of sand.

"Don't let it run out, Beth," Marissa commanded. "Dig deep."

"And she told me I'd been pregnant." Her mother's words coiled inside her, and she found herself reflexively pressing a palm to her stomach. "I lost it." She listened to her hollow words reverberating around the office, couldn't bring herself to look at Marissa. She hadn't known she was pregnant. A patchy diet and a healthy amount of stress had kept her periods irregular for years, and she'd been too distracted with work to keep track. "When she told me, I felt like she wasn't even worried. It was like… it was like she was ashamed." She shook her head, the memory so visceral it was like it was happening all over again.

Until then, she hadn't considered whether she would have children one day or not. But hearing her mother telling her those words had unlocked something in her. Looking up at her mother from the hospital bed, she'd been aware of something deep and powerful; the layers of it all; her, her mother, the baby that might have been: a palimpsest of motherhood. She'd felt the desire squeezing her insides, the loss of it suffocating. And her mother's disapproval made the loss seem double.

"Stay in the moment," Marissa counselled. "How did that make you feel?"

Beth pressed a cheek into each shoulder, wiping the wetness from it. "Alone." She let out a juddering breath. "Like… like I had no one to look out for me anymore. No one to care. I had to get away from it all. All that shame. All that judgment. And I figured, if no one in London cared I was there, why stay?"

She felt light-headed, her brain pulsating inside her skull like the time she'd tried to run up Lombard Street forgetting she hadn't eaten for nearly twenty-four hours.

Marissa's arms found her, pulling her into a hug. "You're not alone anymore," she whispered into Beth's neck. And Beth clung to her, her body growing limp, spent. "You have us."

"I was proud of you yesterday," Marissa said now as they sped faster, the bridge's burnt-orange suspension cables whipping into a blur.

"Really? You were?"

Marissa's eyes were fixed on the road ahead, but Beth saw the curvature of her lips bend upwards. "Really, I was." Beth watched the dip of Marissa's chin as she bowed her head into an almost imperceptible nod. "And Tate is too."

"Tate?"

"Mm-hmm. I told him about you. He's excited to meet you."

Beth didn't know why – she'd never even exchanged a single word with him – but the idea of Tate talking about her made her feel lightheaded.

Marissa reached across to turn on the sound system. Ruby Rae, her favourite singer blasted through the speakers. *"With every tear that hits the floor, I'm a warrior, hear me roar!"* Ruby trilled, and they both joined in with the chorus: *"I'm strong, I'm powerful, breaking through. My head is high, I'm born anew!"* Beth felt a rush of energy, a goofy grin spreading so wide across her face it hurt her cheeks.

A cloud shifted, exposing a burst of sunlight. She tilted her face upwards, letting the glare warm her cheeks.

And she felt it – the possibility of renewal stretching across her like the wide expanse of the sky overhead. Matt, London, and her family narrowed into a distant vanishing point. They couldn't touch her now.

"Woohoo!" she howled. Lifted her arms up to feel the pull of the sea breeze.

"What?" Marissa called, amused, over the roar of the speakers.

"Nothing. It's just… This is… This is awesome."

Marissa turned the volume up. Rolled her shoulders to the beat. "Yeah, baby!" She reached her arm across to squeeze Beth's thigh. "And this is just the start."

13
Muswell Hill, London
6th July 2023

∞

I retreat home, not wanting to look back at Mia. The pleasantness of the morning seems sullied, like food left too long in the sun, and I have the unsavoury sensation of witnessing something I shouldn't have. An unsettling sense of familiarity.

I turn the key in the lock and step into the cool relief of the hallway, trying to shake off my disquiet, to reason with myself. I can't read my own past into every situation. It was probably just a typical couple's spat. But if I do find out there is more to it, I need to let Mia know that I'm there for her, that I understand. I'll mention it, subtly, next time I see her.

Next time.

I roll the phrase around on my tongue. I like the idea that there might be a next time.

I push the pram into the corner and lift Etta onto my shoulder, her grey cellular blanket still tangled around her legs.

"Shall we have some lunch, little one?" I try out the breezy sing-song tone Mia had used in class. As I do, I feel the weight of something loosen itself from the tangle of the blanket, skitter onto the stone floor. "What's that?" I ask, aloud, bending awkwardly with Etta in my arms to retrieve it.

The object – plastic, hard – has rolled to a stop at the bottom of the stairs.

"How did that get there?" My voice ricochets off the empty walls, unnervingly loud. Was it something from the music class, or maybe from the café? One of Astrid's toys? No, no. My memory might have been sleep-dappled, but we hadn't used anything like that in the class, and Astrid had been in a floor seat the whole time we'd been in the café. I would have noticed if she'd had a toy.

And then my chest goes tight as I pick it up, hold it out in my palm.

An hourglass.

A plastic sand timer, encased in a sunny yellow frame.

The sand whispers through it as I turn it round, eyes looping around the interior, the familiar outline that reminds me instantly of…

"Come on!"

Instantly I am slammed back through time.

My chest is pressed onto concrete floor. A naked heel digs into the small of my back as I taste my own tears. "Stop being so weak. Can't you see that you're only hurting yourself? How can I help you if you won't help yourself?"

"Beth!" The door to the ground-floor flat bangs open, crashing me back into the present as our downstairs neighbour, Ingrid, appears. My shoulders jerk, fingers flaring open.

The hourglass falls from my grasp, rattling to the ground.

"Sorry, I didn't expect to see you there," Ingrid stands in the doorway, a hand pressed to her ribcage.

"Hi, Ingrid," I say distractedly, trying to see where the hourglass has landed. "Sorry if I disturbed you. We're just heading up."

"Not at all. I'm just on my way to meet a client." Ingrid is a physiotherapist who works with older people, helping them in their rehabilitation after hip replacements or falls. Walking past their doorway, I always catch the faint medical whiff of Tiger Balm. "But actually, I'm glad I bumped into you. Hardeep's mum came over a couple of days ago and cooked this massive feast. We're going to Sweden tomorrow to visit my brother and we'll never finish it. Would you and Adam take some?"

"Um, sure. That's great, thank you." I'm not fully taking in what Ingrid is saying, my eyes still roving the hallway in search of the hourglass.

"Great. I'll pop by later and bring it up. Don't stress about returning the Tupperware right away; we're coming back late on Sunday." Ingrid closes her front door fully behind her, loops a bag over her shoulder. "Oh, is this yours?" she stoops to pick up the hourglass from where has rolled to the edge of the welcome mat by the front door. Holds it out.

"Oh. Yes." I take in the yellow plastic loop in Ingrid's palm. My stomach twists. There is an awkward moment when she extends her hand out further and I hesitate too long to take it.

Ingrid's smile gets tighter. "Need something to count down the hours till bedtime?"

I force my arm to stretch, compel my fingers to grasp it. "Ha-ha." I eject the laugh from my chest. "Yes, exactly."

I feel Ingrid trying to read me. Widen my eyes in the hope of demonstrating sanity.

"Okay... Well, I'll see you later, then." But at the front

door she pauses, turns. "By the way, did the health visitor catch you?"

"Hm? What?" I ask distractedly, eyes still on the timer.

"Someone came by the other day. You were out."

I rack my brains, trying to remember the last time the health visitor visited. Not for months, surely. Did I have an appointment? The nagging feeling of being followed washes over me once more.

"What did they look like?"

"Normal?" Ingrid grimaces. "Sorry, I was rushing out. They said they'd pop a note through your door and try again another time."

There was no note.

"Beth?" Ingrid nudges at my silence. "Look, I have to get to my client, but I'll see you tonight, okay?"

"Okay." I force my lips to form the words. I feel paralysed, even though inside my mind is whirling.

Ingrid leaves without looking back.

14
Muswell Hill, London
6ᵗʰ July 2023

∞

Upstairs, I try to put Etta in her bouncer – I need space to breathe, to think – but she wriggles in protest.

"Etta, please don't do that." I try to control the anger teetering at the edge of my voice. I am still holding the hourglass, the plastic pressing awkwardly into my flesh as I try to clip the harness. Etta jerks, undeterred. "Come on now, sweetheart. Just give me a minute." I squeeze my eyes tight shut, trying to centre myself, inhale calm, realising – too late – where I have learnt this technique just as Etta kicks, the ball of her foot connecting with the soft part of my stomach and I find myself shrieking, the words ripping out of me before I can stop them: "Stop that now or I will *make* you!"

Etta flinches. Stills.

And I am drenched in regret.

I sound just like one of them.

"Please… darling… I didn't mean it. I am so sorry." I pull Etta into me, burying my face in the crook of her neck. "Mummy's sorry. Mummy didn't mean to shout." I try to ground myself in our mingling scents, feeling our pulses, mine slightly faster than it should be. More kisses. Fierce. "I love you so much."

I take a long, slow breath.

It's just a plastic toy. It probably belongs to another child from the class. Maybe it did belong to Astrid and I just didn't notice. I layer excuse on top of excuse, hoping to believe just one of them.

Etta calms, but the interaction leaves me feeling dizzy, and I force myself to make a sandwich, remembering that I haven't eaten all day. But when I sit down on the sofa to eat, I find I've lost my appetite. Can't bring myself to put the sandwich to my lips. The cheddar cheese smells faintly of sick. My hands tremor as I push the plate away. It reminds me of those early days – after – how I had to retrain my brain to view food as something other than the enemy. But then I look at Etta, now beside me on the sofa, and think of my milk supply. The guilt creeps in. It's not good to skip a meal. Etta will suffer because I've been selfish. I can hear his voice in my head telling me so.

And then I do something I know I shouldn't. I spy the hourglass where I left it haphazardly on the kitchen counter, the sand now having run to the bottom.

I stand.

Take my plate over to counter and pick up the timer. As I tilt it, I hear the susurration of the grains inside, sending shockwaves up my spine.

I look down at the sandwich, suppressing another ripple of nausea. Back at the hourglass. And before I can muse on it further, I twist the hourglass over, setting it down on the wooden countertop. I take the sandwich between my hands.

Hesitate a millisecond before the compulsion over-whelms me.

And then I begin. Ripping off chunks with my fist. Cramming pieces into my mouth as far back as they'll go, index finger reaching so far into the depths of my gullet I gag. Chew, swallow, chew, swallow, as fast as I can, bread and cheese mulching together, sticking to the roof of my mouth. My eyes, fixed on the sand flowing through the hourglass's neck, begin to stream.

The plate is finally empty.

A sound wrenches from me, somewhere between a groan and a gasp.

The last trickle of sand runs out.

I am caked in sweat. Panting. I should want to be sick. I should want to cry. But I feel strangely… elated. Lightheaded. The ingrained satisfaction of having "beaten it" is still buried there, under all the layers I've tried to hide beneath. I remember how good it feels, to prove myself. To have won.

And it is this realisation that brings me back to myself. That makes my stomach acid bubble around the ball of gluten and dairy congealing in my stomach.

No.

I snatch up the hourglass. Stalk across the room to the bin and throw it inside, releasing the pedal so violently that the lid closes with an unnerving *clang*.

"Stay away from me," I say out loud.

But as I make my way across the room, compelled to pick up Etta, to feel my daughter's safety in the flesh, I catch sight of my reflection in the blank television screen. My eyes are wild. My hair is a mess. And it is as though I am looking at my shadow self.

A reflection of a past that is now unnervingly present.

I set Etta on my lap and switch on the television, drowning my reflection in a wash of too-bright children's cartoons.

With the baby momentarily distracted by the colours, I try to keep my mind focused, my thoughts rational.

What do I actually know, for fact?

The Baby Sparks flyer, the hourglass – they could both be explained away. Couldn't they?

The health visitor. I twist, scanning the floor near the front door for a note. Could I have swept something up when I was cleaning? Or maybe they didn't leave one after all? It's not like they'd broken in, hidden in the closet. Even as I think it, I find myself turning to the cupboard, eyeing the closed door.

You're being ridiculous.

Mia? But we'd been together all afternoon. If she'd wanted to get to me, she'd had ample opportunity.

But the invitation – *that* was real. I'd seen it with my own eyes. And Adam had, too, as had that woman in the park.

He must have known it would have this effect. He wanted my attention. Why?

Because of what I did.

Because of what I did to get away. And after.

But why now? Why leave it so long?

I'd assumed we'd had a silent understanding, both holding up our ends of a bargain created, unspoken, in the void of the years. I had stayed away. I had stayed quiet. I had barely even dared to say his name out loud, as if doing so would conjure him, like saying Bloody Mary three times in a mirror. I'd let him have his life and he'd let me have this one.

So is he really getting in contact now, after nearly a decade, just to mess with my head?

I have to believe it. That this is just his usual brand of mind games. I have to hold on to the hope that he won't really come for me.

I hold Etta tighter. Kiss the top of her head.

Either of us.

I am changing Etta's nappy when I hear my phone buzzing. I retrieve it from the arm of the sofa to see a message from Mia.

Hi, Beth! Today was fun! I was wondering if you're around tomorrow? There's a Baby Sensory Class I go to sometimes. To be honest, I'd love the company. x

Guilt washes over me. I'd been so focused on myself that I'd totally forgotten about Mia, what I'd witnessed. I recall the violent expression on her boyfriend's face.

To be honest, I'd love the company.

I zero in on the phrase, trying to unpick the meaning behind the syntax. Didn't it sound almost confessional? Like she needed my help? And I am good at this, helping people, especially when I can understand at least some of what she might be going through.

I need this, I realise. And hadn't I made a promise to be Mia's friend?

I type out an enthusiastic response: *Hey! Tomorrow sounds great.* Can't help adding, *Btw, I think I might have ended up with one of Astrid's toys in my pram? A yellow sand timer? I can bring it with me tomorrow? Thanks.*

I pause for a moment, staring at the black letters on the screen. She'd added a kiss, hadn't she? It wouldn't look weird, or desperate, if I wrote one too? Add one, before I can change my mind.

I feel a little rush as I see the message disappear from the typing window and reappear on the body of the exchange. The hourglass probably was Astrid's. Mia had talked about that Danish shop, Flying Tiger. Said it was good for finding cheap things to amuse the kids with. I'd filed away the information mentally because I'd assumed Mia would be the type to only buy wooden things; was secretly pleased to hear her extol the virtues of "cheap plastic crap."

Buoyed, I set the phone aside and retrieve the hourglass from the bin, turning it over in my hand. *There, see? It's exactly that sort of primary yellow they'd have in the shop. Nothing like the other one, matte black and curved like a bullet, primed and ready to strike panic. I'll pop it in the changing bag now, give it back to them tomorrow.*

Relief runs through me like an ice cube melting.

"You'd like it, wouldn't you, darling, if we saw Mia and Astrid again?"

As if in response, Etta jerks her legs, lets out a raspy squeal.

"Then that's exactly what we'll do."

Elixir Manifesto
by Tate Larsen

The Hourglass Method

What does a successful person have that an unsuccessful person doesn't?

Money, you might say. Intelligence? Luck?

No. The answer is something much simpler. Something that, in theory, should be attainable for all.

DISCIPLINE.

Successful people are focused. Efficient. They have an innate understanding of time, and how much that time is worth, to themselves and to others.

So, by having the discipline to complete tasks within a certain time frame, you can take on more tasks, achieve more things and, ultimately, have more success.

But how can you train yourself to be more efficient?

The answer is: the Hourglass Method.

At Elixir, we have researched extensively the time-management techniques utilised by world leaders: the Eisenhower Matrix; the Bronze Age timeblocking method; Francesco Cirillo's Pomodoro technique, which utilises a simple kitchen hourglass to break tasks into intervals. We have combined this with our knowledge and expertise of popular HIIT (high-intensity interval training) exercise classes to create a system which harnesses muscle memory and the subconscious to have an innate understanding of how long a minute lasts.

An Elixir hourglass is necessary for entry into all our classes, and it will be your responsibility to bring one to class. When you sign up for any course package from Beginner Plus level or higher, you will receive your very own Elixir-branded one-minute hourglass, exclusively designed for us by New York fashion designer Jesús Hernández, for FREE (subject to availability, only when taking out an annual package).

Hourglasses are utilised in all our exercises, but exercise is only one facet of the Elixir program. Which is why the hourglass is yours to keep. Think beyond the studio – where does your life need streamlining? Grocery shopping? Laundry? Management meetings? We guarantee, once you begin using the Hourglass Method in your day-to-day routine, you'll never look back.

By training your brain to understand the value of a minute, and pushing yourself to see what you can achieve within that time, you will become smarter and faster, creating a sense of flow which allows you to focus on the task at hand and block out those extraneous voices that can distract and detract.

Don't forget to celebrate your unique breakthroughs by posting them on the Hourglass Honours Board, where our monthly winner will receive a $50 gift card and an Elixir-branded tote.

Together, we will help you find your discipline.

Together, we will help you find success.

#ItWorks

Please note: Members who arrive without their hourglass will not be admitted to class. They will have the option of purchasing a new hourglass for $59 ($99 for two).

15
Marin County
July 2013

∞

It was still morning when they got to Tate's place, right at the tip of Marin County, on a stretch known as Toledo Sands. It was greener there, more bucolic than Beth had been expecting, the unending route lined with yellow-flowered California laurel, broad-leaved oaks, and coastal grasses. The clean scent of pine was refreshing after the mongrel smell of the city.

Eventually, they turned off the main road and onto a dusty track, where they finally came to a halt in a sweeping double-width drive, where she caught a glimpse of Tate's mansion for the very first time.

"Wow," she breathed, craning her neck to take in the full view. "This is it?"

"This is it." Marissa stepped out of the car, closed the door with a snap of her hip. "Welcome to The Jungle."

It was immediately obvious how it had earned the moniker. Unlike the distinct ruggedness of the landscape they had driven through, the mansion was surrounded on all sides by thick palms, the spear-like leaves throwing a pattern of shadow onto the stone drive. Beneath them, in thick clusters that lined the path, tropical blooms exploded in multicoloured hues: sugar-pink hibiscus, dusty-blue bougainvillea, enormous Birds of Paradise that looked almost ready to take flight.

It was dazzling. Otherworldly. And that was before they even got to the house itself, a palatial expanse of soft, sand-coloured stone that soaked up the early-morning sun and projected it outwards, casting a warm glow across the front court. Italianate porticos ran the length of the ground floor, duplicated along the balconies on the floor above, each one framing floor-to-ceiling French doors whose wide-panelled windows sparkled in the light.

She followed Marissa inside, marvelling at the double-height ceilings, feet clipping on the grey-veined marble floor as they stepped into an open-plan space that occupied most of the ground floor, populated with minimalist occasional furniture, clusters of pot plants and bronze sculptures in curious, contorted shapes. Beyond, single-pane floor-to-ceiling windows afforded views onto a flagstone terrace punctuated by a rectangular swimming pool. Beyond that, accessed by a winding set of wooden steps, the Pacific Ocean glimmered.

She had never been anywhere like it. She had never even *seen* anywhere like it.

She had no idea that, in the not-too-distant future, it would become home.

"We must be the first ones here," Marissa wrinkled her nose. Her voice bounced off the cool stone walls. "Or everyone's still asleep."

It struck Beth then how comfortable Marissa seemed. How fluidly she tossed her set of keys into a china bowl on a counter, slung her overnight bag onto a chair and led Beth to the kitchen, where she heaved open the double doors to a gleaming Sub-Zero fridge and pulled out a couple of bottles of Fiji Water, reaching above a counter for glasses.

"Wait, Marissa, do you... do you live here?" she asked, taking the glass from her, a strange sensation pulling at her. She thought of Marissa's apartment in the city, how tidy it was. Now that she really thought about it, had she noticed a single personal item? Perhaps not. Even the fridge rarely had more than a clutch of apples and a bottle of vodka in it. Beth had put it down to asceticism.

"I crash sometimes." Marissa shrugged, brought the glass to her lips. Set the glass on the marble counter with a confident chink. "Tate's so generous. He says he has so much, it's important to share it with the people he loves."

She turned and walked out onto a terrace, a nudge of her head beckoning Beth to come with her. Selected a towel from the top of a matching stack folded in a wooden cupboard before laying herself onto one of the sun beds that lined the pool. Beth mirrored her but was unable to relax. Watching Marissa sigh, the rise and fall of her chest slow, Beth realised she really knew nothing about Tate – what he looked like, who he lived with, if he had a wife, children, girl- or boyfriend. It seemed so odd, to be sitting there in the middle of a vast, empty house, almost like they were breaking and entering, even though Marissa had a key. And she'd thought it was supposed to be a party, so where was everyone?

It was so silent out there, the only sounds the shush of the ocean, the occasional bird's chirp. She tried to manifest calm but instead felt distinctly unnerved.

"Um, Marissa?" she tried again, although she thought she heard the other woman tut under her breath. Her sunglasses were on, her head lolled to one side. Perhaps she'd actually fallen asleep? "Sorry, it's just… Should we be doing something? When does everything start?"

"Beth," Marissa sighed. "I was the first one in the studio yesterday, and I closed down last night." She roused herself. Raised her sunglasses to the top of her head, the two gold bracelets she always wore on her thin wrist catching the light as she did. "And now I've been driving for an hour and a half. Can I just… have some peace?" Added softly, after a moment's hesitation. "Don't worry. When something happens, you'll know."

Beth had only seen Marissa's face in profile in the car. Now, seeing it in full, she was shocked. Her friend did look exhausted, the whites around her eyes dull, their rims tinged in pink, like she'd been crying. When she looked closer, she could see the skin around her right eye was slightly mottled, the tone uneven and matte, like she'd used the wrong foundation.

"Is everything okay?"

Marissa inhaled, sharply. Replaced the sunglasses and turned her head to the side, away from Beth. "Why wouldn't it be? Relax. Everything's great."

Beth did what she was told. Pressed her head into the back of the sun bed, trying to switch off her mind. But she was restless.

She didn't even know what sort of party this was meant to be. Marissa had been infuriatingly vague about the actual details, relying on platitudes about how "awesome" it would be, how "baller" the guest list was. Marissa never sounded more Californian than when she was expressing enthusiasm. But Beth didn't even know what the dress code was. Should she have brought a present? A bottle of wine? No one in Elixir seemed to drink anything apart from vodka, and she didn't know the first thing about wine, or mansions, or parties in them. Her thoughts tangled around one another: perhaps she shouldn't have come, she was going to do the wrong thing, she was going to feel completely out of place.

The sound of a doorbell reverberated through the ground floor and out onto the terrace, making her snap to attention.

Marissa was now fully asleep and didn't move, but curiosity got the better of her, so Beth wandered back into the living room just in time to hear footsteps pounding down the marble stairs that sloped up the side of the house. She saw bare legs emerging. A girl with a cropped afro and sharp cheekbones darted across the hall, the half-moons of her bottom jutting out underneath her white T-shirt, betraying a magenta silk thong between the cheeks.

The girl reached the front door just before Beth did, heaving it open to reveal two people in catering uniforms – navy ties and long aprons – each carrying a large Styrofoam crate.

"The kitchen's in there," the girl stepped back to let them inside, jerked her head in the right direction. "You can park anywhere on the street. The forecourt's reserved for guests."

She left the doors open, turned to go. Beth hung back, shifting her body weight awkwardly beside a tall potted plant. The girl spotted her.

"Hi," she said.

"Hi," Beth repeated, blushing.

"Beth, right?"

Beth nodded, once.

The girl headed back upstairs.

From there, the mansion came alive.

More caterers arrived, more boxes. She heard the sound

of glassware clinking as it was unwrapped, vegetables being chopped, the hiss of the gas stoves and steaming pots of water heating above them. More people began to emerge from upstairs, other faces she knew from the studio, yawning and in various states of undress as they directed a bevy of service people through the house and onto the terrace, into the gardens below, to the beach. Two men crossed the living room in front of her, groaning under the weight of a giant vodka luge carved in the shape of the Elixir symbol. A food truck arrived, white and edged in neon pink, the words PERMISSION TACOS, GUILT-FREE VEGAN SF emblazoned on the side. Someone directed the driver to the beach access road.

Feeling rootless, Beth followed the steps down to the beach and watched a crew erecting a stage, rigging up lighting and sound. At one point, a woman in a floating silk gown with trailing batwing sleeves walked past, her platinum-blonde hair in rollers, and Beth realised too late it was Ruby Rae – *actual* Ruby Rae!

Back inside, the front door had been propped open and the place was filling up. A flock of guests dressed in casual chic daywear: printed sun dresses and silk jumpsuits for the women, men in a unanimous uniform of converse trainers, slim-fitting jeans and immaculately pressed white T-shirts. *Everyone* wore sunglasses. Beth stared down at her Elixir-branded leggings and felt acutely embarrassed, watching in the background as the noise grew louder, bodies converging, spilling across the levels, taking iced shot glasses from trays and studiously ignoring the plates of exquisitely small canapes that were being handed out.

When she checked outside, Marissa had vanished, so Beth decided to minimize her exposure by hiding in a corner next to a bookcase filled with weighty coffee-table books, the spines shiny and uncracked. There was electricity in the air, an excitement that was intoxicating. The name *Tate* fizzed on everyone's lips, but from her vantage point, Beth couldn't see anyone who seemed to bear his name.

And then Marissa emerged, ethereal in a diaphanous coral maxi dress, her hair scooped into a loose bun, tendrils escaping at the nape of her neck. She was wearing full make up, eyes slicked in smoky kohl – a feline flick, no hint of the tiredness from earlier.

"What are you doing in here, silly?" she slurred, and Beth saw the looseness of her smile, wondered what might be running through her system. She had done coke plenty of times in London – it was sometimes the only way to get through the long nights – but that had always sharpened her, not blunted her edges like this.

Marissa grabbed her by the hand, her palm warm and soft.

"You took your bracelets off?" Beth noted, surprised. Marissa always wore those bracelets, even in class. She'd said they were a christening present from her grandmother, the one person in her life who'd seemed to care about her. She'd died when Marissa was eight. Her wrist looked strangely bare without them.

"Oh." She flexed her fingers, staring at the empty stretch of skin. "They were just junk. I'm working on being less materialistic." Shrug.

Beth found herself being dragged into the grounds and down onto the beach. A band was playing, guitars slung lazily around their shoulders, a sea of people watching, limbs moving in rhythm. Marissa kept hold of her as they moved through the crowd, greeting this person or that, whispering their histories as they passed – this person was Hollywood royalty, that one an heiress to a chocolate-making dynasty, the guy in blue had sold a Fortune100 company before he turned twenty-one.

Beth pressed her lips against the frozen base of the ice luge, felt the hit of a three hundred dollar bottle of vodka land in a stomach that had been empty for going on sixteen hours. When she surfaced, she felt something rough and dry pressed into her hand, looked down to see a tangle of wrinkly, tan-coloured mushrooms.

"Don't look so worried," Marissa whispered when she started to refuse. "They're natural." Her smile tightened. "Anyway, it's supposed to be a party. It'll help you relax."

And Marissa was right. Almost as soon as Beth had swallowed the things, the parched unpleasantness washed away with another swig of vodka, she felt the tension leave her body. They oozed together along the beach, and it was almost as though they were one entity – her and Marissa; her, Marissa, and the crowd – their bodies knotted, arms in the air, the steady rhythm from the band matching the beat, beat, beat of their hearts. And then it was as if an invisible undercurrent had picked up, dragging all the guests into their wake, pushing, shoving, shrieking, two-hundred-odd people vying for prime position at the front of the stage.

"What's happening?" she asked Marissa, a thin spear of anxiety cutting through the fog.

But she didn't need to ask, because around her a chant began to sound, slow at first, and then louder, more frantic, as all the voices joined in, reaching a fever pitch: "Tate! Tate! Tate! Tate!"

And then, as quickly as it had started, a hush descended, the music screeching to a halt.

A figure took to the stage, palms raised to the waiting onlookers, praying for the silence that they instantly provided. A man with shaggy blond hair and husky-blue eyes, dressed in soft fitted yoga pants and a brilliant-white T-shirt, sporting bare feet.

Tate.

He strutted to the centre of the stage in a silence so profound that Beth could hear the growl of someone's stomach five people along. Laughed as he pulled the mic off the stand, his low chuckle melding with the azure sky overhead.

"Friends," he began. And the crowd collectively pitched forward, desperate not to miss a syllable. "I stand here before you a joyous man. A grateful man." His accent was the vocal equivalent of distilled water, uncannily neutral. "A year ago today, I had a dream. I wanted to build something. Something special. Something that would help people. To give them a deeper meaning to their lives. I wanted to empower them. Cure them. Improve them. An elixir" – he paused, giving the audience a knowing look, and obligingly they laughed – "for the ills of modern life." He picked up a water bottle from the stage and uncapped it, the sound amplified as it knocked against the head of the microphone. He took a drink, and Beth felt the crowd holding a collective breath. "Through the Elixir programme, you will find success. But success is a privilege, not a right. And you know yourselves that the journey there isn't easy. It can be painful, physically and mentally." Around her, people nodded. She felt herself nodding too. "And so I ask you now, on this day of celebration, standing here on the precipice of greatness: how much are you willing to give... for perfection?"

Recapping the bottle, he looked into the crowd. "Parker," he said, and leaned forward, pointing the bottle at someone in a flower crown. "How much can you give?" Before they could answer, he turned to someone in a crystal-studded trucker cap. "Avery, how about you?" One by one, he picked people out, turning from one individual to another: "What can she give? How about him?" Beth felt the energy in the crowd change, people jostling, desperate for him to bend his light on towards them, felt the hunger inside herself, too, her limbs taut, hoping, wanting. Finally, he raised his hands, praying for silence. "The answer, friends, should be *everything*. Because perfection is priceless. But together, we can get there. So today, I want you to make a commitment. I want you to reach deep inside yourself, and I want you to *give*. And then I want you to look to the person on your right, and to your left, and I want you to give to them. Elixir can save you, but only if you let it. Only if *we* let it. Together. As one." And then he replaced the mic in the stand and thrust his fist in the air. "It works!" he hollered into the crowd.

A beat later, the echo came back in surround sound – "It works!" An army of fists punched into the air. Enthralled, Beth found herself mirroring them, the excitement tangy, battery acid.

And she felt it now, in full. This thing she had somehow stumbled into being part of. The thing that would save her. That would fill the ache inside her that had become a cavern – her father's death, her mother's disapproval, Matt and the unspeakable incident that had crushed her, slowly making her, inch by inch, *less*.

But none of that mattered now – not her job, or her old life, who she was or had been trying to be. Nothing mattered now but being part of Elixir.

Elixir would save her from herself. For that, she would give everything.

She watched Tate curl his hand around the microphone, his face breaking into a heart-melting smile. Found her feet begin to stamp, the palms of her hands stinging as she cupped them, again and again, her lungs tingling with the ferocity of her ululations.

"All right, Elixir: are you ready to party?!"

She'd never been readier.

16
Muswell Hill, London
6th July 2023

∞

"So, how was the class?" Adam asks at dinner.

We're having the leftovers Ingrid has brought over, way too much for us to eat in one go. The smell of cardamom and ginger fills the flat as I heat up the Tupperware and take it to the table, and I force myself to take an interest in it. Hardeep's mum is an excellent cook, and ginger is good for my supply.

Etta has been difficult to settle, so she's in the Moses basket beside us, chewing on her hand. I look across at her conspiratorially as I bring plates and cutlery over.

"Good. We made friends."

"Oh?" Adam pauses, spoon poised over a tub of chana masala. "Who?"

"Mia and Astrid." I take a seat opposite him, pour us both a glass of water from the jug on the table.

"Mia?" There's something about the tone of his voice that makes me laugh.

"What, you think you know her?" I suddenly have an image of Adam in his suit and tie, sitting cross-legged on the floor of the church hall. Adam is delightful with Etta, but hands-on he is not.

"No, no, of course not." He takes a glug of water, shakes his head. "I used to work with someone called Mia. I thought for a second she had a daughter called Astrid, but actually I think I'm wrong. I think it's Saskia."

"Those sound nothing alike." I shouldn't be, but I'm annoyed at him for taking the wind out of my sails. I'd been waiting all day to tell him about Mia, to show him I'm not a complete recluse, and now we're veering completely off topic.

"Yes, yes, of course they're not. But you know what I mean, though, a sort of ethereal name?" He looks to the Moses basket and his expression softens. "Not like Etta."

It had been an in-joke of ours, calling her Etta. We hadn't managed to stick on a name the whole pregnancy. I'd keep suggesting things and Adam would turn them down.

"Charlotte?"

"Like the pig in that children's book?"

"Charlotte was the spider, not the pig."

"Doesn't matter – now all I can think of is pigs."

"Flora?"

"Too prissy."

"Georgia?"

"I had an aunt called Georgia – I hated her."

Round and round. Nothing landed. It drove me crazy.

But Adam had tasked himself with making a playlist for the birth. When it had all gone wrong, he'd been frantically trying to make it up to me, and in the operating theatre he'd brought his phone out, timed it perfectly so that, as they lifted down the blue surgical curtain and held her up for us to see, Etta James's "At Last" began to play. It was corny, but it was also perfect. And the sweetness of it, of Adam's delighted expression as I focused on the lyrics to the song – at last, at last she was there – overwhelmed me. As they placed her wrinkled, wriggly body onto my chest and I began to cry with the enormity of it all, Adam had stroked my neck and said, "What about Etta?"

It was perfect.

The memory wraps itself around me now. I smile, shake my head. "No, not like Etta."

He snakes a hand across the table. I take it.

"Sorry. We've digressed. Go on then, tell me about this new friend. What does she do? Where does she live?"

I cycle back through the chat in the café. We were there for a good couple of hours, and by the end of it I felt as though we were old friends. But actually, now that I think about it, I couldn't recall Mia talking about what she did before Astrid was born, or where she'd been born. Or where she lived. Funny; we'd circled around the ins and outs of motherhood and all the multifaceted emotions that went with it, but when I thought about any factual details about Mia, I drew a blank. I didn't even know her surname; she was down in my phone as simply "Mia Astrid Mum."

I wrinkle my nose, trying to pretend I am more nonchalant than I'm feeling. "Hmm. I'm not sure she mentioned where she lived. We mainly talked about baby stuff."

"Well, I assume it's nearby if she was at the class? Why didn't you ask?" He probes. I feel a bit embarrassed, as though I'd been caught out missing some social cue.

"I'll ask her now – I need to text her back anyway." I stand, grab my phone from the coffee table and thumb through to

her name. "She's really fun, though. I think you'd like her."
I scroll over to Mia's message and can't help telescoping
ahead: dinner parties, picnics with the kids in Alexandra
Park, Mia's boyfriend a shadowy figure, if present at all.
"She's super-relaxed about motherhood, you'll be happy to
hear," I continue. "I might even learn to take a leaf out of
her book."

I click the message box. Type.

*Hey, sorry to bother you. Just wanted to see what the details were
for tomorrow? Let me know what time to meet and where? And if
you want the sand timer or shall I bring another time?*

Feeling bold, I add, *Love, Beth x*

Two blue ticks appear next to her message almost
instantaneously and I see Mia's status change to online.

I feel oddly shy, like I'm asking her on a date.

Typing… appears under her name.

I wait.

"What's she said?" Adam asks, supportively enthusiastic,
leaning across the table to see.

The notification vanishes. Reappears. Stops.

"Um… nothing. Yet." I try to shrug off the disappointment,
but I can hear it in my voice, and I know Adam will too.

"I'm sure she'll get back to you later." He gives me an
encouraging smile as I turn the phone over, set it next to my
plate. "You know what it's like with babies. You probably
caught her right in the middle of some sort of nappy
explosion. Let me know what she says."

When I don't respond, Adam carries on with his typical,
unabashed confidence, piling food onto his plate. "Honestly,
I think it's really great, darling. It's healthy for you, to have
friends with babies the same sort of stage. She'll just be busy,
that's all. Stop stressing."

"Yeah." I nod, still unconvinced. "I'm sure that's it."

I check my messages sporadically throughout the evening, but Mia still doesn't respond. I watch the notification under Mia's name update itself: "last seen at 20:34," "at 21:03," "at 22:11." She's clearly using her phone, and I know she's seen the message, so why doesn't she just reply?

"Beth, you're getting a little obsessive about this." Adam tries to console me as I pull back the duvet and get into bed beside him.

"I'm not obsessive." The word jars, even though he doesn't mean it to. It's a trait I've tried so hard to unlearn. "It's just…" I hesitate, wary of saying too much, of exposing myself. "She was fighting with her boyfriend. I'm worried."

"Her boyfriend was at the café?"

"Not at the café. After." Adam still looks confused. "I left my cardigan behind. I went back to get it." As I say it, I remember it's still there. My eyelids feel heavy, the exhaustion of the day overwhelming me.

"And they were fighting?"

I nod.

"Elizabeth," he consoles, pulling me in for a cuddle.

The name makes my limbs contract, and I shrug him off. "Please, don't call me that."

"Sorry." Adam bares his palms. "Beth. My love." Sighs. "They have a baby. Of course they were fighting." He laughs softly, cajoling me. "Come on, imagine what she'd think if she witnessed one of our spats." When I don't reply, he sighs, brushes the hair from my face and kisses my cheek. "I honestly think you're reading too much into this. I'm sure she'll reply later. And if she doesn't, there are other friends to make. Other classes. To be honest, maybe it's for the best to keep your distance if there's something going on with her

and her partner. You don't want to get mixed up in all that."
I feel myself sinking into him. He kisses my forehead, my eyelids. "My sweet girl. You're always such a worrier."

I listen to him, knowing logically that what he says makes sense.

But as I close my eyes to sleep, the image of Mia's partner swims before my eyes: the clench of his jaw, the grip of his fist on her upper arm.

Adam hadn't seen the look in the man's eyes.

I knew that look. Dominance. Control.

And now Mia isn't replying to me.

Why does it feel like the two things are connected?

Why does it feel as though something isn't right?

Twitter Transcript
July 2013

@ThePaintedLady Has anyone else tried one of those Elixir classes in SoMa? I signed up for the taster course and it felt, I don't know, a little bit suss...

   @SFMomma Elixir got my bikini body back in three months after my second kid AND helped me get over my PND. It's legit. Now I just need to sell my kidney to afford the next course, LOL!

@Jen_123 I read the @Glowess article. $80 for sweatpants? No thank you!

   @SFMomma *@Jen_123* They're leggings, actually.

@BayAreaBabe86 I saw Tate Larsen in Cow Hollow last week. So hot. He wasn't wearing any shoes though – super weird!

   @Jen_123 *@SFMomma* Same thing.

    @SFMomma *@Jen_123* No, it's not the same thing. They're 100% Lightesse™ fabric. It's not just any

old cotton. Ruby Rae wears them. You've obviously never worn workout clothes in your life, ROFL.

@GlamGurl88 @ThePaintedLady You can't put a price on your health and well-being. If you believe, you'll find a way. #ItWorks

@ItsMeDan @GlamGurl88 Did you just legit tell her to sell her kidney?

@Jen_123 @SFMomma Whoa, someone woke up on the bitch side of the bed.

@SFMomma @Jen_123 Someone woke up on the lazy ass fat whore side of the bed.

@Jen_123 @SFMomma @ThePaintedLady Blocked and reported.

@MyFitnessJourney12 @ThePaintedLady A friend of a friend is doing it. She said it changed their life. I'd love to give it a try, but I don't want to commit to a whole course and she doesn't have any free class passes left.

@GlamGurl88 @MyFitnessJourney12 @ThePaintedLady I've got a code for a free class. DM me, let's connect! #ItWorks

@MyFitnessJourney12 @GlamGurl88 @ThePaintedLady OMG!! Seriously?! DM'ing now.

17
Marin County
July 2013

∞

Tate finished his speech. Applause broke out, a rumble she felt in her chest. He had moved the woman beside her – several women, in fact, and a not-insignificant number of men – to tears. Tears sparkling on their cheeks as they clapped harder, exultant. And she knew in that moment that she was standing at the precipice of something great. Something she was a part of, would do anything to stay a part of if it made her feel even half of what she was experiencing in that moment again.

And then he was moving, towards the front of the stage and then further, twisting his back to them and crossing his arms over his chest before dropping backwards, effortlessly, as eager hands lurched and jostled to steady his fall. He found his feet and moved through the core of them, parting them like Moses and the Red Sea, kissing cheeks and high-fiving hands, greeting everyone like they were special, an old friend. Stopped when he'd reached the back of them, to turn, address them as one.

"And now, we swim."

The effect was instantaneous. All around her, two hundred

bodies began wrenching, tugging at their clothes, discarding shoes and swirls of fabric in piles on the sand. Beside her, Marissa was twisting her bun higher on her head, paused in the middle of unclipping a gold hoop earring to stare at Beth as she hung back, fiddling uncertainly with the waistband of her leggings.

"What?" she hissed, and Beth saw a look of distinct displeasure mar her features.

"I don't know," Beth contorted her face into a frown. A breeze grazed her skin, drifting in from the ocean. The weather wasn't that warm. And neither was the Pacific. But bigger than that, more encompassing, was the fact that she hadn't been undressed in front of anyone since Matt. To break the seal of that now, in front of all those people, seemed...

"It's a bit..." She tried to make her voice light-hearted, jokey. "...embarrassing."

Marissa gave her a long look. "Beth, if you want to be truly open to Elixir, you need to question why that is. If you are embarrassed by your body, it's a sign you don't fully believe in The Work. Do you understand?" she prompted when Beth didn't reply immediately, eyes fixed on a woman a few bodies over fiddling unselfconsciously with her nipple piercing.

"Yes, yes." She heard Marissa, but still she hesitated.

Everywhere, naked bodies were emerging from their chrysalides. The effects of whatever Marissa had given her was starting to wear off and the touch of other people's skin, their intermingling scents, felt suffocatingly close.

"Don't do this to me now. Not now," Marissa urged. And Beth was surprised when she looked into her eyes to see fear sparking there.

But before Beth found a chance to question it, she felt Marissa's hands at the base of her hoodie, felt the swift motion of it being ripped over her head. She wrapped her arms around her bare torso, the ocean breeze biting against her skin. "Please, Beth. Don't make us the last ones in."

The tremor in Marissa's voice caught Beth off guard, but whatever was implied was lost as Marissa's fingers found the clasp of her bra and pinged it open, then glared at Beth's leggings with such vehemence that she found herself pulling them down just to avoid the conflict.

"Clothes are just a mask anyway," Marissa parroted as Beth slunk out of her knickers, instinctively curling over to cover her breasts and groin. "What are you trying to hide?"

And then she was propelled towards the sea, hearing the surf booming deafeningly close, feeling the icy spray of the ocean licking at her. And then they were wading, the water burning cold on her ankles, turning first her calves then her thighs numb as she gasped, letting out an involuntary yelp.

She tripped on something – a stone, a shell, someone else's foot – and found her body jerked down, down, under the waves. Sea water choked her lungs, invading her nostrils.

When she emerged, gasping, Marissa was gone. She twisted, wiping the salt from her eyes, to find Tate beside her, laughing and splashing as though they were in the Caribbean. She found herself meeting his gaze as she became palpably aware of her nakedness, the hardened peaks of her nipples, the goose flesh that pocked her skin.

"Hey, there." He smiled, flashing a Colgate grin. "Everything okay?"

"Hi," she bleated back, aware her teeth were chattering

and sure her lips were blue. "Yes. Nice to meet you. I'm–"

Before she could finish her sentence, he dove beneath a wave.

Later, wrapped in one of the wide-striped matching towels that an invisible network of hands had strategically positioned on the shore, she saw Tate leading a man back into the surf and watched, eyes widening, as the man sunk beneath a wave, Tate's hands pressing him down. No one seemed to notice or care, breaking off into small groups to resume their chatter as casually as if they had just nipped out for coffee. But something about the man just before he went under the water struck her. The look in his eyes. The terror.

"What… what's going there?"

Marissa gave her a tight-lipped smile. "I told you we didn't want to be the last ones in." But then her expression shifted and she nudged Beth through her towel. "He'll be fine. It's just a little test of endurance."

From then, the mood of the party seemed to sweeten and change, as though whatever freneticism had driven people into the water had been exorcised by it, and she soon forgot about the man, the press of Tate's palm against his shoulder blades, the roundness of his pupils as the water sucked him under. She found her clothes among the piles and dressed quickly, efficiently, her skin still sticky and flecked with sand crystals as she pulled her leggings over her hips. Ruby Rae took to the stage, performing a mellow acoustic set that soared above their heads and melded with the rhythmic pull of the waves. The crowd dispersed afterwards, chatting in groups on the sand or wandering up to the terrace above, sunbathing or dipping into the pool. The sunlight swelled and then softened, deepening the sky into mellow pinks and burnt-orange hues.

She still hadn't talked to Tate since she'd arrived, but she'd been watching him. Had seen the way he'd threaded effortlessly through the crowds, shaking hands or stopping to sit and chat, the neck of a vodka bottle clutched in his hand. She'd seen, also, the way Marissa straightened whenever he was close, as though she was always on the verge of calling out to him before pulling herself back. She'd stuck close to Beth, though, hovering beside her like an emissary, though Beth wasn't sure whether this was for her own comfort or because Marissa was anticipating she would make another faux pas.

As dusk settled, the guests thinned out and only a select party remained, Beth among the chosen few, by Marissa's grace. Somewhere in the background, a dinner table was set up – thick knots of driftwood legs supporting a rectangle expanse of glass, elegantly set with neutral linens and hand-shaped pottery. Marissa motioned her towards a chair, told her to sit as a member of staff appeared, pouring wine the colour of clarified butter into a thinly stemmed glass in front of her.

"Oh, I thought..." Beth gazed intently at the yellow liquid, wondering if it was a test, whether she should raise her hand to stop it.

"For special occasions," Marissa drawled. "Tate says it's not about denial but appreciation..."

"...*Tate* says it's a shame to let good Napa Valley grapes go to waste." A voice inserted itself into the conversation, and Beth looked up to see him there, right there, taking a seat beside her, raising his own glass to his lips. She watched the pulse of his throat as he sipped, silent. Positioned the glass beside his plate and cocked his head to look at her, mouth chiselling into a smile.

"Tate," he offered, the verbal equivalent of a handshake.

"I... I know who you are." Her throat felt thick. Somehow, being beside him in that moment made her feel even more undressed than she'd been in the water.

"Ah, but who are you?" he mused, Delphic.

"This is Beth, Tate." Marissa, now seated to her left, leaned eagerly over Beth's place setting. "The one I was telling you about? She's been with us three months and is practically Advanced Level II. She's shown amazing dedication. I think she has great potential. I think–"

"Beth?" Tate cut across her. Marissa stiffened, then withered, defeated, into her seat.

Beth nodded slowly.

"Is that short for Elizabeth?"

She nodded again. Just about managed a guttural "Mm-hmm."

He carried on: "Shame to curtail such a pretty name. Does anyone ever call you Elizabeth?"

She looked down at her place setting, white light bouncing off the charger plate in front of her. "It's what my dad used to call me."

"Used to?"

"He died."

"Ah. Yes. When you were ten."

She gave a jolt. Of course, Marissa had said, once, that Tate listened to the tapes. But realising it now, in front of him, she felt so... exposed.

But then, without warning, Tate lifted her chin to meet his gaze, the press of his fingertips soft and warm against her jawbone. "Elizabeth is a far better name for you, don't you agree?". Before she could respond, he went on: "That is what we'll call you. To honour his memory." His blue eyes stared back at her, two icy pools. "Some scars can't heal if you don't let them breathe."

Then the first course was announced, breaking their conversation. Tate turned to the guest on the other side of him, a man with skin so smooth it looked like it had been poured on. Beth found herself concentrating heavily on the food in front of her, a curl of exquisitely plated vegetables she would later learn had been curated by a Michelin-starred chef, the menu provided to each of them at the end of the meal printed on a sheet of rice paper and written in haiku. She tried to eat, tearing a strip of courgette with her knife and fork and laying it on her tongue, but the proximity of Tate's presence overwhelmed her, and she found herself moving the food around the plate, going through the motions, hoping no one would notice and think her rude. But then she saw the other guests were hardly eating either, all of them making the same show as her.

Instead, she drank; the wine lubricating her, loosening the clench of her shoulder blades and dulling the embarrassing ticker tape of her heartbeat whenever Tate's body brushed against her own. No matter how much she drank, her glass never seemed to be empty, topped up by some spectral staff member hovering in the background.

Beth leaned over in Marissa's direction, trying to keep up with what she was saying, the atmosphere growing warm and hazy around her, but the other woman's conversation was full of riddles, terms she didn't understand, and when she pressed her for explanation, Marissa would wave her away with a shake of her hand or head: "You wouldn't understand. You're not there yet."

"So, you're English?" Halfway through the third course – a bowl of mushrooms, their stems tentacled together – Tate turned to her.

Beth put down the chopsticks they had been eating the course with, grateful for an excuse not to fumble with them. "Yes." She cleared her throat. "From London."

"I love England!" he declared heartily. "I studied there for a year as a boy. I believe my old school mate Harry Wales took one of our classes recently." He let the sentence land, but when she didn't bite immediately, realising too late who the Harry in question was, he carried on: "So, I hear you had quite a trauma before coming to San Francisco?"

Beth's cheeks burned and she whipped her head towards Marissa, anger and embarrassment firing within her. "You... you know about that?"

Tate nodded. "I've listened to the tapes."

"Oh. Yes. Of course." Beth swallowed air, wondering if she might faint. Sometimes she came out of those sessions feeling like she'd been hypnotised, never quite believing how much of her subconscious she had given away.

"Hey, now. There's nothing to be embarrassed about." Tate pressed gently on the back of her hand. "It's all part of the programme. Extraction." A grin. "It works. Now," he lowered his voice, confessional, "I'm going to let you in on a little secret. The recordings themselves aren't important. It's the *act* of recording them that's important." His voice was soothing, honeyed, and she tried to focus her mind on it. "The tapes are a vessel, caging your past trauma in something external. This helps you treat them more objectively, because they become a separate entity rather than festering away in your core. See?"

She felt herself nodding dumbly. It made sense, it really

did. She thought of Matt's retort when she'd discovered the cold coil of Kate's bracelet in their bed: "Well, you were never around." The sting in her mother's words: "What on earth were you thinking?" She pictured the ribbon winding in the cassette tape, her voice extraneous to herself.

"Yes."

Tate licked his top lip, his tongue a succulent pink as it shaped his mouth into a smile. "See, I knew you were smart. That you'd get it. But the tapes have another purpose. They're vital for me, so that I can get a full picture of all our members. Particularly ones with as much potential as you." He made a teasing motion, pretending to doff a cap, and Beth felt a little fluttering in her heart despite herself. He thought she had *potential!* "Otherwise, how else can I help?"

Beth tried to allow her jangled feelings to subside, but the aftershock wouldn't leave her, her confessions replaying themselves as vividly as though Marissa was playing back the Extraction recording right beside her.

She pincered a mushroom with her chopsticks, tried to chew, but the stem was rubbery, the oil it had been sautéed in coating her lips with grease.

"It's okay to feel shame, you know." Tate's cheek pressed against hers, his hair tickling her chin, making electricity prickle down her spine, the closeness of it. "It's what we do with that shame that's important. Harness it." And then, unexpectedly, she felt his palm pressing against the base of her stomach. "The ability to grow life… that is a gift. And you threw it away. You need to live with that. Grow from it. You were still a seed in the ground of your development, stuck in the dark, in the earth. Let the flower I see within you bloom."

Desire gripped her. The tantalising promise of her potential.

Of people believing in her, the way Tate and Marissa did, rather than feeling like a constant disappointment.

"I want it." She heard the tremor in her voice. "I... I love Elixir." She added, quickly, before he could turn away, "I want... I'm *hoping* to join the Elite programme. When I'm ready."

The Elite programme. An exclusive, invitation-only level of Elixir for the creme de la creme that Beth had overheard mentioned in changing-room whispers after class. It granted access to exclusive events, members-only content, the classes were led personally by Tate. Marissa had told her it didn't exist, that it was all just rumours. But she'd said it with a glint in her eye, as if that was exactly what the Elite-level members wanted you to think.

"Patience, young grasshopper," he intoned. Was he being funny, quoting the trite line with such gravitas? Before she could decide, he rose, the scrape of his chair against the hardwood floor causing several of the dinner guests to pause their conversation, look up. He tilted his chin towards a staff member loitering expectantly halfway towards the kitchen and raised a finger in a gesture of pause before turning back to her.

"Wanting is the first step. Having the willingness to prove it? That's what matters most."

18
Muswell Hill, London
11th July 2023

∞

Mia doesn't reply for four days. The waiting makes me sick. I keep replaying the scene I witnessed outside the café, wondering if I should have intervened. I think about searching for her online, but I don't even know her surname, have nothing to go on.

It isn't good for me. This fixation on Mia is reawakening the memories of everything that happened to me, and I know that my deep-rooted desire to save *her* is kindled by guilt, over the one I couldn't. But, in a way, this obsession with Mia is also a tonic, distracting me from thinking about Elixir, the invitation. What his next move will be.

But then, on the fourth day, there it is: a message, delivered seven whole minutes before Etta wakes us up at 5 a.m.:

Hey, sorry I missed this. There's a class at 10 today in Archway. Let me know if you can make it. M

No kiss, I notice, regretting my own. But still, she'd replied.

It had been a rough night, and when I'd opened my eyes this morning, my first thought had been how I was going to survive the long stretch of hours until Adam returned from work. I hadn't worked up the courage to return to the music class again, and without it I have felt the rigmarole of my routine with Etta closing in on me. That afternoon with Mia had exposed me to a different sort of rhythm, and I'd clutched tightly to the feeling, not wanting to let it go. Perhaps now I wouldn't have to.

"What are you smiling at?" Adam asks, returning from the cot with Etta in his arms.

"Nothing." I take Etta from him as he slips into bed beside me, kisses my forehead. "Do you remember that friend I mentioned, Mia? She texted. I think we're going to meet up."

"The domestic-violence one?" he says with a frown.

"*Adam.*" The way he says it makes it sound lurid, gossip-y.

"Are you sure she's really someone you want to be spending time with?"

"I don't know if that's really what I saw. Anyway, I got on with her." I am instantly defensive. I have been on tenterhooks for the best part of a week, and now he's spoiling it. "You're the one who told me to get out of the house."

"You're right." Adam shrugs. "I just don't want you to be disappointed." And then, addressing Etta: "Do you think Mummy's going to end up queen of the Mum Squad, then?"

I snort. "Hardly." Push him away playfully as he takes my phone, holds it up above us like a faux fashion shoot, lips pouted as he lisps, "Mum Squad, Mum Squad."

Adam's teasing, but I can't help projecting a vision of myself as that woman: confident, self-assured, surrounded by friends. It is so vivid I can almost grasp hold of it; perhaps, with Mia, it could become my future. As long as Elixir remains firmly in my past.

She's waiting for us as we get off the bus at Archway Station, slipping her arm into mine by way of greeting. Astrid is in a pram this time, a slick black Bugaboo that still looks brand new, putting my wobbly second-hand Yo-Yo to shame.

"The entrance is a bit hard to find," she starts as she leads us down the hill, "so bear with."

I give her a tight smile. "Sure." I'm not a fan of secret locations. Enclosed spaces.

There is something different about Mia today though. I notice it as soon as we start walking, even though it's ephemeral, hard to put my finger on. She is still immaculate – hair tied back in a slick ponytail, dressed elegantly in three-quarter-length black trousers and a Breton-stripe top, a thin cotton scarf looped around her neck – but something about her manner is distinctively off.

"Is everything all right, Mia?" I ask, hopeful that she'll confide in me, the spectre of her boyfriend not far from my thoughts.

"Of course. Why wouldn't it be?" She lets out a tinkling laugh, and try as I might, I can't see anything in her expression to indicate anything to the contrary. Paranoid, Adam had called me. A worrier. Maybe he was right.

"I need a coffee. Want one?" She comes to a halt outside a small coffee shop on the strip. "Oh, sorry, I forgot." She eyes my chest. "I'm sure they've got juice or something?"

I blush. A headache from my broken sleep has been lingering in the pinched skin between my eyebrows all morning. Maybe it's me who's off. "Actually, I'd love an oat flat white."

But the feeling lingers throughout the Baby Sensory class, a strange experience where mothers grouped in a circle sit on a brightly patterned playmat using props – fuzzy bits of material, textured balls, felt puppets – to elicit some sort of reaction in their befuddled infants. Mia seems to close in on herself, her shoulders tight, practically flinching when I tap her knee to pass her a fuzzy bee Astrid has dropped. Still, I feel her eyes on me once or twice, turning just in time to see her jerk her head away, throw her focus onto Astrid. And several times, she looks as if she is poised to say something to me, lips parted in a half-formed thought, but then whatever it is either dropped or distracted in a froth of toys.

I don't want her to miss the opportunity to confide in me, though, and find myself plucking up the courage, sidling up to ask, as the class winds to a close, "Fancy grabbing lunch?"

She fixes me with a long look, considering, before answering, a beat too long, "Okay."

We go to a café on the corner of Highgate Hill, all exposed wood tables and avocado toast, and I watch warily as Mia settles Astrid into a highchair and places the contents of some Tupperware onto the table in front of her: broccoli spears, lozenges of soft carrots, fingers of toast. I know baby-led weaning is supposed to be fashionable, but the thought of letting Etta loose on chunks of food like that is mildly terrifying. I can't quite hide the alarm on my face as Astrid fists a hunk of steamed carrot into her mouth and makes a horrific gagging noise.

"It's normal!" Mia laughs, looser here than in the class, fishing the carrot out of Astrid's mouth and handing her a sippy-cup of water. I tried to hide my grimace behind a smile of encouragement.

I park Etta's pram beside me, pressing the brake down with my heel and reaching to stuff a muslin into the changing bag underneath it. As I do, my knuckles knock against hard plastic, and I pull out the hourglass, wedged right at the bottom under nappy sacks, spare clothes, and other infant debris. I'd forgotten I'd stashed it there to give to Mia. The shape still makes me queasy, but I know if I can just prove it had got there by accident, it will put at least part of my anxiety to bed.

"Oh, by the way." Casual, cool. "Here's that sand timer I mentioned. Sorry." I place it between us on the wooden table. "Hope Astrid wasn't missing it?"

I wait, anticipating Mia's answer. The sand rushes through the hourglass, and my heart rate involuntarily quickens.

Her fingers pause on the laminated menu she's reading through. She glances at the toy, shakes her head. "That's not mine."

I'm surprised by the abruptness with which she answers.

"Are you sure?" I can't help myself nudging it towards her. The sand shushes through it, a fine mist. "It's not ours. I thought it might be something you'd got from Flying Tiger…?"

Mia shakes her head. Her ponytail whacks back and forth. "No. It's not mine. I didn't bring any toys with me that day. I packed light because I had the sling, remember?"

The thud of my heart grows louder. I do remember, but once again I feel a fog come over me as I try to pick through the fragments of the day. Had I wound up with it from somewhere myself? The music class? The café? I mentally replay the day, searching for something I may have missed. The memories cling together, murky and indistinct.

"Yes." I swallow thickly. "Yes, sorry. Never mind. It's probably from the music class."

"It can't be from Baby Sparks. They're eco-friendly. No plastic."

I want to be annoyed by the callousness of Mia's casual

tone – her gaze is already up, trying to catch the attention of a waiter, palm raised mid-air – but of course there's no reason she'd understand why I'm so bent on finding an answer.

"Oh, yes," I murmur. "I knew that." I feel my face grow hot. "Only… I don't know how it could have got in my bag." I *need* this. I need to find an explanation. Because the more possibilities I eliminate, the more I see the looping hourglass's symbolism, the more I see it connected to the invitation. To Elixir. To the lengths I went to escape it. "Maybe…" I stare so hard at the hourglass that my vision blurs, the edging of the yellow plastic softening, as though it's burning. "Maybe you got it from the play café?"

"Hunnh?" Mia is distracted now, lurching against her seat, sticking her hand up higher. The waiter's moved to another table, taking an order. She tuts loudly. "For God's sake, can't he see we have kids? The service culture in this country stinks."

There's a change in her demeanour again, I notice; her fluid body language turned uncharacteristically jerky and sharp. I twist to get the waiter's attention, and in doing so, my elbow connects with the hourglass across the rickety café table, sending it flying onto Astrid's tray. Astrid shrieks, flails her arms and knocks it to the floor along with the sippy-cup and various sticks of food.

"Fucking hell, Astrid!" Mia snaps, leaning over to retrieve it all as the little girl looks at her in dismay, begins to wail. I sit there, momentarily paralysed, not quite sure how the mood has managed to sour so quickly, before springing from my seat, bending under the table to help.

"It's fine, look…" I reach under the table, scoop everything up and deposit it back on the tabletop, ignoring the gummy residue of half-chewed banana that sticks to my palm. "Don't worry about the hourglass." I watch it roll to a stop at the leg of my seat. "I'll go to the play café later and–"

"Can you just get that fucking thing out of my face?" Mia barks.

I flinch, mouth falling open in a surprised O.

It is at that exact moment that Astrid chooses to pick up some banana, launch it at Mia's face.

"Astrid!" Mia aspirates in disgust, recoiling, and presses a hand to her cheek. And it's as she does this that I see Mia's scarf loosen around her neck, am sure I see a purple bloom of skin beneath it.

"Mia, what's that?" Instinctively I reach up, fingers grasping for the spool of black cotton.

"Hey, get off me!" she snaps, lurching back against the seat.

I am alarmed by the vehemence of it, almost as if it's me she should be afraid of, so I change tact, lowering my voice and speaking gently, in the hope I'll calm her down.

"You know I'm always here to talk, don't you? I know we don't know each other that well, but if there's something you want to tell me, if there's something going on with your boyfriend, if you need help…" I am burbling. I don't know the right things to say, but I so want to help. Want to explain somehow that I get it without giving it all away. And yet even as I'm speaking, Mia is shaking her head, lips tightly pinched. "I understand," I try. Place a hand on her knee. It feels intimate.

There is a moment, barely a second, when I feel Mia yield to me. Where the silence between us feels open to possibility and I am sure she is going to confide in me.

But then Astrid squawks, and I feel the muscles in Mia's thigh twitch. And then she is standing, jerking the chair backwards with an unpleasant screech, grasping at the Tupperware, coat, baby.

"I – I don't know what you're talking about." As she speaks, she wrestles Astrid into her pram, holding firm against her squeals of protest. "I shouldn't have come here. This was a bad idea. James said–" But she shivers her head, whatever thought she was about to utter, lost. "I have to go. I need to…" She reaches into her bag, pulls a ten-pound note out from the fold of her wallet and taps it on the tabletop. "Here. For a tip." She fills in, when I start to protest: "To apologise. For the mess."

I watch her flurry of movement, too dumbstruck to answer. Watch as Mia wheels the pram round and bends to press her cheek briefly to mine. I catch a breath of floral perfume, the lingering whiff of clammy deodorant-scented sweat.

"I'll – I'll call, okay?" she says loosely, but her eyes don't meet mine.

I nod. Watch her back out of the café. Hear the jangle of the bell as the door opens and Mia disappears through it.

"That was weird," I murmur to Etta, sitting back down beside her. She hiccups.

But the comment is deliberately trite. And as the dust seems to settle around me, I can't help wondering what secret Mia is hiding.

And whether it's really just a coincidence that she's walked into my life, now.

19
Marin County
July 2013

∞

Tate disappeared for the rest of the dinner. When it was over, the guests shifted, some making their goodbyes or drifting off to lounge on the sofas or out by the pool. At some point, Marissa was gone too, and when she returned her mood seemed different, jumpier somehow, as though she wasn't quite in the room.

The mood turned soporific, the sky outside the vast windows deepening to a velvet blue, and as Beth lolled her head against one of the overstuffed cushions, she began to wonder where she was supposed to sleep. She burrowed down, eyelids heavy, about to drift off when a voice made her suddenly come to.

"Elizabeth." Marissa had been deep in conversion with a man in a lime jumpsuit, a principal dancer in the New York City Ballet, but now she leaned across the sofa to press a hand on Beth's shoulder, warm and supple. Her full name sounded clunky and unfamiliar on Marissa's lips, and she didn't respond immediately. "Elizabeth," Marissa said again. "Are you awake?"

"Yes, sorry." She tried to suppress a yawn. "But I think I should probably go to bed. Where do I...?"

Marissa stared down at a fingernail, picked at a chip at the corner. She seemed to be toying with saying something. "You've done really well today, but there's something we need to discuss. The next step you need to complete, to advance in the programme."

"Oh?"

"Come." She rose, stepping over a tangle of bodies, dislodging sofa cushions and stray glasses, not bothering to turn back as she made her way through the living room and into the kitchen.

Beth followed, her tongue thick with stale wine and the unquenched desire for sleep.

The bar stools made a shrieking sound as Marissa pulled two back from the black granite island unit that punctuated the centre of the kitchen. She nodded at one for Beth to sit, perching on the other.

"You've been doing really great work here, Elizabeth. Really great work. But it's not enough." Marissa rested her forearms against the cool surface, and Beth saw the fine hairs on them bristle. A shiver ran down her own spine in response. What did Marissa mean? She'd done everything she was asked to do, hadn't she? She thought she hadn't put a foot wrong. Was it something she'd said to Tate? She chewed at her bottom lip, playing back the conversation at dinner, searching for an indiscretion.

"You're still hooked on Matt."

"*Matt?*"

Marissa fixed her vision on her wrists, joined together on the countertop. "It's obvious to everyone that you can't stop thinking about him. And it's holding you back."

Beth fought against the urge to frown. "Marissa, I've barely thought about Matt, certainly not since we've arrived at The Jungle. I promise. Nothing about him is holding me back."

"But you spoke about him at dinner tonight, didn't you? To Tate?"

Beth's cheeks burned. "Yes."

"It's okay." Marissa impulsively reached across the countertop and pressed a palm over Beth's hand. "It's hard to let go. No one's judging you. But if you really want to move forward, you need to prove it."

"Prove it?"

"Don't look so scared." Marissa laughed softly. "It's nothing difficult. But I have an assignment for you, as your mentor. It'll be the next step in your progress. I'm sure you won't find it a problem, only… if you don't think you can complete it… well, I'm worried that we won't be able to carry on." She bit her lip. "You do *want* to continue, don't you? I would hate you to lose all this after all the achievements you've had so far."

Beth thought of how euphoric the day had been. Being with Elixir was like being on a drug, and the thought of not getting the next hit terrified her. "Of course I do."

Marissa templed her palms. Pressed the tops of her fingertips into her lips as she observed Beth, paused for a moment before answering. "Then you need to sleep with Tate."

The missive was so jarring, so unexpected, that at first she couldn't form the words to speak and instead let out a garbled collection of sounds. She stared at Marissa, aghast.

"That… That's the assignment? You want me to…" She felt too embarrassed to even say the word. "…with Tate? Marissa, I don't know, I…"

"You mean you don't find him attractive?" Marissa

sounded almost insulted, and Beth realised the offense she was implying.

She squirmed against the cool seat, thinking of Tate addressing the crowd, of the way his blue eyes had pierced the very depths of her at dinner. "It's not that he's not attractive; it's just that I don't understand... I don't see..."

"Listen." Marissa reached for her hand again, her tone soft. "I know it's difficult for you to appreciate this right now, at the level you're on, but I *know* this is the way to move forward. It's how you can truly heal. Tate says in the manifesto, 'It is only by breaking down the barriers of the past that we can progress through the gates of the future.' And sex... That's your barrier."

Beth swallowed, trying to take it in. "You... you think so?"

"Elizabeth, of course!" The name slipped so easily from Marissa's tongue. It was taking some getting used to, but wasn't that what Tate had said, that it was part of the healing process? Marissa squeezed her hand tighter. "Look, Elixir is all about taking control, about regaining power and responsibility for your actions. Matt and Kate's betrayal took sex from you. They made you passive, a victim. So now you need to take it back. Don't you see?"

She began to picture it: Tate's skin pressed against hers, the feel of his smooth, hairless body, so different from Matt's. It terrified her. But a tiny part of her also felt... excited?

She looked back at Marissa.

Taking back control. Regaining power.

Somehow, it was beginning to make sense.

"This is a test, Elizabeth," Marissa carried on, her words intoxicating. "It may have been handed down by Elixir, but really the only judge is you. If you can seduce Tate, sleep with him. Then you can conquer that demon. You can prove to yourself you've truly moved on."

Elizabeth. That name again. It still sounded odd, a relic of the past. But maybe it didn't have to. What if it *didn't* connect her to family, her old life… What if could signal her *future*?

She had been Beth for so long, and where had it got her? Maybe being Elizabeth would be a fresh start.

She exhaled. Tried to reshape herself in her mind's eye. Not Beth, but Elizabeth. Straightened herself up on the stool. "You really think this is what I need to do? You think… you think it will help me move forward? With Elixir, too?"

"I promise you," Marissa reassured, no hint of doubt in her voice. "It's like an even more intense Extraction session. Rather than just talking about the problems of your past, you'll be actively ridding yourself of them. You'll be ready to grip hold of the future with both hands. It's exciting, isn't it?"

Beth thought.

She hadn't slept with anyone since Matt. She hadn't even touched herself. Every urge, every sexual thought brought her back to the discovery of that bracelet, to what had come after it, her own body hurting, bleeding, thanks to him. And that wasn't fair, was it? It wasn't right. The thought of being finally done with him was so tantalising. So freeing.

"So, you think…" She cleared her throat. "You really believe that if I sleep with Tate, it will help me get over Matt? And the… the baby?" She realised she had been chewing at a loose corner of skin on her bottom lip, and now she'd bitten too hard, tasted blood.

"Oh, Elizabeth," Marissa breathed, radiating warmth.

"What?"

"Didn't you realise?"

"Realise what?"

"Just now. That's the first time you've called it a baby. You're owning it. Taking control of the trauma."

"Oh." Hearing the word echoed back at her again, she wanted to jolt, to run. For so long she had tried to smother the word in her mind, although it was indelible, bound up with her memory of her mother's confrontation, that day at the hospital: "What have you done? You were pregnant, Beth. You've lost the baby."

"Can't you see, Elizabeth?" Marissa pulled Beth into her, extinguishing the memory. "Even the idea of what I've proposed is giving you strength, healing you. Every other time, you were holding back, talking around it. And now you're facing it head on. This is proof: it works!

Through the thin coral fabric of her dress, she could feel Marissa's heart beating a frenetic trill, like fingertips tapping on glass. Her own joined it. She was suddenly aware of their presence in the kitchen – every sound, every smell heightened. The murmuring of the last stragglers from the living room beyond. The rhythmic tick of a second hand, the clock itself unseen. The lingering cooking scents intermixed with the smell of organic citrus cleaning sprays the caterers had used to leave the place spotless. Time stretched before her, unending, in which she became a new person. Happy. Complete.

"You're right," she whispered, in awe of her own possibility. "It works." And she reached her arms around Marissa's thin shoulders, hugging her back. "I'll do it. I'll sleep with Tate."

"Oh, you star. You absolute rock star," she murmured into her hair. "You'll see, I promise you. You'll see. Only…"

Marissa paused, her breath hot on Beth's neck. "You mustn't let Tate know we've discussed this. You can't make it seem like an assignment. It defeats the whole purpose. You understand?"

"Yes… yes okay."

Marissa sighed. "Thank you."

And she felt the sigh, felt the loosening of Marissa's shoulders as she released it. And it seemed odd, this phrase, in the moment. That Marissa would be thanking her when it was Beth it should be helping.

"Marissa," she began as her friend loosened her hold. And she saw it, then, a fragment of a fragment; a tiny hint, in the corner of her eye, of something that looked like fear.

"What?"

But Marissa was already raising herself up from the stool, moving as if to signal the conversation was over, and when she looked again, her expression was clear, and Beth wondered if it wasn't Marissa's trepidation she had seen but her own, reflected back.

"Um… When do you think should I do it?"

And Marissa blinked at her, smiled indulgently, as if the answer was blindingly obvious. "Tonight."

Extract

Elixir Manifesto
by Tate Larsen

"Fail Harder"

You are not a victim, so stop acting like one.

As soon as you frame yourself as a victim, you are denying yourself agency. And a person who lacks agency, lacks culpability, which means they also lack the power to change.

Think about it: You accept praise for your successes, so why would you not also accept blame for your failures? The lazy person, aka the victim, thinks, "Why is this happening to me?" When instead they should be thinking, "What have I done wrong?"

Realising that only YOU are at fault, that only YOU are to blame, is one of the most powerful tools we equip you with in Elixir.

We give you the grit to dig deeper.

To be better.

To fail harder.

So, the next time something bad happens or something doesn't quite go your way, I want you give yourself a good, hard look in the mirror and ask yourself, "Am I a victim, or will I be victorious?"

20
Marin County
July 2013

∞

The hallways were quiet as Beth ascended the curved staircase to the upper floor. Quiet, and dark; the shards of moonlight that glowed through the windows onto the thickly carpeted floor barely had an effect. She reached into the overnight bag she had stashed into a corner that morning and pulled out her phone from the inner pocket to check the time. It was gone 2 a.m.

She gazed down the wide expanse of corridor. Noted the row of doors, all shut. Marissa hadn't given her any detail. She didn't even know which room was Tate's. And so she braced herself as she moved her palm over the handle of the first door she came to. Clenched her upper body tight. Turned the knob.

A bathroom. She exhaled into the empty space. A walk-in shower. Toilet. Sink. All neatly neutral. Closed the door with a soft click. Hesitating, before moving on.

The drunkenness that had weighed her down by the end of dinner was starting to fade, replaced by the dull ache of a pre-emptive hangover pressing at her temples. God, she needed sleep.

The next room was even less helpful – three girls lay

tangled in the sheets of a double bed, another one cramped on a camp bed in a corner, who sat up and hissed audibly as soon as Beth edged open the door, "Fuck off, there's no room." In the next, two bodies writhed beneath the covers, their enthusiastic groans loud enough to mask the sound of her swiftly closing the door. The next room was locked, the handle stuck fast, and when she looked up, she noted a keypad lock beside the door frame. Then another bathroom. A small room that might have been a walk-in wardrobe. A personal gym, smelling faintly of sweat and cleaning material. Another bedroom whose occupant was snoring so loudly she could have sworn the lamp on the bedside table was rattling.

By the time she got to the next door, she was already contemplating going back downstairs, calling the whole thing off, but when she creaked it open to find a soft light on inside, there was Tate lying on the bed, reading, his legs crossed at the ankles.

Entirely naked.

"Oh!" she gasped, instinctively turning away, shielding her eyes. The whole idea suddenly seemed ludicrous. She should go downstairs, tell Marissa she couldn't do it. "Gosh, I – I'm so sorry. I–"

"Don't be sorry." Tate laughed softly, propping himself up against the pillows and placing the book by his side. "It's only a body. It's not something we should be ashamed of, Elizabeth." Paused. "Unless we let it." Bent his leg at the knee. Beth observed the way the muscles on his thigh contracted. His voice was softer in that space, lazier, losing the masticated American consonants for a sibilance that hinted at his Scandinavian roots. "I work hard on my body. I admire the way it looks. Don't you?"

Beth was sure she was now beetroot. She hadn't even

slept with that many people; she had been with Matt since their last year of university, and before then it had been little more than a handful of one-night stands, most of them involving copious amounts of alcohol and not very much effort. She had no idea how to seduce someone.

But it was undeniable that Tate was attractive. He had a great body. And from the little proximity she'd had to it, she knew that he wielded it both with calmness and confidence, that he had a natural tactility that made it easy to yield to him. That he was grounded in himself in a way that was both reassuring and compelling.

Matt had had a good body when they'd first started going out, but he'd grown lazy, giving up the football sessions that had once kept him lean. Favoured ready meals that used to stink up the flat, ignoring her when she suggested, surreptitiously, they "both try to eat a bit healthier." When she found out she'd been pregnant, alongside the pain and the trauma, there was also an edge of surprise – she'd loved him, but by that point she'd barely found him attractive.

There she was, thinking about Matt again.

She found herself moving to the foot of the bed. Swallowed, her throat clenching and releasing audibly. "I… I do. Think you have a good body. I think you're very attractive."

Inwardly, she grimaced, sure she sounded wooden, clunky. But Tate's face curled into a lazy smile. "Well, thank you very much. You could have a great body too, you know?"

Somehow this released her tension, and she had to laugh. "Oh, thanks a *lot!*"

She was reminded that she liked this man. That she'd had a good time with him that evening. Sleeping with him should be easy: a privilege rather than a task. So why did she feel so nervous?

"I'm being serious." Tate raised himself up, gestured to the bed. As he did, she felt like there was something different about him, something she couldn't quite put her finger on. And then it hit her.

"Wait. Your eyes. They're…" She squinted in the lamplight at the brown-flecked whorl around his pupils. "Sorry." She shook her head, her mind playing tricks on her. "I thought before they looked blue."

He shrugged. "Contacts."

Before she could articulate her surprise, he stretched across the bed to her, licking the pad of his thumb and wiping it across the skin beneath her bottom lashes.

"Your mascara's run." He jerked his head towards a door on the far side of the room. "There's cleanser in the en suite. Help yourself."

"Oh." She worried her head, embarrassed. She must look a state; she had barely looked at her reflection since she'd woken up that morning. And then she caught his eye, the knowing glint in the corner. Realised what he was implying: she amended her appearance; why shouldn't he?

"Don't worry about it now," he soothed, taking hold of her fingertips and guiding her towards the bed. "Where were we?"

Beth sat gingerly at the edge of the bed, half compelled to squeeze her eyes shut as she felt the depression of the mattress, the distance collapsing between them as Tate pressed his body against her back.

"You have some weakness in your upper arms," he began, tracing a slow line from the back of her elbow to her shoulder. His tone was matter of fact, totally impartial.

"But…" He knelt behind her, his breath tickling her right earlobe. "…you do have strong thighs. Good quads." When he placed a warm hand on her upper thigh, squeezed, she involuntarily tightened her core. "A classic runner," he continued, moving his hand away. "You've focused on your lower body and neglected your arms and core. But it's easily rectified. I'll recommend some extra classes at the studio that will help." And then his fingers stroked the nape of her neck, brushing her hair to one side as he brought his hand over her shoulder, pressed his palm against her chest. "And you have a good heart. A strong heart. Listen to that beat. Boom. Boom. Boom." He retreated, and when she turned, he was lying on his side, propping his head up with his fist. "You could do really well." Swallowed. "If that's what you want?"

"It's what I want." she said. Slowly. Deliberately.

Tate didn't answer immediately. She wondered if she had said the wrong thing, if she should make her excuses and leave, but then he asked, "I'm sorry, I didn't ask. Was there someone you were looking for? Something I could help you with?"

"I, um…" She thought her heart would break through her ribcage. Jesus, why couldn't she get a handle on herself? And then, forcing boldness: "I didn't mean to interrupt you. I was just… I was looking for somewhere to sleep."

From her position on the end of the bed, she turned to face him, flicking her eyes deliberately to the empty space next to him, the white sheets crisp and uncrumpled.

"You're more than welcome to crash here." Tate shrugged. "I don't really sleep much; I'll probably read for another hour yet, but I'll try not to disturb you."

Beth tried not to frown. She knew Tate's obliviousness

was a necessary part of the test, but she could have done with a helping hand.

"I'll just... I'll put something on," Tate continued, speaking into the silence, reaching over the side of the bed. "I don't want to embarrass you further."

There was a moment when it hung in the balance. When she might have agreed. Rolled to sleep onto the empty side of the bed and told Marissa she had failed; she couldn't do it. But she didn't.

"No, don't do that." Before she could change her mind, she moved fully onto the bed, crawling across the distance in a way she hoped looked inviting. "What if I... evened things up instead?"

Nerves tingling, her hands criss-crossed around her waist as she found the base of her T-shirt, tugged.

"Oh," Tate breathed, taking her in, eyes widening as she carried on, propelled by the fear of what would happen if she stopped. She reached for the clasp of her bra and snapped it open. *"Oh."*

Her nipples hardened, exposed to the empty air. It was true; she could feel it, the power coming back to her. All the weakness Matt had imposed on her, leaching away. Marissa had been right.

She moved over him, face almost touching his, inhaling the smoky, woody scent that lingered on his skin. He smelt so uncannily familiar, almost as though she had always known him. So much so that she couldn't stop her mind from spinning out, grasping at the significance. What if they were actually soulmates? Their spirits, or something like them, drawn inexplicably to one another through time and space?

And then he shifted, and she realised what it was: the

Elixir signature scent, willow bark and chamomile. He smelt familiar because he smelt exactly like her.

"Elizabeth," he cautioned, hands on the waistband of her leggings, restraining her. "Whatever you're planning here, I don't want this to be something you regret, okay? I'm not in the business of making people do things against their will."

"No. No, I won't." The atmosphere felt heady, their intermingling scent connecting as though they were one entity, as though she no longer knew where he ended and she began.

"Well, I need you to say it." It was somewhere between request and command and his grip around her tightened, fingertips pressing into her backside. "I need to know that this was your intention, that it's truly what you want."

And she felt it then, all of it – excitement, terror, possibility – as she met his gaze in full.

Answered with a conviction she hoped would be borne out: "This was all my idea. This is truly what I want."

In the earliest hours of the next day, the sunlight only just beginning to bleach the edges of Tate's curtains, a sound at the door startled her upright. Made her clutch the bedclothes to her naked body in panic.

"Marissa?" she peered into the grey darkness, her throat muggy with sleep.

"Shh," Marissa murmured, silhouetted in the doorway for a moment, observing them. Tate lay starfished above the covers. He didn't stir.

Marissa glided across the room, coming to a stop on the other side of the bed.

"What are you–?" Beth began.

"Don't worry. Everything's okay."

Tiredness hammered against her skull. She felt the ebb and flow of the bed as Marissa shifted her weight onto it and lay beside Tate. Waited for him to wake up, shout in surprise, tell her to get out. Anything. But he remained still.

"Get some sleep," Marissa urged, her voice low but full of command. "You did good."

She found herself obeying. Sinking back against the coolness of the pillow and closing her eyes. Felt Marissa's body shift. Relax. Grow still.

When she heard Marissa's breathing slow to a steady push and pull, she opened her eyes. Marissa's left arm was torqued away from her body, her hand palm down, resting directly on top of Tate's genitals.

Looped around her arm were her gold bracelets, the bands wrapped around one another as though forming a cross.

Transcript
Audio Recording,

Elizabeth Myers, July 2013

Marissa Reid: Ready?

Elizabeth Myers: Um, yes.

MR: Okay, so let's start by stating your name, age, and today's date.

EM: Um.

[long pause]

MR: What is it?

EM: I just… Do you think we could talk about last night?

MR: [laughs] Of course. That's why we're here. You did amazing.

EM: I – I did?

MR: I'm proud of you. You should be proud of yourself too. That's why I wanted to have this session, before we head back to the city. To check in, see how you're feeling. Good, right? It works!

EM: I guess, I just… I didn't realise…

MR: Tate thinks you're great.

EM: Oh?

MR: Yes. You were really impressive, Beth.

EM: That's great, Marissa. I'm really pleased, I just didn't expect–

MR: [laughs, softly] You really crave praise. Did you know that? Any little compliment and you're like a bee to nectar.

EM: Oh.

MR: Don't be upset. It's a good thing. It's good to know what motivates you. You'll need it if you want to make Elite.

EM: Wait, Elite? But I thought you said–

MR: It's real, Elizabeth. It's real, and I'm part of it. Look.

EM: What is that? A tattoo?

MR: Mm-hmm.

EM: When did you get it?

MR: Today.

[pause]

EM: Did it hurt?

MR: Hurt? [laughs] No, it felt amazing. It's a symbol. Of my commitment, of everything I've achieved. Official entry to Elite. And you could have one, too.

EM: It looks red, Marissa. Is it supposed to look like that? Who did it? Did they know what they were doing? You don't want it to get infected.

MR: Are you even listening to what I'm saying, Elizabeth? I'm in Elite. The best of the best. And one day, you could be in it too.

EM: I... [pause, audible breathing] Do you really think that?

MR: Tate says you have the capacity for greatness.

EM: Marissa... [sighs] I'm... I'm just going to say it, okay? Because you've done so much for me. You've been such a great friend, introducing me to Elixir, bringing

me here this weekend. I don't want you to think...
I would hate it if I–

MR: Tate says the heart can only expand with more love
in it.

EM: You mean...

MR: I'm not jealous, if that's what you're worried about.
I'm... I'm an enlightened woman. Aren't you?

EM: Yes, but...

MR: It was an assignment for both of us. Helping you
helped me. Don't you see? I would never have wanted
to hold you back.

EM: If you're sure...

MR: I'm sure. [pause] Look, we're going to be leaving
soon, but before we do, Tate needs me to confirm:
When were you thinking of progressing to Advanced
Level II?

EM: Huh?

MR: He thinks you're ready. And with me in Elite, I'll
be able to progress you more quickly. But it's a three-
month commitment, so you'd need to sign up upfront.
It's five thousand dollars. Could you make that work
for you?"

EM: [blows air] Oh, God. I... Marissa, I don't know how
I could pay for it. It's way more than my monthly
salary. I–

MR: I get that. It's a lot, I know. But I'd hate you to give it
up now. Not when you're doing so well. [pause] I told
you, I think, that when I first met Tate, I was living in
Palo Alto?

EM: Mm-hmm.

MR: What I didn't tell you was how depressed I was.
My dad had left the country years ago and had pretty

much broken off all contact. My mom was mentally checked out, pretty much always had been. I'd always had a hard time making friends; I was shy, even as an adult. I know that seems strange now, but it's true. [sighs] I felt like I had no one. Nothing. I was so lonely. The day I met Tate, I was... I was seriously considering ending it all. He was on his way to a week-long seminar he was running, and he saw me. I was on the side of the Expressway and I–

EM: Marissa, my God!

MR: It's fine, it's fine, I'm okay! Because of Tate. He grabbed hold of me, stopped me. He saved me. And not just then. He brought me to his seminar. He showed me there was another way. A way to be happy. To see my worth. And it was like... like I'd been seeing through fog my whole life, and suddenly the sun had come out. I went to his sessions for the rest of the week he was in Palo Alto, and when it was over I knew it was my chance. And it worked. It's true, Elizabeth: it really works! What I'm trying to say is that I know everything you've been through, and I know how... amazing... I feel right now. And I would hate for you to miss the chance to put yourself right. Isn't five thousand dollars worth it for your happiness?

[long pause]

EM: Marissa, I'm so sorry. I never knew. I didn't realise. I hear what you're saying, I do. It's just... it's such a lot.

MR: I know. [sighs] Only, is it really? Tate would say, can you put a price on your health? Your mental well-being? Plus, imagine what you'd pay in medical bills if you weren't in peak physical condition. Physiotherapy, from being hunched over a desk all day. You're literally staving off heart disease. Cancer, later in life. Think of the price you'd be been paying in therapy. It seems like a lot now, but think of it as an investment for the future.

EM: [almost inaudible] When you put it like that...

MR: Please, think about it. I wouldn't say it if I didn't believe it was true.

21
Muswell Hill, London
13th July 2023

∞

The morning after my meeting with Mia, I wake early, before Adam or even Etta. Resolved to do something nice for him, I slip quietly out of bed to make him a cup of coffee.

Etta's sleep has been getting worse. The books convince me it's sleep regression, although how it's possible to regress backwards from nothing, I don't know. The tiredness is like being at sea in the eye of a storm: as soon as I find the strength to stand, I am knocked back, dragged down. And Adam may not be the one doing the night feeds, but his sleep is disturbed nonetheless, and *then* he has to pull full days in the office, worrying about impressing his boss, his impending promotion. He thinks the big move will come at some point in the summer, that he will finally get the position he's so desperate for. I know he's stressed about it, exhausted, too – falling asleep in front of the television, misplacing his phone; the fact that he remains so even tempered about it makes me feel even worse.

In the kitchen, I pull out the cafetiere, search for the pot of fancy ground coffee I bought Adam last Christmas. It's not in the fridge, where he normally keeps it, and I chastise myself when I find it in the cupboard under the sink with the cleaning equipment, no doubt due to a combination of my cleaning frenzies and my recent forgetfulness. I hope it's not spoiled.

I look at my phone, at the stream of messages I have sent to Mia, all unanswered. I am clinging on to the fact that I am right about her boyfriend, about the bruise I saw on her neck. Every moment of silence makes me worry more. And yet, despite my worries about Mia, the growing maelstrom of my nights, a lack of anything further from Elixir makes me feel strangely calm. There has been nothing concrete since the invitation, and even that has now literally gone up in smoke.

As my sleep has decreased, I've started to notice how clumsy and forgetful I have become: spending fifteen minutes looking for my keys before finding them in the fridge; forgetting the name of the man who lives next door, and avoiding him until I remember it's Sam, of course it's Sam; finding Etta's washing in our drawers, and vice versa. If I hadn't physically *held* the invitation, watched it burn, I would have started to wonder whether perhaps I really had made the whole thing up, whether a mixture of paranoia and exhaustion could have somehow caused me to imagine the whole thing. Wishful thinking, no doubt. But at least so far it has amounted to nothing more sinister.

I take the coffee to the bedroom upstairs, but when I open the door, Adam's not there. I find him in the spare room, moving silently around the sofa bed, a suitcase open on top of it. The room is supposed to be Etta's, but at the moment it's a dumping ground for all the things we have nowhere else to store, the only place I allow chaos to reign.

"What are you doing?" I ask, low, watching as he zips up his wash bag, places it neatly on top of a folded shirt.

"Manchester." When he sees my blank expression, he frowns. Takes the coffee mug I hold out to him and perches on the arm of the sofa. "Did you forget?"

I shake my head, defensively at first, but then memory does prick at me, indistinctly, a tiny splinter. There had been a calendar reminder, I think, sent to my phone. But I can barely keep track of the days at the moment, and when did I last need to check a calendar? And he hadn't mentioned it last night. At least, I don't think he had...

"I didn't forget," I rush to cover myself. "I just didn't think you were going until tonight."

Adam shakes his head. "No, my train's at one. I have a couple of meetings this morning, so I'm going into the office first."

"Oh, yes." I swallow. "Remind me what it's for, again?"

He gives me a long look. "The training course." I hear the irritation ticking up in his voice. "I told you all about it the other night. Weren't you listening?"

I try, I really do. I scroll back through various dinners, hoping to spark a recollection. "I was... I just..." Stare down at my feet. "I'm sorry. It's not you. I've just... not been myself lately."

Next door, I hear Etta mewling loudly. Move distractedly into the room to peer into the cot, steel myself for the day starting anew. Adam follows.

"Beth." He sets his mug down by the foot of our bed, reaches an arm out for me. When I come to him, he rubs the sides of my shoulders. His palms are warm from the coffee. "Is everything okay? You're sure we don't need to look into finding you someone to talk to? A way for you to get some rest?"

"No." I pinch the bridge of my nose. "Please, Adam, I promise you, I'm fine."

"Okay," he sighs. "But are you going to be all right without me? Because if it's too much, I can always change my train, come back early, or–"

"Don't be ridiculous, it's only two nights." I feel my chest tightening. I don't want him worrying about me when he's stressed about this trip. I have to get through it. I force a smile onto my face. "We'll be fine."

"Okay, good." He speaks over my thoughts, and I see him relax, even though I know I don't sound entirely convincing.

Etta lets out a stream of babble, fully awake, and I go to her, pleased for the distraction. Place a kiss on her cheek. "Good morning, love. Come on, come say bye-bye to Dada." I turn to Adam, Etta in my arms. "You know what?" The thought strikes me almost as I'm saying it. "I'll call my friend, the one from baby class. Ask if she wants to come over."

"Mia?"

"Yes, that's her." I'm surprised he remembers.

"Oh." He frowns. "I didn't know you were still in touch?"

"We haven't been, really." I think of the roll of unanswered messages on my phone. "But this is a good excuse to call."

His frown deepens. "Darling, are you really sure you want to be involved with someone with all that…" He waves his hand in the air. "…drama? Is that really what you need right now?"

I can feel myself tensing at the lingering implication that, once again, I can't cope. "First you worry about me being alone, and now you're complaining I want to see someone?" I snap with more force than intended. "I thought you'd be pleased."

He gives a sigh that fills the silence for too long, and I can tell he is wrestling with something. I worry that he's going to get cold feet, cancel his trip.

"Don't fret about me. Just focus on work." I press a hand to his arm, full of remorse.

"Okay." He nods, unconvinced. Glances at his watch. "I do need to go. Just… think about what I said, Beth? I don't want you to do something you'll regret."

It rains all morning, a fine, misting grey that would be manageable to be out in but not exactly pleasant. I watch the droplets fall from the living room windows as the hours stretch out, turn double-digitted.

I scroll through my phone. There's an email from work to my personal account; something about a "keep in touch" day that I'd missed. It seems pointless, when I don't think I'll be going back. I would have handed in my notice, except Adam – ever the accountant – said turning down maternity-leave pay was "leaving money on the table." There's nothing from Tate, although I keep expecting it, day after day of silence putting me more on edge, to the point when I wonder if that was his intent.

Still nothing from Mia.

I change Etta. Feed and wind her. Change her clothes when she throws up a stream of sick down the new knit cardigan I knew I shouldn't have put her in. Put the TV on to drown out the tiny incidental building noises that make the hairs on the back of my neck prickle.

Her morning nap time approaches and I can't face going out for a walk, but Etta refuses to go down, even after I have hauled the pram up the staircase and spent half an hour avoiding the edges of the coffee table as I pace in circles around it. I find myself overwhelmed by the mundanity of it all.

"Okay," I speak over the white noise I've fruitlessly been playing on Spotify. "Enough. We're going out."

I slip my rain mac on. Put Etta on her play mat, leaving the door ajar so I can listen out for her as I stumble the pram back downstairs before coming back up to retrieve her.

My eyes linger on the post on the mat in the hall. Searching for the figure-of-eight symbol that will once again disrupt my equilibrium.

There is nothing.

Outside, the air is cool, the metallic scent of rain lingering.

My hood gives me tunnel vision, affording me only momentary glimpses of the passers-by, heads bowed, umbrellas high. One of the things that struck me when I had Etta, after years of office nine to five, was the notion of "day people" – this whole new world of people who inhabited my neighbourhood when I was usually only there early morning or evening. I wonder what they're doing, where they're going. I can't help but hope, as I glance at the people shouldering shopping totes or pushing prams like me, that one of them is Mia.

I make a half-hearted attempt to act as though I have no grand plan, but when we find ourselves outside the church, I can admit that I've been lying to myself. The playgroup meets at 11 a.m. every Tuesday and Thursday. I am half an hour early, so I loiter at the entrance, scrolling rootlessly through my phone, looking into the face of each new arrival in the hope that it's her, wondering what I'll say if it is.

"Elizabeth?"

I jump, but it's the course leader, Sally, the box of instruments wedged under her arm.

"Actually, it's just Beth."

"Ah, yes. And Etta, I remember her, of course. Lovely name." She beams down at the pram. "You know, she's your mirror image."

"Thank you, yes, people do say. Here." To mask my disappointment, I push the door with my hand, fingertips pressing into the cool metal panel, "Let me help."

Inside, the women have already assembled in a circle. I recognise some of them from the previous class, but I still have that distinct first-day-of-school feeling, convinced they all know each other, have cliques of their own. Mia had been on her own like me.

I move through the motions of the class, but it feels tarnished somehow without Mia. Etta is grizzly. She looks at me disapprovingly as I wave a hand puppet in her face and make a half-hearted attempt at singing along to "Five Little Monkeys."

"Did you have fun?" Sally asks blandly as we're packing up.

"Yes, really fun. Thank you," I chirp, feeling hollow.

I walk us back onto the high street, the formless expanse of the day stretching in front of me. I reach into the depths of the changing bag hooked over the pram, feeling for the water bottle I'd chucked in there earlier.

As I do, my knuckles knock against hard plastic and I pull out the hourglass, wedged right at the bottom under a dirty nappy I'd forgotten to throw away.

I'd been right: there was nothing like it in the class, or I would have noticed; it would have jogged my mind.

Either way, Mia said it wasn't hers, and I hate carrying the thing around like an albatross, hate its uncanny connection, real or perceived, to memories I'd rather not have. I wedge it between my palm and the leather wrap of the pram handle, and the next time we pass a bin I throw it inside.

As I do, I feel a vibration in my jacket pocket and pull out my phone. See, with a jolt, Mia's name flash up on the screen.

"Hello?" I answer, trying to quash the giddiness in my voice.

"Hey, Beth. It's Mia. How have you been?"

"Fine, thanks. How are you?"

"Yeah, good, thanks." She sounds casual, breezy, and I can't help a tug of irritation at how easily she seems to have glossed over our last interaction, my ensuing missives.

"I messaged you."

Mia exhales. "God, did you? Sorry, I've been having problems with my phone. I cracked the screen, and I've only just managed to get it replaced."

"Oh, that's annoying." I allow a little bit of colour back into my voice. Is it the truth or just an excuse?

"And then Astrid was sick," she continues. "A temperature, up all night. And... well, anyway." I hear her sigh deeply. "It's been one thing after another since then." She swallows. "I've not been coping very well."

And I can hear the exhaustion in her voice, the breathlessness of her confession. And feel relieved. *Of course* Mia had been distracted. *Of course* she shouldn't be expected to reply to every text the moment she has an ounce of free time. The Mia I first met may have appeared cool, calm, and collected, but that doesn't mean she's impenetrable. Particularly if what I suspect about her boyfriend is true.

"Mia..." I broach. "About the other day..." Mia doesn't answer, but I can hear her breath through the phone, an even shush. "I need you to know that I understand. Not the full extent of it, but…" I swallow. "I've been there. Not exactly there, but something very much like it, and I need you to know, I *want* you to know…" I can feel it now, the rising panic swooping over me in waves. Images circle me like an old-fashioned diorama. A face close to mine, barking orders, as I collapse in the heat of the sun. My feet pounding against a treadmill as it's drilled into me, again and again, that I'm not trying hard enough. The open road surrounding me, and the of feel fresh air sucked into my lungs, when I realise I am finally free. "It may seem like there's no way out." I squeeze my eyes tight, pressing away the memories. "But there's always a way. Don't let them win."

For a moment, I think Mia has gone. I press my ear tighter against the cool glass of the phone, straining for the sound of her.

"Okay," I hear at last. Mia's voice sounds small and far away. "Okay, you're right. I'm sorry I wasn't honest with you before. I'm sorry for how I reacted at the café. That's why I was calling. I needed to tell you I… I wanted to talk."

"It doesn't matter," I jump in with eager reassurance. "I'm here now. Can I see you? Do you want to meet?"

"Yes. Please."

I can't quell a resurgence of warmth at the thought of seeing her again. This is something I can do. That I've always done well. I can help.

"What about that play café? The one up the hill we went to before? I'm nearby, actually. I could be there in ten minutes if–"

"I can't, not now," Mia cuts in abruptly. There's a beat, which gives me the impression she's looking around before answering. "How long will you be there?"

I check the time on my phone. As much as I want to

see Mia, I don't know how long I can keep Etta at bay. "A couple of hours?"

"We won't make it." She sighs. "Sorry."

"No, don't be sorry. I get it." I try not to let the disappointment creep into my voice. It's not only about losing the chance to be there for Mia but at being unable to talk to her, however cagedly, about what I had been through. The prospect of exorcising some of the demons that had reared their heads again since I received that damned invitation is too much of a balm to give up. And then I remember what I'd suggested to Adam. "Why don't you come over later his afternoon? We could have an early dinner. Bring Astrid, if that's easier. Adam's away for a couple of days, so it'll be just the two of us."

"Oh…" Her voice tapers off. "Okay, yes, I'd love to come over. Only, I don't think I could do tonight." I might be imagining it, but I'm sure Mia's voice gets softer, more muffled, as though she's cupping a hand over her phone. There's a dull click in the background, like a door shutting, before she continues. "But I could come tomorrow instead? I could probably come alone, then."

"Yes, of course." I feel the beat of my heart accelerate. How much of myself am I willing to reveal? "Come as early as you like. I'll text you my address." I put my phone on speaker, texting the information before I forget to.

"Got it. Thanks." The pace of Mia's speech quickens, I am certain of it. As though she's worried about being overheard.

I'm already thinking about tidying the flat, wondering what I should cook, whether Mia will like it. I know it's not the point of the visit, but all the same, I am pursued by the need for it to be perfect. "You're welcome to stay for dinner, too. Is there anything you don't eat? Any allergies?"

"Mia?" In the background of the call, I can just make out an adult voice, male, low, "Mia, where are you?"

"Sorry, Beth, I've got to go," Mia's voice hisses into the receiver. And then, louder, rushed: "No one, James. Just a cold caller."

"Mia, are you okay? I–"

"No, I've told you, I'm happy with the provider I already have," she cuts me off, speaking in a pantomimic tone. And then, hissed into the receiver, "Got to go, okay? I'll see you tomorrow."

"Yes, but–"

"Okay, see you then. Bye." The line goes dead.

"Please look after yourself," I say into the silence.

22
Muswell Hill, London
13ᵗʰ July 2023

∞

Despite my aborted rendezvous with Mia, I find myself steering the pram towards the play café anyway. Halfway there, the heavens open. The rain falls in thick sheets that seem to lower the sky, and the people around me quicken their steps, beating a rhythmic slap-slap-slap on the wet paving slabs. I stop to retrieve the pram rain cover, am tutted at and jostled as I wrestle with the elasticated edging, trying to figure out which way round it goes. Etta screams in protest at her plastic confines, the sound muffled as I break into a jog, weaving through the crowds.

"Nearly there, darling, come on." I try to hold my hood closed at the throat, but I'm unsteady moving the pram at speed one handed, succumbing to the wind that blows it back, whipping cold water into my cheeks and hair.

The café is busy. People have dashed inside for cover, crowding the tables or guiltily joining the queue at the counter. The air inside has that dank, cooped-up smell, the glass windows thick with condensation. The bottom half of my jeans are sodden, clinging to my ankles, and when

I bundle up my mac to shove it under the pram, water slicks my arms and torso.

I release Etta, whose cries have reduced to a low, persistent caw, and hold her close. "I'm sorry, I'm sorry," I say over and over, feeling the eyes of the other customers on me as I fail to calm her.

"Peppermint tea, please," I say to the waitress when we eventually get to the front of the queue. I'm tempted to ask for coffee – I crave the clarity, the sharpness of mind caffeine will bring. But without Mia, I've lost my edge.

When I try to put Etta back in the pram, her cries begin anew, bucking her torso so much I'm worried she'll tip the thing over. Instead, I attempt, unskilfully, to manoeuvre the pram with my forearm, Etta tucked against me, the teacup balanced precariously in my other hand.

There are no chairs or tables left in the play area, but I manage to find a bean bag and a faux tree stump I can rest the cup on. I prop myself up against a bean bag, legs crossed, Etta in my lap, but she still seems so distressed that I try rocking gently, swaying back and forth against the bean bag, murmuring words of reassurance which seem to have no effect.

"Come on, sweetheart. Is this what you want?" I ask softly, lifting up my top. I hate feeding in public. Hate putting my body on display. Especially my body as it is now, which feels so unfamiliar. "Your body is not just a temple," Tate was fond of saying. "It is an artefact. Meant to inspire others." I wonder, briefly, what he would think of it now. Smack the thought away: I shouldn't care what he thinks.

I unclip my bra and cradle Etta towards me, but she jerks her head away, refusing.

"Come on, baby, please? Do you need a change?" I pat a

hand on her bottom, lean in to sniff. "Are you tired? This is because you didn't nap, isn't it?" As Etta's protests become wilder, my placations become more urgent. It's a battle to keep my voice calm, and I'm sure I can feel the eyes of every mother in the area on me, even if they all seem preoccupied, focused on their own babies, their own lives. "I wish you could just tell me what you want," I beg.

I reach for the tea, holding her closely against my chest, but without warning she lurches, head rolling backwards, body following, and I jerk to catch her, re-balancing us but knocking the cup, in its entirety, over my legs.

"Ah!" I shriek as scalding liquid burns through my thighs and I instantly check Etta for injury. Miraculously, she is dry. What's more, although her face is still a mottled red, whatever demons were plaguing her seem to have been vanquished, because she is now completely calm.

I look down at the wet mess of my jeans, a dank peppermint smell lingering. Liquid has pooled beneath them onto the grass carpet. My left sleeve is soaking.

I eye Etta warily, consider. The toilets are only a few feet away. I can't face trying to get her back in the pram.

I'll only be a few minutes.

"Will you be all right if mummy runs to the loo very, very quickly?" I glance at the woman nearest us, an over-sized mint green cardigan draped over her as she cradles a baby even smaller than Etta to her chest. Harmless. "I'm really sorry to bother you. Would you mind watching her for, like, thirty seconds while I get cleaned up?" I hold my left arm out apologetically, gesturing simultaneously to my jeans.

"Yes, of course." She gives me a weary smile.

"Amazing. Thank you so much. Great." I prop Etta against the beanbag, hold my hands out warily, checking that she's in place. "Great," I say again, swiftly, as if to reassure all of us. "I'll be right back, sweetheart." Give her a kiss on the forehead. "I'm just going to get dry. This nice lady is going to watch you." I smile at the woman, nod as I stand to leave.

I jog over to the bathroom and grab a wad of hand towels, too impatient to wait for the dryer, blotting the stains away as best I can. A brown tinge remains, but I figure it's better than it was and turn back to the play area.

It takes me a second to sense that something is wrong. It takes me no more than two to look over at the bean bag and see that Etta is missing. As is the woman.

"No." I instantly break into a run, skirting around tables and knocking into the back of chairs, hearing the faint tut of customers as I do. "Where is she?" I plead with the confused huddle of mothers, not caring how loud I am being, how they look at me with alarm, arms wrapping round their babies, shielding them from me. Half the napkins fall from my grasp, littering the path behind me. "Etta?" I begin to shout, knocking over boxes of soft toys, a stack of wooden blocks. "Where is she? *Where's my baby?*"

The whole café has turned to look at me now, and I see a member of staff approaching, a young guy with an eyebrow ring and lime-green nail polish.

"Madam, is everything all right? You're upsetting the customers."

"She's taken my baby! Where is she? Why did no one stop her?"

This is a living nightmare. One of my recurring dreams come to life.

"Who? Who's taken your baby?"

Through the blear of panic that now seizes me, I see the repelled expression on the waiter's face, know how I must look to him, half-crazed and still clutching some of the brown hand towels in my fists.

"The woman who was here. In the green cardigan. She was watching her. I was only gone for two minutes!"

I can't speak. I swallow air but can't get a full breath, which makes me panic more. *This is what it's like to drown,* I think, triggering a memory: hands pressing me down into cool, blue water. My body fighting, jerking, liquid filling my lungs each time I try to call, to beg. A voice, muffled, from above: "This is what you deserve. If you were stronger, you'd fight it. This is your fault. You are your own failure."

"Wait, you left your baby alone?" The waiter doesn't bother to disguise the admonishment in his tone.

"Please." I sink to my knees, chest heaving. "Please."

I can't imagine it is possible to hate myself any more.

"Excuse me, is this her? Is this your baby?"

With a jerk, I look up, heart clenching. A woman is standing by the archway that is cut into to the little treehouse fort in the centre of the play area. Inside, I can just make out a tiny foot, a familiar pink striped sock half hanging off it.

"Etta!" I choke, stumbling to my feet and rushing over to the entrance to wrench her free. Etta giggles at me as I check her over, unscathed and apparently unperturbed. Relief washes over me as powerfully as the memory of water, and I mesh her against me so tightly we are practically one. I kiss every inch of her bare skin, powerful, fierce. I want to ingest her. Take her back inside my body, the only place she can truly be safe. But even as I think this, I feel the black seed of self-recrimination growing in my core, blaming myself for every second I had been away from her, for any reason there may be for Etta being unsafe. *This is what you get,* I berate myself. *You don't deserve to be a mother.* And then another thought, the tang of the memory still not entirely swallowed down: *You are your own failure.*

"Is everything all right?"

A voice inserts itself into the now near-silent café. I look up to see the woman in the mint-green cardigan, her own baby tight in her arms. The sound that comes out of me is unrecognisable.

"Where did you go?" Anger pierces through me, projecting my own incompetence outwards.

"Oh, my goodness, I'm so sorry!" She holds up her hands in submission. "He threw up. I was just getting some tissues from my bag. It's right over there." She looks weakly towards the cluster of prams outside the fence. "I was really quick."

I take the woman in properly, see the residue of cottage-cheese whiteness on her cardigan, the shadows under her eyes. She looks even more exhausted than me.

"But why would you put her up there?" I try to soften my voice, to calm myself, even though adrenaline still quivers in my nerve endings, makes my face burn hot. "She could have choked on a toy. She could have fallen out. Anything could have happened."

The woman shakes her head. Her features mottle together, confused. "I didn't. I didn't move her. Like I said, I was really quick. I left her on the bean bag. Right there." She points limply to where Etta had been when I left.

"But then how did she get there? She can barely even sit up."

The fear that has barely dissipated resurfaces as the woman gives me a hapless shrug. "I have no idea what happened, honestly. Maybe I did put her there. I panicked. I didn't get much sleep last night. I – I shouldn't have got up. I…"

I feel a mirror held up to my own confusion, my own

tiredness. I swerve to take in the other parents, paused in their play as they gawp awkwardly back at me, shake their heads. I think of the yellow hourglass burning a hole in the bottom of the bin on the high street, take in the face of each of them, searching for a flash of recognition, something that will strike me, make me *know*, with no hesitation, that it's more than just paranoia fuelling my suspicions, that someone is part of this. They all stare back blankly, anonymous.

"I should go. I..." The café now seems stiflingly hot, overcrowded, and there is a low thudding in my right temple that makes it difficult to focus. "I have to go."

I haul Etta higher up on my torso. Find the pram and settle her inside, retreating from the play area and down the aisle, feeling the café folding back in on itself, the gawking customers in the main area turning their backs, the tension dissipating, the burble of conversation resuming. I walk through the doorway and am about to turn in the direction of home when I see the back of a familiar figure walking hurriedly in the opposite direction.

"Mia?" I call out. I'm sure it's her. It's definitely her. But perhaps she hasn't heard, because she keeps on walking. If anything, her pace speeds up. "Mia!"

Using the pram as a support, I propel myself forwards. Mia has made it after all. She must not have seen me, or thought I'd left. Or else she did see me and thinks I'm insane. I catch up to her, grasp hold of her shoulder with a free hand. Spin her around.

"Hey, Mia! Hey, it's me, Beth."

Mia turns.

As she does something falls from her grasp.

Something small. And hard. And plastic.

Black, this time. And more familiar than the last.

"What...?" My insides turn to stone. It can't be. It *can't* be.

And then Mia swoops down to snatch the hourglass from the ground. I lunge for it, but she grabs it first. Catches hold of my fist before I can pull away. And as I turn, try to fight her, the sleeve of my shirt rides up, exposing the skin on the inside of my wrist.

The mark I always try so hard to hide.

The looping figure of eight etched into the flesh.

The exact branding that matches the hourglass in Mia's outstretched palm.

23
San Francisco Bay Area
May 2014

∞

Like the sand in the hourglass, time slipped through her fingers, one month becoming three, three months becoming nearly a year. And in every millisecond in between, there was Tate.

She hadn't anticipated, after that first night at the party, that sleeping with him would not be a full stop but a series of ellipses, that her "healing" from Matt would not take one try but many.

When she wasn't with him at The Jungle, wanted by him, needed by him, pulled from whatever task she was focusing on to be taken by him – in the bedroom, on the beach, once in the storage room by the pool when there were members right outside – she was brushing past him at the studio, where he would pause, quirk his face into a smile. Their relationship in public was so far undefined, but *she knew.*

Sometimes he would stop. Press her hand into his as he'd murmur some little words of encouragement: "You're doing amazingly well," or "I'm so proud of what you've achieved."

And when he said that, she felt like she could fly.

She knew she wasn't the only one. She wasn't stupid. There was Marissa, for one, the two of them circling around Tate like courtiers at a dance. And there were others, too – she had seen the long looks passing between Tate and various members, walked in on intimate moments she would rather not have seen. There were girls that she herself had introduced to classes, cherry picked to garner good favour – which they had. But she tried to be magnanimous, like Marissa. Monogamy was unenlightened, jealousy tawdry and unfitting of someone of her status. Who was she to keep Tate to herself when he had the power to help so many?

Besides, with her five thousand dollar cheque for Advanced Level II, Tate was never more than a piece of paper away: advancement included a free "bonus gift," the *Elixir Manifesto*, sixty pages of Tate's eloquent, soaring prose, telling her how she could make her life better. Plus, his picture on the back cover, enhanced blue eyes still piercing even in black and white.

She was Elizabeth now, wholeheartedly. She needed to "stop taking a back seat in life and grab the steering wheel with both hands" (*Elixir Manifesto*, page thirty-two) and let Beth go, exorcise her into the netherworld of the Extraction tapes, where she would only serve to help Elizabeth grow.

She didn't mind. Beth was unformed, living in the dark, like the shadows in Plato's Cave. As Elizabeth, anything was possible.

But Advanced Level II also raised the bar. She had already found mental grit; she had found focus and discipline. Now she had to learn humility, to understand that "helping those in a superior position is vital for strength and growth" (*Elixir Manifesto*, page twenty-four).

Tate had promised her, with a serenity that seemed to

radiate from somewhere deep within him, that it would be worth it. That she could achieve Elite status. And that beyond Elite was the ultimate Elixir status known unofficially as Perfection – a status he magnanimously admitted even he was yet to attain. "We are all always evolving, Elizabeth. Let's grow together."

And so she began to accept small tasks – willingly, to prove that she *got it*, that she understood. Could she detour to Whole Foods and pick up Tate's groceries? The list would be sent to her phone. Could she collect his laundry from the dry cleaner in Cow Hollow and walk with it the studio? It was only an hour, and it would crease in a cab. Errands met with gratitude – "You're such a star," "You're such a help!" – so that she didn't really mind when the question mark occasionally got lopped off the end: "Buy a set of scales and report a daily weigh-in. We can't achieve success if we don't measure it." "At Advanced Level II, you shouldn't be sleeping more than five hours a night. Oversleeping is wasteful. I'll be checking in, to make sure."

And then the errand runs morphed, became more physical: "You're needed at the new studio on Mission Street. You'll be building the flooring." "You're on cleaning duty at The Jungle. Make sure it's done by ten p.m.!" The combination of these tasks and her exercise sessions riddled her body with a subtle but persistent ache.

Although she still saw Marissa for her Extraction sessions, it was Tate, now, who gave the commands. When they did glance one another, they were always rushing, smiles tight, nods brief. If she did notice that her friend seemed a little distracted – forgetting to start the tape for their session, occasionally drifting off mid-sentence, a rawness around her eyes that Marissa put down to allergies – the thought was soon lost, swept away by the tide of her busy routine.

She lived her life by the Elixir hourglass, her days broken down into tiny granules of time, the urgency of completing a task as quickly and efficiently as she could propelling her forwards. She was permanently on high alert. If she messed up – if she was late, or didn't do it in quite the way it was envisaged – she knew it was her fault.

"You're repeating the patterns of self-destruction you've already admitted were a problem for you in the past, Elizabeth," Tate explained, patiently. "If you really wanted to move on, you wouldn't self-sabotage."

And so she took on further work to make up for it. She wanted to. She was *glad* to. The only thing holding you back is you (*Elixir Manifesto*, page twelve.) She opened up the studio at dawn, cleaned the bathrooms with a toothbrush, joined a team to re-lay Tate's driveway where it had been cracked and muddied after the onslaught of vehicles from another party. On Tate's advice, she fasted for forty-eight hours to refocus her mind, agreeing with him, when he finally allowed her to break it, that she had never relished the taste of an apple so much.

"This is what I mean, Elizabeth," he said, rapturous. "We restrict so we can benefit. We accept hard work so we can reap the reward."

He prescribed her supplements, showing her the data on how what she put into her body affected what she got out. Potassium, zinc, and L-carnitine were in; toxins like sugar were out. He even warned her of the evils of the Pill, extolling importance of understanding her cycle, the way her hormones affected different abilities at different times of the month. Condoms were riddled with microplastics. Did she really want that rot inside the body she'd worked so hard to keep pure?

"What about, you know, if I get...?" She'd blushed.

"Trust your body, Elizabeth," he had promised, running a finger down her naked chest, circling the peak of her nipple. "If you show it the respect it deserves, it won't let you down."

Still, even with the supplements and training, it was hard to keep on top of all the demands on her brain, the schedules she was constantly darting between. Sometimes her mind felt like a dinghy in a storm, trying to keep afloat.

She had taken to biting the skin around her fingernails in nervous excitement, sometimes until they bled. Completing her tasks at JE&G at lighting speed, fingertips flying across the keyboard, in case she was interrupted, called upon to complete a task.

Refusal wasn't an option.

The Advanced Level opened up new opportunities, supplementary online training courses that popped up in her inbox with enticing headlines: "Introduction to Juicing," "Finding Your True Purpose," "Core Strength Maxx." She wanted to take them all. Found increasingly creative ways to make up the cost – cutting her food budget in half, hauling armfuls of clothes, bags, and shoes to the thrift shops in Haight-Ashbury, taking out multiple credit cards. She downgraded her one-bed in North Beach to sharing a studio within spitting distance of the Tenderloin, where the toilet was permanently overflowing and a crack addict screamed in her face every time she walked out of the door.

Something had to give. She knew it would, eventually.

She just hadn't envisaged the something would be her job.

* * *

The day of a client meeting with Accur8 – a big healthcare IT company – the phone on her desk buzzed for the tenth time that hour. She had felt it vibrating against her leg during the morning pack review, trying to ignore the voicemails from Marissa she saw racking up, the bleat of texts. Seizing a break, she ran to the loo, thick-fingered as she scrolled through the messages sent in escalating throes of anger.

Elizabeth, please call when you get this.

Is everything okay? You went straight to voicemail.

Where are you?

This isn't funny, Elizabeth.

Do NOT ignore my calls.

I need you to call me. I won't wait any longer.

Elizabeth, you have to call me NOW.

THIS IS NOT A JOKE.

"Hi," she choked out, palm clammy as she pressed the phone against her ear. The major commands may have been decreed by Tate, but as her mentor and superior, Elizabeth still needed to answer to Marissa.

"Where the hell have you been?" Marissa snapped in reply. And then, softer: "I was starting to get worried."

"I'm so sorry." Elizabeth swallowed. The cubicle smelt of someone else's shit and she felt nausea wash over her as it invaded her nostrils. "I couldn't get to the phone until now." Added, placating: "Please… How can I help?"

"I need you to cover my two p.m. this afternoon. I have an appointment I can't miss. I'll be back by three." She sounded hurried, distressed. But didn't she always?

"Two p.m. today?" Elizabeth parroted back. The nausea made way for dizziness, and she pressed her free hand against the cubicle wall. She glanced at the time on her phone, trying to control her anxiety. She'd have to leave within the next fifteen minutes. The Accur8 meeting was at three thirty; it would be the culmination of an entire month's worth of work. At her level, she didn't even speak in the meetings, but her presence was still required, in case there were queries about the data. Maybe if she didn't shower, if she took a cab straight from the studio…

"Elizabeth?"

She didn't have a choice. If she didn't agree, it would get back to Tate.

She could make it work. She would have to make it work.

"I'll be there."

She arrived at 2:02.

Marissa glared at the clock. Then at her. Left without a word.

She sleep-walked through the class, a pathetic beginners' session, their movements sluggish, clumsy. When Marissa returned, she led Elizabeth into one of the small studio pods kept aside for the Extractions.

"You were late," She pointed to a treadmill they kept in the corner. "Tate says you have to run."

Elizabeth bowed her head. Stepped onto the black ribbon. Refusal wasn't an option.

"He says you are lazy," Marissa began, cranking the speed up to a power walk.

"I am. I should have got here sooner. I'm sorry."

"He says you are thoughtless. You show disregard for other people's feelings and their time."

"Yes, you're right," she huffed, her pace quickening to a jog.

"He says…" Through her panted exertions, Elizabeth could

sense that Marissa was wrestling with something – her voice was flat, hollow. "He says you deserved what happened to you with Matt."

Her skin prickled, the words making razor marks against it. How could Marissa say that to her? But… it was true, wasn't it? She *had* been thoughtless with Matt. And she had been thoughtless today. She wasn't learning anything. She was failing.

"Yes." Tears stung her eyes, mixed with the sweat beading from her forehead. "Yes, you're right. I'm sorry. Please."

The speed increased "Marissa…!" Her lungs stuttered. She sucked at the air.

She looked down at Marissa's finger, white where the first point pressed against the speed button.

"Tate says," Marissa continued, her voice utterly toneless, "if you don't learn from this, you will repeat these patterns again and again."

Again, the speed increased.

"Marissa!" she gasped, trying to grasp the bar in front of her, but the band kept pulling her back. "For God's sake…"

"Tate would say not to be mad at me," she admonished. "Be mad at yourself."

It was true. She knew it was true. She was focusing the blame in the wrong direction. She could no longer speak, attempted a nod instead.

"Only *you* can change you. All Tate can do is help you find your path. Remember that. Fight it. Be strong."

She knew she would fall before it happened. Saw her feet stumbling before she came down, felt the friction burn against her ribcage as her legs came out from underneath her and she was propelled backwards, landing, hard, on the studio floor.

The effect was like a bubble bursting.

"Oh, my God, Elizabeth!" Marissa rushed over, turned the treadmill off. "Are you okay?" She felt herself being helped to her feet, an arm looping around her shoulders.

"I... Yes, I... I think so." Her heart spluttered, frantically trying to pump oxygen through her blood. But then she looked over at the treadmill, to where her targets were still flashing red. And as her breathing settled, the remorse she had felt was replaced by something else. A buzzing in her ears. A rush of energy that surged through her. A *high*. She *was* okay, she realised. In fact, she felt elated. "Marissa," she breathed, "that was the fastest I've ever run." She took a step closer towards the screen. Her nerve endings were still firing, sending quivers of endorphins down her body. "Marissa, did you see?"

But Marissa didn't seem to be listening.

"Oh, God, I'm sorry," she was murmuring, pressing her hands to her cheeks. "Elizabeth, I'm so, so sorry.

It was then that Elizabeth took in Marissa properly. Her skin was chalky, grey, even underneath the tan, her eyes ringed red. When she looked at Marissa's hands, she saw they were trembling.

"Marissa, that appointment. Are you okay?" She realised she hadn't even asked what it was for.

There was a pause. For moment, they locked eyes, and Elizabeth saw the rise of Marissa's chest, a breath away from saying something. For a second, she looked almost frightened. And then the treadmill sounded a jarring electronic beep. Marissa tilted her chin, flinched. And Elizabeth saw her expression clouding over, re-set itself. Recognised in Marissa same the mental lockdown, the same rigid self-conditioning she had been taught to do so well. "Of course I'm okay. Why wouldn't I be?"

Before Beth had a chance to answer, Marissa wrapped an arm around her shoulders, propelled her towards the door. "Your personal best. I'm so proud," she bleated, her tone flat. "Come on, let's go get you a juice."

The high lingered. As she downed her juice. As she dressed, left the studio.

Only.

Only, when she got back to her desk, it was 3:45 and there was a Post-It note stuck on her screen.

Beth, report to me as soon as the meeting is over.

Ice crystallised in her veins.

She looked over at the glass-fronted meeting room, at the group of people clustered around the table.

Caught David watching her from his seat, his expression fixed in a low stare.

Felt the world spin around her as he slowly, unforgivingly shook his head.

Transcript
Audio Recording,

Elizabeth Myers, May 2014

Marissa Reid: [panicked, cajoling, sound of crying in the background. Voice raised to speak over it] Elizabeth. Elizabeth! Calm down. I've started the recording. You need to stop crying and tell me what is going on. This... this isn't helpful. I need you to... You have to... Just breathe. Remember your training. Count to ten. Focus.

Elizabeth Myers: [through sobs] I... I... [crying recommences]

MR: Come on, you can do this. Let's start the session properly. Your name?

EM: [snatched breaths] My... my name...

MR: Your name is...

EM: My name is Elizabeth Myers.

MR: Good girl.

EM: My name is Elizabeth Myers [sniffs] and... and it's the fourteenth of May 2014.

MR: There we go. You've got this. Remember: *I can't* is only one letter away from *I want.*

EM: [gulps] I thought I did everything right. I took all the courses. I know the manifesto off by heart. I thought I was doing so well. How... how can this have happened?

MR: Tell me what happened.

EM: He... my manager said I'd been pulling back for weeks, that the rest of the team have been picking up all my slack, that someone complained. [whimpering] I... I thought we were helping each other out! [sobs] And I guess I fell asleep at my desk a few times. I don't know, maybe I need to change my supplements? Lately I've just been so tired...

MR: Go on.

EM: I missed a meeting – yesterday, when I... when you... [sniffs] I fucked up the client pack. The data in it was all wrong, and not having me present to explain why was a huge embarrassment to my boss. The lead partner had to offer to reduce the fee, and they're going to have to work for the next two weeks for free to fix everything. Either way, that's it, I'm out. Fired. [sobs] What am I going to do?

MR: I–

EM: I can't stay here. I don't have a visa without this job. And I can't go back to London, Marissa, I can't. I can't leave Elixir. And what about Tate? But how can I pay for classes without a job? How will I pay my rent? Oh God, oh God. [audible hyperventilating] Marissa, I can't breathe. I... I think I'm having a panic attack. I...

[chair scraping, footsteps]

MR: Shh. You're not having a panic attack. Breathe. Come on. I've got you. Deep breaths. [sound of snatched

breathing, intermittent sobs] That's it. Together. Come
on. [more breathing] In, out. I'm counting. In-two-
three, out-two-three. And again: in-two-three, out-
two-three. There. There.

[long pause]

EM: This is all my fault. Tate says we are our own success,
and look – I fucked up. I wasn't concentrating. I should
have taken that meditation class, the one on smart
focusing. I–

MR: It's not your fault. I shouldn't have... I'm sorry
I made you cover my class. I didn't realise... I didn't
have another option.

EM: Marissa, what am I going to do?

MR: [slowly] It's going to be okay. I'll... I'll help you.
I promise. Just like you helped me. You're going to
be okay. You won't have to leave San Francisco. Or
Elixir.

EM: But how?

MR: Let me speak to Tate. I'm sure there's a way. You
can give up your apartment. You can move into The
Jungle... like me. You can... you can work for Elixir.
Tate will sort everything out. He always does. I'm sure
he can get you a visa. He knows everyone. It'll be okay.

EM: You'd do that for me? Tate would?

MR: [pause] Tate looks after those who are special to him.

EM: Oh... Oh, my God. Oh, Marissa. I... I don't know
how to thank you. I...

MR: Don't worry about it. We have to look out for each
other, as much as we look out for ourselves. [swallows]
Leave it to me. He won't say no, especially... especially
if you commit to Elite.

EM: [pause] Elite?

MR: Yes. That's the only way it can work. I'll recommend you, tell Tate you're ready to join.

EM: Oh. Oh… Marissa. [pause] But isn't the course ten thousand dollars? [beat] I don't know. Without my job, even if I'm working for Elixir, I don't know how long it would take me to earn that sort of money.

[long pause]

MR: [sighs] I don't know what to say to you. I really want to help you, but… [pause]. Maybe… I don't know. Maybe you should go back home after all. [quietly] Maybe you would be better off going home.

EM: No! Marissa, you don't understand. I can't go back. I have nothing to go home for. My life is here. I can't go back.

[silence]

MR: [slowly] Wait. What if… Isn't your mother coming to visit next month?

EM: Yes.

MR: And listen, doesn't she owe it to you? After everything you've been through? All the psychological damage she's done over the years? What she said to you in the hospital, after what happened with Matt? [rustling] I can get out the tape if you want to–

EM: No. No, I remember.

[long pause]

MR: She should want you to be happy, Elizabeth.

EM: Yes.

MR: She should want to support to you.

EM: Yes.

MR: To help you out with whatever you needed, to get yourself better. I know… [swallows] I know if I were a mother, I would. I would give anything…

EM: Hey, Marissa, is everything okay?

MR: Fine.

EM: Because you know you can talk to me if... We can stop the tape–

MR: I said I was fine.

[pause]

MR: Think about what I said, Elizabeth. You can join Elite. You can be with Tate. I can help you. But only if you help yourself.

24
Muswell Hill, London
13th July 2023

∞

Mia and I both stare down at the looping symbol on my wrist. The figure of eight on its side. The infinity sign. The black ouroboros whorl whose outline matches the hourglass on the floor beneath us.

The Elixir symbol.

A voice that doesn't seem to come from my body rings in my ears: "I knew it."

The uncanniness of it destabilises me, and I realise why: Mia has spoken the exact same words as me, our voices twinning in unison.

Before I can say more, Mia lunges, teeth bared, fingers snatching at me. In panic, I torque myself away, grip hold of the pram. Realise, too late, that she has possession of the hourglass.

"Stay away from me!" I wheel Etta around, shielding her. "I mean it. Don't fucking come near us." I shake my head, watching Mia pocket the hourglass. "It was you. The whole time, I can't believe it was you. Did he put you up to this? What does he want?"

I'm surprised to see Mia's brows knit together, confusion

creased between them. "What does who want? I–"

But I don't wait to hear whatever lies she starts to splutter. "Stay the *fuck* away from me, do you understand? And stay the fuck away from my daughter. Tell him…" I breathe hard. There are so many things I want to tell him – where do I even begin? "Tell him to remember I've kept my end of the bargain. I know he'll always hold the truth over me, but to remember he's not the only one who has secrets to spill. I know who he truly is, what he's done. If silence buys my freedom, so be it. But if he continues to threaten me, I won't hesitate to pull the trigger."

"What? Beth, wait–"

But I don't want to wait. Anger crackles within me. I swivel the pram, wheel it as evenly as I can down the high street, trying to ignore the tremor in my fingers as they grasp the handlebar.

I won't let myself turn back.

"Stop!" she calls after me. "Beth, listen to me. I don't think…"

I won't let myself give Mia another minute of my time. Won't fall for it a second time.

Eventually, the calls fade into the distance.

And when I round the corner, I allow myself a moment to stop; take a low, ragged breath. Mia has gone.

My hands are shaking so hard when I get to the front door that I drop my keys, twice, and have to press my left hand over my right to guide the key into the lock.

The rain has subsided. There is no trace of it in the thin blue sky, although a murkiness hangs in the air, the pavements slick with moisture. By the grace of God, Etta has fallen asleep on the way home, the steady roll of the pram and white noise of cars shushing through puddles finally seducing her to sleep. She is down so deeply that I am able to lift her from the pram, transfer her upstairs to the bedroom and into the crib undisturbed.

Before I leave the room, I have the urge to look down at Etta's perfect, peaceful face, at the little pout of her lips in repose, the cleft in her chin, so like my own. She is completely unaware of what has just happened. No idea the mess her mother is in. But thank goodness, at least she is safe.

Back downstairs, I bolt the door, then wedge a chair under the handle for good measure.

I stand in middle of the empty space, finally alone. Try to steady my breath.

The living room that had seemed so quiet that morning now feels like a vacuum, the silence of my incarceration broken only by the vibrating fuzz of my phone, which has been going off intermittently on the journey home. I take it out of my pocket and glance at the notifications of Mia's missed calls, then promptly block her number.

Not that it matters, I realise with grim reality. *I gave her my address.*

Not that that *matters*, I realise with a sense of futility. *She probably already had it.*

And the knife twists further as I think back to the invitation.

Recall, for first time, that the envelope didn't have a stamp.

I begin to pace, busying myself, trying to untangle the clutter of the place which seems to have snarled and twisted since Adam's departure without my noticing. There is a smell lingering, faint and indistinct: the box of laundry powder I'd tripped over and spilled across the kitchen floor that morning, last night's pots and pans still in the sink, a nappy bin I'd forgotten to empty. How has this happened? How have I finally lost control?

I look at each offending item in turn, but like the messy fragments of my mind, I have no idea where to begin, and eventually I sit, squashing a dirty muslin and a couple of used wet wipes into the crease of the sofa. Stare blankly at the television screen, biting the cuticle of my right thumb until it bleeds, willing a solution to present itself to me.

I miss Adam. I want to hear his voice, to ground myself in him. Adam, Etta – they are everything to me. If I could tell him the truth, could he fix it? Could he make it all go away? Or would it only make things worse?

As if on cue, I hear the buzz of my phone, a message from him flashes up on the screen:

Look what I found at the station.

Below, a picture of a white circular sweet, stamped with a pink heart within which are written the words *BE MINE*.

Despite myself, I can't help but smile. It's an old joke of ours. I have an irrepressible sweet tooth. Not the fancy kind for the smart bags you see now in luxury cinemas or department-store gift aisles, but the cheap sweets you shovel up with a plastic scoop, as many as you can fit into the bag. The kind I was always forbidden as a child. I had forgotten about it, in the throes of Elixir. But afterwards, my craving was rekindled. And when I was pregnant with Etta it was out of control, to the point where I'd send Adam out to the corner shop in the middle of the night for fizzy cola bottles and double cherries.

He found it amusing. Or endearing, perhaps. When he tried to propose, he did it with a Love Heart.

The same one that's in the photo now.

I miss you, I write back, and the pang of it guts me.

I've barely left! he writes back quickly, jovially. And then: *Everything okay?*

I... I begin, and then, realising I have no idea what to say next, I erase it and try again: *We're both okay but I need to...* Bile rises in my throat and I delete that message too. *I wish I could tell you...*

I still haven't completed the thought when the phone vibrates and I see his name appear on the call screen.

"Hi," I answer, wiping the back of my wrist across my damp eyes, swallowing hard. I try to make my voice sound neutral.

"Are you really all right?"

I look at the time on my phone. It's nearly three o'clock. Where has the morning gone?

"Yes," I say simply, hoping I'm not pushed for more. "How's the journey?"

He'll be about halfway there now. I picture him at his seat, a WH Smith bag folded into squares on the table in front of him, as always. We took a trip to the seaside back when we were in the thick of all the problems with Etta. Adam had suggested: *"Let's get away from it all: You know what they say, about the sea air."* It was the first time I'd seen him do it, and I'd teased him for it, called it his "plastic bag origami," but he hadn't found it funny. He'd grown up with no money. I hadn't realised how little until then. He had to take his things to school in plastic bags. The habit of keeping them nice had stuck. I'd never teased him about it again. *"You don't understand, Beth, you've never had to fight for it,"* he's said to me before, in reference to how he perceives what he gleans to be my staunchly middle-class background. *Not for that, no,* I've wanted to reply, *but that doesn't mean I haven't had to fight.*

"Beth, are you okay? Are you listening?"

"Yes. Yes, of course I am, but…" I poise myself. Adam is my partner. The father of my child. So why is it so difficult to tell him the truth? And then I remember how excited he'd been when he left the house this morning. His hunger for this job – why he's always the last to leave, staying sometimes late into the night. It's all part of that same desire to better himself. He's halfway to Manchester – he's stuck on a train, for God's sake. How could I sabotage him like that?

"But…?"

"Nothing." I shake my head. "I just can't wait for you to come home."

When he's back. I'll tell him when he's back. Unless, by then, it's too late.

"It won't be long," he placates, although I think I hear impatience creeping around the edges of his tone. "Hey, listen. I was thinking, when I get back, why don't I take Etta for a couple of days, and you can have some time to yourself? Go on a spa break, maybe. Pamper yourself."

I try to focus on what he's saying, but his words seem foggy and far away. I try to picture myself in a fluffy white robe and the idea is almost laughable.

"I'm not sure. Maybe?" I answer weakly. Know even before the word leaves my mouth that I've said the wrong thing.

"Never mind," he huffs, curt, and I wish I could take it back, rewind. Adam is my protector. I want him on my side. The image of the Love Heart is still up on my screen. Like a talisman, invoking the person I had fought so hard to be when I first met him. I need to remember who that person is.

"Sorry, no, please... I was distracted. It's a lovely idea, Ads. I'd really that." I try again, the words sticking in my throat. "It would be really nice, to feel like myself again."

"Great," he softens. "Think of somewhere you'd like to go. We'll look at dates when I'm back."

I feel myself unclenching. Allow – *will* – myself to believe that somehow telling Adam will put it all right.

Am about to speak when there's a sound in the background of his call that distracts me.

A long, low beep.

My ears prick up, suddenly alert.

"What was that?"

"What was what?" Do I imagine it, or is there a note of panic in his voice?

"That noise." I press the phone to my ear, convinced about what I just heard, confused as to how I could be.

"Um..." He breaks off as though he's looking around. "Just a kid over the aisle, playing a video game."

"Okay," I concede, not okay at all.

Adam clears his throat. "Well, I should go, Beth. I don't have much signal, and I think we might be going through a tunnel. I'll ring when I get to the hotel?"

Does his speech speed up? Does he sound suspicious? Guilty? My finger hovers over the video call button, considering if I should see for myself.

"Yes, I should go too," I say instead, getting cold feet. "Etta needs me." My tongue feels thick, forced into the base of my mouth as though I'm going to be sick. "I love you," I add.

"Love you, too," he says quickly – too quickly? – and rings off.

And I sit, holding the phone in my hands, staring at the screen until my vision goes blurry. Because the sound I heard was definitely not a video game.

It was a car horn. I'm sure of it.

But why would a car be passing a train?

Unless Adam isn't on a train.

But if he's not on a train, where is he?

25
Muswell Hill, London
13ᵗʰ July 2023

∞

The phone is still warm in my hand as I mentally replay the conversation with Adam. There had been no rumble of the tracks. No sound of the Tannoy. No whoosh of wind. Nothing at all to indicate he'd been on a train. If anything, until the beep of the car, our conversation had been smooth, the line perfectly clear, as though he'd been walking down the street with full signal. Which he probably was.

But why would he lie to me about the trip? Fabricate two nights away from home? If he just wanted to see friends, even, goodness knows, if he'd been compelled to go see his family, why wouldn't he have just told me the truth? And then my brain begins to spiral. Because there is only one reason I can think of, one answer that fits the bill: he isn't going to Manchester. He is somewhere else. With some*one* else.

Adam is having an affair.

I whisper the words to myself. Over and over. Until they become numb, lose meaning.

Adamishavinganaffair.

"Paranoid," he had called me. And perhaps I am paranoid.

But I had been right about the invitation. And I had been right about Mia. So my instincts aren't entirely without merit.

I cast my mind back, looking for clues, little indiscretions that would betray the truth I am now so certain of. Late nights and lipstick stains, unfamiliar smells and shady behaviour.

There *had* been late nights, somewhere on the scale between often and infrequent. But hadn't that always been the case? Adam was stressed. Adam worked hard. Adam liked to see his friends and was no stranger to closing time at the pub. That had always been the man I knew, the Adam I had chosen to share my life with.

Had he smelt different? Like another woman? Maybe. No. I don't know. My memories are clouded by puffs of talcum powder, stuck to one another with breast-milk residue and Sudocrem smears.

And yes, our relationship has shifted, seismically since Etta, but isn't that always the case with a newborn? We'd gone from two to three; a couple to a family. How could I possibly unpick what part of that was typical and what part was Adam turning away from me, towards someone else?

But it's the cliche, isn't it? The newborn phase is one of the most common periods for men to cheat. New mothers have a whole new person to look after and no time to look after themselves, and suddenly they're no longer an object of desire.

I feel overwhelmed by it all. Let my hand go slack, and the phone tumbles from it. It clatters to the floor, vanishes under the sofa. I don't care. Who would I even call? Once, I might have entertained it would be Mia. But I have lost Mia, and now I'm losing Adam, too.

I have no one.

I pull my legs onto the sofa, wrapping my arms around my knees, wanting to shut out the world. I'm cold, I think distantly. The bottom half of my jeans are still moist, and a vague, dank smell lingers. I can't believe the play café was only a couple of hours ago.

I had tried so hard. When I'd first allowed Adam into my life, I had tried to rid myself of everything that had gone before, to show him the very best version of "Beth" I could be. But it was like having Etta had cracked the mask, exposed all the vulnerabilities and weaknesses of who I really was. And now, with Elixir back in my life, the mask is rent in two.

I let the weight of the thought sit on me, crush me. And then I do something I haven't done in what seems like forever: I drink.

I walk over to the drinks cupboard, feet shuffling across the wooden floor before I have a chance to regret it. My knuckles knock against the bottles of cordial, the alcohol-free beer and wine, clinking them against one another as my arm weaves to the back and I retrieve the clear bottle hidden in the back. The vodka.

Like a hiker having reached the summit, my finger fumbles around the bottle cap, fighting adrenaline in my eagerness to open it. Tip my head back. Gulp.

Vodka. Tate's drink of choice. Even when I want to fight it, part of me still seeks out the highs of that time. Like an umbilical cord, the peaks of my release are intrinsically connected to him.

Deep in some muffled part of myself, I think I must be awful. Surely, this is awful? Drinking alone, in the middle of the day, while my baby sleeps upstairs!

But I don't care. For months – no, for years before Etta,

before Adam, even – my body has not been my own. I have been told how it should look, what to do with it, what to put to into it. I have exerted control over and had control exerted over it. And now I am done.

"Hahh," I exhale, wiping my mouth with the back of my hand. The vodka is warm, not ice cold as we drank it back then, but it still numbs my throat as it goes down, anaesthetic-like; still stings my nostrils, the corners of my eyes, just as it always did. And I know the pleasant buzz I crave isn't far behind. And there is something powerful, something phoenix-rising-from-the-ashes about drinking this, of all things: the drink I will forever associate with him. *Fuck you*, I want to tell him. *Fuck you, because after everything that happened, all I did to get away, I survived. Despite you, I survived. And you must* hate *that.*

But the victory is only momentary. Because the vodka doesn't make me vanquish him. Or forget him.

It only makes the memories of him more acute.

I retreat to the sofa, holding the bottle limply by the neck.

He comes back to me in pieces, like a jigsaw puzzle. A flash of brilliant white teeth. Hair the exact colour of spun gold. The warmth of his palm on the small of my back. The sound of his voice, accentless, neutral, calm. Until it wasn't.

I press my head between my knees, hands over my ears. Clench into myself.

When I come up for air, I drink more. The room is fuzzy now, pieces of furniture seeming to bleed into one another.

I think I hear something, a scuffling sound, tilt my chin towards the stairs to the upstairs bedrooms, stretching back through time to remember how long Etta has been down.

But the noise isn't coming from upstairs. It's from the front door.

Slowly, I crane my neck to where the seat is pushed up against it. See something white and hard pushed under the gap under the door, birthed beneath the chair legs.

"Hello?" I call out dizzily, unfurling from the sofa and taking a cautious step towards the door.

And then I feel a chill blast through me as I stoop to scan the white card, take in the gold insignia stamped on the envelope's reverse.

No, no, not again. Not now.

"Hello?" I pull myself out of my stupor, feel for the keys that are resting in the bowl by the door. Unlock it and slam it open to see a figure retreating down the staircase. "Mia!" I howl. "Come back here!"

My bare feet slap painfully against cold wood as I race down the stairs before Mia can escape. At the bottom of the stairs, I reach for her arm, blindly catch a snatch of fabric between my fingertips. And then the figure turns, their face coming into view.

And I realise with a horror that burns like the alcohol in my throat: it's not Mia.

It's Ingrid.

26
San Francisco Bay Area
May 2014

∞

Elizabeth knew she was living on borrowed time.

It had been agreed: Tate would help her. She could work for Elixir. But her space in The Jungle, her Elite position was secured in advance of her mother's visit only on the promise that she would *get that money*.

Tate had made an exception, a sort of loan, but he had also made it clear that a loan was exactly what it was.

"You know how much I care about you. How I want to see you fly." Voice pleading, the tips of his fingers stroking the bare skin on her upper arm, brow furrowed over those ersatz blue eyes. "But it wouldn't be fair to others to give it to you for free. How would it look if they thought I was pulling rank?"

And so every day that drew her closer to her mother's visit made her more skittish, on edge. Wondering where she would go if she was cast out. What her punishment would be if she failed. And as her agitation grew, so did the demands of Elite.

When she received her Elite tattoo, wincing as the black indelible ink seared into the skin of her wrist, she had made a promise. Elite was supposed to be the best. They were representatives for the entire program. For Tate. And that meant they were able to endure the most. High reward came at a high price.

For the first time, quietly, in the deepest recesses of her mind, where no chink of light was let in, she allowed her thoughts to wander back to that first, innocent class. Wondered when the vision had distorted, changed.

But then she would complete a task in record time, see the awe she inspired in the others. Feel her resolve harden. Or Tate would stand behind her, gazing at their twinned, naked reflection in the oak-edged mirror in his room. "You are magnificent," he would say, the back of his nail raking across her taut muscles, rippling a shiver through her.

And the thought would be lost.

As much as she was wary of her mother's visit, as much as she anticipated the long looks, her stepfather Greg's awkward throat clearings, Elizabeth couldn't help the flutter of excitement that knocked against the base of her ribcage as she threaded her way through the day-trippers dawdling on the Embarcadero. The visit was a detour from a medical conference her stepfather was attending at Stanford. "A good excuse for a holiday," her mother, Candice, had said, because obviously seeing her daughter wasn't excuse enough.

Tate had driven her in first thing, thundering them across the Golden Gate Bridge in his cherry-red Tesla Roadster. He was rarely at the studio those days, spending hours locked in his office in The Jungle, planning the next phase of Elixir's growth. They had taken on a new fleet of beginners recently after a landmark interview with him on a women's luxury-lifestyle website had gone viral, and he didn't like being mobbed by the giddy fans who clamoured for his attention whenever he stepped across the threshold of the loft.

"I'm an introvert at heart, my love," he had told her that morning, kissing the Elixir symbol on the underside of her wrist. "But you are our emissary today, and that deserves an arrival in style."

An hour earlier, as the dawn had washed the sky in pale gold, he had guided her down to the seafront, led her three feet into the ocean – gasping as the crystalline waves whipped her skin – and pressed a palm calmly against the top of her head until her knees buckled and she went under, lungs screaming for release.

The insult: she had left a pair of sunglasses out by the pool.

"You can't afford to be sloppy," his voice distorted through the water, barked.

When she'd resurfaced from the depths, skin pink and shining, nerve endings snapping as they adjusted to the sudden heat, she knew he was right. "I deserved this," she admitted. "I'll do better."

"Good." He took a towel, smiled. "The cold water has sharpened your mind." Gently, gently, he wrapped the towel around her, rubbed the life back in. Caressed her cheeks, kissing them. "I'm doing this because I want you to succeed. You needed to refocus. If you make silly mistakes like this over a pair of glasses, how can I possibly trust you with anything important?"

Now, as she stepped into the tourist-trap seafood grill her family had insisted on visiting because they had tickets for Alcatraz, the blasting air conditioning not quite disguising the smell of fryer oil and buttery shellfish carcasses, she saw he was right. She would show her mother how much Elixir had saved her, how instrumental it had been to her recovery. "Not just surviving, but thriving," as the Elixir mantra went.

She was ready. She was in control.

Her mother would see how important that money was. How could she possibly say no?

They were already seated when she got to the table, her stepfather mainlining an icy gun Coke in a branded glass, her mother scouring a laminated menu, reading glasses perched on the bridge of her nose. Her sister was there too, chewing lazily on a bread stick. This made Elizabeth halt her step. She hadn't anticipated her being with them. But that was stupid, she realised in hindsight: she was sixteen, where else would she be?

"Hey, guys. You made it!" She injected warmth into her voice, trying not to notice as Greg knocked into the table in his haste at getting up, rattling the cutlery and nearly sending an empty water glass flying.

"Oh, Beth, there you are!" Candice, as was typical of her ostrich-like nature, welcomed her with all the casualness of someone who had seen her eight days ago rather than over a year.

"I'm going by Elizabeth now, actually." She couldn't help knee-jerking the correction. Her nickname rankled now. So childish.

"Oh. Right." As Elizabeth jostled around the table, to the space next to her sister, she saw her mother give Greg a look. "Well, new beginnings, I guess." She picked up the glass of urine-coloured wine that sat beside her place setting.

"Actually, it's funny you should mention–"

"What's that?" Her sister pointed to the Elixir hourglass Elizabeth had absentmindedly placed beside her napkin.

"Oh, nothing." She reached her fingers to it, masking it.

If she had to start explaining that now, she'd never get the message across. She knew her mother would find that part too complicated to understand. She brushed the hourglass into her lap.

"I've got your garlic bread, and an order of calamari rings." A waitress with a nose ring squeezed around her and put the dishes in the centre of the table. "Would you be ready to go ahead and order your entrees now? Just a reminder that we will need your table back by two p.m."

"Yes, I said that was fine." Elizabeth saw her mother's expression wrinkle. She didn't like being hurried. "I know what I want. I'll have the Cioppino." The Italian syllables bounced around her mouth. "Beth – sorry, Elizabeth – can you look at the menu please? Seeing as apparently lunch will be a sprint race."

The laminated menu wobbled audibly as she took it from her mother, feeling her pulse start to race. She didn't go to places like this. She didn't go anywhere anymore, really, except for The Jungle and the studio.

"Have you... What do you have that's vegan?" The menu items loomed up at her, the words coated with fat, dripping with cheese or tossed with carbs. Fried Prawn Platter, Fettucine Alfredo.

"Um..." The waitress danced her weight between her hips. "Maybe the House Green Salad?"

"It has cheese in it." Elizabeth looked at where the woman's finger landed.

"Okay, then how about..."

Elizabeth felt the rest of the table's eyes on her. Her stomach pulled. "No, don't worry, it's fine. I'll just pick the cheese out. Here." She handed the menu back, avoiding her mother's eye as Greg and her sister ordered.

"Vegan?" Candice asked when the waitress retreated.

At the same time as Greg commented, "You've picked up an accent, love." He blithely dunked a calamari ring into a pool of glistening yellow mayonnaise. She watched a fat blob land on his chin, remain there a second too long before he wiped it off.

"Yes," she muttered, not sure whom she was addressing.

"Hey, cool." Her sister's voice was laced with admiration as she looked down at Elizabeth's wrist, exposed now on the tabletop. "Did you get a tattoo? What does it mean?"

"It's not... I'll explain later." She tugged at the sleeve of her sweatshirt, jerking her body away.

There was nothing linear in this conversation, there was no focus. She wished she could use the hourglass right now.

She was nothing like these people. No wonder she had left.

"Beth, have you been ill?"

She felt a hand on her shoulder, and the genuine concern in her mother's voice made her look up. Shook her head, confused. "Ill? God, no. Not at all. The opposite I... I said it's Elizabeth, Mum."

Candice folded her reading glasses beside her, and Elizabeth felt her eyes crawling all over her. "You've lost so much weight." Her fingers grasped into Elizabeth's rib cage. She twisted away. "I didn't notice it at first. And you look exhausted. Is it your job? Have you been working too hard? Because after everything that happened, I really do think–"

"Mum, no." Elizabeth pressed her palms into the tabletop. This hadn't gone the way she'd wanted it to at all. Tate was going to be so disappointed in her. What if she couldn't pay for the next programme? What if he didn't want to be with her anymore? What if he kicked her out?

Breathe, Elizabeth. Stay in control.

She put her hands in her lap. The stem of the hourglass butted against palm. She squeezed it. Exhaled slowly.

"I'm not sick. In fact, I'm... I'm amazing." She fluttered her eyelids, forcing brightness into her voice. "That's what I've been trying to tell you. I've been on this programme called Elixir and... well, it's changed my life. I feel stronger and healthier than ever. I've been working through a lot of my issues. I'm not even with JE&G anymore, Mum."

"You... you lost your job?" Her mother's horror was palpable.

"It doesn't matter." She shook her head. "Tate says that place was a whirlpool, it was only going to suck me down. He says I've only just started to discover my true worth. He says–"

"Who is Tate?" Candice asked, emotionless.

Her sister was studiously rolling a breadstick between her fingers. Greg was halfway through the calamari. Elizabeth felt her face grow hot. That wasn't the point. Wasn't her mother listening to anything she had been saying?

"He's... he's my boyfriend, I guess." Even the thought of it calmed her. He'd said they didn't need to put labels on things, but she knew what they meant to each other. "He's a great man, Mum. A true leader. And he's a millionaire." Turning to her sister, looking for an ally. "You should see where we live. This big mansion by the sea, and–"

"And what does he do, this Tate?"

She hated the way her mother said his name, like an accusation. The crispness of the T's.

"I told you, he's the Elixir founder." Frustration burned inside her. She'd thought they would be impressed, intrigued. Instead, Candice was looking at her like she'd suddenly sprouted three heads. She clasped the hourglass so tightly her nails dug into her palm, pressed on. "He's the most amazing person I've ever met. He knows everything. And I'm doing so well. He says I'm one of the most impressive students he's ever had in the programme. Which is why..." She steeled herself. "That was part of the reason I was excited to see you today, actually. There is an Elite programme I can join. Only..." She almost faltered, but the memory of that morning – the cold Pacific closing over her head – revived her. "I need your help. I need... I need to borrow some money."

"I thought you said this bloke was a millionaire?"

Elizabeth shot Greg a look as he picked up his napkin from his lap, wiped the tips of his greasy fingers.

"He can't pay for my courses, Greg," she enunciated, her words laced in arsenic. "That would be completely unethical."

"Can I clear those?" the waitress said suddenly, clattering their starter plates together. "I'll be back in a jiff with your entrees. Remember, two p.m.!"

No one said anything. A mushroom cloud of atmosphere surrounded the table.

"I just need a loan, Mum." Elizabeth's fingers loosed from the hourglass. She found the white paper napkin beside her plate and began tearing strips off it, letting them fall to the floor. "I'll pay it back. I just... I have to do this course. You understand, don't you? After everything that happened, everything I went through in London. This is fixing me. You may not see it now, but you will."

Her mother looked at Greg. And then back at her. "How much do you need?"

She felt the napkin tear in two. "Ten thousand dollars."

"You're joking!" Greg snorted messily. Elizabeth snatched him a look of disgust. She turned back to her mother, trying to read her expression.

Eventually: "Beth..."

"Elizabeth," she corrected.

Candice turned to Elizabeth's sister, looking in a very teenage way like she wanted the world to swallow her up. "Sweetheart, why don't you go to the loo before we go?" Added, in a warning hiss, "You don't know what the one on Alcatraz will be like. It *is* a prison."

Once she was out of earshot, Candice leaned in, asked in a loud whisper, "It's not drugs, is it?"

"No." Elizabeth shook her head fervently. "God, no. The opposite."

Her mother's features softened. But then she pressed her lips together, her soft coral lipstick disappearing. "Regardless, darling, I just can't give you that sort of money."

"You wouldn't be giving it to me. It would be a loan." Elizabeth's throat felt tight. She could feel the promise of the morning slipping away from her.

"You say that, but..." Her mother looked down at her plate. "Darling, I don't know what you've gotten yourself mixed up in. You're an adult woman, and I can't tell you how to live your life, but–"

"I haven't gotten myself mixed up in anything! Why aren't listening to me? It's just a loan. I'll give it back."

"Like I said, I can't tell you how to live your life, Beth–"

"It's fucking *Elizabeth*. How many times do I have to say?"

"Hey!" Greg snapped. "Don't you dare speak to your mother like that."

"This is none of your business, Greg!"

She stormed to her feet, her seat scraping against the

wooden floor. The hourglass fell, rolling somewhere on the ground, but she ignored it. Panic dug its talons into her. She couldn't go back to Tate with nothing. She *had* to stay on the Elite programme. She was nobody without it. Turning to her mother, desperation clutching at her, she said, "I want Granny's ring, then."

"What?" Her mother looked down at the ruby on her right index finger. The diamond surround glittered as she turned her wrist, catching the light.

"I want Granny's ring," she repeated coldly. Feeling the conviction Elixir had imbued her with bubbling inside her. "It's mine, isn't it? She promised it to me, in her will. You said you were keeping it for me in the safe, but it's clearly all right to take it out and about, so I'd like to have it now, please." Elizabeth saw embarrassment flush her mother's cheeks; knew she had caught her out.

"Darling..."

Elizabeth held out the flat of her palm. "Please."

She watched her mother hesitate. The intake of her breath. And then, slowly, her fingers went to her knuckle.

"Candice, really?" she heard Greg murmur.

"She's right, Greg," came the reply. And then she twisted the ring around her finger. Pulled.

The gold circle was warm in Elizabeth's palm as she curled her fingers around it, relieved. But before she could put it in her pocket, her mother reached for her, closing both hands over her own like a clam shell. She looked intently into Elizabeth's eyes, forcing her to look back.

"I don't want you to be unhappy... Elizabeth. If this Elixir thing is what is getting you through, then by all means, give it your all. Like I said, you're not a child. You're old enough to make your own decisions. But I want you to have a good hard look at yourself in the mirror tonight and ask yourself if you really, truly believe everything you've told me. If you don't..." Her mother's hands squeezed over hers, and Elizabeth felt the ridges of the gemstones biting into her skin. "...you may need this to get help."

Candice released her. Elizabeth felt her entire body quivering, adrenaline shocking through her.

She had the ring. It was going to be okay. She didn't have the loan, but she had the ring. It was something, at least.

Her eyes swerved around the room. She saw her sister making her way back from the bathrooms. Secreted the ring into the side pocket of her leggings, the prototype of a new model Tate had given her as a gift – burnt orange, set to sell out on launch day.

"I should let you guys go," she mumbled, feeling the urgency to leave, to get out of this sordid place with its combo lunch deal and people who were nothing like her. "You don't want to be late for your tour."

"But you haven't even had your salad!" Her mother blinked at her, and Elizabeth was surprised to see something in her expression like hurt.

"It's okay." She was already backing away from the table, mind bent on freedom. "I didn't want it anyway. I'll... I'll tell the waitress to cancel it."

"Sweetheart–"

"No, it's fine, honestly. It's been really nice seeing you." To Greg: "I hope the conference goes well." Turning back to her mother: "And thank you, Mum, for the ring. You really don't know how much it means. I'll make you proud, I promise. Next time I see you, you'll be sure of it."

She left her mother and Greg staring silently across the table. Blindly made her way around the other diners, pausing only to speak to the harassed-sounding waitress.

Just before she crossed the threshold, she heard footsteps pounding, turned to see her sister standing behind her.

"You didn't even say goodbye." The corners of her mouth drooped, and Elizabeth couldn't help but notice, not for the first time, the flicker of familiarity in her expression that made them kin.

"I'm sorry. I'm so sorry. I just… I need to go. You'll understand when you're older."

Elizabeth touched a hand to the side of her sister's shoulder, attempting comfort. Saw her eyes cloud with confusion, something akin to pain.

"They're not bad people, Mum and Dad," she whispered back.

"I know." Elizabeth looked away.

"Just… look after yourself. For me. And for them."

"I will. I promise." She found herself draping her arms around her sister, pulling her in close. Trying to find words for all the things she wanted to say but couldn't articulate. "I love you. You know that?"

It was only when she'd got to the studio that she realised she'd left the hourglass behind.

27
Muswell Hill, London
13th July 2023

∞

"You."

My eyes rove over Ingrid's soft, blonde features, registering the flush of heat in the woman's cheeks. The pieces begin to stack together. Her constant trips – to Sweden, she said, but who knew where, really? The spare key to the flat we'd given her, "just in case." Her "job" – the medicinal smell of wellness she always carries with her. She even looks like one of them: healthy and lithe. For three years, she's been right here below us, literally under my nose. How could I have been so blind?

"What do you want from me?"

When Ingrid doesn't answer instantly, I shake the envelope in her face. "I said what do you want? Why are you sending these? How do you know Mia? What does Tate want?" The plosives spray a stream of spittle into the air, and Ingrid's eyes widen. It is now that I notice the slur in my voice. The wobble in my legs. The smell of vodka on my breath. See Ingrid's forehead crease into something like concern. And as the initial heat of adrenaline begins to evaporate, the first trickle of something else rises in its place: embarrassment. And doubt.

"Beth…" Ingrid raises her arms slowly, cautiously, keeping the distance between us. I begin to feel lightheaded. "I don't know anyone called Mia. Or Tate. No one gave the envelope to me. I found it mixed up with our post."

A tingling sensation sweeps up my spine.

Ingrid is still looking at me with alarm. She has always been so nice. I want to believe her. Besides, Hardeep and Ingrid have lived in that flat for years, way before we moved in. Surely if she was seeking me out it would be the other way around?

"Beth…?"

"No one gave it you?" I repeat dumbly. "It was… it was in your post?" My lips feel thick, numb.

Ingrid nods. Speaks slowly, like she's coaxing a toddler out of a hiding place. "You do remember we've been away?"

"Yes," I bleat, and I do. The trip to see her brother. The leftover food, from Hardeep's mother. But when did they get back? When did I last see her? Why won't my thoughts stick in place?

She continues, placatingly, "And you know how useless Hardeep is at sorting out the post?"

I swallow. "Yes." It's the sort of inconsequential relationship we have. Small talk in the hallway. Hardeep forgetting to pay a bill. A new shop on the high street. Whether the interior walls need repainting. Light. Insubstantial. Safe.

Ingrid shifts her body weight, her lithe limbs moving fluidly from one foot to the other as she takes a cautious step towards me. "So, when we got back, there was a load of post under the door for Hardeep, and I must have scooped it all up together. He only went through it today or I'd have told you sooner."

"Today?" I repeat. "How long have you been back?"

"Oh, a few days?"

My heartbeat picks up. "A few…"

"Yes, it's Thursday today, isn't it? So, four, if you don't count Sunday."

"So it could have been there for a week?"

"Um… I guess?" Ingrid gives an awkward shrug.

The hallway suddenly feels very close. I press a palm to the wall, wishing I could push it away. Push everything away.

"I'm so sorry, Beth." Ingrid reaches a hand out, rests it on my upper arm. "I hope it wasn't something important?" She pauses. And I notice her taking me in in full, her eyes flicking down my body. Down to the bottle of vodka I'd forgotten I'm still clutching by the neck. When I meet Ingrid's gaze, she clears her throat. "Beth, is everything all right?"

Shame washes over me and I look down at my hand. "It's not what you think. I was just… cooking." It sounds hollow. I feel pathetic. Out of control. Embarrassment makes me verbose. "Yes, penne alla vodka. Do you know it? It's delicious." I don't know where the recipe surfaces from. A childhood holiday to Italy? When my mother still gave a shit, so it must have been years ago. "An old family favourite."

"Oh?"

I can tell Ingrid doesn't believe me. And it annoys me, even if it is a lie.

"Yes, I have a friend coming over for dinner. Mia." I allow myself to picture it: the imagined what-might-have-been: the two of us confiding over bowls of pasta, sharing childcare tips and life experiences. I had wanted to help her. I thought I'd understood. And I'd got it so wrong. "In fact, I should get back…"

"Oh. Yes, of course." Ingrid looks up the stairs to the flat and back again, but doesn't move to leave. "Adam's away, isn't he? I bumped into him with his suitcase this morning. Where was it he's going? Leeds?"

"Manchester." I swallow, and the second, earlier lie batters me. I have no idea where Adam really is, *who* he is really with.

"Ah, that's right. Manchester." Ingrid hesitates. "And you're having a friend over?"

I nod, probably a little too emphatically.

"Good for you. It must be a lot, doing that when you're on your own with the baby." Her eyes flick to the bottle again. "You know, if you need any help, if you want me to watch her for you, or if you need any shopping done or anything…"

And then, in the distance, through the open door to the flat, I hear it. Crying.

I turn, eyes fixed up the stairs, narrowing in on the empty void of the living room. Ears straining for the bedroom above it, for Etta, supposedly asleep within.

The cry comes again, louder, more distinct.

And I feel the dull weight of the bottle in my hand. Taste the metallic tang of vodka on my teeth.

I whip my head back to Ingrid, eyes widening.

Etta's awake. And hungry.

28
Muswell Hill, London
13th July 2023

∞

"I have to go." Already, Etta's wails are increasing, becoming more incensed. "Please, don't worry about the letters. It was a mix-up. I – I thought you were someone else." My head throbs, a premonition of the hangover to come.

"Are you sure?" Ingrid follows my eyeline up the stairs, not quite convinced. "I only have one more client this afternoon. Hardeep and I are out for dinner tonight, but I could swing by before we leave, give you a hand?"

"No," I start, with more force than I intended. My mind is already up there, with Etta, but I add, with all the pleasantry I can muster, "That's really kind of you, but honestly, we'll be fine."

Ingrid sucks her lip. "Sure. No problem. I'll leave you to it. And, like I said, I'm really sorry about the letters. If there's anything I can do to make it up to you, if there's anything you need, anything at all…"

I stumble backwards, nodding. "Thank you. Yes. See you soon."

The vodka splashes in the bottle. I fold it into my chest

as I turn, trip back up the steps. I don't look back, but I can sense that Ingrid is still there, watching me.

Upstairs, I slam the door behind me, redo all the locks, fix the safety chain, replace the chair I had knocked aside.

Sealed inside, I am all motion. Etta's cries are much louder now, her fury more insistent, but as much as it pains me, I have to leave her. At least Etta is safe where she is. Safe from me.

My thoughts feel loose and ungrounded, sloshing about in my brain like what's left of the vodka in the bottle. How can I feed her like this? How could I do this to her?

I need to snap out of it. I need to sober up.

I stalk to the kitchen, set the kettle on to boil. Fetch down a mug and open the instant coffee – one spoon. No, two. The irony of my concerns about the caffeine hit hard. What's the point, now, when I can't feed Etta anyway?

You are stupid. You are lazy.

I can hear the snarl in his voice. Imagine the curl of his lip, if he could see me now.

How easily he's got under my skin, without even touching me.

Etta is *howling* now. The guilt washes over me in waves: don't they say babies think you've gone forever if they can't see you?

The kettle clicks. The sound makes me flinch. A jet of steam propels from the spout.

I stir boiled water into the coffee granules and take a swig, not caring if it scalds.

I have to feed Etta. But it'll be two hours, at least, until I'm able to safely.

I look back at the kettle.

And then an idea pricks me. The unopened box of

formula; a clean, new bottle; both stashed under the sink. "For emergencies," Adam had insisted.

My fingers hesitate on the frame of the cupboard door, thinking of all the pain and tiredness I've gone through to exclusively breast feed. All the formula-research rabbit holes I've dragged myself down through: harmful bacteria, risk of asthma, increased obesity. The hissed distaste in the dark corners of Mumsnet threads I've trawled in the middle of the night, nipples cracked and drunk on tiredness: *breast is best; liquid gold; the ultimate sacrifice.*

All of it rekindling in me the ability to exert control over my body, to be part of a collective, the noxious coding that is still, somehow, hardwired in me.

Quitting is not an option.

It was supposed to be what was best for Etta. But now Etta is up there, starving and alone, thinking she's been abandoned. Surely leaving her is more harmful than one bottle ever could be?

Etta shrieks. The sound is almost physically painful.

In one decisive move, I wrench open the cupboard door, pull out the box and the bottle and set them both on the countertop. My hands shake as I open the lid, rip the foil lip so vehemently the box shakes. White powder explodes across the counter.

I try to focus on the instructions on the back of the pack, my head swimming: FILL THE KETTLE WITH FRESH WATER. DO NOT USE WATER THAT'S BEEN BOILED BEFORE.

I look at the kettle, which has barely stopped steaming. Do I really have to chuck what's in there out and start the whole thing again? Surely not. What's next?

BOIL WATER, THEN LEAVE TO COOL FOR NO MORE THAN 30 MINUTES.

Leave to cool? Tears blur my vision. I don't have time to leave it to cool. It's three sentences. How can I find it so complicated?

Etta's cries make me jittery, ignite in me a sense of urgency that makes every wasted second feel like an hour.

In my mind's eye, I see the hourglass, sand whooshing through its neck.

Sloppy. Useless.

Tate's voice curls into my ear.

But then, surprisingly, another of his aphorisms comes to my assistance: *Don't be a quitter.*

I harden myself. *Come on. Think.* Haven't I been conditioned to act under pressure? I look to the sink as something pulls at me: a memory from a movie or television show, a bottle held under a running stream of cool water.

Of course. I grip the bottle in my hand and turn the tap, jaw clamped in concentration. *You can do this.*

You have to. For Etta.

The whole incident must only have lasted ten minutes or so, but I feel as though it's been hours as I enter the bedroom, bottle in hand.

Etta is lying on her back, face puce and streaked with tears, silky hair matted down with sweat against her forehead. The look of outrage she gives me when I enter makes my stomach squirm in a million different directions as I close the distance between us, murmuring apologies that seem insufficient, weak.

"Baby, I'm so, so sorry."

I scoop her hot little body into my arms, pressing her

wet cheek into my neck as I cluck reassurances, listening painfully to her whimpered snatches of breath.

I sit on the edge of the bed, cradling Etta in my arms, but as soon as I do, she begins nuzzling into my chest, Pavlov-like. I smooth a hand across my T-shirt, the guilt washing over me anew. "No, no, baby. Look what I've got for you. A bottle. How exciting. Yum, yum, yum."

I hope Etta can't recognise the quake in my voice.

The liquid swishes inside the bottle as I hold it up, and Etta cocks her head to look at it, brow a deep furrow. My palm begins to sweat against the plastic exterior; what if she won't take it? I hold my breath as I narrow in, stroke the teat against Etta's lips, whetting them with a teardrop of milk. Etta screws up her mouth, wrenches her head away. The anticipation of it makes me think I might throw up. But then she turns back. I wait. Her tongue darts out, chasing the taste. And when I try again, Etta takes the teat into her mouth.

Slowly, reluctantly, begins to drink.

I want to cry with relief.

Fired Up
Podcast Transcript

Brent Peters Interviews Tate Larsen, June 2014

Brent Peters: Welcome to *Fired Up*, the podcast for entrepreneurs everywhere. Today, we are joined by fitness and wellness guru, and founder of the Elixir exercise programme, Tate Larsen. Tate, welcome to the show.

Tate Larsen: [laughs] Well, I would hardly call myself a guru. A humble businessman at most, Brent. But hello. Thank you for having me on.

BP: Modest, perhaps. But not humble, surely? Was that your Tesla parked outside? What does one of those set you back?

TL: Electric cars are our future, Brent. I'm prepared to invest in the safety of the planet. Aren't you?

BP: Ha, okay, you've got a point there. But elsewhere, business is booming, right? Elixir membership is up thirty per cent. You have a slate of new studios in the works. You're thinking of expanding into Europe.

TL: People like what we do. I'm glad we're here to help them.

BP: That's great. That's what we want to hear. So, let's talk about success. Last week on the show, we interviewed Jackson Lange, CEO of meal-replacement disrupter Crayven, who said he owed his success to working hundred-hour weeks and using the critical problem-solving method known as "first-principles thinking." What would you say your incredible success is due to?

TL: So, it's funny you should talk about success, Brent, because success is the guiding light of the Elixir programme. We want our members to find success, in every aspect of their lives. So really, my success is down to adopting the Elixir method myself. Inner strength meeting outer strength. Demanding resilience and grit from both my physical and mental self is what led me to found Elixir in the first place.

BP: Physical grit, I'm sure. What do you bench, three hundred pounds? [laughter] Maybe I need to take some of these classes myself. [pause] But seriously, your members seem super-enthusiastic about the benefits of your programmes. Some may say perhaps a little *too* enthusiastic? I have a tweet here that one of our producers, Craig, has found that I'm gonna read out: "My friend Tara joined Elixir for a month and was forced on a 500-calorie-a-day diet. She developed an eating disorder. This shit is whack, man." [pause] What do you… what do you say to that?

TL: Hmm. That's a real shame. I think I remember Tara. A sweet girl. A little shy. Unfortunately, in the business we're in, we do occasionally have people come to us with underlying issues. We do our best to help, and our methods can have remarkable effects, but some pre-existing psychological conditions are unfortunately best handled by a medical professional. We advised Tara to seek help, and to Tara: if you or anyone who knows you is listening right now, we want only the best for you, and everyone at Elixir wishes you well.

[the sound of a drink being sipped, a glass being set down on a table]

BP: Okay, so you're saying Tara's eating disorder was nothing to do with Elixir?

TL: God, Brent, no! These are adult men and women. We would never make them to do something against their will. All our staff receive training in health and nutrition and are able to advise on diet, should that be something that is asked of us. But to force someone to follow a particular regime? No, no.

BP: Sure. So then, what about the other... Accusations seems a strong word, but what about the other perceptions of Elixir that are, shall we just say, less than complimentary? What about the people who have said that Elixir bears similarities to pyramid schemes, or, perhaps more incredulously, that it's some sort of a cult?

TL: [chuckles] You know, it's funny, Brent, how that word gets banded about. Cult. They called Facebook a cult. Apple. It's amazing how many great organisations these days get slapped with that term because they respond to an inherent social need that a group of people buy into. We provide our members with something they want. And they like it. If that makes us a cult, well...

BP: And a pyramid scheme?

TL: Pyramid schemes are illegal, Brent. Is there something you're getting at?

BP: No, no...

TL: Because I want to make that clear. Nothing of the sort is being offered here. Nothing. I mean, to be frank, Brent, nine times out of ten, complaints are the result of someone who has paid for a course, found it wasn't for them and then tried to get their money back after the fact. You know? Which, I'm sure you'll agree, isn't really our fault, and isn't fair to the hardworking and dedicated team we have at Elixir. In fact – and I'm just going to say now, so that we're clear – despite your playful tone, we have a very low tolerance for any sort of claim that we are operating a pyramid scheme or anything in any way nefarious. It's not only defamatory, but damaging to our business. And we have a very powerful and highly trained legal team who are prepared to take whatever action is necessary against these sorts of baseless allegations. Does that make sense to you, Brent?

BP: Yes, sure. I–

TL: Because if there is something you are insinuating… If you'd like to discuss this further, I–

BP: No, no.

TL: Because I thought this was just a free exchange of ideas. I thought I was here to discuss the success of Elixir and my path to entrepreneurship. That's how Stacey billed it when she booked me. But if there is some ulterior motive, some other reason you wanted to bring me here today, then I'd be more than happy to introduce you to our legal representative…

29
Marin County
June 2014

∞

With the victory of securing her grandmother's ring, Elizabeth's status in Elixir was fully cemented. It seemed everyone in the company knew the open secret of Elite, the importance of the people in it. Members would rush to open doors for her. Straighten up as she walked past. Ask if there was anything they could help her with. She felt powerful, energy snapping in her synapses. She felt special, in Tate's eyes, in the eyes of those who knew what she meant to him. She felt *invincible*.

Only… it was strange. It was as though the more her own moon waxed, got fulsome and bright in the reflected glow of Tate's sun, Marissa's began to wane. And she didn't want to see how far the fall would go.

It was silly things at first. Mistakes that she, Elizabeth, with her renewed focus and keen senses, would try to cover up for. A book Marissa had been reading, left face-down on the coffee table – cracking the spine and potentially scratching the pristine glass surface – that Elizabeth quietly closed and replaced. Marissa's washing, left to moulder in the machine, discreetly moved to the dryer, its owner none the wiser. But leaving the studio doors unlocked after closedown? What if someone had broken in? Turning up late to teach class, so that Elizabeth had to run the warmup until Marissa scuttled in, puff-cheeked and red-faced? Inexcusable.

And those were just the errors Tate missed. But there were more obvious things she couldn't hide.

Marissa had fainted in the middle of one of Tate's exclusive Elite workouts, and refuted Tate's suggested remedy, a juice cleanse, to rebalance and detoxify her system. She'd slept through a sunrise meditation session, then tried to argue with him when he told her she'd lost bed privileges for a week. She'd even driven a wheelbarrow into one of Tate's pot plants and broken it, after they'd spent a month re-landscaping the front drive; had the affrontery to get tetchy with Tate's solution: pay to renew the whole thing from scratch, because obviously now the entire design wouldn't work. It was only fair: she'd broken the thing out of clumsiness or spite, and neither was a good look.

The worst was when Tate announced that someone had made him sick from the mushrooms at dinner one night, and Cassidy – a Florida plastic surgeon's daughter hoping Elixir would realise her dream of winning an Oscar – fingered Marissa as the cook. Watching Marissa from the living room's floor-to-ceiling windows spending the night handcuffed to one of the sun beds, Elizabeth felt the urge to go to her and wrap a blanket around her shivering body, or a towel, at the very least. But she knew it would only make things worse.

"Tate, don't you think... Isn't it enough now?" she asked him in a low voice, watching Marissa twisting in her chair, the ocean breeze whipping her hair into tangles.

Tate followed her gaze, his jaw set. "Elizabeth, I know it's difficult, but I'm doing this for Marissa's own good." He sighed, took hold of her hand and kissed it. "She says she didn't do it on purpose, which means at the very least she was careless. In which case, she's damn lucky I survived." He pulled her into him, wrapping her into an embrace that obscured her view. "A night outside will give her clarity." His features shifted, the edge of his jaw sharpening. "But if you feel so strongly, you could always go out there to keep her company?"

She craned her neck to look back at Marissa, pins and needles prickling her legs at the thought. "No, you're right," she acquiesced, pressing herself into his warmth. "She needs to learn."

After each of these incidents, Marissa would invariably come to her senses. Choke out apologies and beg for forgiveness. She'd tell Tate he was right, that of course he knew best, and things would quieten down. She would be back in Tate's orbit, curled like a favourite cat beside him. But from her silent observations, Elizabeth noticed a steeliness in Marissa's eyes, a cooling of affection, even if Tate himself was oblivious. And she began to wonder if Marissa wasn't curled like a cat but coiled like a spring.

She felt bad for her friend. Sad that, for whatever reason, she was stumbling so far from the path.

But she also felt a whiff of something else. *Embarrassment.* Marred with the faint stench of revulsion, as though Marissa's downfall could be catching. Fear, for what would happen if it was.

She tried to reason with her, in the Extraction sessions that had somehow mutated over time so that Elizabeth was now the one charge. She tried coaxing, asking gently what had happened, what had gone wrong. On Tate's advice, she tried conducting "readiness" drills, ensuring that whenever she gave the word, Marissa would instantly have to stop what she was doing and complete a task of Elizabeth's choosing. She tried endurance tests, flipping the Elixir hourglass over and over as Marissa held increasingly complex stress positions. She tried cold showers, 5 a.m. runs – all the things that she, Elizabeth, had willingly submitted to because she knew it made her stronger, harder, better.

But… nothing. Marissa never seemed to get it. She never seemed grateful. She would endure it all stoically, staring dolefully at Elizabeth with her lips pressed into an infuriatingly reticent line. It was as though the light had gone out of her, and Elizabeth couldn't understand *why*.

And then it was early October. A lovely time of year that always made her think, with muted pangs, of home. The days were warm and mild, but there was a crispness in the air, the sun mellowing to a deep gold that was reflected back in the autumn landscape, the foliage surrounding The Jungle merging into soft browns and ruddy reds more akin to London than California.

She had come back early from the Studio HQ on an important task. They were expecting proofs of Tate's new book – *It Works: The Elixir Way* – and she had been hand-picked to accept delivery. Tate was in Nevada, overseeing the final phase of construction of a new retreat, which meant there would be no one hanging around at The Jungle hoping to catch a glimpse of him.

She would be alone, and she was already planning how she would spend the time: lazing down by the pool, enjoying a blissfully unadulterated stretch of rest. If she happened to doze off, no one would be any the wiser. Although by now she was used to the lack of sleep – her body was constantly awash with adrenaline – it seemed to catch up with her the moment she was alone; a nausea that congealed in the depths of her stomach, pooled distastefully in the corners of her mouth.

Her laziness was covert, though. She knew that if some eagle eye caught her, they wouldn't hesitate to call her out to Tate for slacking. In Elixir, dragging someone else down was as easy a win as raising oneself up.

She opened the mansion door tentatively. Stepped into the coolness of the open living room.

"Hello? Anyone home?"

Silence echoed back.

The anticipation of rest tingled in her nerve endings as she made her way upstairs to change. She could practically feel the impression of the sun bed against her back, the lick of sunlight across her cheeks. But when she got to the landing, she could feel something out of place. Her senses hackled.

There was someone there.

She edged her way along the corridor, remembering her first night in the mansion, how alien it had seemed then. The place she now called home.

"Hello?" she called again, softly.

She was sure there wasn't supposed to be anyone in. She'd checked the rota. It was Saturday, the busiest day for classes, and besides that, half of the Elite members were with Tate in Nevada, so they were even more stretched than usual. If it was that snotty little Angie, thinking she was going to pip Elizabeth to the post in collecting the proofs...

A sound made her ears prick up. A wrenching, human sound. Coming from the bathroom at the end of the corridor.

Tentatively, she reached the closed door. Within, the sound continued. Choking. Guttural.

"Hey, who's in there?" she asked, rapping against the

wood with her knuckles. And then, when there was a momentary still, "Is everything all right?"

"Go away!" the voice was thick, coated in mucus.

"Marissa?" She tried the handle. It was locked.

"Leave me alone, *Elizabeth*." Marissa managed to lace her name in sarcasm. "I'm sure you have somewhere more important to be."

The bitterness of Marissa's tone hit her as forcibly as though she'd been slapped. It was true – recently, Elizabeth hadn't been there for her friend as much as she would have liked. She had been busy; helping Tate prep for the Nevada trip, staying up late into the night to type up the book, which he insisted on writing by hand, filling the pages of a brown leather Moleskine. But she still cared for Marissa, so if she was in trouble, she wanted to help.

"Please," Elizabeth said softly, cheek pressed to the door. "I'm worried. I promise, I'm only here to help."

There was silence at the other end.

She nearly walked away. But then she heard footsteps, slow. The whine of the lock turning. And then the door opened and Marissa's face appeared.

"Marissa, what's wrong?" she asked as soon as the door opened fully. She looked awful, her eyes bloodshot, tears streaming from them. Her skin chalky and pallid. The stench of vomit stung Elizabeth's nostrils, making her stomach curdle. "Are you sick?" Instinctively, she pressed a hand to Marissa's forehead. "Is it a bug? Something you ate? It's not… it's not mushrooms again, is it?" Marissa threw her an acid look and she felt herself blush. "I'm sorry, I didn't mean that. But if you're sick, if there's something wrong, we should get you to a doctor."

"*No.*"

They locked eyes. And then Elizabeth widened her own. Because she suddenly read the emotions that came across Marissa's face in waves: fear laced with desperation. Saw the way Marissa shrunk away from her, curling her body inwards. Saw the way her fingers fluttered to her waist, the barely-there protuberance she now saw on her thin frame.

And she knew, before the words even left Marissa's mouth, what truth they'd bring.

"I'm not sick. I'm pregnant."

30
Muswell Hill, London
13ᵗʰ July 2023

∞

When Etta calmly finishes the bottle, I move us down to the living room. Pick up the bottle of vodka, the envelope down by the front door. I am no longer drunk, or wanting to be, and the acrid smell that lingers at the bottle's neck makes me grimace as I throw it in the bin with a resounding *clunk*. Pause, hand poised over the bin, ready to throw the envelope in after it. Lower it again, and let the lid close as I open the envelope.

It's a photograph. I know which one it will be before it's out of the envelope. Lay it on my lap as I sit on the sofa, Etta propped against cushions beside me.

Elite Members Symposium, June 2014, reads the banner we are standing under.

The last one taken of us all together. Weeks, perhaps only days, before it all fell apart.

I can still remember the first stirrings of the morning sun, warming my neck. The shimmer of it reflecting off the surface of the waves behind us. The crunch of sand beneath my feet. And I remember, too, how hard I had forced the smile that looks so effortless now in print. Know, even though it can't be rendered across time on ink and paper, that beneath the carefree glint in my eyes lies pain, exhaustion, fear.

There he is, beside me, his palm pressing harder than it looks against my shoulder.

And there *she* is, on his other side, chin upturned. Defiant, perhaps? Defiant, or resolute.

Slowly, I turn the photograph around. Read the words scrawled at the back.

Tick. Tock.

The staccato words chime with the beat of my pulse.

I want Adam. The thought gnaws at me. No matter who he is with, what lies he has told, we can work it out. Giving up on him would be letting Tate win. I'll tell him everything. We can start afresh.

I snatch up my phone, nerves creeping with each electronic beep of the dial tone. It rings out, but I try again, undeterred. And again.

But as I stare at the message in the numb silence of the flat, Etta curled beside me, I am surprised to find the anxiety in the base of my belly is replaced by something else. Something dark, and mottled, and powerful.

Anger.

Not just at Tate… but at Adam.

How can he do this to me? Why am I *letting* him do this to me?

I have come so far from Elixir. I have fought for this life. *Our* life. I have looked inside myself and risen above everything that happened to me, and he is blissfully ignorant. I have kept *everything* from him. To protect him. To save him from the reality of who I really am.

To have Etta – to give him the family he has so longed

for – I have been injected, and examined, and pitied. I have been ripped apart and sewn back together. I have bled, and leaked, and ached, and had days when I no longer even recognised the Beth I have attempted to conjure up.

And now, when I need him most, he has thrown me away.

By the time I ring a fourth time, hear again the chirpy tone of his voicemail message –"This is Adam! You know what to do!" – the message I plan to leave is frothing acid on the tip of my lips. Only, when it comes to it, I find I am tongue tied, mute. I manage one strangled sound before hanging up. Am about to throw the damn thing across the room when I notice a red message flag on the corner of my WhatsApp icon. An unknown number.

It's Mia. This isn't what you think. I have to speak to you. Please, call me.

And then I do throw it. Hurl the phone across the room with such vehemence that Etta, scrunching a crinkle-cloth book beside me, squalls.

I can't deal with this. I want to disappear, to take Etta and run. But I am too scared to leave. Even the expanse of the living room feels too wide, too exposed. Instead, I pull her into my arms and retreat to the bedroom, shutting the door and drawing the curtains tight.

I sleepwalk through the rest of the afternoon, a hangover arriving in late afternoon, a dull ache that throbs at my temples, heightened by the heat that now gathers in the room.

Somehow, the hours pass.

I manage to get Etta to sleep.

And then I lie on the bed, watching the light behind the curtains mellow, bathing the room in soft orange that grows deeper and darker as I feel the last of my energy drain from me... and my eyelids start to close...

In the darkness, a scattergun sound rouses me. I raise myself up with a jolt.

I have fallen asleep fully clothed, legs tangled into the mess of covers. I have no idea when, or for how long, but the room is now ink-dark, and the time on my watch says it's just after nine. My first thought is for Etta, but she's still asleep in her cot, unharmed.

The sound is rain, I realise, coming fully to. Hammering on the attic roof, pinging through the gap in the open window beyond the cot. I move to pull down the heavy sash, fingers sliding against the water which now coats the sill, and the noise dulls. But then another joins it. Louder, more insistent. A thundering pulse. Coming from the front door of the flat.

I am suddenly wide awake, anticipation making my nerve endings dance as I open the bedroom door, creep down the stairs. I'd forgotten to switch off the downstairs lights, and in the bald electric brightness I can see the door to the flat juddering. The chair that is still pushed against it quakes on its legs as a fist hammers from the other side. The sound quiets, momentarily, then starts anew, a voice joining it.

"Beth! For fuck's sake, open the door!"

"...Adam?"

I cross the room, crack the door open partway.

He is soaking wet, his hair darkened to black, curls flattened against his temple. His fist is still raised, fingers curled tightly, and I can't help but glance over his shoulder down the dark corridor, wondering what Ingrid and Hardeep must be thinking, before remembering Ingrid said they were going out.

"Where have you been?" he demands. "I've been calling and calling. It kept going to voicemail. Why is the deadbolt on?"

"You were... you were away," I pant, my mind still hazy, trying to place his presence. Did I somehow get the days wrong? Did I – for a solitary moment my mind goes there, although I know it must be impossible – did I sleep longer than I thought? The smell of damp fabric curls against my nostrils and I ask, distractedly, "Why are you so wet?"

He slicks an arm across his forehead. "There wasn't a bus for ages. I couldn't find a cab, so I had to walk." He pushes past me as I shrink back against the door frame. "It didn't start raining until it was too late to change my mind." And then he stops dead, his palm heavy on the handle of his suitcase. "Beth, what's happened?"

I turn, letting the door slide shut behind us; allow myself to see the room through his eyes: the kitchen chair, now knocked on its side. The box of formula, powder spilling out across the countertop where in my flurry I must have upended it fully. The cardboard from the bottle box, littered in scraps across the floor. There are rolled-up dirty nappies discarded on the coffee table next to the half-finished cup of coffee. Toys and board books where I or Etta have haphazardly thrown them. Adam goes to my phone, on the floor next to the sofa. Turns it on to show the multitude of notifications, all from him, against the wallpaper of Etta's toothless grin.

"You leave me all these missed calls – a blank voicemail – and then nothing?" He stalks over to the bin carrying a handful of rubbish and releases the kick stand.

"I tried texting. I tried calling. I even thought about calling *Ingrid*, but I didn't want to freak her out. I thought something had happened to Etta. I thought something had happened to you. Why aren't you saying anything? What on earth's the matter with you, Beth?"

I open and close my mouth, inert. My eyes stray to the photograph, discarded on the countertop, dangerously close to his right elbow. But before he has a chance to notice or I can respond, he stops himself, a hand poised over the open bin. Bends down before turning to face me, holding the neck of the vodka bottle.

"...Beth?"

My brain thuds. My skull feels as though it's about to explode. I say the only thing I can think of in the moment.

"Adam... I *know*."

Adam's expression is entirely blank. He takes a step towards me, fingers still curled around the neck of the bottle. "Know what?"

I swallow. Pull a ragged breath into my lungs.

"I know you weren't on a course." My whole body is quivering, but my voice is surprisingly firm. Of all the things that have happened to me today, it is this that now burns inside me. "I know you weren't in Manchester. I know you've been lying to me. You're sleeping with someone." I squeeze my knuckles into a fist. "Who is she?" I shake my head, trying to stop the tears that threaten. "You owe me that, at least."

I wait. Silently. Watch Adam processing my revelation. Stare, unbelieving, as his features curl into a smile and he laughs.

"Is that what you think?" He closes the distance to go to me, dropping the vodka bottle to the ground with a heavy thud. Holding me steady as I try to squirm from his grasp. "Beth, look at me," he urges as I avoid his eyes. "I am not having an affair."

I look. He feels so familiar. So safe. Tears smart my eyes. He allows my silence. There must be something else. I was so sure, before. It seemed so obvious.

"But you didn't answer your phone..." I say, my voice small, suddenly doubtful.

"I was in talks, and then there was a drinks reception," he says. Gently, patiently. "You know that." Brushes the hair from my head with the lightest touch of his fingers. The lingering scent of the cologne on his skin brings painful comfort. "Look." He reaches for his neck, holds out the lanyard that encircles it. I read the words on the laminated card it holds: *Accountex Summit Manchester. The future of accountancy and finance.* "I called back," he continues, "as soon as there was a break. And then you didn't answer." I slacken and he releases me. "I was so worried, I took the first train back I could. I told Nathan there was a family emergency."

What he's saying makes sense – I know it does. And then the guilt sets in. Nathan, his boss, who he's been working so hard to impress. Tate is messing with my brain so much that I'm accusing my husband of having an affair, when really he's trying his hardest to look after our family.

Still, something nags at me. "But... you weren't on a train when we spoke. I heard a car in the background."

Adam sighs, deep in his chest. "I don't know what else to tell you, Beth. What do you need, photographic evidence?" Presses a hand to his temple. "I knew I shouldn't have gone on this trip. I knew it was too much for you." Pats the pockets of his suit trousers. "You can check my phone. Read my messages. Look, I've even got the train tickets on here, to prove it."

He jerks it up in front of me, holding the app open on his screen.

Heat begins to creep up my neck. London to Manchester, Manchester to London. The typed black letters glare back at me, confirming just how far into madness I have sunk.

"Ads, I... I don't know what to say. I'm so sorry." I feel myself crumpling, shame and embarrassment and exhaustion knocking me from all sides. "I've got it all wrong. I've ruined your trip. Your promotion – I know how important it is. I just... I just..."

As I press myself into him, I hear the warmth flood into his voice. "Hush. It's okay. It's going to be okay." He guides me over to the sofa by the tips of my fingers. Sits down beside me – my kind, patient husband. He says nothing for a moment. In the silence, I can still hear the trill of rain from outside. "It's okay," he repeats. "But sweetheart..." Swallows. Looks away. "Sweetheart, I don't understand what's going on with you. I know it's been hard, with Etta. I know you've always kept certain parts of yourself to yourself. And I get that, I do."

I can see him steeling himself. Wait for the blow.

"But it's like I don't know who you are anymore. You've been so distracted. And distant. I know there's something you're holding back. And if you feel it's something you can't talk to me about, I understand, but I think you need to find someone you *can*." He takes my hand in his, draws slow circles in the centre of my palm. "Beth, I think... I think maybe it's time we talk about getting you some help. There are places you can go, professionals you can talk to, who are better qualified to deal with this than me. I think perhaps it would be what's best for you. For Etta."

"No!" Memories of the Extraction sessions flood my

exhausted mind, and the idea of doing anything similar sends me spiralling. I can't go back to that.

And I know now that I can't go on like this. I can't keep Adam in the dark any longer.

Adam looks grey. And I feel wrung out, too.

Slowly, I rise. Feel his eyes on me as I go over to the kitchen. Retrieve the photograph from the countertop.

I know it is impossible, but I am sure I can feel the tattoo burning at my wrist as I hold the paper out to him.

"There is something I've been hiding. Something I need to tell you. About my past."

I take a long, slow breath. Open my mouth to begin...

... as the sound of the door buzzer rips through the flat.

31
Marin County
June 2014

∞

"What do you mean, you're pregnant?"

Elizabeth's forehead throbbed as she took in Marissa fully against the starkness of the bathroom. Tate had advised her to trial a restricted-calorie diet programme, and she definitely hadn't drunk enough water to balance it.

How could Marissa be pregnant? Was that what this whole thing had been about – she'd been sleeping around? Did *Tate* know? He would be furious: *he* may be sexually itinerant, but it was an unwritten rule that that privilege was reserved solely for him. Why hadn't Marissa said anything in their sessions? What had Elizabeth missed?

"Who...?" The only word she could manage.

Marissa seemed to be staring intently at a spot of lint on the cold tiled floor. "Who do you think? Tate."

"Tate?" The room spun. Unwanted jealousy sliced at her. She knew Tate didn't use protection. She knew, also, that Tate wanted children. Lately, it seemed as though he brought the topic up more and more when they were alone together: a child born out of Elixir, what could be better? But she hadn't felt ready. Every time she pictured it, she would spiral backwards,

to that hospital room, to her mother's face, pinched, accusing. She couldn't take herself back there. Not yet.

And now Tate had chosen Marissa instead.

"What a blessing." She swallowed it down like a stone. "I'm very happy for you."

All this time, she thought she was special. But in the end, it was Marissa. Perhaps it always had been.

She stared numbly at Marissa's abdomen. Felt compelled to reach out to touch it. Was surprised at the vehemence with which Marissa batted her away.

"*Happy for me?* You think I *wanted* this?" Marissa turned her chin, stared back at her pallid reflection in the mirror opposite. Brought the heel of her hand to the corner of her lip, where a thin line of drool lingered. "No, I didn't ask for this, Elizabeth. I didn't *want* it." She swallowed thickly. "Tate raped me."

The word ricocheted off the bathroom's smooth surfaces.

Elizabeth swallowed. The air felt thick, soupy. Carrying with it the sour scent of Marissa's vomit, making her want to retch herself.

"*No.*" Dizziness overwhelmed her. Her eyes went filmy, and she thought she might faint. It was disgusting. What Marissa was saying was disgusting. *Marissa* was disgusting.

She palmed her face, muffling the stench. "You're lying." Shook her head. "He's… he's your…" She struggled for the definition. Tate said labels were unimaginative, designed to put people into boxes. "You've been sleeping with him. *Willingly.* How are you now calling that rape?"

Marissa closed her eyes. Slowly, slowly, blinked them open. When she looked back, it was as though Elizabeth was a tiny child that Marissa had the odorous task of explaining the world to. "Is that really what you believe?"

For a moment, there was stillness. Neither of them spoke, and when Elizabeth trained her ears, she realised she could hear nothing, not a single sound in the house, not even the rush of the waves in the distance. It was as though she and Marissa were the only people to exist in the world.

"Open your eyes, Elizabeth."

She had grown so used to obeying commands that she did. Took Marissa in fully – hair slick with sweat, matted against her forehead. Grey circles under her eyes. Her expression urging, pleading.

"I... I don't understand."

A convulsion rippled through Marissa's body and she looked as if she may be sick again, wrenching her body towards the toilet bowl and gripping the rim. She heaved, but nothing came up. And then she rose, sniffing thickly, wiping snot and sweat onto the back of her forearm. And Elizabeth saw there were tears in her eyes.

"That appointment I went to? Three weeks before, I'd woken up in the middle of the night with Tate on top of me. I tried to stop him, but he pinned me down. Kept murmuring that the 'timing was right.'" She paused to spit into the toilet bowl. "The bastard had me tracking my ovulation. I thought it was to *stop* me getting pregnant." Her mouth twisted. "The test confirmed the opposite."

"What... what are you saying?"

"I'm saying... I truly thought he was trying to make a *difference*. To help people. When I went to his seminar in Palo Alto, I was numb. I had no one. I was desperate to *feel* something, to have a connection with someone. And Tate saw it. That's what he does. What he trains *us* to do. Exploits our vulnerabilities, blows us up and then sucks us dry. I see that now, finally. I was blind to it before. I never would have brought you into this if I'd known the truth."

"Marissa, I don't understand…?" Elizabeth shook her head, trying to keep up with the truth Marissa was dismantling.

"Elixir is… It's like a labyrinth. You go in at one end, and you think you know the path you're on. 'It's just a class. It's just a new top. It's just a diet.' But then you keep going. Twisting and turning. You take a left turn. And then a right. Another course, another self-help session you didn't know you needed. And before you know it, it looks nothing like it did at the start. And you try to turn around, but you discover you can't find your way back. You've gone too far. So you keep going. And going. And going. Hoping you'll find a solution. An answer. Until you realise this *was* the answer all along. The whole point, staring you in the face: there *is* no way out."

"Marissa…" She wasn't making any sense. She was talking in riddles. She was sick. She was… She needed to lie down. "I think maybe–"

"And Elite isn't the end." Marissa shook her head, not hearing. "It's not enough for him to control our money, and our minds, and our bodies. He wants our fucking *DNA*. 'Perfection,'" she spat. "Breeding a perfect little army of Tate Juniors."

"Marissa, *what are you talking about?*" Panic began to sizzle and pop through Elizabeth's body like an electric cable had come loose in her nerve endings, sending them sparking.

"Do you really not understand? Can you really not *see?*" Marissa jerked her hands into the air and Elizabeth found herself retreating to the door frame, pressing the rod of her back against the hard wood, grounding herself. "I'm not the first person he's got pregnant or tried to. You told me yourself you'd come off the Pill, that you wanted to 'go natural,' right? What did you *think* would happen?"

"I was careful!"

"You're an idiot!"

Elizabeth bit her lip. Stared down at her feet.

"I'm sorry." When she looked up, Marissa's face was flushed. "I just…" She fisted a clump of blonde hair, right at her temple, and Elizabeth saw the fist was trembling. "It's painting a picture, Elizabeth. That's what I'm saying. This obsession with perfection. The endless money. The demands. The punishments. Jesus Christ, the *branding*." She held up her wrist, flashed the black symbol that mirrored Elizabeth's own. "What are we becoming?"

Marissa's hand flitted across her abdomen, rested there for just a moment before curling into a ball, falling to her side. Elizabeth had the compulsion to reach out, go to her, but something – a small voice in her head, *Tate's* voice – kept her rooted to the spot. *You are your own failure. The problem is you.*

"Tate isn't some health guru who will solve all your problems." Marissa's voice gathered strength, biting into each word with precise and definite consonants. "He's a crook. A spiritual narcissist with a breeding kink. The night of the Founder's Day party? The night you and he…? It was all *his* idea. The whole thing. He told me…" She laughed bitterly. "No, he *demanded* that I get you to seduce him. Took my grandmother's bracelets as collateral. Told me if you didn't go through with it, the punishment would be worse. It was never for your benefit, your 'healing.'" Marissa narrowed her eyes. *"He just wanted to fuck you."*

"You're… you're lying." Elizabeth's vision blurred, the

image of Marissa in front of her seeming to split in two. "It was an assignment. You said… you said it was like an Extraction. That it would help me get over Matt. The baby. It *worked*."

"No." Marissa shook her head. "Do you really not see it? Elixir doesn't solve your problems. If anything, it creates them. It isn't a wellness programme. It's… it's…"

But whatever she was going to say was lost as a sound inserted itself into the silence.

A long, drawn-out chirrup, resonating from the depths below.

The doorbell.

"The books." Elizabeth sucked in air, snapping to attention. She had forgotten all about the delivery. That was why she was here. For the books. For Tate. Who had rescued her. Given her a home, a job. A reason to get up in the morning. "I – I have to go."

She began to back out of the bathroom, watching Marissa's face contort into something that looked like disappointment.

"Elizabeth, wait–" Marissa reached out a hand.

The doorbell sounded again, eliciting in her a subliminal response.

Elizabeth reached into her pocket, fingering the black hourglass tucked inside. A new one, the hard plastic smooth and untarnished, to replace the one she had lost. He had hit her for that – publicly, making her a warning to others. And he'd been right to. It was unthinkable, a member of her seniority, acting so forgetfully. How could he possibly trust her to look after anything halfway important if she couldn't even look after a simple timer?

Marissa stumbled after her, grasped at the fabric of Elizabeth's sleeve.

"Elizabeth, please, we can leave," she hissed, eyes wide,

pleading. Elizabeth tried to shake her off, but she gripped tighter, urgent. "Come with me. I can get our passports. I know where Tate files them. We can get out. We can tell the cops. The fucking FBI. We can stop this. Elizabeth, please, please… Say you'll come?"

There was a moment, a tiny fraction of a second, when she hesitated. She'd forgotten about her passport. Tate had taken it to sort her visa, had not yet given it back. It had made sense at the time, but what if…?

And then Marissa choked on a cough – messy, indiscreet.

And the spell was broken.

"I can't do this right now." She wrenched her arm out of Marissa's grasp. Stalked back down the hall towards the stairs. Turned the timer in her fingertips so the sand whooshed through it, urging her to get to the door before it ran out. "I have to get the books. I can't let them leave. You should… you should take a shower, Marissa." She couldn't help the bite in her voice coming back, wanting to punish her for distracting her, making her lose focus. "A cold shower. Give yourself some perspective." Wrinkled her nose. "And open the bathroom window. It stinks in there." Already she was at the top of the hall, the power making its way back through the balls of her feet, toes treading nimbly as she prayed to the unseen delivery man, *Don't leave don't leave don't leave.*

"Elizabeth?" Marissa's voice, frail across the distance, agitated her ear drums.

"I'll talk to you later." Hardening herself against it, she pounded down the stairs, wrenching open the door. Hoped she imagined the words that whispered down the hallway.

"Later might be too late."

32
Muswell Hill, London
13th July 2023

∞

The buzzer silences, and I am allowed a moment of reprieve.
But then it starts again, the noise drilling into my skull.

"What on earth?" Adam twists away from me, towards
the front door. I am sure I can feel the blood physically
draining from my face as I watch him rise.

"Wait, don't–"

I try to go after him, but it's as though my feet are glued
to the floor. My mind contorts, trying to figure out who
it might be, telling myself it could be entirely innocent – a
wrong address, a parcel – even though I know in my gut it
won't be. Who would be calling now, in the middle of the
night? "Don't answer it. Please." The photograph flutters to
the floor. "Adam–"

Too late.

"Hello?" He speaks into the intercom.

I press against his back, straining to hear over his shoulder
as he loops the cable over his wrist.

"Open the door!" The voice is muffled, but I can just
about make it out. "I need to speak to her. I need to know.
Where's Beth?"

Mia.

"Who is this?" Adam's forehead wrinkles as I clutch hold of his upper arm, try to wrench him away from the phone.

"Tell her to go away, Adam. Please, don't listen to her." I am shaking so hard my teeth begin to chatter.

"I know she's in there. Let me in!" I hear the pounding of Mia's fist against the front door below, even from beyond our door and down the stairs.

Adam places a hand over the mouthpiece, hissing at me, "For goodness's sake, she's going to wake the whole street."

The buzzer goes again, a persistent drone.

"Just leave us alone!" I reach around him, press my own cheek against the receiver. "Leave *me* alone!"

A pause. And then the voice on the other end replies, coldly, "He doesn't know, does he?"

I turn, numbly, to look at Adam. The expression on his face tells me he's heard.

"Who is this?" He takes hold of the receiver, presses me back when I try to stop him.

"She isn't who she says she is," Mia warns.

"No!" I lurch, make a play for the receiver.

"She's been lying to you," she continues.

"No, no, no…" I want to run. Or hide. Do *something* to make it all go away. "It – it's not true," I stammer lamely instead. "It's her who's been lying. She's been stalking me. She tried to take Etta!"

"Let me in," Mia's voice spits out of the receiver, "or I'll call the police."

The threat lands. "No police." I watch my arm stretch in front of me as though it's divorced from my body. A dummy hand, reaching for the intercom, presses the button with the pad of its right thumb. "Top floor," I say hoarsely, forcing myself to ignore Adam's penetrating gaze.

I drag myself to the front door. Heave it open to the sound of footsteps echoing up the staircase, their pace frantic, quick.

"Beth." It is a statement, not a question. Mia stretches an arm for me as I instinctively jerk myself away.

"I asked you to stay away from me. What do you want?"

Mia sighs deeply. "Answers."

"To what?" I palm my temple, grasp a fistful of hair in frustration. "Why did he send you? Who are you?"

She worries her head. "I told you before, I'm not… I'm not one of them." She grimaces, fine features puckering. "Look, I don't know what happened to you out there, but I just want answers. I know you're not who you say you are, so please: talk to me. Tell me the truth."

And then I take Mia in fully. She is shivering, her thin shoulders slick with rain, hair matted against her forehead. And I see, in relief, the slim nose, something in the area around her mouth and chin. The pull of familiarity I had felt the first time we met.

Realise, with a rush, who Mia must be.

"Answers to what? Can somebody please tell me what the fuck is going on?"

Adam storms towards us, tugging angrily at the knot of his tie. I'd almost forgotten about him in the fray, and now the smell of his rain-drenched suit pulls at my nostrils. Poor Adam. If he thought I was cracked already, his boundaries are about to be tested to the limit.

I am about to answer; open my mouth to speak, when another noise insinuates itself upon the room: Etta, crying.

Adam looks from one of us to the other, and then glances up the stairs towards the closed bedroom door.

"This is madness," he mutters under his breath. "Just… Everybody stay put. I'll resettle her. I'm getting out of these clothes. And then I want us to all just take a breath. Sit down and tell me, once and for all, what is going on. The *truth*, Beth." As he says it, I wince, look across at Mia. "As your friend puts it."

He picks up his suitcase, makes his way up the stairs.

"Your boyfriend," I start, staring up at the empty stairs where Adam has disappeared out of sight. The knot of Mia's story is beginning to unravel, but there are sections that are still snarled that I can't make fit. "He wasn't trying to hurt you?"

Mia stares at me, shakes her head. "No."

"But I saw you with him, that afternoon at the play café. You were fighting. He looked angry. I thought…" I shake my head. It seems so base, now, what I believed I had seen. That I'd actually believed I could help.

"I called him that day. Told him what I suspected. He was angry because he thought I was putting us in danger. Me and Astrid. He wanted me to stay away."

Mia rakes a hand through her wet hair. Now that I watch her, I recognise the uncanniness of the gesture; I can't believe I hadn't noticed before.

But then, before I had only seen what I'd wanted to see.

"I thought there was something going on the first time I met you," she enunciates slowly, tangling a tendril of hair. "When you said your name, I knew–" She glances up, catches my eye. I read a whole history in her gold-flecked irises: hurt, betrayal. A dark tinge of fear.

I look away. All the time I thought I was the victim, but now I see myself reflected back to how I must look to Mia: the villain.

"And the bruise? On your neck?" I feel lightheaded. The storm outside hasn't broken and the living room air is soupy, dank.

"There was no bruise." Mia's reaction to my frown is surprisingly cutting. "I'm not the one lying."

I swallow. My thoughts are swimming. Everything I know, everything I *thought* I knew, has been turned on its side. Like that optical illusion of the rabbit and the duck, I no longer know which way is up.

"I didn't mean for any of this to happen." And as I say it, I feel myself breaking, my entire sense of self splintering; tiny fragments I'm not sure I will ever piece back together. "I didn't mean to hurt anyone. I – I just had to get away." The words feel stuck in my chest, each one coated with mucus, the sobs I am doing everything I can to hold at bay. "I'll tell you everything I know. I promise. Only… How much do you know?"

But whatever Mia is about to say is swallowed by an almighty crash from upstairs. There is a sound of glass, smashing. And then Adam appears at the top of the stairs, his tie loose around his neck, half his shirt buttons undone. Etta is in his arms. His face is white.

"What the *fuck* is going on, Beth?" he hammers, footsteps thudding down the stairs.

I am doused in panic, as though someone is holding me under the depths of the icy Pacific. "What?"

"Someone threw a brick through our window!" When he reaches the bottom of the stairs, I see he's holding it out, and I think I might faint. "It landed in her crib. If I hadn't already picked her up, it could have killed her."

Wrapped around the brick is a piece of paper, crumpled and torn in parts from the impact. As he brings it closer,

I see the unmistakable looping symbol, make out the words written beneath:

Time's up.

"No." As the panic grips hold of me, I find myself bolting out of the flat and down the stairs. It's all too much, all these threads, pulling across me as tightly as a corset. If it wasn't Mia who was after me, that means someone is still out there, someone who knows who I am.

Someone sent by Tate.

I slam open the front door of the house, gulping in the fresh air, rain lashing at my cheeks as I search the street, heart pounding.

"Come out, coward! Show yourself!"

Nothing.

Opposite, there is the sound of a window being levered, a man's head craning out of it. "Everything all right, love?" he asks.

I agitate my head. Turn. Behind me, Mia and Adam are standing in the open doorway, their mouths agape.

And I know I have nowhere else to go. I know that all the running will never be enough.

Wordlessly, I take Etta from Adam's arms, pull her close.

Snake past them both, heading back up the stairs to the flat.

To confront the past.

In the living room, I sink into the sofa, feel the relief in my quivering legs.

I take in Mia, looking sad but resigned.

I take in Adam, the desperation in his eyes.

Heave a low, deep breath.

And begin.

"Nine years ago, I was part of an organisation called Elixir." I squeeze my eyes shut, fighting to keep the memories at a distance. "I did something. Something bad. To get away from them." Bile lurches in my stomach. I palm my mouth, resisting the urge to vomit. Close my eyes. Breathe.

"And now they want me to pay."

33
Marin County
July 2014

∞

Elizabeth had kept quiet about Marissa's revelation, instead focusing all her efforts on her next project: the Founder's Day party.

For this, Tate had promised an even more extravagant celebration, telling her there was something magnificent he wanted to reveal. He wouldn't tell her exactly what he was planning, but she thought – she hoped – he might ask her to marry him.

Ever since he had returned from Nevada, Tate's mood had been euphoric. The build had gone well, and he'd secured a high-profile new client: the heiress to a luxury hotel dynasty who wanted to roll out the Elixir product line across their estate. He was dreaming big, picturing Elixir studios across the globe, providing complimentary taster sessions for the chain's high-net-worth guests. Holding court in The Jungle's vast living room, Tate would talk in rapturous tones about next steps, the people they would help, the growing squadron of Elite members jostling for attention at his feet, hanging on to his every word.

"This is it, guys," he rhapsodised one evening, swirling

a frosted glass of vodka in his fingertips. "We're effecting change. We're saving people from themselves. Making a true difference in the world. Together. My announcement on Founder's Day will cement that." A squeeze of Elizabeth's thigh, in her coveted position beside him, and she was sure her hunch was right.

He was softer towards her then. The edges around him sanded down. As though his absence had made him realise what an asset she was to him. Gone, at least for now, were the punishments; instead, he was all smiles and praise, telling her how important she was, how far she had come, how Elixir fitted her like a second skin.

And it was true: she *had* done well. The best. No one had come through the programme so quickly. No one had won as many rewards as her or had taken punishment more stoically. And no one could match her recruitment skills: her consultancy background made her diligent, able to tell in an instant which members were valuable, and which were wasting their time. She had excellent powers of persuasion, able to elicit exactly the right reason why someone would want or need to take their training to the next level. She even proposed a new feature: Extraction mentors should be addressed as *"maestro,"* their mentees available at a moment's notice, responding to a text alert within a thirty-second window, no matter the time, day or night. Tate loved it.

"We're two halves of a whole," he told her, pressing his palm against hers so the tips of their fingers touched, making pride swell within in her core.

The only thing she was worried about was Marissa. Ever since that day in the bathroom, she had gone quiet. Too quiet. Yes, she turned up on time. She listened, willingly.

She performed whatever tasks were asked of her without confrontation. She was, to everyone who witnessed it, a model Elixir student.

But Elizabeth didn't buy it. She found herself obsessing over Marissa's movements, making subtle shifts to the class timetable so that they top and tailed, shadowing her as she moved through the mansion to pull a water bottle from the fridge or take her turn on laundry rotation.

"Can you quit breathing down my neck?" Marissa finally snapped when Elizabeth found her in the study allegedly working on the Member's Newsletter. "You're going to make me press the wrong button."

It was the day of the party, and Elizabeth had been bubbling with nervous energy all day; a boiling pot with lid clattering, threatening to spill over. Nothing could go wrong. Nothing.

"Sorry, of course," Elizabeth held her palms up in submission, eyes frantically scanning the black text glaring on Tate's iMac screen to make sure nothing was awry. "I was just stopping by to see if you wanted lunch. After all, you're eating for two now." Marissa's pregnancy was still their unspoken secret, clinging in the air between them like the orb weavers' nests she was continually having to clear from the garden's tropical foliage.

"I'm fine," Marissa responded curtly, not even bothering to turn from the desk.

Elizabeth watched the muscles of Marissa's shoulders clench and release. She was wearing a racerback T-shirt from last year's fall collection, a powdery lavender Elizabeth owned herself. The cut showed off Marissa's tanned skin and strong torso, as it was designed to, but Elizabeth couldn't help but notice there was a rip on the top right seam, that the fabric on the back was wrinkled, like it had been screwed up in the back of a drawer. She tutted, inwardly. Marissa really didn't help herself.

"The caterers are arriving at two," she spoke meticulously; squashed down the urge to admonish. It wouldn't do any good to rile Marissa up. "I'll need you to power-wash the terrace before then so they can set up. And string up the fairy lights in the front. Cassidy can help you if she's finished her list."

At Tate's request, she had sorted the specifications herself. Secured the city's hottest caterer and presided over his detailed menu requirements – vegan, organic, produce from within a five-mile radius. Talked Elixir's newest, celebrated member – the frontman for a hot new boy band – into performing an exclusive concert of his new album in exchange for a one-on-one session with Tate. She'd even specified the theme: "Diner En Blanc" – an all-white dress code. It was perfect for Tate: elegant, iconic. Plus, the dress she had bought – ice white, bodycon – would be the perfect outfit for a proposal.

She waited now, dancing on the balls of her feet. Marissa couldn't fuck this up for her.

"Yes."

"Yes… what?"

Marissa remained stock still. Elizabeth watched the nape of her long neck, where curlicues of soft baby hair had escaped her messy bun. Not a flinch. Not a whisper.

And then Marissa spoke, her voice entirely devoid of emotion, "Yes, maestro."

Elizabeth almost missed it, but just before she turned to go, she saw a flicker of movement in the fingers of Marissa's right hand, hovering over the mouse. Watched as they lifted. Curled. Tightened into a fist.

The unease stayed with her as she moved through the house, overseeing the final touches, ordering the bookshelves to be rearranged alphabetically, running the pad of her index finger across surfaces and demanding their immediate cleaning. "Did you really think this would be acceptable?" She was jittery, lightheaded. Tate, the guest of honour, would be arriving late. The success of the evening rested on her.

The panic fluttered in her veins as she showered, retreated to her bedroom – not her room, really, they all chopped and changed, but the one she liked the best, painted the softest dove grey, with uninterrupted views of the sea. It was like sleeping in a cloud. She tried to soak it in. Breathe in the calm.

Nothing was going to happen. Everything would be okay.

She took her dress down from where it was hanging on the back of the wardrobe door. Held it against her naked torso as she admired herself in the driftwood-framed mirror propped against a wall. Wondering when he would do it, how he would ask her. Tate was always one for a big occasion.

Somehow, a thought, untethered and without warning, drifted past across her mind, like a child's balloon on a gentle breeze: her mother.

Somehow, without really thinking about it, she grabbed hold of the string. Pulled.

Her mother wouldn't be there when she got married.

Or her sister. Or Greg, even.

No one, in fact, who knew the old her.

The thought was amorphous, bigger than her, and she found herself struggling to get a full breath, found the room was suddenly airless, devoid of anything but herself.

She pressed the heel of her hand to her sternum, feeling the imprint of bone against it. Was surprised to find her cheeks damp, tears leaking unbidden from the corners of her eyes.

No.

In the mirror, she watched her reflection harden, her gaze become steel.

Tate had told her, holding her close in her darkest moments as she'd sobbed into him, that it wasn't her fault. Her mother had abandoned her. Just as Matt had. After that horrible lunch at Fisherman's Wharf, she hadn't even bothered to call.

But Elizabeth wasn't alone. She had Elixir. And tonight, Tate's proposal would cement her position.

She wasn't going to let anyone – her mother, Matt, least of all Marissa – fuck that up.

Quickly, she dressed. Left her hair loose, cascading down her back the way she knew he liked. Stepped towards the pair of sandals she had laid out before pausing, her toes flexing against the soft carpet. No, tonight she would go barefoot. Show Tate she was truly ready to be by his side.

And then she took a bottle of the Elixir Signature Scent from the bedside table and spritzed the air in front of her before stepping forwards, twirling gently, letting the fine particles mist her cheeks, her bare arms. Inhaling relief.

Toeing carefully into the quiet corridor, she saw the door to the room at the far end was slightly ajar. It wasn't much bigger than a walk-in wardrobe. In fact, she was sure that's what it had been once, though it was now decked out with a squeaky camp bed, a single lamp on the floor beside it. Tate referred to it as the "contemplation room," used for when he felt members were in need of isolation. She had been in it once herself – twenty-six hours she had felt every minute of – and she still remembered the closeness of the air, how she had craned her neck to see her friends from the single sealed window, listening to the faint echoes of their enjoyment from below. How, as time loosened and stretched away from her, she had hammered on the door, begging to be free. Lately, it had become Marissa's room, because no one but Elizabeth seemed to want to share with her, and Marissa herself didn't seem to care.

She was in there. Elizabeth could make out the curve of her leg, looped over the edge of the camp bed.

Good.

She crept, half-ducked, towards Tate's study. Pressed the code on the pad outside, ears pricking at the chime of the buttons in case they alerted others to her presence.

Inside, she was swift, agile. Moving elastically towards the desk drawer, where she knew Tate kept the keys. Grasped them, hand sweating against the heavy bunch of metal, exacerbating the bitter, blood-like scent.

And then she was standing by the bedroom door. Limbs quivering. Arm reaching. A figure moving, leaping from the camp bed.

"Elizabeth? What–?"

The rest of the sentence was obliterated as she snatched the door handle, pulled. Thrust the key into the lock and twisted. Heaved the breath she'd been holding into the air in a messy blare of sound.

"Elizabeth, what is this?"

She looped the keys onto her index finger, listening to their pleasant jangle as they spun around.

"Elizabeth! Please! Come back here! Let me out!"

The banging sound had faded by the time she'd left Tate's

study, the keys safely re-secured. By the time she'd reached the foot of the stairs, she couldn't hear it at all.

"Oh, Elizabeth, thank goodness – the caterers have a question!" A member came hurtling towards her, hands flapping, eyes desperate.

And she rolled her shoulders.

Slipped a smile onto her face.

No, no one would stop her.

No one.

34
Marin County
July 2014

∞

The Jungle was throbbing. There were people everywhere. Curled on the flax-coloured sofas, leaning insouciantly against the cool stone of the mansion walls. Hunched around the vast dining table, some perched two to a seat. There were people on the terrace surrounding the rectangular perimeter of the pool, whose cool waters danced and rippled in the light of the storm lanterns that studded it. There were people in the kitchen. There were even people heading down to the beach, and from Elizabeth's vantage point, she could just make out their silhouettes, picked out by the flaming tiki torches that lined the path.

Their smiling faces and brilliant white outfits gave the whole place a glow. A glow that radiated out of them and bathed Elizabeth in a breathless, incandescent pride. She plucked a canape from a tray – a coconut-oil-roasted celeriac "scallop" served in an individual pink-hued shell, a nod to Tate's love of the ocean – and ate the whole thing in one, feeling ravenous for the first time in forever.

"Hey, turn the music up!" she commanded Cassidy, who was charged with manning the Sonos speakers. The band was waiting for Tate's arrival, so in the meantime they were blasting the playlist that Elizabeth had curated, afternoons trawling through trendy music websites to seek out tracks she thought aligned with Tate's exacting taste.

The volume increased, and she felt the tension between her shoulder blades release. Her ears had been trained upstairs, convinced that even if she couldn't hear Marissa, someone else would.

Now no one would hear a thing.

"Great party, Elizabeth!" someone called across the room. And she saw several heads swivel in her direction, nod in appreciation.

Joy flamed through her, making her cheeks flush.

She sensed his presence before she saw him. The way the crowd seemed to quieten. How, when he moved through them, there was an instant ripple effect, their bodies rotating towards him like a field of sunflowers.

He moved diligently past the guests, greeting each of them as they waited, patiently, for their moment in the sun. A grin here. A slap on the back there. The aura he gave off was palpable. He was so good at this. Remembering everyone's name, some little detail that made them unique. *We must be active participants in the world around us,* it said in the Elixir manifesto. *To be involved is to learn.*

Soon, he was close enough to where she was standing, by the sliding glass doors leading to the terrace, so close that she could make out the peaks of his stomach muscles beneath his thin white T-shirt. The knot of the signature grey yoga pants he was wearing, she noted with a flash of disappointment. Didn't he like the theme?

She straightened her spine, readying herself. Plastered an expression on her face she hoped was both winsome and subservient, that said, "I know I have done well, and I am ready to hear your praise."

"All right, everyone, outside!" he commanded, beckoning behind him as he moved first close to and then past her. "It's too nice a night to be in here. And who shut these doors? You know I like to smell the ocean when I've been at work all day. The sea air is life-giving! Energising! No wonder you're all slumped in here, half asleep."

Idiot, she cursed herself. She watched him heave open the doors and walk through, his chin barely tipping in her direction. She should have known.

She followed the surge of the crowd, feeling the sea breeze whipping her cheeks. The flagstones were rough against her bare feet as she hurried to keep up with him through the swarm. Someone collided with her, knocking her hard onto the floor, and in that moment she lost him.

No! She scrabbled to her feet, resigned to find some lonely corner of the space to retreat to, but just as she was about to give up, fingers found hers and she turned to find Tate, his handsome face cocked to one side.

"It looks good," He nodded. And she watched the roundels of his cheekbones twitching as he smiled. "You did good."

Her heart swelled, but as she curled into him, hungry for further praise, some sixth sense made her hackles raise, ice water dripping down her spine. She twisted to look up at the façade of the house.

Saw Marissa's face appear at the tiny bedroom window.

"*No.*"

She didn't realise she'd spoken aloud until Tate, preoccupied with selecting an iced vodka glass from a proffered tray, glanced back at her. "What was that?"

Her insides lurched around the celeriac, the fatty coconut oil erupting in her gullet.

"I said, 'Oh,'" she stuttered quickly, "I – I didn't see the tray," careering her body around him and towards the server in a well-executed move to keep Tate's back turned. "Thanks." She took a glass between her thumb and forefinger, nodding to the waiter. The alcohol stung her lips as she gulped it down.

When she looked back up the house, Marissa's face had gone.

As the evening flowed, her tension began to dissipate. She tried to pin herself to Tate as he worked the crowd, reading everything into the looks he would throw her, the small asides that would bring her into the conversation. Her whole body was on fire, the slightest brush of his skin against hers sending shivers of pleasure through her.

And then he leaned into her, the supple skin of his closely shaved cheek caressing the side of her neck. "I think it's time."

He took the now-empty vodka glass from her hand and used it to clink together with his. "Friends!" he called, taking a step back to address the crowd. A single look in Cassidy's direction and the music was cut. The crowd surged forward, and she found herself jostled, sucked backwards into the fray. "Now, as you know, I have been looking to take Elixir to the next level…"

"Excuse me, sorry, excuse me…" She contorted her shoulders, pushing her way through the jostling bodies to reclaim her place. A stiletto heel came down right on the fragile skin next between her toes and she yelped in pain.

"The ethos of Elixir is always to aim higher, to reach further. To better ourselves, and, in doing so, the world,"

Tate continued, shooting her a brief look of irritation at the disruption. She was now in the front row of the circle that had formed around him, making her way around its periphery to join him. "I am sure you are all by now aware of the not-so-secret Elite level our most driven members aspire to. But today, my friends, I am delighted to announce that I am preparing to ascend to the next level. Yes." He paused, nodding at the collective intakes of breath, the amazed expressions of his spectators. "It is true: soon, I will reach Perfection."

The gasps grew louder, the word reverberating on the lips of the guests: *Perfection, Perfection, Perfection.*

"But I haven't risen to this state alone. Perfection requires a partner. Someone who will help Elixir soar. To fully realise this beautiful dream we have all created."

Somehow, she found her way to his side, her heart felt like a hummingbird frantically beating its wings against her ribcage. She was sure there was a stupid, soppy grin on her face, but she couldn't make it go away. This was it, this was it, this was *it.*

"Which is why I am delighted to announce–"

But whatever Tate was going to announce was lost, drowned out by a guttural shout from the back of the crowd. His voice tapered off, his lips puckering in displeasure, as his audience began to turn, distracted by whatever was happening behind them.

After that, everything seemed to happen from a distance, as though Beth was watching it from up high, one of the myriad tiny stars that picked out the velvet sky overhead.

There was scrambling. People jostled each other aside.

Bodies parted.

To reveal...

Marissa.

"Tate."

Acid pooled in the corners of Elizabeth's mouth. How had she got out? And then she looked at the unpleasant grey hoodie Marissa was wearing, marring the pretty sea of white, the gashes across her arms, a vast rip down the right shin of her leggings, blood pooling on the torn fabric. There were streaks of blood across her forehead, ragged cuts across her hand, and she was panting, hard. She must have battered down the goddamn door.

"Ah, Marissa. Just in time." Somehow, Tate's voice remained steady. But Elizabeth knew every crevice of his face, every subtle change of expression. She saw the way his jaw was set, read in it the clench of his back teeth. He may have been hiding it well, but he was worried. "I was about to announce–"

"Shut up, Tate," Marissa spat, interjecting. In contrast to Tate, she wore every emotion plainly. There was a sheen of sweat to her skin. Her voice shook. "Whatever you're planning to say... don't. I won't be a part of this. I refuse to let you use me like some sort of *fulcrum* to destroy anyone's life further."

Beside Elizabeth, Tate licked his lips. Let out a deliberately nonchalant laugh.

"I'm *destroying lives?* What, by helping people? Making them better? *Saving* them?" His voice curled around the words. Every letter, every syllable was exacted with precise, definite, aim.

Marissa shook her head. "What you do is the *opposite* of helping."

Elizabeth watched her eyes, roving the gaping crowd. They had repelled away from her to the edges of the terrace, like wrong ends of a magnet. "Can none of you speak? Can none of you *see*?" she urged. Her voice tacky with mucus, and Elizabeth grimaced inwardly. "Are you all so stupid you don't realise what's going on here?"

Silence.

"He doesn't care about *any* of us," she continued. "He's *using* us. It's all for his own gain. The courses, the classes... we're just lining his pockets. And the 'Elite'...?" She let out a bitter laugh. "We're his fucking slaves." Marissa's mouth twisted, ugly, cynical. "It's all *bullshit*, his whole manifesto. It's cobbled together from different practices – a copy-and-paste job made to fit exactly what he thinks you'll respond to. I doubt he even believes it himself!" Marissa paused, sucking in a breath, clearly waiting for someone to jump in. When no one did, she balled her fists, rolled her eyes to the sky. *"Jesus Christ, are you even listening to me?"*

Elizabeth gaped. Marissa looked, she thought, like a madwoman. Hair plastered to the side of her face. Spittle glistening on her chin. There was no trace of the manicured, put-together woman she once knew. It was painful, watching her, but out of some sick fascination, she couldn't bring herself to make her friend stop. "You all think he's such a fucking *genius?*" Marissa jeered. She took a step forward, making the crowd around her recoil in response. "Every word he says is a lie. His degrees, his success, it's all made up. Nothing checks out. He says he studied medicine at Dean College, Cambridge University? There *isn't* a Dean College at Cambridge University – the only one I could find is in Cambridge, Massachusetts. There's no record of him at Harvard. And the Extraction tapes? They're his *blackmail*. He has *everything* on you. Don't you see? Every secret, every worst thought. All there, in case you ever dare to challenge him. He can ruin you with the flick of a switch. How can we believe anything he says? Even his *eye* colour is fucking fake!"

Elizabeth looked from Marissa to Tate, Tate to Marissa. Waiting. Hanging on his next move. She watched the rise and fall of his Adam's apple. Saw him smooth his palms against the side of his yoga pants. Willed him on, internally: "Come on, Tate, prove her wrong."

Finally, he pressed the palms of his hands together in prayer. Put them to his lips. Spoke. "Marissa, insurrection is such a bad look on you."

A pause.

Then someone in the crowd let out a nervous titter. Another laugh joined them. And Elizabeth felt it: a chink in the tension of the air. It was going to be okay.

Tate stepped back, addressing the crowd with raised arms, magnanimous. "Does anyone here really believe these lies?"

He paused, drinking in the complicit silence.

"Good." He nodded. "And does anyone feel that they are a *slave*? No? Well, that's a relief. Does anyone feel, in fact, that they have been lied to, cheated, or *blackmailed*? Raise your hands – go on, anyone, anyone who pleases – if you have any grievance to share. If you feel that Elixir hasn't worked for you and is, in fact, *one, big, fat, fucking, joke*."

Elizabeth could hear the growl of the ocean. The rustle of breeze through the palms. The subtle call of cicadas. But not a sound from any of the guests.

"Excellent." Tate nodded, succinct. "Well, now that that's out of the way–"

"No."

When Elizabeth remembered it later, it was as if time seemed to both explode into motion and slow down simultaneously.

There was a flurry of movement.

She saw Marissa's hands, reaching, fumbling. Her wrists shaking as she aimed something at Tate.

A glint of metal.

A gun.

Elizabeth's eyes swerved to Tate, saw the horror and fear rip through him, every modicum of control vanished.

There were screams from the crowd. Bodies ducking, as people hurled themselves out of the way, making for the house, the beach, some even diving into the pool.

And then a sound, cracking the air in two.

And with a rush, she felt something. Her body propelled into motion.

Palms pressing against her bare arms – Tate's palms, she realised, heart momentarily swelling. Reaching around her shoulders. Pulling her – *that must be it* – out of the way.

And that *was* it. Surely. Because what other explanation could there be? Tate was saving her. Moving her away from the bullet.

But then, somehow, she wasn't moving *away* but *towards*.

And then there was pain. Bright, fire-hot. A dull ringing in her ears.

A… smell? Metallic.

Wetness in her lower abdomen. Her hands, pressing unthinkingly into herself, came away a vibrant, sticky red.

And somehow, Tate was… behind her? Lowering her to the ground.

And then a wooziness overcame her, like when she'd proven to Tate how long she could stay beneath the waves for him, blood pulsating in her ears, inside her skull.

And just like when she'd proven to Tate how long she could stay beneath the waves for him, she was cold, *so cold*, her teeth chattering uncontrollably.

Someone rushed towards her, their face a blur. Hands pressed into her, trying – she assumed, clarity amidst the madness – to stop all that red.

Elsewhere, jaws were gaping. Figures were rooted to the ground.

Black spots began to creep into the corners of her vision as she searched their faces.

Found Marissa's. The terror in it. Fear raked across it with a pen knife.

Saw her turn.

And run.

The crowd, moving en masse, seething as one, reaching for her, grabbing.

And then she heard Tate's voice, calm and in control as ever, as the blackness began to envelop her.

"Don't touch her. Let her go. She can't run forever."

And I ran.

Fuelled by the last ounces of strength I had punished my body to develop in Elixir. Trying not to think of the thing inside me, the presence that had churned my insides for the last two months, even now making me fight against the bile that burned my throat, ignoring the threat of my tongue depressing against the floor of my mouth, making me gag.

I didn't dare look back. I didn't dare stop. My ears – tuned to the frenzied whoosh of my breath, the repetitive thwack of my feet against tarmac – pricked up at every intermittent, unfamiliar sound.

I expected at any moment to feel hands on my shoulders, my body pulled back. To admit defeat.

Still, I ran. Away from the shoreline and up through open fields. Trying not to be spooked by the clusters of black cows who stared at me with a menacing stillness, lowing into the navy night sky. Considering each car that passed and not knowing, not trusting, not daring.

Slowing, eventually, at the low heave of a monstrous red eighteen-wheeler. Daring myself to pause, extend my arm... raise a thumb.

And finally, after hauling myself up, up, onto the worn fabric of the passenger seat, I did stop, physically. But my mind was still running. Looping the scene back, over and over: Tate – the gun – Elizabeth – the gun – Tate – Elizabeth – the images jerking and screeching past one another like an old VHS tape, until I wondered whether, like an old VHS tape, if the film of memory would eventually snarl and snap.

"Thank you," I gasped at the driver. A woman: red hair, the colour of a maple leaf, tied in a tight ponytail at the nape of her neck. Dragged the door shut behind me and heard the rattle of my breath in the close silence of the cab.

The woman said nothing. Nodded.

But as I pressed the back of my head against the seat, trying to still the twitching and jerking that danced through my nerves, I felt the strap of the backpack loose itself fell from my sweaty grasp.

It thunked, loudly, metallically, as it hit the floor, and I side-eyed the woman, trying to still the alarm on my face.

There was a moment, as the woman's hand froze against the wheel. A pause as we both looked down, before she shifted her gaze to me, shivering against the sweat that drenched my torso and stuck my thin sweatshirt to my skin. A cough.

And then she stretched an arm into the depths behind her, brought back a rough tartan blanket, the edges frayed.

"Hope you don't mind dog hairs." The woman's voice was softer than I'd expected, a honeyish warmth that didn't seem to match her thin arms and dry, brittle skin. "Where do you need to get to?"

Hope prickled inside me as I curled the blanket around myself. "As far as you're going. If that's okay?"

I saw the loose skin beneath the woman's neck tighten and clench as she swallowed, considered.

"I reckon I could take you as far as Tijuana." She curled her hand into a fist and held it to her lips, clearing her throat before reaching to adjust the rear-view mirror. "But your best bet would be to cross the border." Pulled the stick shift back and wound the wheel with the palm of her hand before glancing back down again at the backpack, raising a bushy eyebrow at me. "He'd have to be a real piece of work to follow you there."

35
Muswell Hill, London
13th July 2023

∞

I stand between Adam and Mia, a lifetime lived in minutes in my mind.

I cannot read the expression on Adam's face. It is as though he is a different person – which is ironic, really, when the person who is different is me.

"You're… you're not Beth?" he asks.

I shake my head.

"Your name is Marissa?" It is barely a question.

Etta shifts against me and I press my lips against the top of her head, the reminder of her presence awakening in me a desperate, clenching ache. *I am, I am Marissa*. I want to explain to him, excuses tripping over themselves in my mind, *but I am still me. This is still us, our family. Etta is still ours*.

"Yes." The word comes out gluey. I lower my eyes to the floor. "I never… I hated lying to you." Looking to Mia: "And I didn't mean to take her name, it just…"

The memories assault me now. I have kept them at bay for so long that it has been like holding a door against the ocean. The darkness, the rumble of the truck eventually lulling me to sleep. Stirring briefly when the driver – I later learnt her name was Emmy – pulled over at a rest stop. Waking fully to the bitter smell of coffee and gratefully slurping down the muddy liquid as Emmy eyed me warily. "I didn't pitch you as the kind to take creamer."

Arriving in Tijuana later that day and watching Emmy from the window, exchanging words with a skinny guy with a sweaty moustache and, inexplicably, a faded Twilight T-shirt that said TEAM JACOB across the front in yellow.

"Andrew'll take you as far as Sinaloa. He owes me. Got your passport?" I'd nodded, and then she'd jutted her head in the direction of the bag at my feet. "*That* needs to go in the back." Shielding the contents from view, I'd unzipped the bag. Reached a hand, unseeing, into the bowels. Felt my fingers stumble and trip over not one passport but two.

"I'd taken both of them from Tate's office." Adam and Mia are observing me wordlessly, and I wish I could hide somewhere, put my hands over my eyes, so I won't have to face their accusation. "Mine and Beth's. I'd hoped I could convince her." I shake my head. "I'd forgotten until that point that I still had them."

I look down at my hands, notice Mia's across from me, the tremor in them. I don't want to carry on, but I know there's no going back now. The only way out is through.

"I didn't know if Tate realised I had them, but either way, travelling under my own name seemed like a bad idea from the start. Andrew and Emmy were standing right behind me. Arms folded. Waiting. And then I flipped to her photo and looked at the likeness and thought, 'What if…?' Figured if I was caught, I could just claim a mix-up, retrieve my own. I couldn't believe it when it worked."

Adam walks over to the kitchen. Pulls a glass from the

cupboard and runs the tap. Drinks. Slowly. "And then?"

The journey to Sinaloa in Andrew's truck, pine-tree air freshener doing little to cover up the stench of fast-food wrappers and old gym socks. Handing over a wad of cash from the stash I'd been saving to pay for a motel for the night. More on a bus ticket down to Mexico City. Sharing a seat with a lady who carried a crate of chickens and told me, "Eres demasiado delgada," – "You're too thin" – as she'd tried to feed me cookies from a bag in her pocket.

"Back in San Francisco, I'd been squirrelling cash from my bank account for weeks," I tell them, "although it wasn't like there was much there to begin with. Tate had seen to that."

Lingering in a city back street, I traded the gun for cash, laughed at for my polite grade-school Spanish, "Disculpame, por favor…"

When that ran out, I pawned the trinkets I'd managed to secrete into the backpack before leaving: an antique enamel pill box of my grandmother's that wasn't worth much but that I was inordinately fond of, a pair of cufflinks I knew Tate never wore and wouldn't miss. Later, I traded… other things I'd rather forget, for a clean room for the night.

I managed to convince a motel owner to let me help out cleaning and sorting the place in exchange for the smallest room plus a little extra cash for food, but it wasn't enough. Not enough to sustain me. Or to abate the constant need to look over my shoulder, the fear that one day I'd stumble round a corner and there he'd be.

Then, one night, wondering what on earth I was going to do, I'd looked down at the twin passports and wondered, just wondered, if it could work a second time. If the likeness would be enough. I figured by now I looked just as different from my own photograph – my face drawn and grey, my eyes dull – as I did to hers. That our discrepancies would be less obvious in Mexico, as tourists, than in the States.

I sold the last thing I had to get the plane ticket: tiny diamond earrings I'd been given as a sixteenth birthday present and managed to hide from Tate. It was silly, holding on to them as long as I did, but they felt like they belonged to another me – a naive, innocent, carefree me I didn't want to let go of. And then, somehow, there I was, on the plane: a new identity just there for the taking.

One whose owner may never be interested in having returned to her.

Beth Myers, I rehearsed to myself, the English accent feeling ungainly at first, taking years to sink into muscle memory. *My name is Beth Myers.*

"Why didn't you just go to the police?" Mia's voice cuts through my reminiscences, incredulity barely disguised. "Surely that's what anyone would do, if Tate had done all the things you say he had?"

"Because of what *I* did." I squeeze Etta tighter, wrapping her chubby arms around my neck. "To Beth." This is the curse that has marked me, the longer it has been, the further I feel I've forgotten him. That the more I have built my life up, the more I have to lose; for one accusation to take away. "I never meant to hurt her – if anything, it was the opposite. I tried to tell her. I wanted her to come with me. But then, after, I knew that any attempt to point the finger at Tate would only have it turned directly back at me. It would be my word against his, and at the end of the day, who was the one holding the gun? Tate had the money, the power, the legal muscle behind him to make it all go away. What did I have, except a target on my head?"

It was that realisation that would come crawling up my

spine with the bedbugs from the Mexican motel in the days that followed. As I twisted my torso to find a comfortable position on the lumps and bumps of the mattress, listened to the sound of laughter pulsating from the streets through the thin walls. On those endless nights, I would think to myself, *All I wanted was to belong, and now I'm more alone than ever.*

"What about your mum? Why didn't you try to call her? Surely any sane parent would–"

"I did."

I feel as though the top layer of my skin has been ripped away. Bad enough to reveal to Adam that I'm not who he thinks. But exposing the real me – the raw vileness of it – is as painful as physical flagellation. And I am there again, in the shade of the Zócalo, pressing the cold plastic of a burner phone into my ear as I dial the number I somehow still remembered by heart. The voice at the other end, anonymous, unfeeling: "We're sorry, you have reached a number that is no longer in service. If you feel this is in error, please check the number and try again." And I did try again. And again, and again.

"She'd moved." Tears sear the corners of my eyes. "I had no way of knowing where. I tried to look her up, once a year or so, but even if I did find her, what do you say to a mother who doesn't want you? After all this time. After what I did."

"I always thought there was something you were keeping from me." Adam presses his temple into his hands. "You never wanted to talk about your family. I knew you'd spent time in the States, that something had happened with an ex, but I thought…"

And then his vision shifts, locking onto Etta, and I know before he speaks what his next question will be. "And the baby?"

Etta wriggles, as if in response. I cast my eyes around

vaguely for a watch or phone. It must be past eleven. She should be asleep. We should – I realise the absurdity of it – be waking her for a dream feed. I look at the formula scattered on the surfaces from what feels like years ago.

"I couldn't keep it."

I hold her tighter. The skin pressed against my T-shirt and Etta's pyjamaed torso is clammy. I can't look Adam in the face.

Of all the things that happened to me since joining and leaving Elixir, the ghost of this has haunted me more than anything else. The doctor had been pleasant, his clinic clean and orderly. When he'd asked me, his voice gruff but friendly, why I wanted an abortion, I had struggled, the weight of it crushing my mind, and he had nodded, patted my calf. "Esta bien. Todos tienen sus razones." Everyone has their reasons.

It was never the act itself; despite, or perhaps *because*, of my struggles to have Etta, the thought of a woman being driven to have a baby she doesn't want appals me. It was the fact that I had been forced to *make* that choice. I had always assumed I would have children. Often, even as a child myself, I would dream of righting the wrongs of my own upbringing. But the moment I was given the opportunity, I couldn't go through with it.

"It wasn't even the fact that the baby was Tate's. But I didn't even know how I would make it to the next day. If I would be discovered, taken back to them. Worse: if I would be caught and sent to jail. How could I bring a child into that?" I feel heavy, dragged down by the weight of what might have been. "I always wondered if that was why... why we had trouble with Etta." Etta snuffles, and I wrap my arms around her tighter, walk us both over to the sofa, sinking into it. "Like it had caused some sort of problem. A problem I deserved. Like it was some sort of karmic punishment."

"You did what you had to do." It is Mia, not Adam, who speaks. "And I don't believe in karma. Only opportunity." She looks at me plainly, and I see in her eyes perhaps not forgiveness but something close. Understanding.

I turn to Adam, hoping, praying he'll offer some comfort of his own, but his gaze has shifted, and he is staring at Mia, forehead creased as he takes her in.

"I'm sorry, I still don't understand. If Beth is really Marissa, and the real Beth is in San Francisco, how do you fit in? Who *are* you?"

Mia rouses, moves to speak.

But I answer before she has the chance to.

"She's Beth's sister."

36
Muswell Hill, London
13th July 2023

∞

The feeling is akin to travelling up in a lift, the moment when the carriage jerks, rattles, before finally landing in place.

"When did you realise?" Mia breathes, confirming.

Etta worries against my chest and I hesitate, allow her to settle before adjusting, turning. Try to put into words the uncanny feeling that had sat with me since the first time we had met but hadn't, until now, had life breathed into it. Because it is more than just their likeness – I, more than anyone, could testify to that – but something intrinsic: the way their voices rest on certain words, a particular twitch of their facial expressions or their dual habit (now, I see it; before, I couldn't place it) of coiling their index finger and pressing it to their lips when in thought. I had been so eager for a connection with Mia, and then so fearful of what I thought that connection might be, that my vision had been warped, the wrong elements enhanced, like I'd been looking in a funhouse mirror.

"When you arrived, I think..." Now that I know, the weight of who Mia is – who she knows *I* am, and what I've done – sinks into me.

"Mia… *God*…" It's like a tiny part of Beth is sitting there beside me, making me face her. "You have to understand, I never meant to hurt her. I swear to you. I tried to get her to *listen* to me. To *leave*. She wouldn't. She was totally brainwashed. It's what he does best, sucks you in and pulls you down, until before you realise it, you're caught in this whirlpool where you can't think and you can't breathe and you–"

I gasp for air. Am surprised to feel the warmth of Mia's hand on my shoulder. "Beth… I mean, Marissa, it's…" She stops short of offering complete comfort, lands on: "I understand." She takes a seat beside me on the sofa, hand reaching into her pocket. And then I see, stark in her palm, the black hourglass.

"She – Beth – left it behind. It was the last time we saw her, at that lunch in Fisherman's Wharf. Mum and Dad didn't notice, but I took it. I kept it all these years. I hoped…" Mia looks down at her hand and I see a tear ski down her cheek and come to rest on the tip of her nose. "I thought maybe she'd come back for it. Ask us about it." She sighs. "But she never did."

I can't remember Beth ever referring to Mia by name. She only ever called her "my half-sister," the *half* pointed, almost sad.

I remember the day of her family's visit, though. She was good at hiding it, but she was nervous about seeing them again, although Tate had coached her to focus all her energy on getting money out of them instead. I remember, now, that she'd left the hourglass behind. She'd got into trouble for it, but by then she was so far entrenched that she'd accepted it, gladly. And she'd got what Tate wanted, hadn't she? Returned, not with money, but with her grandmother's ring. The ring that had paid her entry to Elite. So she was happy. Even if she'd sacrificed her family for it.

"She became a different person with him, Mia," I try. A petty reassurance. "We all did. I was just lucky I realised before it was too late. Even renaming her Elizabeth, it was all part of it. Divorcing her from her reality, recasting her as someone new." I press my lips together, my mind stumbling over memories I thought I'd lost. "He tried it with me in the beginning. Asked if I'd ever thought about being called Melissa. But he was subtle, Tate. I'll give him that. He'd never push if he didn't think he had a bite. I think that's why he's so successful at what he does – he has this innate ability to read people, knows exactly how to use them to get what he wants. And he makes sure that it's always them doing the asking, so it's never him at fault. That was why I went by Beth. I wanted…" I realise how trite this sounds now, a pathetic thing to be proud of. "I wanted to remember the old Beth. To pay penance to the person I helped to destroy."

Bitterness curls around me as all the ugly thoughts I've hurled at myself over the years come to a head. Mia should be screaming at me, accusing me. Calling the police. Instead, she waggles Etta's toes, covered in the soft grey cotton of her babygrow, deep in thought.

"Her dad called her Elizabeth," she says distantly. "I remember there was a period when she was a teenager – I can't have been more than three or four – when it was the only thing she answered to." She lets out a low hum; releases a smile that doesn't quite make it up her face. "I was desperate to please her, but I could only pronounce it 'Lizabuff,' and obviously that became the family joke. My parents would call out, 'Lizabuff, time for dinner! Lizabuff, we're leaving for school!' until she became so irate she called the whole thing off." Mia releases Etta's toes, puts her hand in her lap. "She was such a hormonal teenager."

Silence falls between us, the heaviness of all the things unsaid pendent in the air. Eventually, I can't take it any longer.

"Mia," I begin, moving Etta onto my shoulder only to find her taken by Adam, who has been hovering around us, nervous energy making him unable to stay in one place.

"I'll take her," he says. "Try and see if she'll settle upstairs." He is already moving towards the stairs, but I find myself reaching for him, fingers knotting around the sleeve of his suit jacket.

"Adam, are you…? Are we…?"

He has said very little to me since Mia's arrival. Barely even made eye contact. Our past sits in the empty space between us, the smooth pages of the stories I have told him now ripped ragged. Now he turns his cheek, presses the butt of his chin into Etta, and I see the way his grip tightens. Protective. Possessive. See the danger he clearly thinks I have put them in.

"Adam, please." I push myself up from the sofa, wanting to bury myself in him, in them. To tear myself away from the horridness of this evening and feel the strength of the only thing I have: my family.

But Adam shifts away from me. Places a foot on the bottom step.

"I need some space," he mutters as he walks upstairs. "I should tape up the window, anyway, in case it rains again."

He's gone before I can say anything to convince him to stay.

37
Muswell Hill, London
13th July 2023

∞

In the living room with Mia, Adam's absence is deafening. I realise how vulnerable I am, sitting here with a woman whose sister I–

"Mia," I ask, turning to her. She knows all of my story, but I know so little of hers. "I don't understand. If you're not part of Elixir, what *do* you want?"

When she speaks, I hear the hurt in her voice. That desperate, urgent need. "I want my sister."

And I want to help her, but how can I?

"I haven't spoken to her for ten years. I don't..." I press my hands to my temples. "I don't know why Elixir wants me now." A nauseating headache insists itself on me and I realise I am desperately thirsty, paying the price from my earlier binge. "I'm sorry. Do you... Can I get a drink?"

Without waiting for a reply, I go to the sink, pour us both a glass of water and return to the sofa. I gulp, desperately. I haven't let it cool and it is barely less than tepid, the metallic bitterness of London-tap never more apparent. I think with a faint, ironic longing of Tate's fridge, stocked full of ice-cold bottles of Fiji. Would everyone have been better off if I'd just... stayed?

"I understand what happened to you was awful," she speaks carefully. "I thought... I don't know, when we first met, I thought that you were one of them – *still* one of them. And I know now that's not the case. But I can't just leave her there. Not now. Now I'm more worried than ever."

I shake my head, the thing that's been puzzling me ever since I realised who she was now looming large. "But how did you even find me? How did you know who I was?"

Mia plays with her own glass thoughtfully, rolling it between her palms. "I've been following you."

And I feel again, as she says it, as though someone has walked over my grave. That unceasing sensation that someone has been watching me. I hadn't been imagining it. "How?"

"By chance, at first." She lets out a cynical laugh. "I told you I don't believe in karma, so I suppose 'chance' is what I'd call it. Mum got a letter about a missed appointment – a six-week postnatal checkup." Looks down her nose at me. "Addressed to Beth Myers."

I frown, think back. Had anyone contacted me after we'd been discharged? The six-week checkup – had I been at that appointment? That time was all such a blur. There was so much chaos in the hospital after Etta's birth, because of course I'd never registered. I'd given my passport as ID, and they'd obviously tracked my – Beth's – NHS number through that. But then I had called to check up about Etta – I remember, now, vaguely muddling through what I'd told them must have been a mix-up with addresses, redirecting everything to the flat. Even then, I'd been anxious, convinced I'd find the police waiting for me when

I brought Etta in, the whole illusion revealed. That was why I'd been desperate for a home birth in the first place: the fewer eyes on me, the better.

"But why did it go to your parents? Didn't she ever change her GP?"

Mia shrugs. "I guess not. She was always pretty healthy, so I'm not sure she used the doctors that much, and then her work had health insurance, so knowing Beth, she went private. Mum assumed the letter must have been for me and they'd somehow mixed up the names, but it was obvious it wasn't – I was well beyond that stage. And besides, I'm registered near me in Wimbledon."

Wimbledon. So Adam had been right: Mia didn't live anywhere near us. She'd been travelling up here just for me.

"I tried to tell Mum that something was going on, but she dismissed it. She said it was probably just the surgery's error. But something kept niggling at me, something that didn't seem right."

"Didn't your mum wonder if it was Beth herself, if she'd come back?" I ask, trying to get a clearer picture of the woman I had heard only negative things about. "Why didn't she message her? Why did she never try to contact her after your visit?"

"She did." Mia frowns. "She emailed her, the night after that disastrous lunch. But Beth told them to respect her wishes and leave her be."

"She did?" Something pulses in my brain. Something that doesn't feel right. Beth mentioned once, before things between us had fallen apart, how hurt she was that her family had never contacted her again. The final nail in the coffin for her old life. Why would she lie?

"Yes." Mia stares at me, lips parting, body suddenly tightened, alert. I thought I had hidden the alarm in my voice, but I know she has sensed something. "They tried again, over the years – both of them. I know Beth's relationship with my dad was hard, but he cared about her. *All* of us. He just wants everyone to be happy. But it was always the same story: when they called, they got Tate saying Beth didn't want to speak to them, and when she emailed, Beth would say Mum and Dad didn't understand, they didn't want her to be happy. If they pushed too hard, she'd just ask them for money, and then they'd back off."

Mia's memories unsteady me. Beth had always depicted her mother as unforgiving, the root of all her issues. But wasn't that exactly what Tate's Extraction sessions were designed to do, isolate us from our friends and family, make us think the only life worth living was Elixir? Would my tattered relationship with my own parents have had a hope of being mended if I hadn't taken the same bait?

"And you?"

Mia shakes her head. "We hadn't spoken since she'd left, but I'd always held out hope that she'd come back, that one day we'd have a relationship. And when I saw the letter, I thought…" She swallows. "I called the surgery pretending to be her and said there was a mix-up. Gave Beth's date of birth and acted a bit vague and dopey. It's amazing how little faith people have when you play the new-mum card." Her comment stings, and I think of all the times I've seemed dazed in her presence. "They gave me the hospital name, and then I rang up with some lie about being a gift company having an item returned, pretended I'd get fired, cried until they gave in and told me your address." Her eyes flick around, taking in the wreckage of the house. "Then I came here.

"I was just a teenager when Beth left," she sighs. "She was always this impossibly glamorous figure in my life. A straight-A student, so driven, and then she had this cool job in the city, the handsome boyfriend. She was literally perfect." There's a glint in the corner of Mia's eyes that makes it obvious how much she had idolised her. "When she came to visit – which wasn't often – she always brought fancy gifts: Michael Kors perfume for our mum, whisky for Dad, even though I don't think he drank it. I remember once she got me a Ralph Lauren teddy bear with a red tartan bow around its neck. She pulses her shoulders. "I think she was always trying to impress." She stares down at her drink, and I wonder with a flash if I should have offered her something stronger.

"I didn't know the real reason behind her moving to San Francisco until much later. They just told me she'd been sick. But I knew Mum was worried about her. Not sleeping. I'd hear her roaming about the house at night. And she lost loads of weight. When Beth moved to San Francisco, it seemed like this amazing opportunity." She looks down at the glass again but thinks better of it, putting it down on the carpet beside her feet, undrunk. "I mean, imagine," she continues, her fingertips moving to the sleeve of her jumper, pulling at a loose strand. "I was sixteen; my cool big sister was going to live in America, home of Lizzie Maguire and Abercrombie & Fitch!" She rolls her eyes wearily. "Ultimate kudos."

"And your parents? They didn't think about going to the police?"

"Mum tried. They asked how old she was, what exactly the allegations were. But Beth was an adult, and whatever she was doing was of her own volition. She was capable of being in contact and she wasn't showing any signs of being mistreated or abused. They didn't know the full extent of what she... what you both were going through. They had no choice but to leave her be."

I think of the irony here, of how well Tate has played this. On the outside, there is nothing to convince anyone of wrongdoing. The sex was consensual – at most, his word against ours. The money was handed over willingly. It would need someone from the inside to shine a light into the dark corners of Elixir, to expose him for what he really is. And like the coward I am, I had blown any chance of doing it myself.

"So you came here to do... what?" I ask, and my stomach knots.

"I didn't know at first. I didn't even know exactly who you were. I followed that blonde lady for a bit – your neighbour? She looked so put-together, so self-assured – from what I knew of Elixir, she'd fit right in." I can't help a small huff of agreement. I'd thought it myself, hadn't I? "And then I saw you, and Etta. You looked so lost. I didn't understand how you could be connected. I followed you, though" – she allows herself a small smile – "to the park. You dropped a muslin, remember?"

My brain aches. There she was, in the peripheries of my memory, handing me the muslin on the fringes of Alexandra Park. The day I'd received the Elixir invitation. I'd been too preoccupied then to take her in properly, too tired after to have recognised her in the playgroup.

"You do look like her, though – enough to make me think there was something to it. And after following you in the park, I knew for sure. So, I followed you home. Saw you leave a while later in a hurry. And I..." Here she has the decency to look awkward. "I went through your rubbish. I found the flyer for the Baby Sparks class inside it, and thought if I could just find a way of getting close to you, getting you to confess..."

The Baby Sparks flyer. Despite myself, I can't help but feel a wave of satisfaction: I *knew* I hadn't moved it. I wish Adam was here so I could prove to him I had been right – but Adam is upstairs and probably hates me.

"You broke into my flat?"

"I wouldn't call it *breaking in*." She pouts. "I waited for you to go out and then rang your neighbour's bell. Told her you had a midwife's appointment you must have forgotten about. I was going to slide it under the door of the flat, but then I saw you'd left it open."

My spine tingles. It must have been when I'd gone out shopping. I'd been so distracted by the invitation, I probably hadn't even noticed. "And you put it in the bin?"

She shrugs. "It was a brand-new bin liner. I figured if I rested it on the top, it would be subtle enough to look like a coincidence."

"But... why? What was the point?" Despite everything, I was impressed by Mia's chutzpah. Saw in her the same keen-eyed determination as her sister. Only in Mia, hopefully, the skill would be used for good.

"I wanted to get to know you, Marissa. I just wanted to try... to try to understand." My real name jars. It feels so odd, hearing it here in this flat that has always been 'Beth's.' "But I didn't know if you were dangerous. That's what James thought. Why he wanted me to stay away."

A vision of Mia and James outside the café. I feel dizzy.

"Your argument – it was about me?" I couldn't believe my stupidity. I'd been so convinced Mia needed my help, and the whole time it was *me* she'd been scared of. I'd only seen what I'd wanted to see.

Mia nods.

I exhale, putting the pieces of the jigsaw together. "So it was *you* who moved the flyer? And the hourglass?"

She blushes. "Yes. At the time, I'd wanted to... I don't know, rattle you? Get you to confide. But I'd promised James I'd stay away. I shouldn't have asked you to come to that baby class or gone to lunch. When you took out the hourglass, I freaked out. I thought James was right, that I shouldn't have meddled. But I was angry. And I wanted to get to you, to hurt you. But moving Etta in the play café – that was wrong." She lowers her head. "I'm sorry."

I reach for her, resting a palm across the hands that sit coiled in her lap. Trying to convey all the things I can't say in words. Because in terms of wrongdoing, who am I to judge?

But as we sit in silence, each of us contemplating the truths that come to light on this dank, dark night, something isn't adding up. The pieces I have gathered are jumbled, don't fit right.

"And what about the invitation? The photograph? The brick? How did you...?"

And then I look at the expression on Mia's face. "What invitation?"

And my heart begins to thump.

Slowly, slowly, I crane my neck towards the stairs, recalling the sound of the brick crashing through glass. It's so quiet up there. How long has Adam been gone? What's he doing?

And then a feeling prickles through me, fire and ice shooting up my veins as I leap from the sofa and pound up the stairs to the closed bedroom door.

To find the smashed window wrenched open, glass still scattered.

A black timer on the dresser, the sand run through it.

And Adam and Etta gone.

38
San Francisco Bay Area
14th July 2023

∞

The flight to San Francisco takes eleven hours and ten minutes and I don't sleep for a single second of it. Haven't slept, in fact, for the previous eleven hours either. Crammed in the seat beside Mia, the air scented with industrial catering and sterile air conditioning, I am physically, acutely aware of where I am, but my mind is back in London, in the emptiness of the bedroom.

I can't move. I can't make the plane go faster. But internally, my thoughts gallop.

I have failed. I have failed Etta. And Adam. I have failed to outrun Elixir. And now I am paying the ultimate price.

I think of all the times I'd choked on telling Adam the truth. If I had, would he have been more vigilant? More prepared? Would he have persuaded me to have done something the moment I'd received the invitation? Avoided the horror show I'm now living through? I'll never know.

My fruitless searching of the flat seems so redundant now: calling their names, knocking into furniture, throwing off the duvet, searching – blinded by madness – under the bed, in the wardrobe, in the spare room. Hoping, for a moment, that Adam had taken her somewhere, to safety perhaps. A hotel? His family?

But one look at the hourglass and I'd known.

Adam and Etta are in danger. They are in danger and it's all my fault.

The top drawer of Adam's bedside table had been open. The one where we kept the passports. All three were gone. And I'd had little doubt about where they've been taken.

"We can call the airlines, get them to ground the flights," Mia, in her naivety, had suggested. As if Tate would ever fly commercial.

Her next suggestion made me sink even further.

"No, no police." I'd agitated my head. How would I have explained it? What if they'd arrested me? "What if–" The room had spun 180 as I tried to explain myself. "What if by the time we unpick it all, it's too late?"

On the plane beside me, Mia shifts, the tips of her fingers brushing against mine.

I still can't believe she is here. That when I'd reached for the box hidden under winter blankets, pulled from it the eagle-embossed US passport – six months and one day left on the validity – she'd declared, "I'm coming with you." Adding, even when I'd winced, holding the credit card linked to our non-existent bank balance aloft, "Let me help." Admitting, when I'd demurred, "We've got the money. I told you James was away a lot for work. It's true." An ironic smile. "He's a consultant, so I guess that means I married my sister?" Shrugged, awkwardly, as she reached into the depths of her coat pocket to produce her wallet. "Let me do this. Let me help. Let's get them back."

It's 5 p.m. when we arrive in San Francisco, but nearly midnight in London, and I sway as we make our way through security, the fuzziness of my brain dulling the fear that would otherwise be palpitating in me – that I'll be seized at the border, tipped off by Tate for my litany of crimes: Beth's shooting, the debt I had left behind, credit cards maxed out, loans unpaid, the money all gone to him. Not to mention the identity fraud I had been committing for nine long years.

In the moment, I'd hoped using my real passport would stop Elixir tracking me as fast. But now that we're on their home soil, I feel as through their eyes are on me more than ever.

I try Adam's phone for the millionth time, the vacuum of eleven hours in air space making me hope I'd finally reach him, that there would be a benign reason for their disappearance. But of course, it goes to voicemail, my message sent back from the ether with a single tick, like all the others.

"Here, take this." Mia presses something into the small of my hand as she propels me towards the car-hire booths. A round, yellow pill. "Diazepam," she confides, closing my fingers around it. "You need to stay calm," she argues, when I tried to protest, "if we want to get them back."

The city looks so different, I notice numbly, nose pressed against the passenger-seat window as we wend our way through the Bay Area. It's always had a drug problem and a housing crisis, but in the years since I've left, those twin blights have spiralled. The opioid crisis has ravaged through the huge numbers of mentally ill and addicted unsheltered residents; the cost of living has been driven sky high by the myriad tech companies who made the city their home, only to retreat during the pandemic due to "poor trading conditions." There is something particularly unsavoury about Tate peddling fifty-dollar hand lotion in the same city where plastic tents and belongings-stuffed shopping carts line the streets.

"We're not leaving here without them," Mia promises as we make our way over the Golden Gate Bridge, and I fight the urge to open the car door and run.

I clutch Etta's grey bunny to me, the one Adam had bought in the hospital, trying to extricate whatever I can of her scent. A talisman.

"Whatever it takes," I agree.

And I look at my reflection in the wing mirror.

See Marissa staring back.

Finally ready to fight.

39
Marin County
15th July 2023

∞

We park in a lay-by half a mile out from The Jungle. The sensation of being back here is destabilising, the memories of my final escape snarling around me like tree roots, every crunch of path or snap of a twig making me halt, snatch a breath.

And then we reach it. The thick palms and creeping vines look even greener and more lush than in my mind's eye, the mansion's façade is grander and more imposing. The exterior is speck-free, windows buffed and shined, and I wonder whose job it was to see to it, who had choked on their willingness to prove themselves a worthy servant.

"This is it?" Mia breathes, staring up at the behemoth.

"This is it," I agree, resignedly. "The Jungle."

Saying it here, out loud, I am struck by a wave of inertia. What am I doing back here? Why, *why* have I allowed myself back into this bear trap? But then I think of Etta, hidden somewhere within. Picture Tate, his manicured fingers touching her unsullied skin, his breath against her cheek, and I ball my fists. Running didn't work. Fighting has to.

I take Mia by the fingertips, pull. "Let's go."

"What do we do?" Mia asks as we stand facing the front door. "Knock?"

I can tell that she is scared too; I can see the quiver in her limbs and know if I were to press a hand to her heart it would be beating a tattoo as fast as mine. I shake my head, plunge a hand into the back pocket of my jeans to retrieve the other object from the shoe box I'd secreted inside.

Answer, deadpan, "Still got my keys."

I'd hoped that the house would be quiet, given the timing, but as I push open the door and enter the vast, light-flooded entrance room that has haunted so many of my dreams, I am surprised to see there is a stirring of activity.

The place hasn't changed. The smell of eucalyptus is thick, making my nose twitch. Still the clean lines, the neutral Scandi tones. The heavy coffee-table books, bought for effect. The expensive artwork, purchased with other people's money. The place hasn't changed... but many of the people have. True, a few I recognise. They're all women. The little redhead that always got Beth's nose up, Mackenzie or Camilla or... No, Cassidy. That was it. Ife, a mainstay from before even my time, whose father was a Nigerian ruler. A girl I recognise but never caught the name of, sporting the same thick black braid, now sitting cross-legged on the floor.

But it's not the women who surprise me. What surprises me are the children.

Three of them sit around the edge of the dining table, dressed identically in muted pastel leggings, legs swinging as they scoop some sort of grain-and-vegetable combo neatly into their mouths, not missing a crumb. A toddler squats on the marble floor over by the French windows stacking plastic-free blocks in various shades of beige. Babies rest in arms or sleep in wicker Moses baskets, attendant mothers cooing. It could be an advert for a trendy nursery.

The door clicks shut behind us, making Mia flinch, and I see them all turn to stare at me, the eyes of the ones I recognise rounding as they, in turn, recognise me.

"Is that...?" one of them asks, a half whisper that is quickly shushed, but then another hisses, "She came back?"

"Where are they?" I demand of the amorphous collective, my voice ricocheting off the cool stone walls.

They say nothing.

I try again, louder, the anger fizzing through me. "Are you all deaf? I said, where. Are. They."

Two of the women place protective hands on the pudgy limbs of the children. There's movement, and Ife rises and bolts upstairs. I reach out to grab hold of her but she's too fast for me, long limbs springing easily across the room.

"Marissa," a voice calls, distracting me. I turn. Cassidy is picking her way across the room, a baby clutched to her hip. "Just stay calm, okay?" She closes the gap between us, places a firm grip on my upper arm, squeezing tighter when I try to resist. "This is a *calm* space," she repeats, synthetically zen. "There are *children* here. We don't want anyone to get hurt." She gives a knowing look to the other women, and I see the threat laced within her coolness. They are all tensed, ready to spring. If anyone were to make the first move, it wouldn't be me.

"Cassidy, you just need to tell me where they are, and we will leave without another word." I close my eyes. Bite my lip before adding, "Please."

She shakes her head, her voice still maddeningly placid. "I'm sorry, I can't do that."

"Cassidy..." It takes every ounce of restraint to stop

myself from lashing out at her, knowing that it will lead to nothing. Mia and I are outnumbered. And once the Elite get going, they have no off switch.

Instead, I try to breathe. Find myself choking on air. The room, despite its open-plan structure, its gaping floor-to-ceiling windows, is suffocating. I can't bear that I am back here. I can't bear the thought that Etta could be here somewhere, hidden in The Jungle's cavernous rooms. That I am the *reason* she is here.

Cassidy pinches the bridge of her nose, adjusting the baby on her side. He has her red hair, the same smattering of freckles across the bridge of his nose. I don't want to think who his deep brown eyes belong to.

"Jenna, take Axel," she commands, speaking through my verbal inertia, thrusting her chin towards the group on the sofa.

A small girl springs into action, bleats, "Yes, maestro," and Cassidy releases the baby to her. She scuttles back to her place, watching us cautiously. She can't be more than sixteen.

"Listen," Cassidy resumes, once Jenna and the baby are settled. She rests a hand on my shoulder, her voice turning silken, adopting that coaxing, mellifluous inflection they use to lure someone into accepting orders. "I know you probably have a lot of questions. But first of all, I need you to understand that it had nothing to do with us." She gestures with her chin, encompassing the other women. "So, anything you do to us won't make your situation any better."

"Don't let him do this, Cassidy. Can't you see, even for Elixir, this is wrong?" Frustrated tears blur my eyes.

"I'm sorry." She presses her lips together, a thin line. She is so slight that I don't know how she could have carried that child to full term. Her hip bones jut out from the sky-blue leggings that slick her body like sealskin. How has she survived this so long? How is she still under his spell?

"Then just tell me where they are. Tell me they're safe. Anything. Just... help me. Please."

"I – I can't."

"Cassidy, it's my *fucking daughter.*" I feel something inside me bending, and then breaking, all the reserve I'd held at bay shattering. The anger sears through me as I lurch towards Cassidy, going for her hair, her throat. There are screams from the other women as they leap to their feet, hands grasping for me as they try to release my grip, pushing Mia out of the way as she comes to my defence.

But then a voice freezes us all in place, exuding instant control.

"Stop this!"

A figure stands at the top of the sweeping staircase.

And all of us turn to face it.

"She's not *your* daughter," the voice says, each letter an ice pick of enunciation. And I feel the chill of it run through me, freeze my veins.

Because standing at the topmost step is Beth.

40
Marin County
15th July 2023

∞

"Beth…" I release her name from my lips, feeling the strangeness of it, of handing her identity back over.

"*Elizabeth*," she hits back, not missing a beat. Her lip curls. "You were pleased enough call me that once."

I feel a wrenching, a wordless guttural sound pulled from my chest as I make for the steps. I'm barely halfway across the room before Elizabeth has turned her pale eyes to Cassidy. She calls her name once, and the woman leaps for me, taking hold of my arm with unsurprising strength. She in turn calls for another woman and I am caught fast. The pads of their fingers digging into my upper arm, the herbaceous stench of Elixir's signature bouquet thick on their skin. It turns my stomach. How did I ever think it smelt nice?

The rest of them move in chorus, clustering around me and Mia, ready.

I take them in, Tate's army. How desperate they all are to be in his good books.

"I know Cassidy said none of you are part of this, Elizabeth, but I'm sure Tate must have confided in you." Trapped, I try appealing to her superiority, keeping my voice deferential, contrite. "Are you able at least to tell me *why* he's doing this? Couldn't you... Can I just speak to Adam? Or see Etta? I won't do anything. I just want to know they're all right."

Slowly, she shakes her head. "I'm afraid I can't let you do that."

Our eyes lock and I allow myself to look at her in full. All these years, I had held in my mind the image of her the night I had left, and although she is now hardly old – in fact, probably looks young for her age – I can see the indelible marks the last nine years have left on her. Her skin, although dewy and clear, stretches over her hollow cheekbones. Her lips definitely have an unnatural plumpness. And her tanned arms, visible in the sleeveless tank, are sinewy, thick stripes of veins running their length. At first glance, she looks the picture of health. But I see under it the effort that has gone into it, what it has cost her to have achieved each step. An unnaturalness that pushes far beyond simple "good health."

Is this what I would have become, if I'd stayed?

"This wasn't exactly how things were supposed to happen. Everything got a little... messed up in the end. But I have to say I'm surprised you made it here so quickly, without my passport." Her top lip quirks. "Thanks for looking after that, by the way. But then, you were always very determined."

"I used my own." I look to the floor. "I never wanted to become you, Beth." Out of the corner of my eye, I see her nostrils flare. "I mean, *Elizabeth*. I never wanted to take what was yours."

"But you did."

She moves one step down the staircase, fingers skimming the banister. As she does, I see for the first time that she walks with a barely perceptible limp, right hip jerking ever so slightly to meet the rise and fall, hand grasping the banister tighter to take her weight. My eyes go to the band of skin at her stomach, exposed beneath her tank top. To the spiderweb scar I see creeping from the waistband of her leggings.

I remember the bite of metal between my palms, fingers trembling as I had aimed the gun at Tate. And then the flurry of movement as I had squeezed the trigger. But then I remember Tate's arms dragging Elizabeth into the bullet's path: a human shield. An explosion of red. Nothing I could have done to stop it.

She catches me looking and her fingers flutter to her stomach, adjusting her top.

"I'm sorry," I whisper, knowing the words will never be enough. "Elizabeth, I don't know what he's told you, but you have to know I never wanted to hurt you. Tate is the reason for all of this. Everything I told you back then was true. He's a liar. And a bully. And so much more. He's not the great man you think he is." As I say it, the terror rises in my throat, burning it. "And now Adam and Etta could be in danger. Please… please, you have to help me."

My words peter out into silence. None of the women speak. For a moment, I think I've made a difference. But then Beth presses her hands to her ears, shakes her head "You know nothing."

"Elizabeth!" With a jerk, Mia stumbles forwards, resisting the women who rush to grab her, hold her fast.

I see Elizabeth's eyes narrow, confusion knitting across her face as she searches the cluster of women. And then her manicured mouth hangs open as the confusion morphs into disbelief.

"Mia?" And Mia nods. Takes a step closer. "Why are you even here?"

"For *you*."

There is a moment, a semicolon of time, when I think that this it, that we've finally broken the spell. But then Elizabeth stiffens, a mask coming over her face.

"You shouldn't have come. You should never have got involved with any of this." She shakes her head. "In fact, it's thanks to you that everything has been so messed up in the first place. It was all planned out – the invitations, the timing – and then you had to get involved and spoil everything. At least he had the sense to get out when he did." She is spooling facts faster than I can keep up: What plan? What did Tate get out of? But then, to my surprise, Elizabeth's voice softens. And as she takes in Mia, I notice the smallest, slight tremble of her bottom lip. "What I can't understand is why were you even bothered about me in the first place? Why are you pretending to care?"

"I *do* care," Mia whispers, words laced with hurt. "I've always cared. We're family." She jerks towards the stairs and the women instantly tighten their grip in response, until a look from Elizabeth makes them relax, hang back.

"You're lying," she challenges, although there is an upward inflection in it, the possibility of a question. "You, Mum, Greg – you were all happy to see the back of me. You never even tried to contact me. You were all glad to see me go." She juts out her chin. "So now this is my family. My real home. Here."

"But we *did* try!" Mia takes another, cautious step. "We didn't know the extent of what was going on here. None of us would have if I hadn't found Marissa. But Mum called and called. She always got Tate. And then voicemail. And then *nothing*. And she emailed – you *replied*." She shook her head. "You told us to leave you alone, that you were happy.

God, Mum even tried calling the police, but they wouldn't do anything because you were a consenting adult. What else could we do?"

And for the first time, I see a flicker of confusion pass over Elizabeth's face. A momentary disarmament. "I never got any emails," she murmurs, turning her head away.

And suddenly, Mia and I share a look as the truth dawns on us both: *Tate.*

"Elizabeth," I placate. "Elixir has made us both do things we should be ashamed of." We have been through so much together, she and I, and now it needs to end. Exhaustion washes over me. The longer we remain talking, the more my concern for Etta grows. The knowledge that she may be here is physically painful. And Adam – is he hurt? Will he ever forgive me? *Where is Tate?* "I should never have made you a part of this. I should never have left you behind. I will always live with the shame of that. I should have told people the truth about Tate when I had the chance, but I was too much of a fucking coward." Tears sting my eyes. At that moment, I truly hate myself. "But we can put it *right*." I look up at her imploringly. "Stop protecting him. Don't let him do this. You were my friend once. Can't you find it in your heart to be one again? Please, whatever Tate's promised you, it's not worth hurting my daughter over." At the thought of her, I feel my chest cracking. I'm not a good enough mother. I could never protect her. I should never have had the gall to have her in the first place.

But at the word *daughter*, Elizabeth seizes up. "She's *not* your daughter." Thumps her fist against the banister. "She's *mine*. Mine and Tate's."

Electricity shoots up my spine. When I look at her, Elizabeth's expression is steely, one hundred per cent conviction.

"Is that what Tate's told you?" I ask, trying to bury the incredulity in my voice. Elizabeth speaks with such determination that I am truly worried she must be mad. "Elizabeth," I coax gently, "Etta is *my* daughter. Mine and Adam's."

She doesn't flinch. She doesn't move. Instead, she stares coldly past me. And then, the left corner of her mouth twitches.

"Jenna," she addresses the girl who took Axel from Cassidy. "You and Crystal take the children and go down to the beach until I say. Ife," she calls backwards, into the hidden depths of upper house, "it's time to fetch Adam."

41
Marin County
15th July 2023

∞

The silence that follows seems to drag on for hours, although it can't be more than a few minutes. The group of women seem so inert, so emotionless that it's unnerving. But of course, I have forgotten what it means to be in Elixir. How easy it is to stand to attention when the threat of punishment outweighs any discomfort.

And then there is movement in the corridor behind Elizabeth. And I see them.

"Etta!" Her name rips from my lips as I lunge towards the stairs, fighting the bodies that converge to hold me back.

Behind me, a shriek: "*Jesus,* Elizabeth! Your sister just *bit* me!"

"Stop this!" Elizabeth snaps. "Stop fighting! Both of you! Unless you want someone to get hurt."

I look at my daughter, my tiny, fragile daughter and instantly freeze.

Elizabeth shakes her head, turning to Mia almost regretfully. "I told you, you weren't supposed to be here. Why didn't you leave things alone?"

"We won't fight," I promise, a glance at Mia to ensure

her cooperation. I let my body go slack in Cassidy's grasp. "Just… don't hurt them."

And then a sound jars me. Hearing my voice, Etta jerks, her little body pulsating. She lets out squeal of recognition that knots my heart as I stare past Beth to the figure holding her.

Adam.

Relief breathes through me that they are both safe, that she has had him to protect her.

Until I take him in fully.

Read the expression on his face.

And the knot in my heart twists, tightens.

"No…"

It is like falling backwards into a black abyss. Every simple explanation, every realistic reason that I try to grasp hold of is slicked in Vantablack, edges impossible to find.

Because as I search his body, looking for signs of injury, a fight, I see there's not a scratch on him. He looks… well. Washed, clean shaven, none of the signs of poor sleep that rightly should be carved into his face. Wearing clean clothes: soft grey tracksuit bottoms and a crisp white T-shirt. Clothes, I see on further inspection, that bear the neat looping logo of Elixir.

And then, I realise how odd it is that he stands so freely. No one holds him, coerces him. He's not resisting or trying to run. He looks, in fact, entirely and utterly at home.

And that's when the bottom falls out of my stomach, the truth winding me faster than I can stop it.

"Surprise," he says, as our eyes meet. He gives me a steely smile. "It's always the husband, right?"

Adam isn't their captive. He's one of them.

"How… how long?" I do my best to quell the tremor in my voice. "When did they get to you?"

He waits for Elizabeth. She nods, once.

"Always."

The word razors through me as I take in the man I loved, lived with, created a child with. I search the familiarity of his features – the exact pattern of his hairline, the bump of his nose, the certain crease in his right eyebrow: try to find in them some small kindness, a sense of remorse. There is nothing. The life I thought we had created together – his job, his childhood, *Jesus, his lactose intolerance* – what, if any of it, had been real?

"There was no conference in Manchester," I stammer, grasping hold of the first scab of information I can pick.

"*Technically* incorrect." He adjusts his hold on Etta, and it takes everything in me not to rush to her. "There *was* a conference in Manchester. I just wasn't there. The devil's in the details, and all that. I was supposed to be overnighting here, to meet with Elizabeth, but when I saw all your missed calls, I knew something must have happened." He jerks his chin towards Mia. "I didn't realise she'd be there in the house, though. Complicating things. Having to stage the brick through the window, getting someone on the ground to help me get out of the flat... That took some planning."

At this he looks with giddy pride towards Elizabeth, who rewards him with a magnanimous smile: "Don't worry; your efforts have been noted."

"The invitation, the photograph... it was all you." It doesn't warrant a question. "You wanted to get me back here. Why?"

"That was the original intention," Elizabeth speaks before Adam has a chance to. "To get you here. The big reveal on Founder's Day. The culmination of *everything*," she adds, with surprising bitterness. "How was I to know Mia would fuck everything up?"

There are now so many pieces of the jigsaw that I can't hold them in one place. I try to focus on what she is saying, what she means by a "big reveal," but my mind is still on Adam, on the lie we've been living.

"How..." I squeeze my eyes shut. "When did you join them? You said... You told me you'd never even left the country."

"Well, we told each other a lot of things, didn't we, *Beth*?" The name is an acid drop on his tongue, and I look away, trying to hide the tear that snakes down my cheek.

He sees, though, and despite himself, Adam sighs.

"I *am* an accountant – that part is true. Nathan would have been lucky to have me take over the firm." So his job was real, at least. But his friends? His likes and dislikes? Our life together tumbles through me, each possible truth snared by a lie. "Tate was a guest speaker at a conference I went to years ago: *Make It Happen: How to Master Your Life and Control Your Own Destiny*." He waves his hands over an imaginary banner. I can hear the awe in his voice. "I was hooked. Spent almost all my savings on moving out here, more on all the classes and seminars, moving my way up. But after a year, I was almost finished. I thought I'd have to give up, go home, but then this opportunity presented itself, and I knew I'd be the perfect fit. I can be pretty charming when I want to be."

I see his lip curl over the top of Etta's head, my insides squirming as I remember our first meeting, how he'd spilled his drink on me in the pub, how we had laughed over my wet tights, Adam apologetically blotting them with blue roll. How he'd seemed so warm and easy, and how, for perhaps the first time since arriving in London, I had allowed a tiny part of me relax. It was all a set up.

"You never loved me?" Part of me doesn't want to give voice to it, but I need to know. "Not at all?"

He holds my gaze. "Like I said, we're obviously both well-versed at playing parts."

The tears sting. My limbs slacken fully against the women holding them. I don't know how long I can keep up the fight.

"Why?" I look at Etta in his arms, the life I thought we had both struggled so hard to create together. "What did I ever do to you? What was it *worth*?"

"You don't understand." He adjusts his grip on Etta tighter as she wriggles in his arms and my stomach lurches. "You've never understood. You always had it easy."

"*Easy*?" I hiss. Everything I've escaped. Have continued escaping from. The last thing any of it has been is easy.

"Yes, *easy*," he sneers. "Don't try that little-girl-lost act on me. Remember, I know who you really are. Five years of you acting all meek and mournful, pretending to worry about money when you knew one call to your rich parents would have solved everything. Happy for me to slave away all hours while you limped through one dead-end job after another."

"You know that's not true!"

"It *is* true," Adam spits back. "You're a leech. You always have been. Spent all the money your parents gave you, used Tate for everything he had, and when the good life ran out, you took someone else's."

My eyes flick to Elizabeth, watching us with a silent smirk. My lip trembles. "That wasn't what happened."

"You've never worked for *anything*," Adam continues, his

voice gaining momentum. "People like you always land on your feet. Well, unlike you, I *earned* my way to the top." His right eyebrow is quivering, like it always does when he's antagonised, and the familiarity of it, the sham that such familiarity is built on, sickens me.

"Then what about her; what about your daughter?"

"She's not mine." Adam lets out an acerbic laugh. "She's Tate's."

"Will you both stop saying that!?" I can't take it anymore. The lies. The gaslighting. With all the force left within me, I rip my right arm out of one of the women's grasp, clutch air as I launch myself towards the stairs. The momentum of it unbalances me and I stumble, trip, my shin connecting painfully with the marble floor as I cry out in pain. "Adam, are you even *listening* to yourself?" I cry, even as I feel hands on me again, clawing me back. I grunt as they pin me to ground, elbows pressed against the length of my spine. "You can't seriously let Tate do this – take our daughter!"

Desperate, I stretch an arm up to Elizabeth, standing immobile on the stairs. *"Please,* Elizabeth. Let me speak to Tate, make him see sense. I came back, okay? That's what he wanted, wasn't it? The cards, the threats? The night I left – he told me I'd be back. And he got his wish. I'm here. Please. Don't take Etta from me. If it's me he wants… I'll stay." I think of the freedom I had fought so hard for. How not one part of it mattered: not without Etta.

Elizabeth folds her arms, and I see something cross her face, a softening of her lips, jaw, that almost looks like amusement… or pity.

"You think this is about *you*?"

I feel as though I'm in a movie, stuck in a freeze frame.

I had assumed that taking Etta had been a ploy, the

ultimate way to get my attention, to bring me back. But now I think of the children the young girl, Jenna, had led away. How uncannily well behaved they had been. Model Elixir members. Even the babies.

At the top of the stairs, Etta bats her arms and lets out a shriek into the stale air, oblivious to any of it.

I think of the child Tate had tried to force inside of me, once before. Hear the blood whooshing in my ears. Feel the room begin to spin.

It isn't me he wants. It's Etta.

"Elizabeth," I begin, the words wrenched from my lips slowly, painfully. *"Where. Is. Tate?"*

But she doesn't have to answer. Because at that moment there is the sound of a key in the lock. The front door scrapes open.

And all of us turn, in unison, to see Tate's blond head appear from the other side.

42
Marin County
15th July 2023

∞

"What the is hell going on in here? Why is everyone standing around like this? Don't you have work to do? And where the fuck are the children?"

Tate, unchanged after almost a decade, enters The Jungle with the full force of his personality.

But then he stands stock still, allows the door to crash shut loudly behind him, as he notices me, the entire gamut of reactions crossing his tanned features, before settling on his signature impassivity: forehead unwrinkled, mouth sewn in a thin line – the quintessence of a poker face.

"Marissa?" He punches a laugh into the air. "What are you doing here?"

It takes everything in me not tear at him. To rent my nails across his cheeks, his lips; rip the smugness right out of him. But I think of Etta, feet away and so vulnerable, of the women who now hold me tightly, the half-moons of their fingernails score my upper arms. I squeeze my eyes shut. "Don't play games, Tate."

The house is silent. When I was here, The Jungle always seemed so full of noise, of people, the whir of activity, the hum of music on the sound system. Now, there is nothing. Even Etta is quiet, convinced by some sixth sense to be still.

Tate swallows. I watch the pulse of his throat clench, unclench. His synthetic blue eyes are clear as he holds my gaze. "I don't know what you're talking about."

"You've got my attention. What do you want?"

I search his face. He seems to have aged barely more than a day since I last saw him. His skin is smooth, unlined, his blond hair still as fulsome and neatly coiffed as it was nine years ago. He would be sure to say this was emblematic of Elixir's promise, #ItWorks, rather than the truth: that it's easy to look unmarred when you have lived your life off the blood and sweat of other people, a modern-day Báthory, with better-smelling bath products and a more compelling sales pitch.

"Marissa, I don't even know what you're doing back here."

He has the temerity to look confused, and it makes me clench my fists tight enough to pierce skin. "Are you joking? For months you've been taunting me – no, not months, *years*." I throw a glance at Adam. "You set up this elaborate plot to entrap me, bring me back here, you steal my fucking *daughter* to get my attention, and for what?" The rage is now steaming inside me, a kettle whistling, and I don't know how long I can hold down the lid. "I kept your secrets. I kept away. I've caused no harm to you or the vileness you've created here. So why now? Why take Etta? What do you *want*?"

"It wasn't Tate." From her vantage point, Elizabeth speaks, her voice tremulous, laced with something – excitement, maybe, or fear. She takes one slow, cautious step down. "It wasn't Tate; it was me."

The world spins off its axis.

I look from Elizabeth to Tate. See the conviction in her eyes, the cloud in his.

I look at Adam, the way he has his chin tilted to Elizabeth, almost in admiration. At Mia, confusion sparking, her belief that her sister is an innocent victim beginning to waver.

"Can someone please tell me what the fuck is going on?" I hear the venom bubbling up in Tate's voice and am amazed at the power it has, even now, to make me quake with fear.

All of us, collectively, look to Elizabeth.

"It was for you." The desperation of it, the yearning in her voice, punches me in the gut. What monster have I created? "I was going to tell you at the Founder's Day party, but it's all gone wrong. I wanted to tell you that... I can finally reach Perfection."

Perfection. Hearing the word is like being plunged into a bucket of ice.

"Elizabeth." Tate sighs, shaking his head. "We've been through this..."

As Mia overlaps him, "...What do you mean, perfection?"

"'Perfection,'" Elizabeth quotes, verbatim, eyes locked on Tate. "'Elixir Manifesto Addendum, July 2014. Imagine a world in which Elixir is king. Imagine the things we could achieve, the beautiful earth we could create together. That world is in our grasp, if we work together to achieve it.'" She pauses, swallows. Mia frowns in confusion, but I realise I know what is coming. I remember what Tate spoke of; the night I saw him for what he truly was. "'When two Elite souls come together in the creation of new life, a child made in their image is a blessing to Elixir, and blesses the giver of life in return. Together, they enter a new status: Perfection.'"

Slowly, slowly, I look away from Elizabeth, towards Etta. "No..."

Tate was the only man to be a member of Elite. Like so many things in Elixir, it was an unspoken rule.

Which meant all those children, those perfect, passive children, must be Tate's.

"It was the announcement he was supposed to make the night of the party." This, Elizabeth directs at me. "*You* may not have wanted *your* chance, but I hoped I'd have mine." She sniffs, teeth clenched against tears. "When you shot me, you took that chance away from me. Do you see? The damage from the bullet destroyed my ability to have children. You took away my chance at Perfection. You ruined everything."

The weight of what I have done is like an anchor, dragging me down. The night I left Elixir, I had tried to destroy Tate. To free Elizabeth, to free us all. Instead, I had taken this from her. I think of the trauma I had suffered trying to conceive Etta. The thought that I had been the cause of the same problem, irrevocably, for Elizabeth, was heart-breaking.

"They told me I was lucky to be alive, even if I couldn't bear children. But what sort of living has it been to be cast aside, to have to sit there and watch child after child be born when my own chance had been ripped away from me? And *you*" – she whips her head towards me – "you had it right there in your grasp." She presses her hands to her gut. "His child. And you threw it away. It wasn't fair. So, I put things right." She beams at Tate, arms raised in supplication. "I made us a child, Tate. Yours and mine. See? We can finally be together! We can achieve Perfection."

"She's not *your* child!" Horror flushes through me. "She's *mine*, and..." As much as it disgusts me to say it now, I add, "And Adam's."

And then Elizabeth does something I don't expect.

She laughs. A low, sinister laugh, rising from her gullet. It is somehow more threatening than if she'd extended a blade.

"You're right. She's not my child, not by blood." She licks her lips, wolfish. "But whose name does she have on her birth certificate?"

It winds me. And I see it now, the way she has twisted my own betrayal to her advantage. I took her name, and so now she is taking my child.

But why would Tate raise a child that wasn't his?

And then, almost as the realisation is worming its way into my mind, she launches her next attack: "And she's not Adam's. He's not her father. Tate is."

I feel as though a hand has been thrust inside my chest, is squeezing my lungs. I rove Adam's features, searching for some sign that she is either lying or has gone completely mad. "How could that even be possible? We had sex. We were...we were *trying*."

"Frozen sperm is flown all around the world on a daily basis, didn't you know?" Elizabeth flicks a hand onto her hip. "There are companies dedicated to it. Ours was called Cryostork, which I thought was cute. And Adam was very, *very* dedicated to his role." Slowly, she raises her fingers in the air, making a crude scissoring gesture. When I gasp, she tuts. "It's not that bad. Vasectomies are reversible, you know."

"I'm sorry, are you saying you..." Tate interrupts. "You *took my sperm?*" To his credit, he looks horrified. *"When?"*

Elizabeth pouts. "My love, for a person vain enough to have full monthly medicals, it wasn't difficult to persuade Dr Stone to throw a sperm analysis into the mix."

Dr Stone. The name rocks me. Another setup. The fertility doctor who had "fixed" me. Who had been so encouraging and kind. So happy for me when the embryo had implanted first try. All the pills and the tests and the injections. All the self-hatred I had hurled at myself, convinced that it was a problem I had caused, my karmic cross to bear.

"There was nothing wrong with me?"

Elizabeth shakes her head. "But don't worry. Dr Stone is a first-rate physician. You were always in safe hands."

I press a hand to my abdomen, to the potential for life it could now hold. "This is sick, Beth."

"*Elizabeth!*" she spits. Huffs a breath. "And it would have all gone so easily if we'd been able to stick to the plan. The invitation was just the start. Moving things around the house to make you think you were going crazy. Waking the baby up in the night. We figured you'd finally tell Adam the truth, and then he'd persuade you to come out here to confront Tate. Right in time for the Founder's Day celebration, where Tate would receive his gift."

It is Adam I look to now. Adam, who holds my child in his arms, a child he has no right to. "But why go to all these lengths? If it was Etta you wanted, why not just take her?"

"Because I wanted to see *you*," Elizabeth answers before he can open his mouth. "Because I wanted to look you in the eyes as you felt the pain of having your child taken away. Just like you took away my chance of ever having one." She screws up her mouth, her face turning ugly with hate. "Tate told me you were jealous of how close he and I were. That you had shot me because you couldn't *bear* the thought that I was his favourite, and then you ran away like a coward. He knew you couldn't stay running forever. And I wanted to prove him right."

"God, *no*!" I look at Tate in disgust. The lies are astounding, even for him.

"Do you see, Tate?" Elizabeth steps delicately down a couple of the steps, ignoring me; her eyes are wide, her desperation pure. "What I've done for you? We can be happy together! Reach Perfection together. Etta may not be my blood, but she bears my name. I'll love her like my own. I even named her after you!" Her expression freezes as she waits for it to click. "It's an anagram, don't you see?" she urges. "I know how much you love those!"

And with that, she pushes the knife in to the hilt.

As I picture the operating room. Adam's carefully curated playlist. The melodious croon of "At Last" filling the air as he looked at me, grinned, "What about Etta?"

Now, the name rips apart, the letters rearranging themselves in my mind.

E – T – T – A becoming T – A – T – E.

43
Marin County
15ᵗʰ July 2023

∞

Etta… an anagram of *Tate*.

How could I not have seen it? I feel violated. It is the final blow in how Elixir has infected every part of my life, has continued to infect it even when I had thought I was free.

"How could you do this to me?" I gaze up at Elizabeth, the hurt radiating through me. "I was your *friend*. I tried to *save* you."

Her jaw tightens. She clicks her teeth, immutable. "Friends don't shoot friends, Marissa."

I look at Tate, his expression stony. How can he just stand there, so passive, so calm?

"I wasn't trying to shoot you! I was trying to shoot *him*!"

"Stop lying to me!" Elizabeth stamps her foot, pressing her hands to her ears like a child having a tantrum. "Tate told me everything. You couldn't bear that you were having Tate's child and he wanted me more. So you ruined my chance at happiness. And if it hadn't been for Tate–"

"If it hadn't been for *Tate*," I insist, unable to hold myself back any longer, "who *pulled you in front of him*, you would have been fine!" The anger I feel is exquisite. Not at Elizabeth, mind-muddled, brainwashed Elizabeth. But at Tate. And with a burst of strength, I hurl myself forward. The movement is unexpected, taking the women holding me by surprise, and I feel the wrench and pull of their limbs, the change of weight, as I finally find myself free.

"He used you as human-fucking-shield, Elizabeth! Are you really so far gone you can't see it? All of you!" I stumble back, the nerves on my loosened limbs twitching, to address the room full of these idiotic, innocent, wrecked women. "Wake. Up!" Nine years of pent-up rage pours out of me. "Can you really not see what he's done? What he will continue to do, if no one puts a stop to it?" My voice reverberates off the cool stone walls, and I feel the power of it. I will no longer be silenced. "I was a coward. I was a fucking coward, and I admit it. I shouldn't have run. I should have stayed. And I should have fought. And I should have shut the whole thing down when I had the chance." There is no turning back now. I wasted so many years thinking Tate had mastery of me. I am done.

The women are staring at me now with a mixture of horror and awe. "You don't have to be afraid of him," I urge them. "He is *nothing*. Don't you see? He picks people apart. He drags them down. He makes them think they're alone in the world, and that the only thing that matters is him. But you're not alone. You can fight him. *We* can fight him. Together, our voices are more powerful than his. All the awful things he's done to us, made us do to each other. We can tell the truth – Elixir isn't a wellness group, it's a fucking *cult*! And it has to go down."

A long silence.

No one speaks. No one moves. A sneer slicks itself onto Tate's face, and for a moment, I think it's all over.

And then…

A voice to my left. Cassidy takes a step towards me. And I feel her fingertips lace between mine.

"I… I was fifteen," she whispers. "He told me my father had unhealthy desires for me. That sleeping with him, Tate, was a way of overcoming the trauma of it." A tear slicks down her cheek. "My father loved me, and I told him if he contacted me again, I'd call the police and get him kicked out of his company."

"He took my inheritance." A throat clears. Ife, standing at top of the stairs beside Elizabeth. She takes a step towards us. "He said I was materialistic. That keeping it was a sign of weakness."

"He raped me," one of the women holding Mia murmurs, letting go of her arm to join me. "That's what it was, but I've never used the word, until now."

"He messed with my birth control." Another. "I kept finding it in different places, getting confused when I'd taken it and when I hadn't."

"My periods stopped. I guessed because I was so thin. I don't even know how I got pregnant. But he told me it was my good work, rewarding me, that I should be grateful."

They come forward, one after the other. Stories of humiliation. Coercion. Fraud. Rape. Stories that sound so much like my own. And as they gather round me, I feel the strength rising from within me.

"Beth?" Caught up in the fray, Mia takes a step towards the base of the stairs, looks up at her sister with pleading eyes.

Elizabeth presses her lips together, shakes her head. But the tears are falling now, freely.

Mia hesitates. And then she reaches into her pocket, pulls

out her phone. Scrolls for a moment before her finger pauses on the screen, and she begins to read. "'Dear Mum and Dad, I want you to understand that the life I have chosen is here. Stop trying to contact me. Stop your threats and your lies. Your presence in my life is only harmful to me and I won't have you as a part of it any longer. I won't surround myself with oppressive forces. I am an adult, and I have made my choice. Yours, Elizabeth.'" Silently, she puts her phone in her pocket. Stares up at her sister.

"I... I didn't that write." Elizabeth's voice is small, uncertain. I see her eyes flick towards Tate, assessing him.

"I know." Mia nods. "He tripped up. Didn't call Dad 'Greg.'" She laughs softly. "My poor dad. Even when you didn't hate him, there's no way you'd call him that. At the time, I thought it was a mix-up. But when you said you hadn't gotten the emails..."

"And the other times?"

"We *tried*," Mia urges. Looking at them in opposition, I see their likeness mirrored even more clearly. "Emailing. Calling. We never gave up hope that you'd see sense and come home. *Please*, Beth. Marissa wants her daughter back. I want... I want a chance to know my sister."

It is as though I can see the synapses of Elizabeth's brain firing, as though she is trying to wrap her mind around the new reality that is being presented to her. She looks at the women. Back at Tate. Finally, at me.

And I know, finally, in that moment, we've got her.

"You..." She swallows, looking at me. "You weren't trying to shoot me?"

I shake my head. "I know that things weren't right between us when I left, but I would never... I begged you to come with me."

A tear loosens itself from Elizabeth's eye, slicks down her cheek and disappears on her chin. "Oh, God…"

"It's over, Tate," I look down my nose at him, feeling my strength surging, surrounded by the women whose lives he has tried to ruin. "You, Elixir, all of it. You're done."

I wait, breath held.

The women look from me to Tate.

Waiting.

Until, eventually, "Well, this has all been a very exciting afternoon, hasn't it?" Tate puts his hands together as if in prayer. Presses them to his lips, as he often did when giving a speech. "So many revelations. So many false accusations." He blows air. "But that's what they are, of course: accusations. Not facts. Not proof. In fact, what we *do* have is an attempted murder." At this, he looks at me. "And whatever mess Elizabeth has created here. As for the rest of it…" He shrugs his shoulders, satisfaction smiling across his face. "You were all quite happy paying your membership fees, attending your classes. No one is chained up here. No one is held captive. I'm running a business which you were all willing participants of. And if anyone would like to raise an issue, publicly? I have a team of the best lawyers in the country who will gladly investigate it."

He steps towards us, parting the women with a look. His voice has lost the veneer of charm. I can hear the poison that underpins it, the threat that lurks in his too-crisp consonants. "Defamation. False-light invasion of privacy. Intentional infliction of emotional distress. Harassment." He ticks them off on his fingers, moving towards the bottom of the staircase and then up. "If anyone fancies being slapped with a million-dollar suit, then please." His lip curls. "Be my guest – as so many of you already are."

Several of the women shuffle nervously, look down at their feet. Cassidy has turned pale, and I'm worried she might faint.

"No?" he asks the silent onlookers. "No one's going to fight back now?" He hums. "Just like I thought. All talk. You are all just desperate for attention. Desperate for someone to think you're worthy, that you'll *be* something. My only crime is telling you exactly what you wanted to hear: that you were special, that you were improving." He imbues his tone with a faux Valley Girl whine. "Well, today I can finally tell you the truth: you are not." He is halfway up the stairs now, looking at us all with condescension. "I am Tate Larsen, millionaire, guru and your fucking *king!* And you are *nothing!* No one. None of you are special. None of you are important. None of you are anything... without me."

He has reached almost the top of the staircase now, just one step below Elizabeth. Lording it over us. And I can feel the energy in the group wavering, the women beside me quavering.

"He'll bankrupt me," one of them whispers.

"What if he gets social services to take Celia away?" moans another.

But then I look up at Elizabeth. See the steel in her eye.

And then her face twists, the expression on it so bitter I can almost taste it.

"No, Tate," she murmurs, the ire a low rumble in her throat. "It's you who is nothing."

And then, with all the force and speed honed from a decade of training, Elizabeth raises both her arms, palms facing outwards, and pushes.

Tate wobbles.

For a moment, he is suspended in mid-air, one signature bare foot raised, the other wobbling on the step.

He teeters.

Balancing the entire weight of his six-foot frame on a single heel.

And then he is falling. Arms windmilling. Surprise and irritation fighting for the breath in his lungs. Until, finally, there is an ear-splitting crack.

Flesh and bone against marble.

He barely has time to scream.

A small river of blood flows out from under his skull as he lies limp at the bottom of the stairs, eyes staring blankly upwards.

Dead.

Silence. No one knows where to look. Whether to speak.

And then: chaos.

The women shriek. Several of them run out towards the beach, presumably for the children. A couple huddle on the sofa, sobbing. I hear Cassidy on the phone, panic in her voice. It is a blur of shock, and I find myself unable to move. The memory of the night I left Elixir haunts me, the uncanny likeness to what is happening now.

Only this time, the right person is on the ground.

Adam, in the manner befitting what I now know of him, hurtles down the stairs towards the front door, practically flinging Etta at me. I come to life as I reach for her, bury my face into her neck, sobbing, kissing her cheeks, her arms, never wanting to let her out of my sight again. He is gone with barely a backward glance. And somehow, I feel... peace.

Soon, there will be sirens. Later, questions. Inquiries. Allegations and promises made, all of us trying to salvage what we could of the truth, and our dignity. None of us are entirely innocent, and I know, whatever the consequences turn out to be, I will have to live with the part I played in Elixir for the rest of my life.

But for the moment, I watch as Elizabeth descends the staircase. Steps nimbly over the body at the base, accidentally-or-not kicking it with her heel. Our eyes meet, and without a word I take hold of the hand that stretches out to me desperately. I see the spell broken in her finally as she sobs into my shoulder.

"I'm sorry," she whispers, barely audible. "I'm so sorry, I'm so, so sorry."

I squeeze hers as I answer in return, "So am I."

Together, we stumble-walk towards the glass French doors of the mansion – Mia by our side, Etta in my arms. Look up at the wide Californian sky that had been both our prison and our release. Beyond, the Pacific Ocean glimmers in the softening evening sun, the ripples of white catching the light. Shifting, mutating, but always that unending, constant blue.

I had thought that I was unworthy of being Etta's mother. That everything I had been through had made me rotten, unfit. But now that role has been tested to the limit, I know, deep within my core, that whatever happens, my love for her is like that ocean: constant, unbroken.

Marissa. Servant. Beth. Mother. It seemed as though all my life I had been trying to work out who I was, that I'd never truly believed I deserved any of these roles.

Now, I finally had the freedom to try.

"What's going to happen to us?" Elizabeth whispers, looking out into the light.

"I don't know, Elizabeth." I press Etta closer to me,

breathing in her familiar scent as the sound of sirens start to grow closer. "But I think we'll be okay."

And then she takes a step forward, presses her fingers to the glass.

"Please... call me Beth."

Bay Area Chronicle
10th August 2023

"I WAS BRAINWASHED!" FORMER ELIXIR MEMBER RUBY RAE FINALLY SPEAKS OUT

Pop sensation and recently announced *Dancing with the Stars* contestant Ruby Rae is the latest voice adding to the controversy surrounding deceased fitness guru and alleged "sex cult" leader Tate Larsen. Since the entrepreneur's demise, alleged to be an accidental death during a gathering at his Toledo Sands mansion, known to his followers as "The Jungle," there has been an outpouring of accusations of criminal activity, with several members of Tate's organisation held on charges of racketeering, modern slavery, and sex trafficking.

"He put me on an extreme calorie-restriction diet, telling me that my relationship with food was holding me back from success," Rae reveals, talking for the first time from her home in Presidio Heights. "The diet tied in with my album *Stardust* going platinum, and so I became convinced he was right. Now I know it was just a way to control me, to manipulate me into coming back, wanting more. It was brainwashing in its truest form."

Larsen's wellness brand, Elixir, was known for its expensive and *extreme* health and fitness programs, but what has only emerged since the founder's death is the lengths to which its participants were forced to go. "There was always another level," says one former member who wishes to remain anonymous. "More money to give, more demeaning tasks to undertake. If we hesitated, it was seen as a sign of weakness, a lack of commitment." Several of the highest-ranking members were bound to bear children for Tate, convinced that by doing so they would attain the ultimate Elixir tier, known chillingly as "Perfection."

Rae, who cut ties with the organisation several years before the incident in Toledo Sands, confirms that she never had sex with Larsen, although more than fifty former members have come forward to say that they did, either through seduction, coercion, or outright rape. "He tried, though," Rae nods soberly, twisting a lock of her iconic waist-length platinum-blonde hair. "I think the only thing that got me out was my relationship with my parents. His signature move was trying to cut you off from your friends and family, but he wasn't counting on Mom. That woman is hard as nails," she says, proudly, adding, "She's the real reason I am where I am today."

With the help of her parents, Rae privately cut ties with Larsen and spent time in a facility in Arizona before getting back on her feet, but for a long time she felt too scared to go back to the thing she loves: music. "Being in the public eye, you try and avoid controversy, so I was terrified to speak out about my own experience with Elixir. I had no idea what sort of power he truly held, if he was able to totally destroy my career, and so I made the decision to take a career break, and just put myself back together," Rae explains, defending her recent absence from the music scene. "Of course, I had no idea that this had been going on – and far, far worse – with other women." She hastens to add, "I feel awful for any part I had to play in not bringing down this vile and evil man earlier, and as a gesture towards making this right I am announcing today that I will be making a $1 million personal donation to the Bay Area Women's Shelter."

Now, with Larsen's demise and several other key members awaiting trial behind bars, Rae finally feels able to truly be herself. "I've been writing again," she says hopefully. "It's like a weight has been lifted. I finally feel free. I only hope Tate's other victims are able to find their peace."

The trial continues...

Euston, London
September, 2042

She pinches the screen on her phone, zooming into the tangle of lines on the map and trying to pin one of the unfamiliar street names to her location.

"Come on, it's not rocket science," she mutters to herself, hurrying to reach the next street corner before the light turns red, rotating the map to match the name on the side of it. She can't let herself be defeated so easily. London is bigger, noisier and dirtier than she had anticipated, but it isn't Outer Mongolia, and she isn't an idiot. She can do this.

"Excuse me, are you lost?"

She looks up from her phone to see a girl smiling at her. Not much older than her, with two auburn braids wrapped round her head and a navy T-shirt bearing the slogan POSITIVE VIBES ONLY, but still she feels herself tense, her inbred mistrust of strangers – particularly having grown up in a village where everyone was on first-name terms – rising to the surface.

"Sorry, do you speak English?" The girl's smile wrinkles. "Um, *hablas inglés*?" Her voice is warm and has a pleasant sing-song tone to it, like a perfect note played on a violin. She points to the phone screen, enunciates loudly, "Do you need help?"

They both look to the screen as a message flashes across the top.

MUM: *Are you okay? Are you lost? I can see on Find My Friends you've been going up and down Euston Road for fifteen minutes. Can't you find the right turning?*

She feels her cheeks sear, quickly swipes the message away with the point of her index finger. Her mum had begged to come with her, but she had insisted: she wasn't going to go to university with her mummy by her side. She had to start somewhere.

"I'm trying to find Gordon Square" she explains to the girl, who is still waiting patiently beside her and has had the decency not to look embarrassed for her. "The UCL Department of Philosophy?"

"Oh, I know where that is. It's right next to where I work." The girl cocks her head in the opposite direction to where she'd been walking. "Come on, I'll walk you. I'm Samantha, by the way."

She hesitates, eighteen years of stranger danger warnings thrumming at her temples. But then she takes in Samantha's neatly made-up face; clean, manicured hands. If this was a serial killer, they had serious game.

"Thank you so much. I probably sound like an idiot, but I've never been to London before."

"Not at all! I'm happy to help."

They fall into an easy tread, skirting the stream of office workers clacking down the pavement in a strangely choreographed rhythm. The sea of grey is so different from the green, uneven paths of home, the smells of coffee and fast food and pollution a far cry from the country air, but there is something thrilling about it, electrifying. A sense of adventure.

"So are you studying at UCL?" Samantha adjusts the beige tote bag on her shoulder as she steps out of the path of a tourist rolling an enormous wheelie bag.

"Hoping to. There's an open day today. It's my first choice."

"To study philosophy?"

"Yeah." She blushes again. Saying she wants to study philosophy always sounds so self-important, particularly when they didn't even study it at school, but she is drawn to the idea of it, of delving into the way different people made sense of the world, particularly when her own world always seems like such a mundane and uninteresting place. But her mother doesn't like it. Both the choice of subject and her desire to study in London. Then again, her mother would be happy if she spent the rest of her life in Throckbridge, taking a job in a local shop and living on the same street as her – better yet, the same house. There has to be more to life than that.

"Wow." Samantha's mouth rounds into an impressed O. "That's such a cool thing to study. The way different people make sense of the world is so fascinating."

"Yes… Yes, exactly." A shiver of deja vu runs down her spine. She cocks her head to take in the girl in more detail, feeling the warmth between them, a sense of a connection. Samantha isn't conventionally beautiful, but she has an energy, an assurance, and by comparison she feels clumsy, awkward.

"This is where I work," Samantha stops, looking up at a modern building with floor-to-ceiling glass doors, beyond which sits a trendy-looking entrance hall, rattan chairs, blush-pink cushions, lots of potted plants. "I think the UCL Philosophy Department is just a few doors down."

She looks down the road to where Samantha has pointed

but finds herself reluctant to leave. She has felt so lonely all morning: she'd arrived far too early for the start of the open day, then had been shouted at for colliding with a woman with a pram, knocked a coffee all over herself at Pret before ordering another, at which point she had to admit to herself that she didn't even really like coffee. She'd tried to be brave, responding chirpily to her mother's messages that she was "loving it so far!" But the truth was she felt completely out of her depth.

"Hey," Samantha speaks softly, running a small pink tongue across her top teeth. "What are you doing after the open day? Do you have friends in London?"

Instantly, she feels a little flutter in her chest, tries to disguise the hopeful grin she is sure is forming on her face. "Oh! Um, nothing, actually. My train's not until four, so I was just going to wander around." As she says it, she feels deeply uncool.

"Ach, surely you don't want to be alone on your first day in the city?" Samantha turns her head towards the glass doors, and then back again. Her eyes widen. "I'm going to be here all day. Why don't you stop by when you're done, and we can go for lunch?"

"Oh, really?" the flutter in her heart turns into a thud. The thought of eating lunch on her own had already filled her with dread. "You're not busy?"

Samantha giggles. "I'm never too busy for lunch." And then she reaches into her pocket and pulls out a small piece of white card. "Actually, as a potential philosophy student, you might find my job quite interesting."

She hands the card over. It has a single word on it, emblazoned in gold: EUPHORIA. Underneath it, a phone number. Nothing else.

"We run self-improvement seminars," Samantha says, tapping the card with a fingernail. "You'd be amazed at how much you can learn about yourself, and other people, even from a single session." Talking about it, her whole face seems to light up. "I've only been here a year, but I've developed such a deep understanding of myself, and the world." And then her eyes widen, as if she'd just had the best idea. "Hey! If we have time after lunch, why don't you try out a seminar?"

"Oh, wow." She looks down at the card. It shimmers in the light. "It sounds really interesting." She holds the card between her thumb and forefinger but hesitates, resisting taking it fully. "But I don't really have the budget to pay for something like that. I'm saving." She shrugs apologetically. "For uni."

"Oh." Samantha looks at her feet, a wrinkle scoring across her smooth forehead. When she looks up, it disappears. "Look, I shouldn't really do this, but as you're new to the city, and you'll hopefully be studying right down the road, why don't I give you a session for free?"

She opens her mouth, thinks about it for a second before answering, "Are you sure? That's really kind of you but I feel bad about taking something for free. I don't want to get you into trouble or anything." She doesn't fully understand what a self-improvement seminar consists of, but Samantha seems so confident and at ease that it must be something good. And the thought of having a readymade friend just down the road is reassuring. Maybe it will even make her mum stop worrying.

"Don't be silly. It would be my pleasure!" Samantha winks, the top of her button nose twitching. "I get a couple of free credits a month to pass on to people anyway. I'm happy to use one for you. I'm feeling a really positive energy from our encounter. It's like fate." She shrugs her shoulders jauntily. "And hey, if you really like it, you can pay me back when your student loan hits."

"Oh. Okay, then. Yes, that would be great," she answers enthusiastically, trying to imbue her voice with the same confidence the girl exudes so effortlessly. "I could come back here for... twelvish, if that would work?"

"Sounds great." Samantha holds out her hand. "Just ask for me at the front desk. Oh, silly me, I didn't catch your name...?"

"Sorry." She holds out her hand in return, feels the warmth of Samantha's palm enclose it. "It's Etta."

"Pleased to meet you, Etta." Samantha pumps her hand enthusiastically. "See you at twelve."

Acknowledgements

Authors don't have colleagues in the traditional sense, but I am sure I speak for many of us when I say that author friends are as vital as any work mate – they cheer your wins, raise you up from your lows and truly understand the crazy, beautiful, privileged, insanity-making world you inhabit on a day to basis. Charlotte Duckworth, Emily Freud and Liv Matthews: you are the best work wives I could ask for; thank you for bearing with the many highs and lows this book has taken me on.

As always, thank you to Luigi Bonomi, Amanda Preston and the LBA team for your constant support and advice – and to Luigi in particular for planting the seed, "you do enjoy a good cult…".

To my wonderful editor, Gemma Creffield: your huge enthusiasm for this crazy book has meant the world. I have loved working with you, and particularly enjoyed the side bar chats during edits – red flags all over the shop! Caroline Lambe, April Northall and the wider Datura team: you are all SUCH a pleasure to work worth, it has simply been a joy. And to Mark Swan for the note-perfect cover design: thank you for capturing the essence of the book so beautifully.

To the hugely talented Rebecca Millar, thank you for all of your advice and help with the early drafts of this book. I genuinely don't think I could have finished it without your keen eye and cheerleading. And to Travis Tynan for such insightful proof reading!

Mr Adrian Lower and your team, Gill Holland and Edi Silva, you may be a little surprised to discover yourselves in these acknowledgements, but your support on a personal level during the writing of this book cannot go unnoticed. Your kindness and generosity during such a difficult period in its own way gave me the strength to keep writing. And to Mr Lower: thank you for a very detailed explanation of where exactly one would need to be shot in the vagina!

To my poor friends and family, who have had to live with my hair pulling over this book largely without complaint: thank you for lending your time, ears and thoughts. I *would* say it won't happen again, but we all know that's not true.

To everyone who has borrowed, bought, sold or recommended my books: thank you, thank you. You are the reason authors keep writing.

And lastly to George: you are and will always be my best friend. You, Marlowe and Juniper are my world, and I can't quite believe as I'm writing this that our little family is finally complete.

DATURA BOOKS
catering to the armchair detective,
budding codebreakers, the repeat offender
and an emerging younger readership.

Check out our website at
www.daturabooks.com to see our entire
catalogue.

Follow us on social media:
Twitter @daturabooks
Instagram @daturabooks
TikTok @daturabooks